Y0-BQW-520

Mendocino California

November 2011

Todd Walton

"A splendid novel of great and magical stories."

— Elizabeth Marshall Thomas, author of *The Hidden Life of Dogs*

Other books by
TODD WALTON

FICTION

Inside Moves

Forgotten Impulses

Louie & Women

Night Train

Ruby & Spear

Of Water and Melons

Buddha in a Teacup

NONFICTION

Open Body: Creating Your Own Yoga

The Writer's Path: A Guidebook for Your Creative Journey

Under the Table Books

A Novel of Stories

(with drawings by the author)

todd walton

LOST
COAST
PRESS

Under the Table Books*: *A Novel of Stories
Copyright © 2009 by Todd Walton

All rights reserved. No portion of this book may be reproduced in whole or in part, by any means whatever, except for passages excerpted for purposes of review, without the prior written permission of the publisher.

For information, or to order additional copies, contact:

Lost Coast Press
155 Cypress Street
Fort Bragg, California 95437
800-773-7782
Fax: 707-964-7531
http:\\www.cypresshouse.com
Book production by Cypress House
Cover and interior illustrations by Todd Walton

Library of Congress Cataloging-in-Publication Data
Walton, Todd.
Under the Table Books / Todd Walton. -- 1st ed.
p. cm.
ISBN 978-1-935448-02-0 (casebound : alk. paper)
1. Bookstores--Fiction. 2. Marginality, Social--Fiction.
3. California--Fiction. I. Title.
PS3573.A474U53 2009

813'.54--dc22 2008054973

Manufactured in the USA
2 4 6 8 9 7 5 3 1

This book is dedicated to:

Ginger Malisos

Rico Rees

Cynthia Frank

Peter Keat

Pattie DeMatteo

Scott Soriano

Melinda Welsh

Kathy Mooney

Dave Peattie

Marcia Sloane

and all the librarians

and bookstore people

who lovingly tend

the gardens of literature

Contents

Dream of Breaking

Do you know the meaning
of this oldness?
The ancient quality
of time that this
clay pot holds?
Listen to it.
The earth is there.
The sky is there.
Hold it in your hands.
Drink from it.
Dream about being
molded, dream
of breaking
and being found.

Ann Menebroker

Under the Table Books

Operating Procedures

(subjects of change)

My father was an idealist caught in the backwaters of capitalism, a man sickened by the wasting of our world in the name of Progress—otherwise known as the slaughter of Nature. Even so, he believed he needed money, actual dollars, in order to survive, and so he opened Lord Bellmaster's High Quality Previously Owned Literature with the intention of making enough to feed his wife and two children.

His best year—the year I turned twelve—Lords (as it came to be known) showed a profit of nine hundred dollars. My mother, a fiercely pragmatic social worker, was hardly impressed and predicted with vitriolic accuracy the following year's collapse.

When I was fourteen, my father hired his first employee—a defrocked Anglican priest with feminist pretensions—and the business ground to a screeching halt. Literally. My father closed up shop, took a job at Deaton's Hardware, and for the first time in a decade my parents had sufficient funds for a three-day vacation to Yosemite with*out* the kids. Nirvana, according to my mother.

My father marked the occasion of my fifteenth birthday by forgetting all about my "special" day. Seven days later, no doubt reminded of his lapse by my mother, he begged me to tell him how he might make amends for his forgetfulness.

And I said, "Father, it would be my great honor to assume the lease of the bookstore and take over the business."

The blood drained from his face. "What about school?"

"School is a devastating waste of my precious time, as you know. I will, however, soon pass my high school equivalency exam, at which point I will need ways and means to accrue sufficient funds pursuant to attending college."

In truth, I never intended to inflict the didactic spasms of higher education on my person, but I knew how my parents reasoned and I was certain the evocation of university fantasies would stir their fear-driven hearts. I even said something about majoring in Pragmatism.

So they acquiesced, I took the helm, as it were, and instituted a system of anarchist exchange that has caused Under the Table Books to flourish. The following philosophy, now a popular poster reproduced by young people everywhere, is my own adaptation of the natural laws espoused by Buckminster Fuller, Ann Menebroker, Fools Crow, Jane Blue, Nikos Kazantzakis, Charlotte Kasl, Julius Erving, Ella Fitzgerald, Rudyard Kipling, Pema Chödrön, Philip Whalen and, of course, Groucho Marx.

To wit:

ALL BOOKS ARE FREE.

If you want to leave something you value
as much as the book you're taking, cool.

Have a book you don't want? Drop it on by.

And don't get us wrong.

We enjoy receiving stacks of quarters
and piles of dollar bills.

We delight in all forms of currency,
including tasty comestibles.

Yes, and keep those potted plants coming.

May all beings be well read.

At last count (earlier today) Under the Table Books was supporting (in minimalist style) eleven *Homo sapiens*, seven felines, two tortoises, a shell-shocked raven, and the sociocultural needs of several hundred spirits dancing in the bodies of human beings.

Moustafa, Frisbee guru and master baker, calls Under the Table Books "a fine specimen of improvisational reality." My mother calls us "plain cuckoo." Jenny, my housemate and a bold sentimentalist, calls us "beautiful chaos."

I just love what happens here. I find the comings and going and givings and takings an endless source of inspiration.

We sincerely invite you to believe in us in theory if nothing else.

Yours truly,
Lord Bellmaster
freelance human being

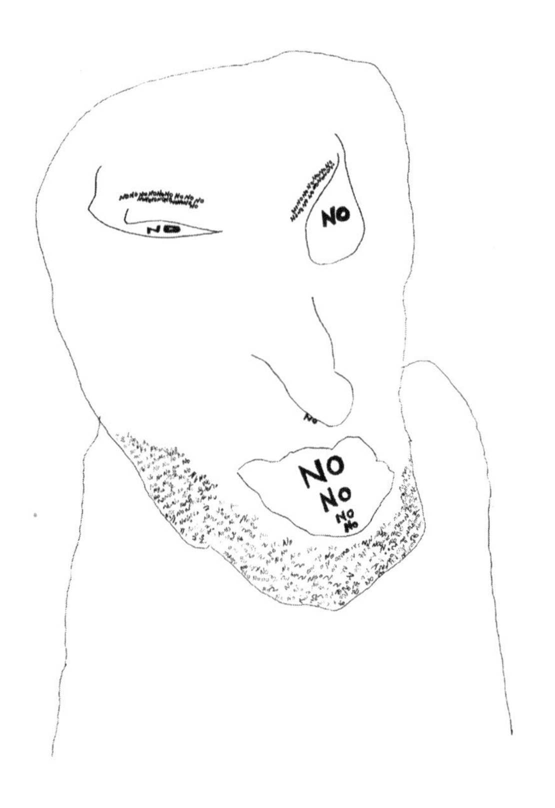

The Big Green

(told to Lord Bellmaster by a man wearing a *Save the Endorphins* T-shirt in exchange for a well-thumbed copy of Buckminster Fuller's *Critical Path*)

People have always told me I'm weird. But who isn't a little weird? You know what I mean?

In first grade, I would stand barefoot by a tree at the far end of the playground and I could feel stories coming into my feet and traveling up my legs and through my heart and out my mouth into the air. At first, the other kids laughed at me, but I *had* to do it. Every recess I would run to the tree and pull off my shoes and start babbling.

I didn't have a single friend when I started telling the stories, but one day this boy sat down nearby and listened for a few minutes. Then he got up and ran away and came back with four other kids, and pretty soon *they* got up and ran away and came back with more kids, and I just kept telling about the children lost in a mysterious forest called the Big Green. Pretty soon there were dozens of kids sitting around me, and when the bell rang none of them would budge until I said, *The End.*

Well, from then on I had lots of friends and my teacher invited me to tell stories to the class while she took little naps and pretty soon I was going to other classes and telling them stories, too, until finally I was named the official storyteller of the school and I was interviewed and photographed for the school paper. And then there was an article about me in the local newspaper, which is when my mother and father found out about what I was doing.

I'll never forget that night—the day before my seventh birthday. My father came home from his office and my mother showed him the article in the paper about me and he became furious. "What are all these stories *about?*" he wanted to know.

I told him they were mostly about lost children and he said, "*You've* never been lost. That's *lying.*"

"They're just stories," I said, trying to defend myself. "They like us to make up stories."

"*Who* likes you to?"

"The teachers."

"Why didn't you *tell* us about this?" He glared at my mother. "Did *you* know about this?"

"Heavens no," she said, cringing. "He doesn't tell me anything."

"So now all our friends are gonna see this and..."

"We've had five calls already."

"Sonofabitch," said my father, clenching his fists. "That does it. No more storytelling. You hear me? No more."

"But..."

"But nothing. You quit telling stories or you'll be in big trouble."

So I stopped. It wasn't easy, but I did it. I lost most of my friends and I got beat up by some older kids who tried to force me to tell them stories, but I'd been in big trouble with my father before and it wasn't something I would risk again until I was seventeen and left home for good.

Now here's the amazing part. I didn't remember any of this until last year when I went to a psychic astrologer to celebrate turning forty-seven. The first thing she said to me was, "Your great gift emerged when you were six, but something happened and you were forced to squelch it."

"Gift?" I said, remembering only my profound loneliness. "What kind of gift?"

"You were psychic. And judging from your chart, such a gift would have been unacceptable in your family. Even dangerous for you."

"I don't remember," I said, straining for any sort of memory from my early years.

"Then you turned to the physical. Sports?"

"All I did," I said, remembering the endless baseball—the safe simplicity of bat meeting ball, a boy drifting back in left field to catch another towering drive, never wanting the day to end.

"And now?"

"I work at a preschool. I'm a teacher's aide."

Then it hit me, the way I keep the kids entertained between four and six waiting for their mommies to pick them up. I stand barefoot by a tree at the far end of the playground and tell them stories about the children lost in the Big Green. And though the children in my stories are definitely lost, they are not alone because they have each other, and so they never lose hope of finding their way home.

Where House?

(location location location in a somewhat derelict part of town)

The bookstore portion of the anarchist collective known as Under the Table Books occupies the entire second floor (approximately ten thousand square feet) of a three-story warehouse on High Street, so named because the wide avenue runs along the spine of a hill. Hence, when you enter the bookstore from High Street, you may think you are entering the ground floor of the old building, where (when?) in reality the *actual* ground floor is down a steep and dimly lit stairway opening into a large yoga dance music sprawl overflow space known as the rumpus room.

Adjoining the rumpus room is a commodious kitchen wherein Moustafa bakes his delicious breads and cookies, and members of the commune gather for food, chat, coffee, tea, cards, laughter, and the inevitable tears that punctuate life in a large ersatz family.

Bedrooms abound on this actual ground floor, their usage governed by something like a rule (only not so hard and fast as an *actual* rule) to wit: members of the *sangha* should first and foremost think of these bedrooms as guest facilities and/or temporary havens—which is not to say long-term occupancies are unheard of here. Carl Klein, for one, has "camped" in one of the more remote bedrooms down under for the past seven years. Nor are such lengthy stays frowned upon so much as occasionally (volubly) wondered at.

Why, you might ask, is there almost a rule about the ground-floor bedrooms when the two oddly configured apartments on the third floor are so blithely rented ad infinitum to the luckiest of peeps? Because vivid revelations over time have informed the collective that *flow*—good *strong* flow—is essential to the health of a successful sodality. Why? Because flow is the antidote to Stagnation, Exclusivity, Hierarchy, and Redundancy—major threats to the vibrancy of a creative community.

Should a person such as yourself open the sliding glass doors on the south-facing wall of the commodious kitchen and cross the brick terrazzo shaded by the grand old olive tree, you might very well be tempted (and welcome) to step onto the flower-lined path that meanders through a scrumptious quarter acre of vegetables, herbs, berry bushes, and fruit trees—a wonderland tended avidly by Under the Table booksters, notably Moustafa, Jenny, Lord, Natasha, Ben, Denny (when he's not on the road) and the Spinelli sisters, Iris and Leona.

Numero Uno, the poet laureate of the local watershed and a frequent visitor to the bookstore, recently spent a hot afternoon with his feet in the fishpond—shaded by the grand old olive tree—writing the following ode to the bookstore garden.

Sunflower Satori

Look what love makes!
Look what death provides!
The soil made fertile by infusions of
the breakdown of everything.
The ground seeded by luscious people
eager to help things grow.
And here comes water — rain from a hose!
Here come the bees and butterflies!
Here come the worms!
Here come the weeds!
Here come the precious baby plants
to be nurtured into
flowering and fruiting and ripening
so we may eat before
it is our turn to be eaten.

Numero Uno

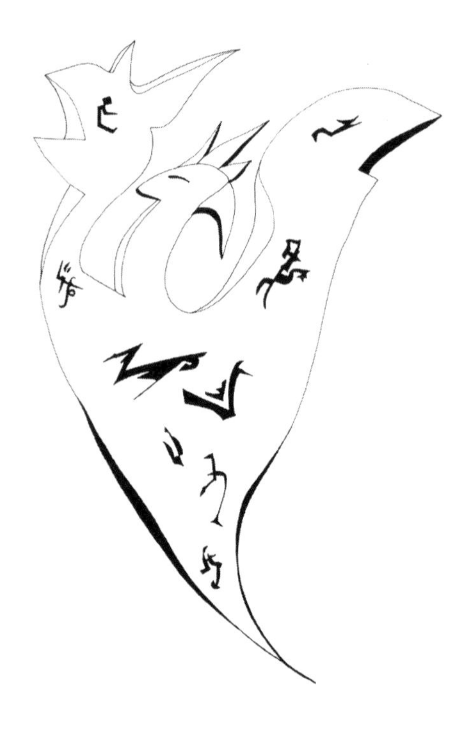

Hawk

(as told by Lord Bellmaster)

My darling apartment mate Jenny—ten years younger than I but every bit as wise—came home last night from two weeks in New York City, her drawings and paintings rejected by galleries large and small, her confidence badly dented. I ran her a hot bath and made pesto pasta and opened a bombastic Zinfandel while she soaked. When I brought her a glass, she looked up from the bubbles and said, "I'm shit, Lord. Total shit. Some of them even laughed at me. They said I was hideously naive."

"What do they know?" I said, handing her the wine. "They live in New York. They know nothing of your life, your visions."

"They define art," she said listlessly. "They are the supreme arbiters of taste."

"Please," I said, grimacing majestically. "That's..."

"Hideously naive?" she snapped, downing her Zin in a single gulp. "Just leave me alone."

This morning I woke to the pleasant smell of a fire in the hearth. I showered and shaved with the expectation of finding Jenny in a better mood—more the person she was before she ran the gauntlet of the New York galleries. Cloaked in my Jackson Pollock bathrobe—the gray splattery one—I padded down the hallway and found Jenny feeding a pile of her drawings to a blazing inferno.

Discretion being the better part of my occasional valor, I chose not to interrupt her crematory activities, changed into my black burnoose, grabbed my notebook, and hurried down here to the store. It is fast approaching two in the afternoon, and every time the bell above the door jingles I expect the jingler to be Jenny, but she has yet to appear, yet to call.

Business is good today. Sixty-seven books taken, forty-seven given. We have also received three lovely bonsai fuchsias, four frozen catfish (boned), a Mickey Mouse watch that keeps excellent time, an Adlai Stevenson for President button, and seventy-seven dollars and seventy-seven cents (some sort of omen, I'm sure.)

Old Mrs. Armitage has treated the cats to lightly fried nuggets of chicken breast, the Spinelli sisters, our resident identical twins (wearing matching blue kimonos today) have dusted and alphabetized the *British Romantics (female authors)* section, Carl Klein (with a fishing story recently published in *The Tule Review*) has done his admirable vacuuming, and Cecily Considine, the brilliantly buxom diva of Weatherstone coffeehouse (her shockingly white blouse all but unbuttoned) has tempted me for the better part of an hour with promises of unparalleled erotic satiation. A good day, all in all, Moustafa due to spell me any minute now.

What a tyranny it is for anyone to judge the flowering of Jenny's spirit. How sad and frightened those New York people must be to strike her so cruelly, to slander her visions.

Moustafa enters in his baker's whites and salaams to me, his dark brown eyes shining brightly, his mahogany skin glowing as if lit from within. "Bellmaster is sad," he says, narrating my life. "Bellmaster is feeling assaulted. Bellmaster needs to take a long walk and get some sun on his skin and his heart beating faster."

"Correct," I say, "but first answer me this. Why would anyone want to denigrate Jenny's beautiful pictures?"

Moustafa removes his red bandana and releases his enviable Rasta tumble. "Why does the snake eat the mouse, the hawk feast on kittens?"

"Natural?"

"Necessary."

At which moment Jenny enters wearing a knee-length skirt of black denim and a purple Under the Table Books T-shirt—a tall broad-shouldered beauty with shoulder-length reddish brown hair and limpid green eyes and a delightful dancer's ease imbuing her every movement. And though my rational mind tells me I'm imagining things, she seems much taller than she seemed yesterday, and older, too—more woman than girl—and more complicated and more mysterious and more...better.

"Jenny," says Moustafa, bowing politely. "Welcome home. Your trip was marvelous, I see."

"Fabulous," says Jenny, salaaming to her Frisbee master and friend and instructor in the ways of yeast and dough.

And I can barely keep from shouting, *Liar! You hated New York. They demolished you!*

"Though it may not have seemed so fabulous at first," says

Moustafa, winking at me. "For it often takes time to digest a feast."

"I burned all my drawings," she blurts. "Everything back to the very first ones my mother saved from nursery school. Thousands of them. And all the photographs I ever took and all the pictures ever taken of me. And all my clothes except this skirt and shirt. It took me most of the night and all of today until just now."

"Good," says Moustafa, placing his hands together and bowing deeply. "How good and brave of you."

I am frozen in dismay, my knees shaking, my head throbbing.

"And you?" asks Jenny, looking at me, *into* me.

"Going," I murmur—mouse hypnotized by snake.

I arrive home—the smell of burned paper still strong in the air. I gather the pages from my desk and carry them to the fireplace, the remnants of Jenny's drawings glowing red in the depths—my own pages bursting into flame as they touch the embers of her art.

My work has just begun—millions of old words to burn before I rest—my heart full of blessings for those people in New York.

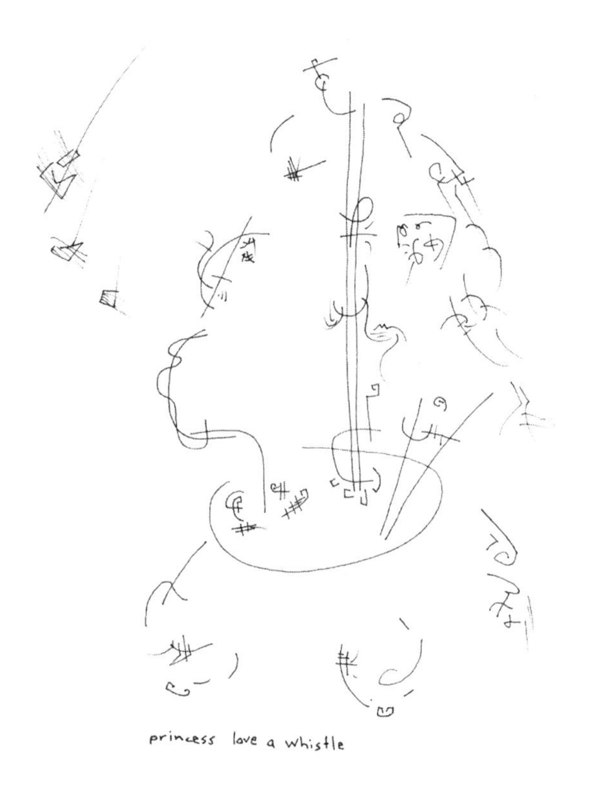

Lovely

(a warm day, the air suffused with the intoxicating scent of mock orange)

"Sweet brown girl, where you learn to dress?" asks the graceful young black man, feeling oh so dashing in his sleek gray jumpsuit belted with a purple sash. "You choose your own color combinations or is this the work of some genius friend?"

Natasha, the Tuesday morning Friday afternoon Sunday noonish counterperson at Under the Table Books, glances up from her notebook and arches her right eyebrow. "Self-taught," she says, scanning her suitor with a practiced eye. "Are you a fashion authority?"

"Just might be," he says, removing his dark glasses to give her a peek at his pretty brown eyes. "Something so very Bette Davis about this arrangement. Kinda busted Deco the way you fill things out, the way this soft red burns so sweet on you. Plays so clean off your pale blue scarf. We very much like the whole ensemble, though truth be told, you would make a paper bag look good."

Natasha is twenty-three years old, her long black hair coiled atop her noble head. Her mama white, her biological father black, she has been a prime target of male admiration since her eleventh year when her breasts first budded and she changed from cute to lovely. Born as brown as her father, she has spent her entire life with her white papa Felix and her white brother Ben.

Mashman Z, the cat from the hood they call Ground Zero, has traveled perilous miles to catch a glimpse of the woman his main man Harold "Cush" Rrradman calls "chocolate goddess perfection."

"Are you seeking any book in particular?" she asks, shading her eyes, though there is no visible glare in the cavernous store.

"They have one about you?" he asks, batting his lashes in a blatant mockery of innocence. "With pictures? I love a good book with pictures."

Natasha sighs. "What's your name?"

"Mashman Z," he says proudly. "And you?"

"Natasha," she replies, disliking the task at hand. "And I'm formidably busy."

"I see that." He smiles benevolently at the words on her page. "Poetry?"

"Private," she rejoins, closing her notebook.

"Listen," he begins. "How 'bout..."

"How 'bout nothing," she snaps. "How 'bout I don't like men who tell me to listen? I listen to what I want to listen to."

"What'd I do?" asks Mashman, stunned by her vehemence. "Just saying hello."

"Goodbye," she says, closing her eyes. "And when she woke up, the storm clouds had given way to sunshine."

"Do I deserve that?" He glances around the funky old bookstore.

"I don't remember being mean. I'm just trying to be real."

Her eyes pop open. "Hardly call *you* real."

"Why? What's unreal about me?"

"The whole ensemble," she says, throwing his words back at him. "Mashman *Z*? You get that from a comic book or something?"

"Earned that name," he says, frowning quizzically. "Stopped two deaths in a single bound. Besides, there's more to comic books than meets the eye." He cocks his head. "I'm not what you think, Princess."

"And what do you think I think you are?"

"Stupid dumb from down," he says, nodding. "Stupid dumb lookin' for pussy y nada mas."

"I have little sense of your intelligence," she says, folding her arms. "But the pussy part rings true."

"Thus you believe my motivation is little more than tail?" And being an unconscious mimic, he folds his arms, too. "You *are* dazzling, Natasha. I confess to a sexual pull, but surely you can't gas me for that. I'm human. Yah?"

Mrs. Armitage enters, her black eyes shining as the bookstore cats crowd around her—a stern old lady in a faded blue gingham dress with a matching floppy bonnet. She waves to Natasha. "Hello, dear," she says dryly. "Threatening rain. Awful humid."

"Hello, Mrs. A," says Natasha, beaming at the cat lady. "The kits have been mostly melancholy today."

"My children," says Mrs. Armitage, peering down at the seven cats. "Soon the clouds shall burst."

The cats reply with meows and mewing as they follow their favorite human to the Reading Circle—a goodly expanse ringed by a menagerie of mismatched chairs and vaguely Persian pillows. Mrs. Armitage raises the hem of her tattered dress above battered combat boots and kneels on the fraying carpet to give each of the kitties a brisk massage before serving their lunch—*diced turkey liver l'Arlesienne*—into seven silver bowls.

Mashman Z watches Natasha gazing at Mrs. Armitage and a

tender song bursts from his lips—his voice a warm falsetto.

Oh lovely world where sweet brown princess
kiss her queen of cats with tender smiles

"Nice," says Natasha, surprised into opening her notebook so Mashman Z can read her poem. "Wouldn't have guessed you'd sound like that. Here's something you might want to sing."

"An honor and a delight," he says, smiling down at the page where the first word to come into focus is *Now*.

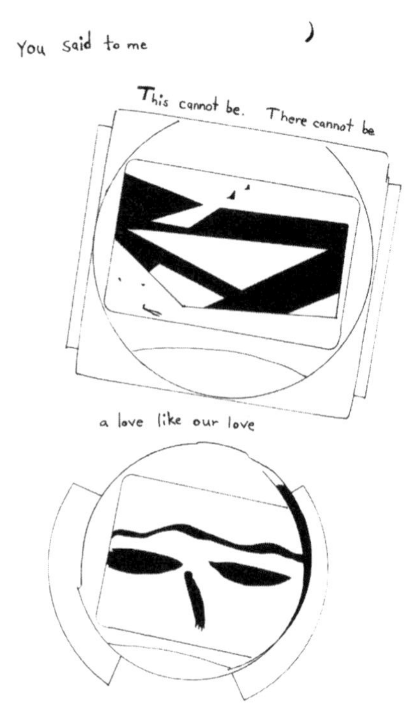

Florence

(as told by Felix, devoted patron of Under the Table Books—
papa to Natasha and Ben)

Florence was the only lover I longed for, but I was one of many to her. Our time together was always miraculous for me, and once, after an evening of stupendous lovemaking, I couldn't help but ask, "Don't you want this *all* the time?"

"I *have* it all the time," she replied simply. "With all my men."

"And women, too?"

"That's none of your business."

"Why not?"

"I'm gone."

And she left. I swore I'd never speak to her again, but when she called the next day, I was available, desperate, in fact, to spend however many hours and days of her life she'd give me.

A month later, both of us happily drunk, she stunned me with the news that she'd changed her mind, wanted it *just* to be me, and I whooped for joy, she moved in, and before the dust could settle I found some other guy's underwear in the dirty clothes hamper.

"So?" she shrugged. "So I had a bit of fun with somebody else. He's no big deal. You're my main man now."

"*Main?* What about *just* me?"

"I'll try," she said, looking into my eyes. "But I'm weak about certain things."

Fair warning. Six times in six months she confessed to new affairs, and then she got pregnant.

"The father?"

"Odds say you."

"Odds?"

"Two other long shots."

"Again?"

"Doing the best I can, lover."

"So what do you want to do?"

"Get married. Have the kid."

"Marriage? You can't stay true to me *now*."

"I'm true to you," she said simply. "You're the love of my life. I just need other lovers to keep me going."

"Then marry somebody else. Torture some other sucker."

"I'd rather marry you," she said, weeping. "I love everything about you except you don't like me having other lovers."

"Men," I said, surprising myself. "I can't stand the thought of you with other men."

"Women be okay?" she asked hopefully.

So we got married and she had our beautiful boy Ben, and I believed all her other lovers were women until she got pregnant again and suggested her next child might be possessed of darker skin than ours.

"No."

"A friend of Sheila's. We didn't plan it. Things got out of control after the drumming and the hash."

"Hash? You're still nursing Ben, aren't you?"

"He doesn't seem to mind."

"But *I* mind," I said, grabbing her and shaking her. "He's my child, too. I love him more than anything in the world. I don't want him drinking your milk laced with hash."

"Oh, yeah," she said, as if waking from a trance. "Of course."

She stayed with us until Ben was six and Natasha was four—her farewell note a revelation.

> Dearest Felix,
>
> Four years seven months you my only lover. Never thought it possible. Only possible with you. But now I have to go. Or die. The children will be better off without what I will become if I stay. They are both strong and smart and good, as you are. I'll be in touch.
>
> Flo

When Ben was seven and Natasha was five, we got a postcard from Bali—palm trees on a white sand beach by a turquoise sea.

> Dear Felix and Benny and Natasha,
>
> So beautiful here. People very kind. Sometimes I feel horrible for leaving you, but I know it was the right thing to do. I pray for your happiness every day. Loving you.
>
> Flo

On Ben's ninth birthday, Florence wrote from Los Angeles.

Dear Felix and Ben and Natasha,

I work for a movie producer, reading scripts and evaluating them, and I'm writing one of my own about a woman who can't stay anywhere for very long. She starts out thinking her wanderlust is a bad thing, but she comes to realize that roaming around is what keeps her sane. She is a bumblebee in the garden of life.

There is a park where I like to go in the evenings. I love watching the children on the swings. I love watching the tiny children stumbling through the sand. I love it when they fall down and cry for their mothers, and sometimes, if their mothers are distracted, I will go to these crying children and comfort them. Sometimes they are afraid of me, but almost always when I hold them in my arms, they stop crying and look into my eyes and I look into theirs and I see *you*, all of *you*, looking out at me. Loving me. Happy Birthday, Ben. I'll kiss you in my mind nine times, *you* seven, Nat.

Flo

Eleven years old, Ben began dazzling friends and neighbors with culinary marvels, and soon our home was a magnet for hungry artists—an impromptu salon from which Natasha emerged a poet.

mother

I remember you and I don't remember you.
I look at Papa's pictures of you but they don't
move, don't have voices can't hold me won't
give love. I dream of finding you and peeling
away your white skin to see if you are brown inside—
the reverse of me—my brother your son
had two more years of you than I.
Does that make my loss less than his?

It has been nineteen years since we last saw Florence. She should be here any minute. Ben and Natasha are in the kitchen concocting gastronomical masterworks. I have dusted and vacuumed and straightened everything. Our house has rarely seemed so orderly.

I stand in the living room immersed in a memory of Florence, her face aglow. Ben enters with a spoonful of pesto and sticks it in my mouth. I nod my approval and return to my memory of Flo—no other woman so deliciously suited to me.

Now Natasha fires up the stereo and gets me dancing. "Hang tough, Papa," she sings, whirling away to the kitchen.

I never wanted to see Florence again. I could never forgive her for leaving our children—for leaving me to raise them without her. Then, a year ago, as I was sinking beyond salvation into the wreckage of wine and dope and depression, my children intervened and took away my bottle and my pipe and my pills.

And Natasha said, "Papa, we have forgiven her. We want to see her. We have forgiven her."

And Ben said, "Papa, she wants to see you. She wants to see all of us together. She wants to be with us for a time. We want that, too. We have forgiven her. Truly, we have."

Now I have gone without wine or dope or pills for a year.

Soon Florence will be here to join us for my birthday party—our magnificent children proving the wisdom of her choice.

I say, excuse me, could
you wait one moment please,
I seem to be lost and I'm
hoping you can point me in
the right direction, help me
get my bearings, even, perhaps
answer that most basic of
questions: what is my
purpose in life, not
that you would
necessarily know
my purpose in life,
although I suppose
you might, in the
sense that everyone,
perhaps, shares
a greater purpose,
the details of which
embody the more
personal...
I say, please.
could you
Hello?
Please.
I say.

Fire Books

(a cold rainy morning, the bookstore slowly warming)

"No, no, no. Cay*uga*," says the elderly man—shrewd gray eyes twinkling in a satyr's face. "*Fire Over the Cayuga*."

"Mystery?" asks Natasha, frowning at him. "Has anyone ever told you how much you resemble..."

"Alec Guinness," he nods, smiling wistfully at the buxom young brown woman—his favorite of all the Under the Table booksters. "Ten thousand times. I've been told it so often I sometimes think I *am* he. With amnesia. I've even developed his accent, though I've never *been* to England." His smile broadens. "I'm from Cayuga,

Arizona. Unless I'm Alec Guinness. Wasn't he fabulous in all those Dickens movies?"

"*Star Wars*," says Natasha. "He *made* that movie work."

"I agree. And as for *Fire Over the Cayuga*, it's a history book detailing the only skirmish of the Civil War fought in that part of Arizona. *I* wrote it. Unless I'm Alec Guinness, in which case, *he* wrote it. Perhaps. The point is, I no longer possess a copy."

"Of your *own* book? Why not?"

"I gave it to a woman I loved. To prove she meant more to me than anything else." He bows to the bygone spirit. "She's buried *with* the book, her special request, and I've been desperate for a copy ever since." He lowers his voice. "I don't feel quite whole without one."

"She took part of your soul," says Natasha, nodding. "I've been there. Fall for a guy. Boom. I lose myself. Pieces of me disappear into him. Not enough comes back. I fragment." She sighs. "Gotta get your soul back any way you can. Let's take a look."

He follows her through the store to the *Very Old & Esoteric* section. Three big cats block their way, demanding to be petted. Natasha reaches down and gives them cursory strokes, but they want more.

"I'll deal with the felines while you look for the book," says the old man, squatting down to pet the cats. "My eyes are not so good anymore."

"What's your name?" asks Natasha, scanning the faded spines of the ancient tomes.

"Alec," he replies absentmindedly. "Alec Guinness."

"But I thought you said..."

"Yes?"

"Oh, never mind," she says, finding the Fire Over books. "*Fire Over China, Fire Over America, Fire Over Iraq, Fire Over Boston, Fire Over Los Angeles, San Francisco, Beirut, Chicago, Berlin, Moscow, the Cayuga, Buenos Aires...Fire Over the Cayuga*. I found it. By Peter Franklin."

"That's it," he says, rising slowly. "That's my name. Peter Franklin. Of course." He takes the book from her and gazes at the tattered cover. "I have a sister. Melissa. Have you pen and paper? I'm getting a rush of data. My first dog was named Cozy. Mother's maiden name Rubenstein. I lost the third grade spelling bee to Carol Moonie. I spelled *scissors* s-i-z-z-o-r-s."

"Follow me," says Natasha, leading him out of the maze of books. "I have just the thing."

Peter fills ten pages of Natasha's notebook, murmuring and sighing and chuckling as his memories return to him.

Maria Fernandez—first girl kissed, warm lips, brown eyes, knobby knees

Alexandra G—first lover. Her parents were gone for the weekend. She knew what she was doing. Bed huge

Seventh grade allowance—fifty cents per week

Chores: mow lawn (push mower), take out garbage, ants on can, watering fruit trees, pulled weeds for neighbor, Mrs. Small—money for movies

Danny Kaye in The Court Jester

Box of toy soldiers—favorite white horse, tail missing, detachable saddle

Gin Rummy with Jewish grandfather—moustache, gin and tonics, real estate

Slapjack with sister—jack of hearts, sting

Mother in curlers on the phone, laughing

Natasha carefully places the pages of Peter's memories inside the precious copy of *Fire Over the Cayuga*.

"I don't know how I can ever repay you," he says, wiping away an invisible tear. "I understand the policy of this store is to leave whatever we feel a book is worth, but how does one determine the value of memories?"

"Up to you," says Natasha, closing the book and kissing its spine—a habit she's had since childhood—books the salvation of a motherless child. "Anything you want."

"What if I were to tell you an amazing story?" he asks, his eyes sparkling. "Would that cover it?"

"Perfectly," says Natasha, imagining a ceremony in the garden to make this delightful man her grandfather.

"Well," he begins, "when the book came out it caused quite a splash in Civil War circles and there was talk of it being made into a film. I was flattered, naturally. I'd never published anything before and it felt wonderful to be so lavishly praised, but I never *believed* a movie would be made. Publishing a book was one thing, but a major motion picture was quite another. I worked at the post office, after all."

"In Cayuga?"

"In Cayuga. Where I was known as good old Peter the Civil War fanatic, the funny fart who looked very much like Alec Guinness."

"Even then?"

"More so then than now," he says, seeing his dapper self mounting the marble stairs to his post behind the iron grate. "But then the talk turned serious and before I knew it I was flying to New York with a famous movie producer. Oh, what was his name? He made westerns and gangster films. Shoot-'em-ups. He purchased the film rights to my book for fifty thousand dollars, which was a huge sum in those days and freed me forever from my postal drudgery."

"Amazing," says Natasha, wanting so very much to believe him.

"And he," says Peter, dismayed by the lack of a name to attach to the fast-talking movie mogul, "wanted *me* to help him convince Alec Guinness to play the part of Major Bidwell, not the *biggest* part, mind you, but certainly a pivotal role."

"Can this be true?" asks Natasha, her disbelief swiftly gaining ground. "Alec Guinness? Him*self*?"

"It's all true," says Peter, nodding sagaciously. "I was born bereft of imagination."

"So then what happened?"

"We took a taxi from the airport directly to a Broadway theater and watched Alec Guinness as Hamlet. In *Hamlet*. The greatest performance I have ever seen."

"Wow," says Natasha, her doubt dissolving. "Wow."

"We went backstage afterward," says Peter, reliving those moments of glory, "and we had champagne with Alec, and he went on and on about *Fire Over the Cayuga*, how he was dying to play the part of Major Bidwell, how he was *born* to play the part, and I was bursting with happiness."

"And then?" asks Natasha, holding her breath.

"That's the end of the story," says Peter, sighing contentedly. "That's how I like it to end."

Don't Be Sorry

(morning fog showing signs of relenting)

"There are things I could tell you," says Mrs. Armitage, sitting at one end of the bus bench, her scowl barely discernible in the shade of her floppy bonnet, her oversized old-fashioned dress giving no hint of her true shape. "Things that could save you lots of trouble."

"Too late," says Cassandra, a handsome young black woman in blue jeans and a bright red sweater, her hair short and curly. She holds up her hand to display the slender gold wedding band yoking her finger. "Shoulda talked to me three years ago."

"*Leave* him," says Mrs. Armitage, scowling at the yellow stripes separating the lanes. "I spent nine years with a man I should have left after five seconds." Her fury subsides. "You're what, twenty-four?"

"You're so *nice* to me," says Cassandra, liking the old gal. "Where you going so early in the morning?"

"Anywhere," says Mrs. Armitage, nodding slowly. "It doesn't matter. Something always happens. Later on, I'll go to the bookstore and feed my kitties. I can't have cats at home because I have parakeets, though I'm feeling less and less good about keeping birds in cages."

"Twenty-four," says Cassandra, checking her face in her compact mirror. "I wish."

"It's irrelevant," says Mrs. Armitage, sitting up straight. "I'm sorry I asked. Maybe I'll ride out to the college with you. That's where you're going, isn't it? I never went to college, but I'm an avid reader. I'm particularly fond of the history of food."

"Good for you," says Cassandra, remembering her mother's admonition: *Be polite to old people, you hear me? They worked hard and long just to survive, so you must show them respect.*

"How old *are* you," asks Mrs. Armitage, squinting curiously at Cassandra.

"Would you believe thirty-seven? Married two days before I turned thirty-four." She laughs. "I was *so* relieved."

"Take it from me, get out as soon as you can."

Cassandra frowns. "Honey, you don't know the first thing about me or my marriage."

"You're an Aries," says Mrs. Armitage, nodding assuredly. "Moon in Capricorn. Libra rising. Loyal to a fault."

"How'd you know I was Aries? I don't know about my moon and that other thing, but the one I read in the newspaper is Aries."

"Cosmic download," says Mrs. Armitage, folding her arms. "He'll take everything from you. He can't help it. It's how he was programmed. Which is why it's imperative you break free as soon as possible."

"What's your name? I'm Cassandra."

"Cassandra," says Mrs. Armitage, wrinkling her nose. "You were born with that?"

"Truly. And you?"

"Mrs. Armitage. Can you imagine a more boring name than that? Before I got married I was Olive Olson. Hard to say which is worse."

"My daughter is named Olivia."

"My husband called me that once, and only once. I was so shocked I smacked him." Mrs. Armitage glares at a memory of her treacherous mate. "I was not a happy soul in those days, not that I'm particularly happy now, but comparatively speaking, I'm overjoyed."

"You have children?"

"Two daughters."

"They live here in town?"

"No."

"Grandchildren?"

"Most likely, though I can only surmise that from my daughters' charts. I haven't seen them since they were children, but every now and then I'll check their transits to see what's going on with them. Difficult lives, both of them. We don't speak."

"Why not?"

"I'll tell you a little story," says Mrs. Armitage, moving over beside Cassandra. "Have you got a moment?"

"Until the bus comes," says Cassandra, warming to the old woman. "You know, I've seen you before. I drive this route. I'm a bus driver when I'm not in school or taking care of my baby."

"I appreciate this," says Mrs. Armitage, smiling painfully at Cassandra. "I'll even pay you, if you'd like."

"Don't be silly. Tell me your story."

"It's this," says Mrs. Armitage, opening her purse and bringing forth a box of breath mints. "Care for one?"

"Merci."

Mrs. Armitage sucks hard, organizing her thoughts, wanting very much to get her story right. "My daughters were six and eight. I was all of twenty-seven when I caught him in our bed with another woman. I threw him out and told him never to come back, but by then he'd brainwashed the girls against me. I'm not sure how he did it, but he did, and they swore they'd run away if I didn't take him back. So I spanked them. And every time they even *mentioned* him, I spanked them. Hard."

"So they ran away," says Cassandra, knowing this particular story all too well.

"Yes," says Mrs. Armitage, nodding numbly. "So I called the police and they found the girls at the other woman's house. She'd been my husband's lover for years. Since before I married him. So I gave him the girls, though I loved them more than I loved myself. I was sure I'd die without them. Absolutely certain. Do you know what I'm saying?"

"Yes," says Cassandra, thinking of her own little daughter dancing to their favorite music, already dancing a woman's dance. "I know."

"But what I'm telling you is it's *wrong* to love them that much. And it's wrong to stay with a man who doesn't love you enough to let you be your*self*. Because if you stay with him, you'll end up like me. All alone."

"I'm sorry," says Cassandra, taking Mrs. Armitage's hand. "I'm sorry you've had it so hard."

"Don't be sorry," says Mrs. Armitage, squeezing Cassandra's big warm hand. "Just start doing what's good for *you*."

"Honey," says Cassandra, taking a deep breath. "I left my old man seven months ago for the same reason you tossed yours, only my little girl hardly knows the man is her father. And just now sitting on that bench, I was about to call him and forgive him because I've been so lonely. But I decided to pray first and ask God to help me know what would be the best thing to do. And that's when I heard you saying, *There are things I could tell you. Things that would save you lots of trouble.*"

The Roar of Time

(a bench in Plaza Park, pigeons and squirrels vying for crumbs—
Mr. Laskin about to make his daily trek to Under the Table Books)

"Everyone agrees the ozone layer is disappearing," says the slender boy with a mess of blond hair.

"Do tell," says Mr. Laskin, an old man with a long white ponytail.

"The ultraviolet rays are coming down and killing everything," says the boy, gazing fearfully at the sky.

"Who is *every*one?" asks Mr. Laskin, closing his detective novel—*FLINT*.

"Scientists," says the boy, nodding confidently. "They have satellite pictures and everything. It's just *gone* over Australia most of the year."

"Scientists used to say cigarettes were good for you, too," says Mr. Laskin, wishing he had one right now. "Doctors used to prescribe them as a cure for the jitters."

"No," says boy, frowning in dismay. "Come on. Really?"

"How old are you?" asks Mr. Laskin, wondering what the boy's mother looks like, imagining her as the heroine of *FLINT*.

"Ten," says the boy, wondering if Mr. Laskin could possibly be telling the truth about doctors and cigarettes. "Do you know Mrs. Armitage? From the bookstore? Where you get your sandwich?"

"Don't let her fool you," says Mr. Laskin, arching an eyebrow. "There's more to her than meets the eye."

"Well, she says I'm Sagittarius with my moon in Leo, Aries rising."

"So what?"

"She says it means I'm inherently optimistic and creative and my life is about to take off in a good way once I get over my fear of rejection."

Mr. Laskin closes his book. "Is your mother named Fiona?"

"Carol," says Derek, his voice dropping to a whisper. "But I don't live with her anymore."

"Why not?"

"There wasn't enough food. So finally I left." He shrugs. "So what do you think I should do?"

"You can live with me," says Mr. Laskin, putting his hand on the boy's shoulder. "I have a variety of camping spots hereabouts. Just don't bother me in the morning. Unless it's an emergency."

"Well, thanks, but I meant about the ozone layer disappearing. It's killing all the phytoplankton."

"Why are you asking *me?*"

"Well, because you're wise. Right?"

"Says who?"

"Well…in all the books I read, you know, whenever people get in trouble or some crisis is coming, they go on a journey and they almost always end up finding some really wise old person."

"And what do they say? These wise old people?"

"Oh, you know, they usually ask a riddle or propose some sort of quest, and if you survive…"

"Like what?"

"Oh, in this one book this boy had to scale the inside of a whirlwind and it took him up to this peaceful sky country."

"What good did that do him?"

"It was very quiet there, so he could hear the universal mind."

"Yeah," says Mr. Laskin, smiling at the sky. "I call her Lulu."

"Well, in this one book, the voice knew everything."

"And it gave him the answer?"

"In this one book."

"Called?"

"*Beyond the Roar of Time.*"

Mr. Laskin looks down at *FLINT*. "Ever read any of these "F" mysteries? *FRESNO, FLORIDA, FRANCE, FLETCHER, FORTUNA?*"

"No. Are they good?"

"Always the same basic story structure. Somebody gets killed. Always several suspects, each with a powerful motive. The detectives, a man and a woman, always figure out who did it by studying the history of the place. The solution is always there. In history."

"So what are you saying?"

"I'm saying," says Mr. Laskin, excited by a sudden upsurge in lucidity, "that you must scale the whirlwind to the peaceful sky country and study the history of the world to find out what you need to know."

"About the ozone layer? How?"

"I'll make a wild guess," says Mr. Laskin, feeling moved to oratory. "Pure conjecture, but then what isn't?"

"Wait. I want to write this down," says the boy, bringing forth a notebook from his back pocket. "Okay, go."

"But first," says Mr. Laskin, holding out his hand, "allow me to introduce myself. I am Alexander Laskin."

"Derek," says the boy, the warmth of the old man's hand bringing tears to his eyes.

"So here's what I would guess," says Mr. Laskin, giving Derek a reassuring smile. "People lived under a brutal sun for thousands of years. We've all seen pictures of cities made of mud in the desert, and you'll notice several things in those pictures. First, most everybody stays inside most of the time because there are no trees for shade. And when people *do* go outside, they cover their bodies from head to toe, except at night when they dance by their tiny fires. Tiny because wood is so scarce. Mostly naked, I'd imagine, night being the only safe time to do so. And they're all skinny because they've learned to survive on very little. So maybe that's what we'll have to do when the ozone layer is mostly gone."

Derek keeps writing. "So do you think the ozone layer will ever come back?"

"*That* you'll have to ask the universal mind, *if* you make it up the inside of the whirlwind. No easy feat, I imagine. And now, if you'll excuse me, I must finish my mystery. The cause of the crime is apparently inextricably enmeshed with the manufacture of automobiles."

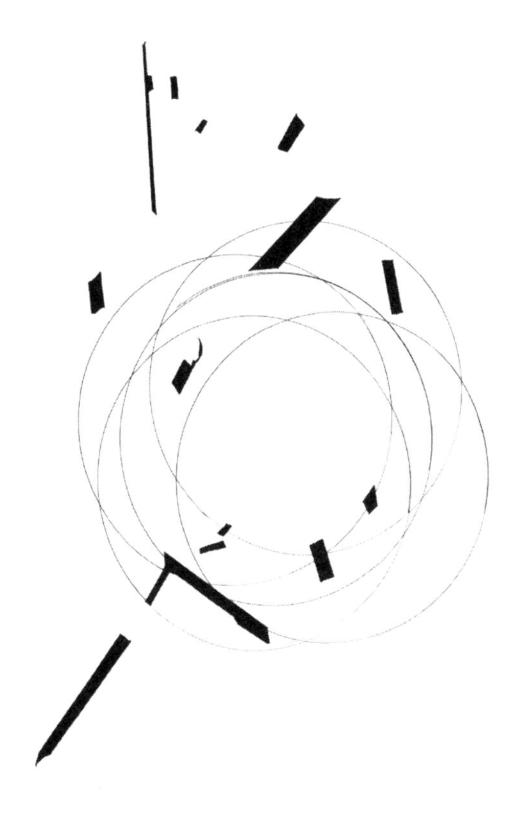

Venus & Mars

(confirming a fundamental Under the Table Books axiom)

Two huge white trucks pull up in front of Under the Table Books, and a man with flaming red hair and heavy black-framed glasses barges into the bookstore yelling, "Is it true the books here are free?"

Lord Bellmaster, in pink paisley pajamas and lost in amorous dreams, stirs on his stool behind the counter. "Our philosophy states..."

"I know, I know," says the red-haired man, trembling with rage. "If we take something, we're supposed to leave whatever we think it's worth, but I don't think anything here is worth a goddamn *thing*."

"So be it," says Lord, smiling affably. "Care for some coffee? Tea? Moustafa just brewed a stunning pot of stick-to-your-ribs Darjeeling."

"So I'm taking *all* the books," says the enraged man, gritting his teeth. "How do you like that?"

"Off the top of my head," says Lord, stifling a yawn, "seems kind of greedy. But what do I know? Do you have the time?"

"Yeah," says the man, signaling six burly men to enter the store with red dollies. "It's time to say bye-bye to your phony idealist stupidity."

"Not idealist," says Lord, piqued by the insult. "Fully operational pragmatic anarchy."

"Hackneyed spiritual crap!" screams the man, grabbing an armload of books. "Moronic mystical barf!"

As Lord watches the men loading their dollies, he resists the urge to call for help. *If our operating principles are sound—and they are—precisely what is needed will come of this.* Still, he finds it challenging to watch thousands and thousands of wonderful books being carted off by a man motivated by hatred and contempt for a community based on love and generosity.

The trucks pull away. The man with flaming red hair and heavy black-framed glasses wipes his brow and scans the shelves, the fabulous inventory barely dented.

Now several people enter the store with boxes of books. Winking and nodding to Lord, they begin distributing the volumes to the appropriate shelves, replacing what has just been taken.

The flaming man sneers at Lord. "Made a few phone calls, huh? Well, call all you want, because I've got more trucks coming."

"I called no one," says Lord, studying the man's tortured countenance. "Word gets around."

"You don't impress me," snarls the man. "Not one little bit. And you'll soon see how *stupid* you really are."

"Let me get this straight," says Lord, making an effort not to shout. "You believe that by taking all our books you will prove *my* stupidity?"

"I'm not talking to you anymore," growls the man, stalking out to greet the next two trucks as his burly assistants resume their work.

Mrs. Armitage arrives to feed the bookstore felines—a fresh batch of *lamb noisettes Melba* in her *Howdy Doody* lunch box. She glares out from under her bonnet at the men filling the trucks with books. "Things are moving fast today," she says, turning to Lord. "Neptune tugging on Mars. And *Venus*..." She bursts into uproarious laughter—highly uncharacteristic of the old gal—and can't finish her sentence.

"What's so funny," snarls the man with flaming red hair and heavy black-framed glasses. "I'm *emptying* this place."

"Venus," she says, catching her breath. "She's been so *active* of late, bopping us with all her big...passions." She takes a step closer to the angry man. "Change or be changed."

And now, as the trucks rumble away with their tonnage of books, an enormous school bus pulls up in front of the store. Painted various shades of turquoise, the behemoth coach brandishes on her flank the words BOOK SCAVENGER in block letters identical to those that previously spelled LODI UNIFIED SCHOOL DISTRICT.

"Hey," says the man with flaming red hair and heavy black-framed glasses, "I didn't order a bus like that." He glances around at the dozens of people filling the shelves with books from their private collections. "But I guess we'll need it."

He orders the six big men to get back to work, the biggest of them retorting, "That bus ain't ours. Besides, it's already bursting with books."

"Oh, of course," says Lord, smiling at the man with flaming red hair and heavy black-framed glasses. "Denny's home. He's our long-range book scavenger. Roams far and wide. It's in his blood."

"Oh, I get it," says the man, seething with fury. "Emergency backup, huh?"

"I suppose you could call it that," says Lord, gazing raptly at the open door. "Look. Here's Denny now."

The man with flaming red hair and heavy black-framed glasses gasps in horror at the sight of Denny—a rangy man with flaming red hair and heavy black-framed glasses—the furious fellow's identical twin.

"Hello, hello," says Denny, holding his arms open for a hug—Mrs. Armitage the first to give him one.

"Just in the nick of time," declares Lord, smiling gratefully at Denny. "Always and only in the nick of time."

"Good books raining down on me wherever I went," says Denny, releasing Mrs. Armitage and moving to embrace the man with flaming red hair and heavy black-framed glasses. "God, you look familiar."

"Stay away from me," shouts the man, dashing out the door and running away as fast as he can, never once looking back.

"Who was that," asks Denny, perplexed by the bizarre reaction of the man with flaming red hair and heavy black-framed glasses. "I hope I didn't offend him."

"He was taking all the books," says Lord, laughing reverently. "Making room for all of yours."

"What a guy," says Denny, reaching down to pick up a cat. "What a wonderful guy."

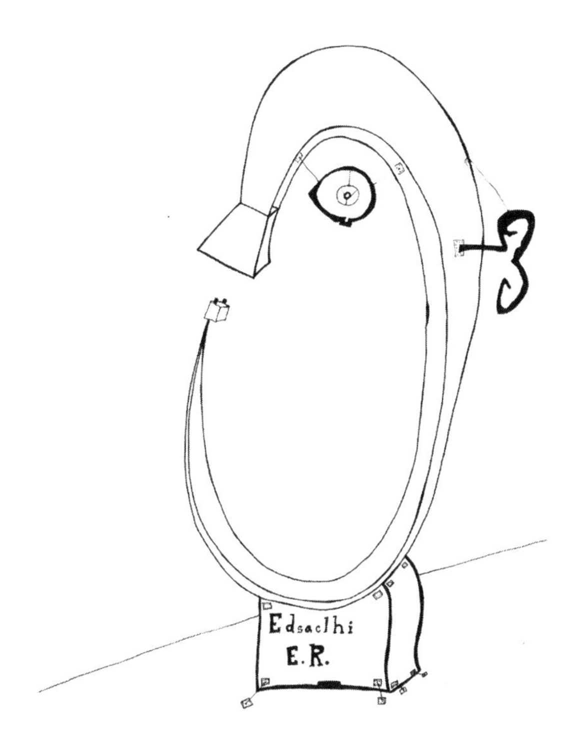

Idols

(whatever will be we'll be)

"I wanted to be a pirate," says Lord Bellmaster, smiling over the counter at the boy. "What do *you* want to be?"

"You," says the boy, a slender child of ten. "Have a bookstore."

"Ah, but I don't *have* this store," says Lord, pointing declaratively at the very high ceiling. "I share it. You can share it, too. And by the way, what's your name?"

"Derek," says the boy, squinting suspiciously at Lord. "What do you mean I can share the store? When I'm older?"

"I mean anyone who wants to be part of whatever goes on here may do so if he or she wishes to."

"I could *live* here," asks Derek, gazing around the massive room. "Where would I sleep?"

"Myriad possibilities," says Lord, winking at the boy. "Now if you'll excuse me for a moment, we have a customer. Yes, my good man? How may we help you?"

A portly chap with a blond mustache places a stack of poetry books and ancient cassette tapes on the counter. "How much for these?"

"Ah," says Lord, smiling magnanimously. "First time in Under the Table Books? Basic policy: you leave what you think they're worth."

"Aw for chrisake," says the man, wincing. "I *hate* stores like this. I hate making subjective decisions. Just give me a goddamn price."

"Okay," says Lord, rubbing the stubble on his spacious chin. "Eight hundred dollars."

"*Nine* hundred," shouts Derek, surprising himself.

"For *these*," says the man, horrified. "Nine *hundred*?"

"Too much," asks Lord, blinking at the man.

"For two Scott Soriano first editions, a *signed* Pat Grizzell, a hand-scribbled D.R. Wagner, a lipstick-smeared Ann Menebroker, and possibly the only known recording in the whole world of Robin Rule reading her Italian love sonnets? These are worth tens of *thousands!*"

"Well," says Lord, holding up his hands in surrender. "That's the way it goes."

The man forks over nine big ones and dashes out the door shouting, "Yahoo! I *stole* them! Yippee!"

Lord takes the nine bills and hands one to Derek. "Here. You earned this."

"A hundred dollars," says Derek, staring in disbelief at the money. "For what?"

"For whatever you want," says Lord, leaning over the counter and peering down at Derek's bare feet. "Please don't take this as parental, though that's exactly what it is, but given the cold mornings of late, why not buy yourself some shoes?"

"I've never even *seen* a hundred dollar bill," says Derek, frowning curiously at the faded green paper. "Was this old hippie guy a president?"

"Invented bifocals and libraries," says Lord, dropping the other eight bills through a small hole in the floor—money raining down on Denny Blumenfeld banging on the piano in the rumpus room and singing a bluesy version of *The Star Spangled Banner.*

The bills flutter around Denny as he finishes the old anthem with "Home, let me hear you say, home, oh yeah, *home* of the bray–yay–yave."

He pockets one of the bills and carries the remaining seven into the kitchen where Moustafa Kahlil and Jenny Morgan are playing gin rummy and waiting for their dough to rise.

"Here," says Denny, putting the money in the center of the table. "Next winning hand takes the pot."

"Gin!" they shout, slamming down whatever they've got and scrabbling for the hundreds.

Jenny gets four, Moustafa gets three. They hold their loot for a full minute—Denny watching the Groucho Marx clock over the stove—and when the second hand bisects Groucho's forehead, Denny calls, "Time."

"Here," says Moustafa, handing Jenny one of his bills. "These two I will keep to pay our outstanding grocery bill."

"Correcto," says Jenny, keeping one bill for herself and carrying the remaining four into the garden where she places them in a shiny brass bowl at the feet of the granite Buddha—weighing the money down with a polished black stone.

Derek and Lord are seated in Fleet Feet—Tracy the Good kneeling before them plying shoes.

"These are the best ones," says Derek, wiggling his toes in the Super Space Catapaulters. "Do you have any old beat-up ones?"

"Why not get them new?" asks Lord, eyeing a pair of burgundy high-tops that would go nicely with his magenta jumpsuit.

"I'll get robbed," says Derek, shrugging. "One kid I knew almost got killed by somebody who wanted his shoes."

"Well, we *do* sell a spray," says Tracy, grimacing. "It's called Glow No More. Dulls the shine, makes hideous greasy stains. Highly effective."

"Yes," says Lord, nodding encouragement.

"Yes," says Derek, blushing as he hands her the hundred-dollar bill. "Please keep the change if there is any."

"Change will be thirty-seven dollars and sixty-seven cents," says Tracy, holding her breath. "You couldn't possibly want me to have all *that*, could you? I mean...that's like half my take-home."

"Oh, well," says Derek, holding up his hands in surrender and winking at Lord, "that's the way it goes."

On their way back to the bookstore, Lord asks Derek, "How do those catapaulters feel?"

"Like walking on air. Like I could jump to the moon."

"So...where do you live?"

"In the bookstore," he replies, afraid to meet Lord's questioning gaze. "If it's still okay."

"Parents?"

"No."

"Anybody know you're alive?"

"Only you and Mr. Laskin and Mrs. Armitage."

"Then we'll find a place for you. And do you know why?"

"Why?"

"Because you're such a wonderfully fast learner."

"Oh, *boy*," says Derek, leaping high into the air. "Oh, boy."

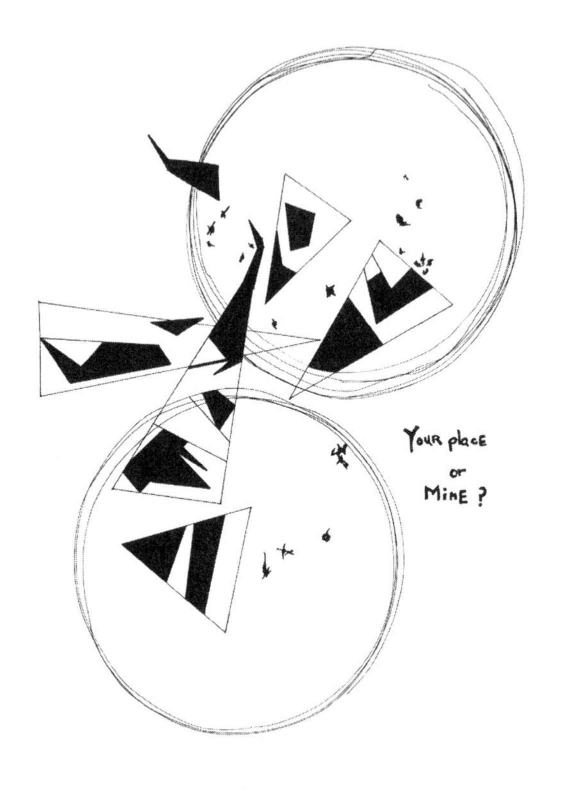

Denny

(being a book scavenger and a very honest dude)

Nobody gets it like my friend A.J. gets it. He gets it so often, if I didn't *know* he got it, I would think he was such an outrageous liar I wouldn't respect him even slightly. In fact, I would think he was kind of despicable. But I *do* know he gets it and so I respect him even though the reality of his getting it is kind of overwhelming and I haven't quite sorted out how I feel about it but I don't find him despicable or a liar because he's not a liar, at least not about how often he gets it.

So two days ago, I can't take it anymore, A.J. describing the latest entree in the sexual smorgasbord of his life and me getting it so infrequently as to be a source of embarrassment and pain and me finding him despicable and dishonest (though I would later alter that assessment) I finally explode, "I don't believe you, man. So why don't you just shut up and let me do my work?"

Well, A.J. is a very sensitive guy. He's hurt I don't believe him, and he says if I want to come to his apartment and verify what he's saying, I'm more than welcome. And I'm so pissed off and curious I agree to go.

So when we're done looking through the books in Napoleon Diaz's mother's attic (we're book scavengers for an anarchist bookstore called Under the Table Books, which, believe it or not is a great job, especially if you like books, which I do) we walk the seven blocks to A.J.'s apartment.

On the way I ask, "So should I hide? Or what?"

"Hide?" He frowns at me like I'm deranged. "Why hide? Just hang out. Meet the women. Enjoy yourself."

"You mean..."

"I mean stay as long as you like. It's a party. You'll see."

We get to A.J.'s building, a beautiful old brownstone, and we take the old-fashioned copper elevator up to the third floor and I wish I lived here instead of in my bus because it feels so rich here, so serene, and the richness and serenity nearly make me cry.

So we're coming down the hall to A.J.'s apartment and up ahead are two luscious women standing there talking and laughing and I'm thinking, *God, A.J.'s got spectacular neighbors.* I mean, these gals have fabulous bodies, lovely faces, and they know how to hold themselves, if you know what I mean, proud and confident, and it never occurs to me they could have anything to do with A.J. because they're so extraordinary, and A.J....

A.J. is a nice guy, okay? He's about my height, not big or small, not particularly handsome, but he has a good smile and a very direct way of looking at people when he talks, but he isn't anything special in the looks department, at least not physically, and he's a book scavenger, not a corporate whatever or some independently wealthy Romeo, and honestly, until I found out otherwise I considered him a nice guy to work with, a guy who lied outrageously about his sex life, and it was getting on my nerves for reasons I've already enumerated, which is why when these extremely beautiful women with their gorgeous legs and flashing eyes and beautiful arms greet him with tender embraces and long kisses, and it turns out to be *his* apartment they're standing in front of, well, I'm speechless and pretty well convinced he *hasn't* been lying, and I'm thinking I might as well go home, when A.J. introduces me as his *very* good friend and these women smile at me in ways I have heretofore only dreamed of being smiled at, and, actually, have never even dreamed of because I have never been the recipient of such open, hungry smiles, so I didn't know about such smiles to dream about them, but now I do.

Here's Susan, a dazzling brunette with big brown eyes and girlish breasts billowing her lacy blouse saying, "*So* nice to meet you, Denny," while Mona, a *zaftig* blond in a sleeveless pink belly shirt pouts at me says, "So maybe tonight there'll be enough to go around."

I decide to stay.

A.J.'s apartment is profound. I never in a thousand years would have expected A.J. to have such a home, decorated so tastefully, so artfully, very much like I always imagined *I* would decorate a place if I could afford the deco furniture, the snazzy lights, the Persian rugs—the painting behind the leather-cushioned rattan sofa an African market scene of smiling women with red bandanas balancing baskets of fruit on their heads—and I can't help saying, "A.J., this is fabulous. Absolutely stupendous. How can you afford all this on what we make?"

But A.J. isn't there. Susan is, dazzling me with the unerring honesty of her posture and the vivid promise in her shining eyes. She's looking deep into me and liking, apparently, what she sees.

"They couldn't wait," she whispers, handing me a brimming glass of excellent red wine. "If you know what I mean."

We hear big fun afoot in the bedroom down the hall—the very best kind of groaning and shouting—easy raucous love.

I blush and take the wine from her, or I take the wine and blush, and all I can think to say is, "A.J. What a guy."

"Yes," she says, clinking glasses with me. "Do you know what makes him such a guy?"

"Tell me," I whisper, intoxicated by the sight and the sound and the scent of her. "I'm all ears."

"I hope not," she says, touching me. "I like other parts, too."

"So," I gush, "tell me how he does it."

She moves closer and closer. "He asks so very nicely and he knows all the big and little ways to thrill a woman. And he always takes his own sweet time, and always gives us however much time we need, too."

"I see. And you are..."

"Ready for love," she says, tonguing the rim of her glass. "You?"

"Um..." I say, downing my wine, "that would be true of me, too."

Olivia's Adventure

(Olivia loves coming to Undo Tayba Buke)

The big orange cat named George allows the little girl to pet him, but when she tries to pick him up he runs away. So Olivia turns her attention to one of the tortoises, but he just sits there and won't put his head out and doesn't make a sound. Olivia looks at Mommy Cassandra scanning the shelves of books. Seeing no look of concern from Mommy Cassandra, Olivia decides to venture out of sight, something she has never done before anywhere except in the little apartment she shares with Mommy Cassandra and Teddy Bear and Gooky Rabbit.

"Two, I'm two," says Olivia, starting down the aisle and practicing her newest speech. "Two. I'm two. How ode are you? How ode are you?"

To her delight, a little person appears before her, a being the size of a mouse, his hair a frizzy tangle, his suit made of gray fur. "What's your name," he whispers, every bit as excited to see *her* as she is to see him.

Olivia is amazed. The little person spoke without moving his mouth, yet she heard his voice. How wonderful. She smiles coyly. "It's me, Olivia. I'm two. How ode are you?"

"Ancient," he says with a sigh. "Are you here with your mother?"

"Mommy firty-sebben."

"I'm *much* older than that," he declares. "I'm a book spirit."

"It's me, Olivia. Where your mommy?"

"Haven't got one," he says, tapping a book on the bottom shelf. "See right there? Mildew. Must be tended to. Excuse me."

He pulls the book out from between its neighbors and disappears into the vacant space—the volume falling to the floor. Olivia claps her hands and waits expectantly, but the book spirit does not return.

"Where he go?" asks Olivia, loving how safe she feels in this canyon of books, wondering when Mommy will come looking for her.

"Psst. I'm over here."

"It's me, Olivia," she says, turning in the direction of the voice. "Book spurt?"

"I'm a book," says a book. "I have a ruby red spine. Do you know the color red?"

"Red an blue an yellow an..." Olivia frowns, trying to remember the rest. "Red an blue an yellow an..."

"Yes, yes, yes, that's me, I'm red, and I'm *dying* to be touched. Please? Would you?"

Olivia reaches for the book, whispering, "It's me, Olivia."

"Gentle now."

Olivia pulls the book from the shelf and it falls to the floor.

"Ouch!" cries the book. "Be careful."

"Sorry." Olivia pets the book. "Feel better now?"

"Would you hold me?" asks the book. "Please?"

Olivia squeezes the book to her chest.

"Now look at my pages."

"Weed me a book," says Olivia, opening to the middle. "Laddin rubba lamp. Laddin rubba lamp. *Big* genie come."

"*You* are my genie," says the book. "I live again through you."

Olivia is asleep in Mommy's bed. Mommy is talking on the phone to *her* mommy faraway after long drive. Olivia is dreaming about the book spirit and the red book—having a feast of sand cakes with them at the playground.

Mommy Cassandra says to *her* mommy, "You should see the book Olivia made me buy today. I swear to god, Mama, she had a grand mal seizure until I agreed to get it. Cost me five dollars and my coolest rhinestone earrings. It's kind of a weird bookstore. You're supposed to leave what you think the book is worth, and this is a mint condition hardback copy of *Kim*, by Rudyard Kipling? Mama, I never in a million years thought I'd be saying this, because I *refused* to read this old English stuff in school, but this book is totally blowing my mind. Totally. It's this psychedelic journey through India with these amazing characters, like the absolute best mystery thriller written by some mystic a hundred years ago. You'll love it. I'll send it to you when I'm done."

How I Got Into the Migraine Mitigation Business

(told by Tomas who lives over Under the Table Books)

My father was in the merchant marine and it is no exaggeration to say that we, my mother, my sister, and I, were always greatly relieved to see him sail away and never glad to see him come home. Fortunately, he was often gone for the better part of a year and he rarely stayed home for more than a month. He was an alcoholic, a compulsive gambler, and terribly abusive to my mother. My most vivid memory of him—I was eight—is of my mother receiving word of his death and shouting, "Thank you God," at the top of her lungs.

My mother worked days as a typist at the university and nights as a cocktail waitress at the Hotsy Totsy Club. It was family lore that the very first words I spoke were *Hahzee Tahzee*, which thereafter became our moniker for the club. My mother was still typing at the university and wowing the boys at Hahzee Tahzee when I left home at sixteen to make a brief appearance in college before embarking on a career as a musician. But I digress.

My sister Rose, two years my elder, disliked me intensely for the first seven years of my life. She saw me—and rightfully so—as her main competition for the attentions of our overworked mother. Hence, Rose rarely spoke to me except to snarl. We shared a tiny bedroom in our diminutive apartment, and I have no doubt that her antipathy to me contributed to my zeal for reading, my predilection for listening to music through headphones, and my habit of spending most of my daytime hours outside. I don't wish to paint a picture of my sister as a villain. She, as I, was doing her utmost to make the best of a difficult situation.

I give you this background because my sister was my first client, as it were, in a practice that would become the only consistent work I've had in my fifty-some years of life—migraine mitigation.

I was seven, teaching myself to play the guitar, reading Robert Louis Stevenson and Rudyard Kipling, and building forts with my best friend Lew in the vacant lot cattycorner from our three-story apartment building. My sister was nine. Our father had recently returned to sea after a catastrophic month at home. He had ransacked the apartment several times looking for cash. He had beaten my mother. And he had terrorized my sister in ways I can only imagine, for I spent all but a few hours of his last monstrous residency with Lew and his family five blessed blocks away.

In the wake of our father's departure, my sister began to suffer from murderous migraine headaches that no over-the-counter remedy could diminish. Nor were the drugs prescribed by doctors much help to her. Only one thing seemed to ease Rose's misery, and that only a little—a head rub from Mother. Thus, I diagnosed my sister's headaches as a ruse for getting more than her fair share of Mother's attention, which diagnosis severely restricted my sympathy for Rose.

Then one evening, as my mother was hurrying off to Hahzee Tahzee, Rose begged for a head rub, and Mother said, "Oh, I can't, honey. I'm late as it is. Maybe your brother..."

I was sitting on the living room sofa reading *Treasure Island*. Rose gave me a withering look and stalked off to our bedroom, the apartment reverberating with a profound silence that often fell when Mother left for the club and before the denizens of the apartments above, below, and on either side of us arrived home from their various jobs and ignited their televisions.

I remember the words on the page blurring, and my entire being tingling with a desire to help my sister. But I couldn't conceive of approaching her. She was ferocious. She hated me. So I stared at the page until the words grew clear again, and I forgot all about my sister as I gave myself to the fantasy of being a pirate.

But my sister did not forget about me. She bore her pain for as long as she could and then returned to me, her face drained of color, her brow furrowed, her lips trembling as she squinted through a fog of pain. "Tomas," she whispered. "Please. Anything."

I closed my book and gestured for her to sit on the floor in front of me with her back against the sofa. Then I placed my hands on her shoulders and said, "Take a deep breath and exhale through your mouth."

Amazingly, she acquiesced to my command without an argument, and thus ensued the first massage I ever gave anyone.

I massaged her shoulders for a few minutes, and then worked my way up her neck to her ears, temples, forehead, and finally to her crown chakra, my fingers kneading her skull with uncanny thoroughness and sensitivity—as if I had done this a thousand times before.

When I began to feel what I now refer to as "the divine

accumulation of trauma-infused energy" causing my fingertips to tingle, I proclaimed in a deep voice, "Now your crown will open and your pain will rise swiftly to leave you."

Which it did—with an audible pop.

I sat back, my arms quivering from the unfamiliar exertion.

Rose got up, and without saying a word, went to bed.

When I tiptoed into our bedroom an hour later, my slumbering sister was illuminated by moonlight, a blissful smile on her pretty face.

The next morning, Rose sang *Oh Happy Day* as she made her sandwich for school, glancing my way several times—and not unkindly.

Four days later I was sitting on my bed practicing my scales (electric guitar through headphones) when Rose appeared at the foot of my bed, her shoulders hunched, her face revealing the renewed ferocity of her suffering. She opened her clenched fist to reveal three shiny quarters, while with her other hand she tapped her throbbing head.

I shrugged and looked away.

When she doubled my fee, I got to work.

Art

(wherein Lord and Jenny compress their spirits
for the sake of possibly making some money)

They are coming down the steps from their quaint old apartment, Lord in black trousers and white dress shirt, his wallet fat with five new twenties, Jenny sans bra in a periwinkle dress, her nails painted silver, her reddish brown hair piled beguilingly on her head, her ears bejeweled with rhinestones. They are artists on their way to dine with wealthy patrons, Lord hoping to gain a commission for a sculpture, Jenny desperate to peddle her painting of an impossible bouquet of camellias.

Their path to Jenny's little white car is blocked by a man covered with a film of dust, his ragged clothes stuck to him with the glue of three bathless days. He removes his tired baseball cap, clutches it in both hands, and says, "I hate to bother you good people, but is there any chance you need some work done? I'll pull weeds, anything. I can fix things, too. Leaky faucets? I used to be a plumber. Busted toasters?"

"Make a good name for a band," says Lord, smiling warmly at the man. "Myna Burnt and the Busted Toasters."

Jenny frowns and shakes her head. "Sorry. We pull our own weeds. No busted toasters."

The man turns to go. Lord brings forth his wallet. Jenny puts her hand on Lord's wrist and murmurs, "We're late."

"It is the artist's duty to arrive late," says Lord, bounding down the last few steps. "And besides, I haven't tithed yet today."

"But the rent," Jenny sighs. "Groceries?"

Lord catches up to the man. "Here, my friend, take this."

The man frowns at the money. "Forty dollars? That's way too much. Are you sure?"

"Positive. Good luck."

"God," says the man, big tears streaking the dust on his cheeks. "You gotta let me work for this. Where I come from, when you're in trouble, people help you, you know, give you work or something. Here..." He glances around at the neatly-kept apartment buildings, the azaleas blaring their spring pinks. "I've been walking around for three days. See, I need sixty-seven dollars for a water pump to fix my truck and get us back home. To Yreka. My wife and kids are sleeping on this old lady's porch down here past the park, and..."

"No time," says Jenny, hurrying to the car. "We're *very* late, Lord. Come on. Please?"

"I'll say a prayer for you," says Lord, winking at the man. "We're on our way somewhere."

The man grabs Lord's hand. "Hey, my name is Michael Carson,

and you're a wonderful person. This is gonna do it. This is gonna start the ball rolling big time, I just know it. Thanks."

Engine purring, Jenny says, "Forty dollars? Don't you think that's a bit extravagant considering our rent is due next week?"

"I'm feeling lucky," says Lord, grinning at the passing trees. "Felt like a perfect way to prime the pump. No pun intended."

"Why is that a pun?" asks Jenny, her mind filled with visions of selling her painting for hundreds of dollars. "Pump?"

"Michael needs a water pump to get back to Yreka," says Lord, closing his eyes. "I pray the universe supports him in his quest."

"Seems like a lot of money." She shrugs. "But...I love how generous you are."

"If I can't give to *him*," says Lord, opening his eyes, "how can I expect the universe to support *me?*"

"Mmm," says Jenny, hoping to avoid a diatribe on metaphysics. "You think we'll have those yummy scallops again? In mint sauce?"

"Why didn't I give him all he needed?" asks Lord, peering out at the graceless mansion of their patrons. "I could have. Easy."

Their catered meal—steak and lobster—devoured, Jenny takes her place on the brilliant blue sofa beside Allan, a chubby man with millions made betting on the ever-rising price of gasoline. Mercedes, Allan's excruciatingly thin wife, enters with the evening's sixth bottle of Chablis, while Lord fiddles with the fire and fights his urge to vomit.

"Well, we've decided," proclaims Allan, lighting his chrome

pipe and puffing a rich Orkney blend. "We won't take no for an answer."

Mercedes clinks glasses with Lord. "We want a dinosaur. Twice as big as the one you did for the Bluford's. More blue and less red. Near the bamboo. Primordial." She giggles. "Three thousand dollars?"

"And for your flower thing..." says Allan, turning to Jenny.

"A thousand," says Mercedes, smiling ardently at Jenny. "It will *just* fit above the window in the upstairs guest bathroom."

"Great," says Jenny, sighing with relief. *Rent money for two months.* "Thank you *so* much."

"A *blue* dinosaur," says Lord, pouting at the flames. "I don't know. I'm not much interested in dinosaurs anymore. This would be my third. If I agreed to do it. I'm more and more drawn to the drum."

"Hmm," says Allan, glowering at Mercedes. "Then what about *four* thousand?"

"You know, of course," says Lord, seeing Michael Carson's tears coursing down his dusty cheeks, "the dinosaur won't come out anything like the Bluford's. Nothing I do ever does. Come out like anything else."

"But close?" says Mercedes, clinking glasses with him again. "Only more blue. Shall we say *five* thousand?"

I should have given Michael Carson enough for his pump, thinks Lord, taking a deep breath. "Sure. Five thousand. But only for you."

Beer or Wine

(regarding fate and will)

Reinforcements having finally arrived to handle the dinner rush, Bernie sits on a stool behind the counter in Steve's Stunning Sandwiches, looking out at what appears to be an endless line of customers. He is tired from making two hundred and twenty-eight sandwiches in eight hours, people impatient, Steve in a horrible mood. Fifty-nine years old, his back aching, his feet throbbing, Bernie runs his hand through his thinning hair and dreams of going home to a hot bath and a ball game on the radio.

Popcorn and beer. Did I finish all the beer last night? Yes. Be honest. Maybe red wine tonight. Variation on a theme. A different buzz. Or how about stopping at Lefty's, maybe actually speak to Flora, ogle the birthmark at the corner of her mouth, make eyes, have a little fun? Oh, why not? Because. Because.

He bites into his avocado on rye with artichoke hearts and hot mustard, and remembers a day long ago—he must have been nine or ten—when his father took him to a ball game, the Giants versus St. Louis, a doubleheader. The concessionaires ran out of beer in the seventh inning of the first game and there were big fights and he remembers a man's horribly bloody face—all for beer. He sighs at the memory of his father pointing at the blood saying, "See? See?"

He changes from deli whites to street clothes, recalling the teasing of his first wife. He would rise every morning, sodden with fatigue, to go off to the cardboard box factory, and she would sneer from bed, "First the pants, *then* the shoes." And he wanted to say to her, "Fuck you, you mean-hearted viper." But he never did.

Even so, he looked forward to coming home to someone waiting for him with a hot meal, someone to talk to, as opposed to no one. *I should get a cat. Or a goldfish. No, a cat. Something warm that needs me. Needs me to touch them. But then what if I go away for a few days? When? Who knows?*

Home to his tragic apartment, heaps of dirty clothes in every corner, a sour smell of old pizza emanating from his dank kitchenette, he drops his jacket on a bag of relatively dry garbage near the front door and makes his way through the squalor to the bathroom.

"My life," he says sadly, "is this accumulation of stuff I ate, junk I looked forward to, crap in crummy stinking boxes." *Oh, quit being so hard on yourself. You're just like everybody else.*

Sitting on the toilet, he peers through the cracked half-window that gives a view across the alley to the apartment of a woman he knows only as the woman in the window, the woman who wears puffy down jackets in winter and less and less as the days grow warmer. Tonight, this crisp fall night, she is uncharacteristically naked, dancing to a Doobie Brothers song about a man never good enough for the woman of his dreams.

The song fills Bernie with excruciating longing, and he thinks of his dream that recurs almost every night, of being chased by killers.

Bernie identifies with the man in the Doobie Brothers song. He has never felt good enough to be loved by a woman sane enough to dance naked on a cool night at an open window to a thumping love song about passion unrequited. And he realizes she is calling to him with the song and her dance, and if not to him specifically then to someone *like* him, a mate, a parallel human.

If only I had the courage to call out to her, to invite her over for a beer. Which, of course, would entail cleaning up a bit and, of course, going out again to buy the beer, and the question, assuming by some miracle she said yes, always the question is, do I have the strength?

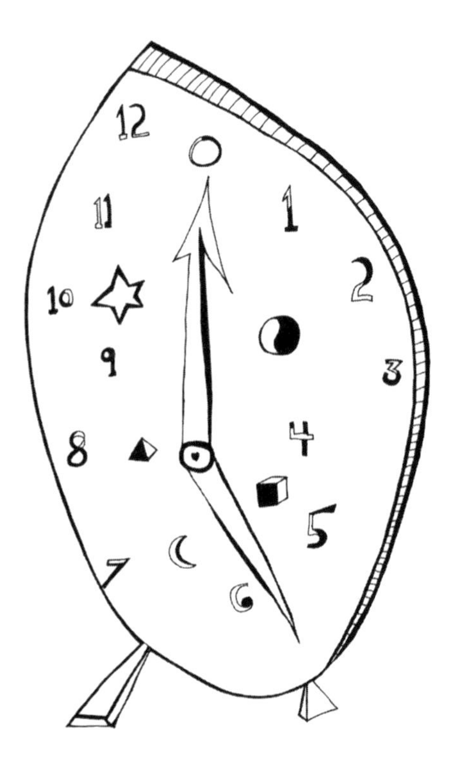

Tomas On Time

(a handsome Spanish Greek guy with a luxurious handlebar mustache)

Shocking to realize how quickly the children become adults, how swiftly they overtake their elders. Yesterday I sat on a beach and watched a little girl and little boy run to the edge of the surf and then run away from the onrushing water and then run back to the edge and then run away shrieking at the tops of their lungs—for an hour without pause. Such wild strength! The momentum of youth.

Lord Bellmaster, for example. I've known him since he was a boy named Theo and I was a young man. Now he is thirty- or forty-something and I am approaching sixty. I remember a day in early spring a thousand years ago—my old red pickup humming like a gang of monks—heading home to my pad above the bookstore after a three-day bash at Lola's farm. Ah, Lola. Where are you now, mistress of lust and hallucinations and the very best *chile rellenos?* I was twelve miles from town, cruising on a dirt road through fields of corn and millet and wheat when I came upon Theo running fast—a boy on the cusp of manhood as graceful as a young deer.

"Ho, Theo," I said, rolling down my window and grinning through the clarity of Lola's mescaline. "How'd you get all the way out here?"

"Ran," he said, keeping up his steady stride. "Running."

"When?" I asked, mesmerized by his feet touching down on the earth and springing into the air.

"This morning," he answered, smiling through his fatigue. "Ran to Otter Creek to see the sunrise on the water. Now I gotta get home before noon or my mother will kill me."

Otter Creek is seventeen miles from town.

"Want a ride?"

"Sure do," he said, petting my truck in thanks. "I'll ride in back."

So this morning I come into the bookstore and find Lord bent over, his back aching from what he doesn't know. I say, "Lord, remember that morning when you were a boy named Theo and you ran seventeen miles to see the sunrise on Otter Creek?"

"One of the greatest days of my life," he says, smiling through his pain. "You came along when I was about to drop. I stood in the bed of your truck with my arms folded on top of the cab my chin on my arms songs gushing out of me as we sailed through a green ocean tires crunching sweet percussion to my bliss."

"I was coming home from three days at Lola's farm—everybody hoping to reach nirvana quick."

I'm about to say more but catch a whiff of Moustafa's bread coming out of the oven and I'm downstairs before I know it, Jenny pouring the blackest coffee into the whitest mugs, the new kid Derek wearing a chef's hat helping Moustafa with the loaves—winter sun slanting through bamboo dappling the garden Buddha.

Oh, this moment.

Pinky Jones

(the other one who lives over Under the Table Books)

On the third floor of the Under the Table Books building, down the hall from Tomas's apartment—before you come to the four creaky stairs leading up to the gray door opening onto the roof where Tomas grows tomatoes and roses in redwood tubs—a brass 3 dangles from a nail stuck in a bright pink door. Tomas's apartment is 1. There is no 2.

A man named Pinky Jones—sixty-four—lives behind the pink door in a big room halved by shoji screens. Three skylights and two small windows provide a modicum of natural light. Pinky has only recently resumed life with other human beings after living alone for thirty years in a cave in the coastal mountains of northern California.

Born John Harlan Weiss, he took the name Pinky Jones when he embarked on his show business career at the tender age of sixteen. You may remember him as the tallest and most appealing character in the moronic sit-com *You Can't Be Serious,* the cast eventually replaced by animated versions of themselves, Pinky the last to lose his job to a highly unflattering caricature exaggerating his height and turning his attractive nose into a bulbous beak.

A gifted singer and musician, Pinky went from television to starring in eleven hugely successful movies about thoughtless idiots, while simultaneously fronting the sextuple platinum pop group *Crotch*. At the zenith of his mega-stardom, he married a hot young movie star, suffered through an ignominious divorce that was the tabloid rage for several months, and then he disappeared—the name *Pinky Jones* synonymous with *Loser* ever after—Pinky, the person, largely forgotten.

"I had no name in the wilderness," he explains to Tomas one rainy morning as they emerge simultaneously from their respective lairs. "I was inseparable from the earth."

"Curious you'd stick with the name Pinky when you came back," says Tomas, recalling the giddy viciousness of Pinky's detractors, the media gorging on the missing carcass of a fallen idol. "Why not go by John? You're a good looking man."

"God says stick with Pinky," says Pinky, blushing at Tomas's compliment. "Or whoever it is that talks to me when I ask for guidance."

"I call her the Mind Boggle of Beingness," says Tomas, leading the way down the stairs.

"Why not?" says Pinky, nodding appreciatively at Tomas's expression for God. "And I understand *why* the mind boggle of beingness says stick with Pinky. I finally understand."

"So why?" asks Tomas, opening the door on a downpour.

"Because Pinky was the name of my fear," says Pinky, holding out his hand to feel the rain. "And the whole reason I came back was to change that fear into love."

"Where you going, my friend?" asks Tomas, about to make a dash for his car.

"Monica's," says Pinky, opening his huge pink umbrella. "You?"

"Laying down tracks at the studio," says Tomas, eyeing Pinky's spacious canopy. "Retro schlock funk. Walk me to my car?"

"A pleasure," says Pinky, overjoyed to be of service. "By the way, if you ever need a male vocalist, I'm a perfect-pitch baritone. Sang day and night in my cave. Glorious echo effect."

"I'll keep you in mind," says Tomas, climbing into his tiny blue Toyota. "Guys who can actually sing are always at a premium."

Pinky loves walking in the rain with an erection.

Standing on the corner of Seventh and Broadway, waiting for the light to change, Pinky senses someone scrutinizing him.

"Yes?" he says, turning to a pretty woman in a yellow raincoat, her long gray hair spattered with raindrops.

"Sorry," she says, averting her gaze—her accent tinged with Czech. "I thought you were someone I knew."

"Could be," he says, awestruck by her aliveness. "Who?"

"A man," she blurts. "Eons ago."

"Eons schmeons, you beautiful girl," he sings in his perfect pitch baritone. "You can't be much over forty, you knockout, you."

"Flatterer!" she cries. "I'm fifty-seven."

"Youngster," he says, offering his hand. "Pinky. Yours?"

"Sharon," she says, taking his hand. "How incredibly brave of you to call yourself Pinky after that old loser Pinky Jones."

"Oh, come on," he says with a twinkle in his eye. "Admit you lusted after him when he sang *Meet Me In The Tunnel of Fun?* Be honest. You wanted him, didn't you?"

"He *was* a fox," she says, mesmerized by Pinky's big soft lips. "And he could sing like an angel. But he threw it all away."

"Have mercy," he says, his hand growing hot in hers. "Haven't you ever gone down the wrong road and gotten lost? And wasn't your only way back through forgiving yourself?"

"Yes," she murmurs, hypnotized by his voice. "Yes."

"So let's forgive Pinky. Together. Okay? One, two, three. We forgive you, Pinky. With all our hearts, we forgive you."

"We forgive you, Pinky," she says, smiling rapturously. "With all my heart, I forgive you."

Pinky smiles up at the sun breaking through a gridlock of clouds—baptized by Sharon's compassion.

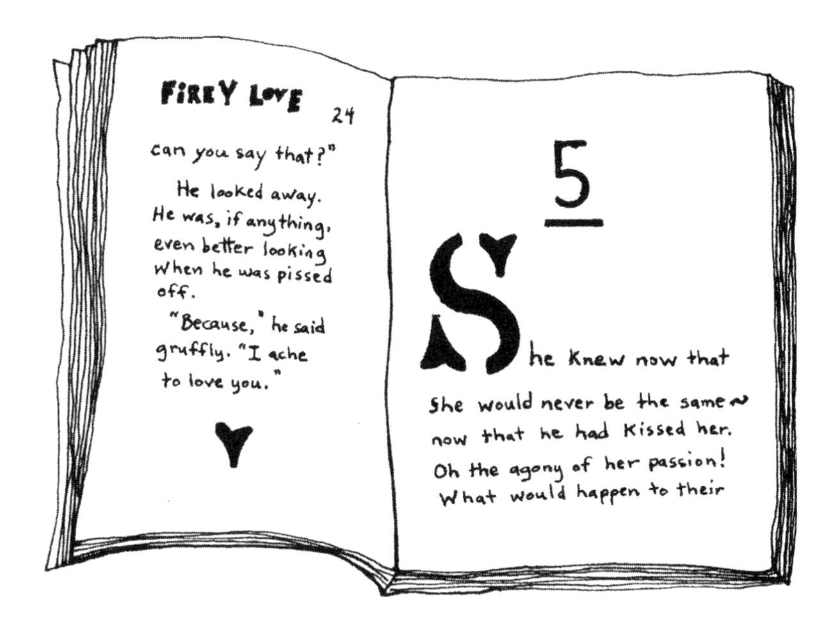

The (Romance) Novel

(whither goest originality?)

Numero Uno—one of the more notorious unknown poets west of Otter Creek, by turns bitter and euphoric, a tough guy with a generous heart and a Bronx accent—is teaching a six-week course on novel writing for women hoping to make the transition from Welfare to Work.

Numero's title for the course is *Sucking The Marrow From the Bones of the Larger Fictive Form*. Never mind that he has never written a novel or even a longish story. Numero has a degree in Speculative Word Ordering from the now defunct Institute of Symbiotic Ideologies.

His students are eight Latino women ranging in age from twenty-three to fifty-nine, only two of them fluent in English. They listen to Numero as if he is some sort of oracular priest, his English words and pidgin Spanish barely intelligible to them, but his enthusiasm—the hope he imparts through his diatribes—excites them tremendously.

"Pith," says Numero, writing the word on the blackboard in the elementary school classroom where they meet every Tuesday and Thursday evening—the women sitting *on* the desks rather than trying to fit into the tiny chairs intended for six-year-olds. "Comprende *pith?* El centro. The heart. Como se dice *heart?*"

"Corazón," says Amelia, forty-nine, a buxom mother of five with long brown hair tinted orange—madly in love with Numero.

"Of course," says Numero, slapping his forehead. "Duh. Eso. El corazón of the story. Es necessario you introduce the reader to some aspect of el corazón del story, el cuento, pronto. En el first chapter. And from then on, chapter after chapter, more and more of the heart is revealed. This is muy importante. Way more importante than el plot. El plot es irrelevante unless accompanied by a stripping away of the veils of emotional deception. Comprende?"

Luna raises her hand. She is thirty-four, the mother of three, a burly brunette who runs an unlicensed taqueria in her tiny apartment and deals dope to local teens. "Es posible hacer mucho dinero con un novel? Ow much moanee I can get?"

"If it's a bestseller," says Numero, closing his eyes, "you can buy a new car, a new house, and have money left over. Mucho dinero."

The women make big eyes at each other. They love the idea of getting new cars and new houses. The other Welfare to Work class they took qualified them for work in preschools where they can't earn enough money to pay for childcare for their own children while they're providing childcare for other people's children. Making novels seems a much better way to go, especially with the new houses and new cars.

"So," says Numero, writing the word *angst* on the blackboard beneath the word *pith*, "que es el corazón of your story? What makes your cuento tick? Because it's pretty clear, es claro, that the great works of fiction are reflectivo de the angst of the author. Entonces, es importante saber que es, what is, el fundamental dramatic equation illuminating your personal saga." He sighs emphatically. "Amelia, por favor, would you translate that?"

Amelia rattles off a staccato volley of words that sounds to Numero like a mix of fireworks and a mockingbird on amphetamines. She goes on and on, the women laughing uproariously before falling silent, as if Amelia has suddenly revealed a painful secret.

Maria raises her hand. She is fifty-nine, roly-poly, with white hair and granny glasses. She speaks no English whatsoever. She asks plaintively, with Amelia translating, how soon can they begin writing their novels. She is hopeful of finishing hers by the end of the six-week course so she can sell it before Christmas. "It will be so wonderful to have money to buy presents for my grandchildren and great-grandchildren, and to buy a turkey for Christmas dinner. Last year we had so little and it was very hard on the children."

Numero feels a major headache coming on. He glances at the clock above the blackboard. Twenty minutes to go. "Yes. Si. Ahora. Let us start writing our novels *now* so we can sell them before Christmas."

"No es difícil we sell novels?" asks Carmelita, the youngest of the women—petite and graceful and exquisitely beautiful. She has three children and works two jobs and lives with her kids in a broken-down car in her cousin's driveway. She holds aloft a paperback romance entitled *El Hombre Con Dinero—The Man With Money*. "Yo quiero escribir...I won to wry a buke lie thees. Okay?"

"Perfecto," says Numero—bolts of pain shooting up his neck and resounding in his temples. "Wry a buke lie that."

Numero eschews the offer of a ride from Amelia and trudges across town to Under the Table Books, praying Tomas will be available to perform some migraine mitigation magic.

He finds Jenny perched behind the counter reading the May issue of *Culture Collapse*, her auburn hair piled high on her head, her cheeks streaked with tears.

"Seen Tomas?" asks Numero, blind from the ache behind his eyes.

Jenny sniffles back her tears and looks up from an article on the plague of illiteracy among college graduates. "I think he's helping Lord cast his dinosaur. Cement."

"Dinosaur?" asks Numero, clutching his head. "Jesus God, I'm going insane."

"A sculpture," says Jenny, wincing in sympathy with Numero. "How about some aspirin?"

"How about a soul transplant?" says Numero, falling to his knees, crushed by the weight of his hypocrisy.

Jenny comes around the counter and kneels beside Numero, her own worries evaporating in the heat of the poet's dismay. "What did you do?" she asks, ever fascinated by the subjective nature of sin.

"I'm teaching a bogus course to a bunch of innocent sweethearts," says Numero, rocking forward and pressing his forehead to the floor. "Because I need the fucking money. I'm three months behind on my child support payments and I owe Moustafa five months' rent for my desk and bed in his penny-ante brokerage bus."

"What are you teaching them?" she asks, wishing *she* felt like an innocent sweetheart—her relationship with Lord fast disintegrating.

"I'm supposed to be teaching them how to write novels," says Numero, gently banging his head. "But only two of them know how to construct a complete sentence. As for paragraphs, forget about it."

"Maybe start there," says Jenny, resting her hand on the nape of Numero's neck. "A good sentence is the foundation of a good paragraph. And so on up the grammatical pyramid."

Numero relaxes—Jenny's touch a salve. "You mean..."

"Start at the beginning," she says, helping him to his feet. "Tell them how you became a poet."

Numero nods, his headache downgrading to a dull roar. "Yes. Exactamente. I'm a poet. What do I know from novels?"

"You have a passion for words," says Jenny, leading him to a beanbag chair in the reading circle. "Every time you come in here, everybody gets excited about poetry again. That's the important thing."

"But what about survival? Carmelita lives in her car with three kids." He sinks into the beanbag, his headache gathering force. "Astrid lives with her five kids in a one-bedroom apartment with another woman and *her* five kids. They *need* to sell their novels."

"They need a new social order," says Jenny, returning to the counter to attend to a customer.

"Yeah, but in the meantime..." murmurs Numero, closing his eyes and surrendering to a vivid memory.

He is sixteen, flunking all his classes—isolated and ignored and purposeless—when something loud and clear interrupts his dismal reverie. With a tremendous effort, he raises his head from his desk and sees a middle-aged woman standing resolutely in front of his English class. She is short and stout, wearing black pants and a cherry red blouse and a blue beret over curly gray hair—a tower of books on the table beside her.

"I am here," says the woman with unmitigated passion, "to awaken you to the mystical possibilities of poetry."

And she reads from the works of her favorite poets.

And Numero feels bathed in a mystic light.

And as the woman closes the last volume of poems, Numero raises his hand for the first time in all his wasted years of high school and asks in a voice choked with tears, "Lady, could you write down the names of those poets you just read?"

Tomas kneels beside Numero in the reading circle. “Hey, buddy,” he whispers. “Jenny says you have a bad headache. Want a session?”

“It’s gone,” says Numero, opening his eyes and smiling sublimely. “I remembered where I came from.”

Moustafa

(telling his story)

In fifty years of life I have called myself many things. Musician, poet, athlete, Buddhist, broker, gardener, dancer, lover. My friends call me Moustafa, and some of these friends refer to me as their teacher in the ways of baking bread and flinging discs. My skin is dark brown. I once defined myself as African American, but I have since discarded this definition. I prefer *earthling*. My house is a former school bus divided into four rooms: kitchen, bedroom, bathroom, penny-ante brokerage office.

I have not seen my father and mother for twenty-five years. I can only imagine what they would think of me if they knew me today. When I was a child, they wanted me to do well in school and go to college. My mother wanted me to be a doctor and have many children. My father wanted me to be wealthy. I didn't complete college and I have no children and very little money.

I was in a band when I was a young man. I played electric guitar and made deafeningly loud music. I slept with many young women who desired me because my band was famous. I smoked marijuana all day long and used cocaine to rouse myself for concerts. Because of these habits, my mind was perpetually clouded and I was unconscious in my sexual behavior. I do not remember any of the women I had sex with because I was not really there.

I was obsessed with making more and more money. It was my goal to sign my life away to a giant media corporation so my loud music would be played all over the world.

One night I snorted so much cocaine my heart ceased to beat. With my last fragment of consciousness I vowed to change if I survived.

Following my near suicide, I gave away all my money and became an itinerant laborer, celibate, and intentionally poor. For six years I had no home. I grew dangerously emaciated. I ceased to speak. I was afraid every minute that my heart might stop again. I was doing penance for misusing young women and wasting my talent. I became too ill to work. Some part of me wanted to die.

Then one freezing winter day I found a book lying on the sidewalk. I stopped to pick it up and lost my balance and fell to my knees. I barely had the strength to move. The book was a collection of short stories by Guy de Maupassant. I opened the volume and read the following words.

> For six years I lived with this thought, this horrible uncertainty, this abominable doubt. And each year I condemned myself to the punishment of seeing this brute wallow in his filth...

How could this be? How could this lost book, opened thoughtlessly, show me myself more clearly than a mirror?

I took the book to Under the Table Books to trade it for a bite to eat. Lord Bellmaster gave me food and invited me to spend the night in a room downstairs. I have been here now for twenty years.

Shortly after joining the commune, I became apprenticed to a master baker, a Jewish Parisian named Myron Kaminsky, who made the legendary breads for the now defunct café Yeast & Cinnamon.

During my second year with Myron I began studying with an elderly philosopher named Rikyu Chin. He introduced me to meditation, tea, and the basic instructions of the Buddha. I taught him how to fling discs and how to make crisp raisin scones.

My father and mother worried constantly about money. I don't worry about money. I am more concerned with being a good friend, though I *am* fascinated by economics, both global and local.

If you have even a few pennies to invest in the electronic markets, I will be happy to facilitate your gamble.

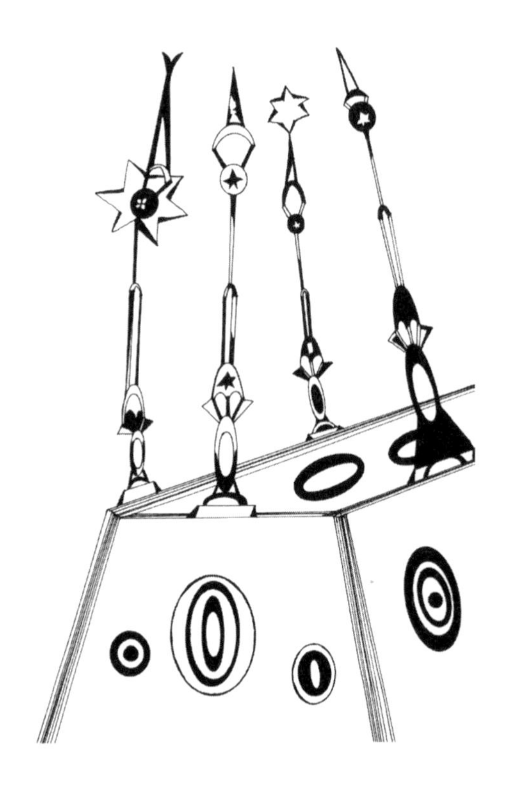

Pinky In Church

(mixing and matching for ultimate tonal euphoria)

Suzie is a round-domed cave in a granite cliff seventy miles from the nearest human habitation in far northern California. Pinky found Suzie—or she found him—thirty-three years ago at the end of Pinky's seventh day of wandering in the wilderness. Feverish and starving and dying of thirst, Pinky happened upon a tiny stream from which he drank the most delicious and refreshing water he had ever tasted. Then he lay down in the crystalline flow, and fell asleep.

He dreamt he was at the kitchen table in his parents' farmhouse. His mother slid a sheet of cookies into the oven. His father came in from the orchard with a basket of pink apples. Pinky felt happiness wash over him as Mother gave Father a kiss on the lips.

"You're alive," he said to his parents. "I thought you were dead."

His mother smiled and picked up her accordion. "There is no death, my darling. Only change."

"A swarm of yellow butterflies fluttered through the trees at dusk," said his father, tuning his guitar. "You could hear the percussion of their wings on the air."

Pinky's mother began to play her accordion and sing a haunting version of *Meet Me In The Tunnel of Fun,* his father accompanying her with a gorgeous run of chords. When they came to the line *We won't come out till we both feel fine* Father sang high and Mother sang low—Pinky's absolute favorite memory of the way his parents sang together.

Pinky woke from the dream to a vast chorus of crickets.

He rose from the creek no longer wishing to die.

"Oh, Mother, oh, Father," he said, opening his arms to the starry firmament. "Thank you for giving me life, for loving me. I've missed you all these years. I felt..." He caught himself, fearing to betray the memory of his parents.

Go on said the chorus of crickets. *We love the truth.*

"I felt betrayed when you died. Betrayed and abandoned and lost."

Then he heard the music of the wind blowing across Suzie's mouth.

"I doubt very much I could stay in town without the churches," says Pinky, kissing Monica's chin. "What am I saying? I couldn't possibly stay away from Suzie without the churches."

Pinky and Monica are snuggling in Monica's bed—rain dripping from the eaves. Monica lives on the second floor of an old Victorian duplex surrounded by towering elms and sycamores. Monica is sixty-two. Pinky is sixty-four. Monica and Pinky have been lovers for seven months—their lovemaking a fountain of youth for both of them.

"You are such a luscious hunk," says Monica, kissing Pinky's ear. "Thirty years alone in a cave. Wish I'd been there with you."

"You'd want your bed," he says, closing his eyes and seeing Suzie's fabulous striations. "I slept on the ground for the first few days, then made a bed of pine needles. I didn't always sleep in the cave. I explored the woods and seashore far and wide, sleeping out under the stars."

"What did you eat?" she asks, trying to imagine life without grocery stores.

"Plants and animals. Grasshoppers. Lizards. Mushrooms. Berries. Eggs. Fish. Crabs. Cockles and mussels, alive alive oh. I think I told you someone lived in the cave before me. They left an axe, a fishing pole, and best of all, a frying pan."

"Breakfast," she murmurs, her taste buds screaming *Coffee.*

"You are one gorgeous animal," says Pinky, watching her slip out of bed and glide to the bathroom. "Maybe make love before pancakes?"

"No need to ask *me* twice," she sings from the toilet. "Never ever."

Pinky stands in the pulpit of St. Alban's Episcopal Church singing a bluesy version of *Meet Me In the Tunnel of Fun*, his rich baritone ringing in the spacious confines. He has the place to himself, having arranged with Carl Klein, the parish janitor, to use the church on Monday and Thursday mornings for communing with the caveness of the joint.

"Living in a cave gets in your blood," Pinky explains to Moustafa over tea in the bookstore garden one nicely cloudy day. "She is so exquisitely responsive. Not just with her echoes, but with her embrace. My God, Moustafa, I lived *inside* her for thirty years. No wonder I sometimes feel lost without her."

"One with her," says Moustafa, reverently.

"The oneness of the lover and the beloved."

"I am you and you are me."

"We are stardust."

"Tea," says Moustafa, laughing. "Bread and chocolate."

"On and on," says Pinky, amazed anew to be alive.

A shadow falls across Derek, blotting out the noonday sun.

"What are you doing?" asks Pinky, gazing down at the slender boy wielding the much too heavy pick.

"I'm digging a hole to make a fort," says Derek, glad for the opportunity to rest. "For when I want to sleep outside."

"How deep will you go?" asks Pinky, envying the boy his task. "Perhaps I could help you."

"Sure," says Derek, nodding agreeably. "The soil is very rocky and the slope is steep. That's how come they didn't plant anything here.

I'll have to make some sort of roof for when it rains, or maybe I won't sleep out here in the winter." He frowns at the stony ground. "I'm not sure how far I'll get. I think I'll have to develop my muscles as I go along."

"A cave," says Pinky, his handsome face going dreamy as he takes the pick from Derek. "With a westerly view. Just like my Suzie. Yes."

"I was thinking more of a fort," says Derek, wide-eyed at how deftly Pinky wields the pick—how easily the ground yields to his mighty swings. "But go as deep as you want to."

"Deep," intones Pinky, warming to the work. "Deep she will be."

Jenny, having eagerly assumed the role of Derek's motherly sister, goes in search of the boy as darkness falls. She expects to find him in the kitchen helping Moustafa prepare supper, for that is where the child has been every afternoon since coming to live at Under the Table Books. But the kitchen is deserted, no sign of any sort of cooking underway.

"Derek? Moustafa?" she calls, her voice ringing in the silence. *How odd.* She can't recall the kitchen ever being empty at suppertime. "Tomas? Denny? Lord? Carl?"

"Out here!" shouts Derek, calling from beyond the garden.

Jenny steps into the twilight. She finds no one on the terrazzo, no one in the hammock, no one in the chaise longue beside the goldfish pond. Now she hears the clank of steel on stone from somewhere down the rocky slope where only cactus and the heartiest weeds will grow—where Derek said he wanted to build a fort.

"Jenny!" cries Derek. "Come see before it gets too dark."

The boy's voice moves Jenny to tears. Every night now she dreams of being pregnant. Every time she sees a baby she feels shaken to the core by the urge to become pregnant.

Now this sweet boy has come into her life, into her extended family of friends, and she feels profoundly connected to him—as a mother connected to her child. How strange and marvelous and confusing and fulfilling and heartbreaking and mysterious and lovely her life has become since Derek arrived—not that her life wasn't fascinating before, but...

She gazes down the rocky incline, the world grown soft and surreal in the deepening dusk, and she gasps at the sight of a boulder as big as refrigerator rising out of the ground and tumbling down the slope through the brittle grass to the bottom of the dry gulch.

"Derek!" she cries, fearing for the boy's safety. "Be careful!"

Derek scrambles out of the ground from whence the great stone came, dancing triumphantly on the lip of the hole. "Wow! Did you see the rock come out, Jenny?"

Now men emerge from the earth—dusty and sweaty and grinning—Tomas and Moustafa and Lord and Denny and Carl Klein, and last of all Pinky Jones.

In the stillness presaging dawn, Pinky steals down the rocky slope and enters the newly made cave to sprawl on the underground earth.

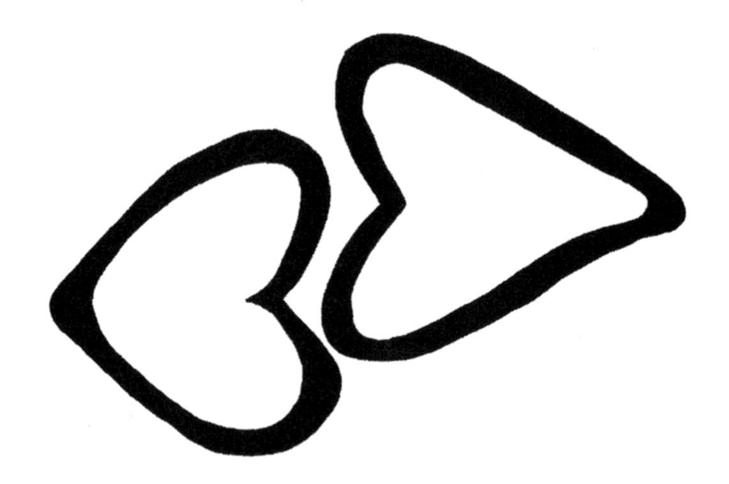

Monica On Love

(for women only, but you know what that means)

On this gloriously warm evening, the bookstore is saturated with scintillating feminine mojo, the male residents of the anarchist enclave having been warned to stay downstairs or upstairs or simply away for the duration of Monica Copia's workshop—a benefit for WRATH—Women Rising Above Theocratic Hegemony.

By 6:30 the bookstore is filled to bursting with women of every age, color, shape, size, and moral persuasion. The volume of chatter is Niagaran, the excitement palpable. Seven great urns of Moustafa's famous papaya tequila punch have been emptied and refilled and emptied again, so it would be no exaggeration to say the girls are ready to rock.

Monica enters at 6:57 to thunderous applause. Garbed in a fuchsia sarong, her glossy gray hair displayed in a five-strand braid garlanded with orange and yellow nasturtiums, her toenails blazing red, her shoulders tanned rosy gold, Monica is a curvaceous two hundred pounds with large cantaloupe breasts and dark wolfish eyes that, to quote her lover Pinky Jones, "take you apart and put you back together and take you apart again, and you're happy to *be* taken apart."

Jenny and Natasha, organizers of the benefit, are also garbed in sarongs, the preferred warm-weather costume of wrathites everywhere.

"Welcome to Under the Table Books," says Natasha, the crowd falling silent as her mellifluous voice fills the cavernous room. "It is my special joy and privilege to welcome our speaker tonight. Her books have been for me, truly, the mother I never had. When I first read Monica Copia's book *I Like Kissing You Out Of Bed*, the portals of sensual and sexual love were opened to me as never before. I felt my every intuition about sex given a basis in solid words. And now Monica has just published her second major work on the subject nearest and dearest to our hearts and minds and labia and clitorises and vaginas..."

The ecstatic mob breaks into ululations and shouts.

"...*A Little Lie Down With Chocolate*," says Natasha, holding the tome aloft. "A manifesto for the life I know *I* want when it comes to love and loving. I give you the high priestess of uninhibited psychosexual intercourse—Monica Copia."

Monica bows to the sizzling throng of well-oiled sisters and says in her deep amorous voice, "Hey you juicy love goddesses, thanks for coming out to party with me."

Thunderous applause recedes into reverent silence.

"I want to talk about kissing while standing," says Monica, her hands describing the shapes of bodies in the air. "The standing kiss when lips meet at the apex of two bodies and the charm of balance dispels all physical disparity. No neck strain, no unequal effort, no arms caught under bodies in bed as we bring our mouths together in the divinity of equality transcendent of gravity."

Natasha and Jenny glide into place on either side of Monica and sway in sexy time to the cadence of their teacher's voice.

"That's why we get so turned on by good dancers," Monica intones. "Because a good dancer knows how to settle into a sensual balance with his or her partner." She laughs uproariously. "I once stayed hooked up with a shithead from hell for seven months because the little prick could dance like an angel." She raises her arms skyward. "Blessings on our ignorant past. May we learn from our mistakes and realize nice guys can dance, too."

"Say more about standing kissing," shouts Mrs. Armitage, folding her arms and scowling out from under her old-fashioned bonnet. "Sounds crucial to me. Sounds like something I've definitely missed out on."

"Equality," says Monica, nodding reverently to the old lady. "Yoga for two. Discovering the nexus of physical harmony—the cornerstone of the architecture of love. In the standing kiss, size and weight gaps disappear if you do it right—the egalitarian starting point for mutual exploration. Parity. Why else does the minister say, 'Now you may kiss,' at the moment the marriage begins? And how often is the future of a relationship revealed in that first kiss? Always."

Downstairs, arrayed around the kitchen table in frozen wonder, sit Denny, Derek, Mr. Laskin, Moustafa, and Carl Klein. In the center of the table is a tiny silver speaker transmitting the voice of Monica Copia from on high, her voice collected by a microphone secreted in the head scarf of a handsome Gypsy woman—Lord Bellmaster in drag, standing in the *Erotic Politics* section well out of eyeshot of those most likely to see through his disguise.

"Should we be doing this?" whispers Derek, frowning worriedly at Moustafa. "I thought they said this was for women only."

"Every man has a feminine aspect," says Denny, wearing red lipstick and dangly turquoise earrings. "My woman is listening."

"Besides," says Carl Klein, wiping the sweat from his brow, "I'm tired of missing the most interesting stuff because I have a dick."

"If you feel uneasy about listening," says Moustafa, gently touching Derek's shoulder, "you are free to go elsewhere."

"But remember," says Mr. Laskin, raising a knowing finger, "they *want* us to know about this."

"I'm sixty-two," says Monica, taking a deep breath. "When I look back over my many lovers, male and female, I see that some of the briefest liaisons were the healthiest and most helpful to me, and I see that my three longest-lasting relationships were the sickest and most dishonest and destructive to me *and* my lover. In saying this, believe me, I am not advocating promiscuity. I am simply challenging myself to consider the healthy purpose of sexual love separate from the contention that longevity is good, brevity is bad, for certainly trust grows over time if well nurtured, and lust expiated with a lover we deeply trust can be as good as it gets."

A lonely woman asks, "But what do we do with our sexual energy in the absence of a receptive lover?"

"Oh, God, sister, I hear you," says Monica, nodding in sympathy. "I feel your anguish, I do. I've been there more times than I can count. But I've come to realize that when we call that energy *sexual* we limit our potential to become irresistibly alluring and happy. I am more and more convinced that what we call sexual energy only *appears* to be exclusively sexual because we are most conscious of it as it arises from sexual arousal. But I say to you, darling woman, to all you darling loveable desirable luscious women, what we call sexual energy is actually an omnipresent power, a metaphysical gravity, love, if you will, that is here all around us waiting for us to open to it in myriad ways so we may become steeped in it, so it may transform us into artesian wells of love. This is our quest: to learn how to access the unlimited reserve of cosmic love—the royal jelly of life."

A silence falls as the gals digest Monica's vision of reality.

"But how do we get over our fear of losing our lover?" asks Jenny, bringing the topic hurtling back to earth. "How do I stop hating the idea of my lover kissing somebody else?"

"By giving up the belief that we *have* our lover to lose," says Monica, looking into Jenny's eyes. "By dedicating ourselves to work and play and creativity and people we love. By ceasing to focus so much attention and *need* on one other person. By transcending the headlock of childhood fears. By...drumroll, please...knowing *absolutely* that anyone who doesn't want to love us is no one we need cling to. By placing *yourself* in the center of your life. And by loving your lover with all your heart, without holding anything back. So that if he or she dances away one day, you will know it was nothing *you* withheld that caused them to withdraw. You will know absolutely that their going is *not about you*."

Little Fart in a Distant Room

(nurturing the divine spark)

Derek, a slender boy of ten, his antecedents Celtic, his skin rosy white, his hair summer gold, stands on a chair at the bread-making table watching Moustafa mix the ingredients for the morning loaves.

Moustafa is a muscular man of fifty, his ancestors African and Caribbean, his skin dark brown, his black hair deployed in seventy-seven slender braids of exquisite knotting—the work of Natasha and Jenny, his adherents in the ways of baking and the flinging of discs.

"The starter, please," says Moustafa, bowing to Derek. "The magenta jar, por favor."

"Magenta," says Derek, leaping off his chair to open the old white refrigerator reserved for baking supplies. "Pinkish purple, right?"

"Or purplish pink," says Moustafa, smiling at the eager lad.

"Got it," says Derek, shivering with glee to have found the right stuff so quickly. "I love the word *magenta*."

"Why, pray tell, do you love the word?" asks Moustafa, feeling a surge of fatherly love for this child so recently freed from homelessness.

"*Magenta* sounds like a poem all by itself," says Derek, giving the jar into the mighty hands of his friend and teacher and protector. "Sounds like *magic* mixed with *gentle* and the name of a beautiful girl."

Jenny is showing Derek how to operate the gigantic copper-colored cash register dominating the eastern end of the counter in Under the Table Books. Money of late has been going out faster than coming in, so the various slots for bills and change are nearly empty.

"Wow," says Derek, dismayed by the paucity of currency. "I've got more than this in my secret stash."

"See," says Jenny, taking a deep breath, "this is where Lord and I part ways. Well...one of the wheres. He *likes* an empty cash register. He says it imparts a sharp tang to life that heightens creativity. Whereas I say an empty cash register creates panic and artistic strangulation." She winces. "Which is why I keep breaking down and taking jobs I hate."

"Why not take a job you love?" asks Derek, waving to Iris Spinelli as she enters the store pulling a bright red Radio Flyer wagon piled high with old *Life* magazines. Iris is a slender big-eyed octogenarian with a splendid truss of pink rhododendrons affixed to her straw hat.

"I can't imagine getting paid for doing what I love," says Jenny, shaking her head. "Except, of course, for working here and selling my art, but those aren't the same as *job* jobs."

"What about teaching kids how to draw and paint?" asks Derek, nodding enthusiastically.

"Oh, you need all sorts of degrees to do that," says Jenny, shrugging dismissively. "A jillion years of school."

"What am I? Chopped liver?" asks Derek, using an expression recently learned from Mr. Laskin.

"Huh?" asks Jenny, frowning curiously at the boy.

"You're teaching *me* to draw," he says proudly. "So why not other kids, too?"

"Oh, but that's for free," she says, hugging him. "For love."

"See," says Derek, reveling in her embrace. "A job you love."

At which moment a handsome hirsute hunk rushes into the bookstore and gazes around in wide-eyed wonder at the treasure-trove of books. "You guys see an old lady with a pink flower sun-hat come in here dragging a wagon full of *Life*s?"

"Iris Spinelli," says Jenny, nodding graciously to the gorgeous hairy guy. "Even as we speak she is adding her wares to our extensive collection of *Life*s and *Look*s."

"I want them all," says the fine furry fellow, whipping out a big wad of green. "Shall we say ten bucks each?"

"We shall," says Derek, striking the SALE button—a friendly clang reverberating through the store. "Right this way."

Derek and Lord Bellmaster are sitting twelve rows behind first base at Willie Mays Park watching the Giants clobber the Dodgers. This is the first professional baseball game Derek has ever attended.

He is so deeply thrilled by the experience, he keeps forgetting to breathe. Their highly prized tickets were acquired in exchange for a battered first edition (1938) of *Larousse Gastronomique.* Jenny made the trade, but finding baseball baffling and boring she gave the tickets to Lord. He, in turn, offered them to Carl Klein who actually played outfield in the Giants' minor-league system for three years in the 1950s and would almost certainly have made it to the majors but for his tendency to strike out and misjudge line drives. Carl stared at the tickets for a long time—untold memories flooding the forefront of his consciousness—and finally declared, "Take the kid. He's never seen the real thing."

Derek had *heard* of Willie Mays, but until Lord gave him a brief history of baseball on the train ride to the ballpark, he had no idea that Willie Mays was a baseball player. Now, having memorized Lord's every word about the game, Derek knows that Willie Mays was the greatest baseball player of all time, and "anyone who says otherwise is an idiot."

*Every*thing about the day has been a thrill for Derek: the train ride, the majestic ballpark on the shores of San Francisco Bay, the brilliant green field beneath a cerulean sky, the bold and graceful players, the fabulous electricity of the gathering crowd, and best of all, getting to spend a whole day with Lord, just the two of them.

In the fifth inning, the Giants leading nine to nothing, the Dodger shortstop dives to snag the hurtling orb, leaps to his feet from full sprawl, and throws out the hustling Giant by a hair. Derek is so moved by the sheer beauty of the play, he leaps to his feet and shouts, "Wow!"

In response to Derek's enthusiasm, a grizzled man sitting in front of them turns around and says, "You should be ashamed to wear those hats." He is referring to the Giants caps Lord and Derek are sporting—vintage black and orange ones from the 1950s loaned to them by Carl Klein for the day, one of the caps autographed by Willy McCovey, the other by Felipe Alou.

Derek feels the man's rebuke as a physical blow—tears of hurt and confusion springing to his eyes.

Lord puts his arm around Derek and whispers in his ear, "It *was* a marvelous play. Very possibly one of the most astonishing plays I've ever seen. The impossible made plausible. Physical genius of the highest order. Blue-collar ballet. But see, kiddo, most die-hard Giants fans, I among them, hate the Dodgers with such a burning irrational caveman stupidity we are incapable of appreciating them even when they do something transcendent of mere rivalry. So don't take it personally, okay?"

Derek sniffles back his tears and says to the man in front of them, "I'm sorry, sir. I'm only just now for the first time in my life learning about this game. I didn't know you weren't supposed to cheer the other guys when they did something incredible."

The man turns around again, his scowl changing to a smile. "It *was* an excellent grab, I must admit. Reminds me of what Omar Vizquel used to do *routinely* three or four times a game way back when. Hey, where'd you get those cool old hats?"

Derek and Mr. Laskin, a white-haired elder with a handsome weather-beaten face and luminous blue eyes, are dumpster diving behind Alberto's Ultra-Gourmet Grocery, the cheeses fabulous today. Dusk is descending. Soon Mr. Laskin will accompany Derek home to Under the Table Books before heading down to the river where he's been camping with his friend Leo since the cold spell broke a week ago.

Derek regales his favorite oldster with a vivid account of the Giants' stirring victory over the Dodgers in the seventeenth inning—after the Giants blew an eleven-run lead in the ninth. Mr. Laskin helps Derek climb out of the dumpster and they plant themselves on a bus stop bench to divvy up their spoils, most of the pungent cheeses destined for the kitchen at Under the Table Books.

"Ah, you see this *Saint-Marcellin?*" says Mr. Laskin, holding the moldy chunk of cheese up to his large Gallic nose. "Unmistakable zenith of rot. Used to buy hundreds of pounds of this every year." He gives Derek a serious look. "Promise me you'll never buy a *Saint-Marcellin* after November or before April. Can't possibly be fresh. And this..." He buries his nose in a barely moldy half-round of Brie. "This is *Brie de Melun*. We'll want to eat this pronto. Already slightly overripe, which is just the way I like it. I'll take a small wedge for me and Leo, the rest goes to the bookstore." He sighs and sits back, suddenly weary. "You know I *owned* a baseball team and a state-of-the-art stadium, too, before they took everything away from me. Loved the game. Loved the suicide squeeze, the hit-and-run, the double switch in the ninth—a transfusion of hope. I was a hands-off owner. I trusted my skipper."

"Do you miss being rich?" asks Derek, leaning against Mr. Laskin—loving him *so* much even if everyone else thinks he's deluded.

"Oh, sometimes," says the old man, gazing up at the first star of the evening. "Not so much the money, but my few good friends. The only people who *really* knew me for the better part of my life."

"Can't you call them up?" asks Derek, overcome with a longing to see his mother again.

"They are all dead now," says Mr. Laskin, nodding wistfully. "Raphael and Jean and Philip and Amy and Louise and Carmen. Gone to whatever comes next." He chuckles and lifts a small wedge of cheese to his lips. "This *Coeur-de-Bray?* I will forever associate this luscious *fromage* with the hot-air balloon vacation the seven of us took from Paris to Brindisi. Just for the hell of it. Just because we could."

Derek and Natasha, a brown-skinned goddess in her early twenties, use three different cheeses rescued from the dumpster to make four enormous soufflés for supper, sixteen mouths to feed.

"Almost more trouble than it's worth," says Natasha, sliding the last of the molds into the oven. "If I didn't have you helping me, my little man, we'd be having good old soup and bread and cheese, believe me."

"I *love* learning to cook with you," says Derek, closing his notebook of pages freighted with myriad steps for making an excellent béchamel sauce. "You're a fantastic chef."

"I'm a novice compared to my brother Ben," she says, stretching her long arms skyward. "Let's go pick salad stuff and then I've *got* to put my feet up."

"I can pick the salad stuff," says Derek, taking Natasha's hand. "You've done more than enough for one meal."

"Oh, child," she says, lifting him with ease and cradling him against her full young breasts. "You are so sweet to me."

She kisses him again and again until he laughs for joy and says, "Stop," meaning *Keep going.*

"I love the earth between my toes," says Natasha, setting the lad down. "Love to get my fingers in the soil."

Natasha and Derek wander through the verdant garden, filling their baskets with lettuce and carrots and spinach and radishes, when all of a sudden the world grows absolutely silent.

They hold perfectly still for a short infinity, and they can *feel* themselves expanding into the mysterious spaciousness of No Sound.

Now comes a little fart from a distant room—the cosmic joke taking a moment to sink in before they both burst out laughing.

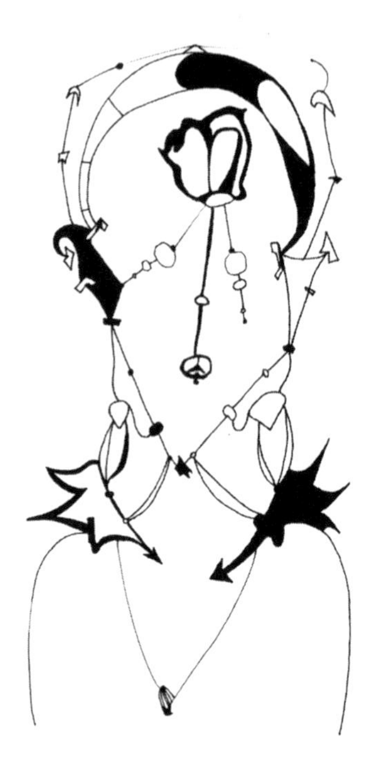

Metaphors & Archetypes

(runnin' round your heart, runnin' round your brain)

Denny, a rangy book scavenger with a self-image as variable as the weather in maritime Canada, is making one of his rare appearances at the helm, as it were, of Under the Table Books. And though he feels completely out of his element manning the bridge (the stool adjacent to the cash register), historical data suggests he possesses an uncanny talent for trading things of little value for things of inestimable worth.

Recently returned from a wooly ramble in his solar-powered school bus through Oregon Washington British Columbia Alberta Montana Idaho Nevada and Southern California, Denny is charging his batteries before setting off for the Southwest, Deep South, Mexico, and Iowa. He longs to be in a relationship with a woman who'd like to go traveling with him, and to that end he is avidly reading Monica Copia's classic treatise on love and relationships *I Like Kissing You Out Of Bed.* Having once heard Monica speak, Denny is now a true believer, truly believing that Monica's text holds the key to his ultimate success as a relationship-worthy guy.

As our story begins, Denny is reading and rereading Chapter Seven of *I Like Kissing You Out Of Bed: The Archetype As Metaphor,* each sentence a revelation to him.

> The Noble Loner and the Misunderstood Genius are two closely related archetypes frequently inhabited by American men born in the latter half of the twentieth century. In either case, or in their hybrid form, The Misunderstood Noble Loner Genius, these archetypes render successful long-term liaisons virtually impossible. Why? Because the maintenance of optimal archetypal equilibrium requires Noble Loners and Misunderstood Geniuses to *remain essentially alone.*

"Whoa," says Denny, looking up from the book as a beautiful buxom blue-jeaned belly-button-baubled blue-eyed blond from Belgrade enters the store, her golden hair in a long ponytail, a small pearly white falcon perched on her shoulder. "She sure nailed *my* ass."

"Excuse me?" says the bountiful Belgradian, impressively arching her eyebrow. "Did you, I hope, just say something about my ass?"

"Oh, no," says Denny, blushing attractively. "This book. Seems to know all about me." He coughs self-consciously. "Are you looking for anything in particular today?"

"You mean something other than a partner? Someone like you,

perhaps? For adventuring through this miraculous life?" she asks, brandishing a vivacious Slavic smile. "Did you mean am I looking for something other than a good strong man to roam the world over with me in search of beauty and miracles and lusciously sacred places for making splendiferous love? Were you asking me if I wanted to get to know you and to overcome the personal and cultural roadblocks to a genuine connection of our chakras one through eight? Or were you being literal? Did you *really* mean am I looking for a book or books about some mildly appealing substitute for the deep and intense partnership of soul mates? You and me maybe. Not really. Just browsing. Tell me, what is the name of this extremely accurate book you're reading?"

"*I Like Kissing You Out Of Bed,*" he says, mesmerized by everything about her and then some.

"That remains to be seen," she says, her husky voice ringing all his bells, one through eight. "But what's that book you're reading?"

"Um...*I Like Kissing You Out Of Bed,*" he gurgles. "Really."

"But how do you know?" she asks, pursing her oh so kissable lips. "We've only just met."

"I...well..." he stammers, as beautiful poems and proclamations of love gather on the tip of his tongue like honey bees on maple syrup. *Oh, if only I had the courage to speak these paeans of love aloud to you.*

She looks deep into his eyes and says with untrammeled, unmitigated, uninhibited honesty, "Please rise above your self-doubt and tell me you very much want to get to know me so we can travel together for a time and taste together our moveable feast."

"Really?" he squeaks, terrified by the possibility she actually means what she's saying.

Sensing his profound unease with the who what why and how of her, she says, "Never mind," and dances off into the *Blatantly Sexual Fiction and Poetry* section.

"I...er...um..." he stammers, glued to his seat by his chronic endemic for all intents and purposes permanent doubts and fears.

"Your archetype precedes you," she sings in clear ringing tones. "But you *can* leave it behind, believe me."

At which moment, the magnificently unkempt Lord Bellmaster enters the store crooning disconsolately. "Ho, Denny. What news?"

"This book," says Denny, holding the volume up so the front cover—a photograph of one of Monica's stupendous breasts—is right at Lord's eye level. "This book is seriously kicking my ass."

"How so?" queries Lord, transfixed by Monica's fabulous boob.

"By lucidly revealing how I am trapped in the metaphor of my archetype," says Denny, still somewhat dazed by his encounter with the bountiful Belgradian. "Do you know which archetype *you* signed up for?"

"Guilt-ridden horny bastard?" guesses Lord. "Is that in there?"

"Absolutely," says Denny, flipping back a few pages. "Only Monica calls you the Sex-Obsessed Moralist, which is often closely aligned or hybridized with the Alarmingly Charming Self-Saboteur."

"Whoa," says Lord, taking the book from Denny and ravenously imbibing the terrifyingly accurate description of his personal modus operandi. "Nailed my ass, too."

"Speaking of archetypes," says Denny, taking the book back from Lord, "here come the men from upstairs."

Enter Pinky and Tomas, the former a boyish sixty-four, the latter a darkly handsome fifty-something.

"Amigo," says Tomas, shaking Denny's hand. "What's happening?"

"Archetypes," says Denny, tapping Monica Copia's treatise on love. "You know yours?"

"Probably same as you," says Tomas with a pliant shrug. "Robin Hood sans Maid Marion."

"And you, Pinky?" asks Lord, inhaling deeply of the delicious scent of freshly baked bread wafting up from the kitchen.

"Well, I *was* a Wounded Innocent Recluse Saint hybrid," says

Pinky, being none other than Monica Copia's current main squeeze, "but I've since morphed into a Lusty Sensual Singing Lover."

"Lucky you," says Tomas, brightening at the sight of the buxom blue-jeaned belly-button-baubled blue-eyed blond from Belgrade making her way to the counter with several volumes of erotic poetry—a small pearly white falcon perched on her shoulder.

"Luck is the manifestation of cosmic synchronicity," says Pinky, bowing flamboyantly to the beguiling mistress of the little raptor.

"I will trade you my falcon for these erotic love poems," says the sexy Slav, deftly aiming her words at Denny's heart. "She requires special handling, but she's worth a small fortune."

Denny takes a deep breath and prepares to break through his emotional logjam into the sensuous reality he has longed to enter since adolescence. He is literally one exhalation away from asking this bewitchingly powerful woman to teach him everything she knows about the handling of her precious bird, when for no good reason Lord Bellmaster interjects, "Just how small a fortune are we talking about?" and begins to giggle like a nervous little boy.

Lord's giggling starts Pinky and Tomas giggling, too, and Denny, despite a valiant effort, can't help but giggle with them, and soon all the sweet male misfits are on the floor laughing their butts off—the Belgrade bombshell vanishing out the door and leaving her falcon perched on the cash register gazing disdainfully at the goofy humans.

"You know," says Denny, the first of our fallen heroes to rise, "I really think she liked me. I really think she might have been the one I've been looking for my whole life. And now she's gone. And all that's left of her is this imperious little bird."

"Don't worry," says Pinky, gasping for breath, "if she really loves you, she'll be back."

"Right," says Lord, choking with laughter. "And Snow White and the prince have great sex every night for all eternity."

"She would devour you," says Tomas, rolling onto his back and staring at the ceiling. "A woman like that..."

"Yes," says Lord, frowning quizzically at Tomas. "A woman like that...what?"

"A woman like that," says Pinky, closing his eyes and imagining how fun it would be to make love to the sexy Slav, "is succinctly described on page seventy-nine, second paragraph of *I Like Kissing You Out Of Bed*.

Denny flips to said page of said tome and reads:

> The Fearless Female Adventurer and her near twin The Woman As Strong As Any Man will find seriously slim pickings among American men born in the latter half of the twentieth century. Why? Because The Supremely Strong Fearless Woman Adventurer's strength and straightforwardness, along with her readiness to immediately move into active intimacy with a man, is fiercely antithetical to the dominant belief underlying modern male emotionality. To wit: there must be something wrong with a woman who revels in her own masculine energy.

"Darn," says Denny, gazing into the stern black eyes of the falcon. "So now what am I supposed to do with *you?*"

Ruby Heartsong

(exquisite lushness of the kitty's fur)

Peter Franklin, famous throughout the local watershed for his striking resemblance to the late great actor Alec Guinness, stands before Lord Bellmaster at the counter in Under The Table Books with two incomparable day-old pumpkin pies secured from the *Baked Goods* refrigerator, along with a magnificent black-and-white photograph of Alec Guinness as Colonel Nicholson in the classic war film *The Bridge on the River Kwai,* framed in dark mahogany.

"For these precious items," says Peter, *sounding* exactly like Alec Guinness, "I will give you this Ruby Heartsong gift certificate, good for one fabulous session." He clears his throat. "Fair enough?"

"I'm sure it is," says Lord, scrutinizing the small white card. "Is this silk? It feels like..."

"Skin?" says Peter, arching an eyebrow and nodding archly. "I don't doubt it. Ruby rarely leaves a sensual opportunity unexploited."

The lettering—sharply rendered Nicolas Cochin Antique with a maddening touch of purple in the black ink—reads

ONE FABULOUS SESSION

Ruby Heartsong, LOTFLC

Sensual Realignment and Ignition

"You've been to her?" asks Lord, his fingers tingling delightfully as he fondles the silky card.

"I *live* because of Ruby's ministrations," says Peter, turning profile and gazing dramatically at the rafters in exquisite mimicry of Alec Guinness as Colonel Nicholson. "I would follow her to the ends of the earth. And so will you, once she's had her way with you."

"What exactly does Ruby do?" asks Lord, imagining a Rubenesque redhead with long arms and a French accent.

"She... oh what's that expression? Damn. I never...because, you see, my generation lacks a point of reference for...ah, here it is... she will rock your world."

"You mean..." says Lord, staring in wonder at the dashing old gentleman, "she...that is...does she..."

"Spit it out," says Peter, frowning at Lord. "I must have these pies to the philatelist society by eight."

Lord reddens. "Um...does she...sex?"

Peter sighs in exasperation. "My dear fellow, Ruby Heartsong is a licensed Liberator of the Five Lower Chakras. She studied for seven years at the Institute For Integral Sensuality where she is now the resident diva of radical touch. A far more salient question would be: are *you* prepared to be changed forever? If not, I suggest you give that certificate to someone who is. Prepared. To be changed. Forever."

"You know," says Lord, thrilled by Peter's challenge, "for a frequently flustered fellow you certainly have your lucid moments."

Peter bows graciously. "So true. That's because certain things in life transcend confusion, and a fabulous session with Ruby Heartsong is one of those things." He makes a mystical gesture and intones, "May the force rock your world."

Lord and Jenny lie side by side in their queen-sized bed, neither able to sleep, the atmosphere stifling despite the windows being open to a cool breeze. They have been bedmates for three years, their sexual relationship preceded by seven years of devoted friendship—and now they're on the verge of hating each other.

"But I love you *so* much," says Lord, wanting to leap out of bed and run away into the night. "Why can't…"

"I feel insane," says Jenny, wanting to scream. "I miss you when you're gone, and when we're together all I can think about is getting away from you." She sighs profoundly. "We haven't made love in three months and eleven days."

"And there's nobody else," he whispers. "At least not for me."

"I fantasize," she says, penetrating Lord's formidable force field to take his hand. "But it never goes beyond fantasy."

"I, too, have imaginary lovers," says Lord, feeling as flaccid as he has ever felt. "But mostly I'm not much aroused."

"We're still so young," she says, biting her lower lip. "Maybe we should make a baby. Would *that* arouse you?"

Lord takes a deep breath and imagines making a baby with Jenny, and the idea *does* send a bit more blood to the appropriate sector—but not much more. "This isn't just about sex, you know," he says, his heart aching. "We have such different impulses, such differing sensory modalities, such contrapuntal ways of improvising, such antithetical notions about money and time and space and..."

"I know," she says, swallowing her tears, "but when I try to imagine *not* being with you, I...I fall apart."

He takes her in his arms, feeling brotherly and fatherly and avuncular, but not especially loverly. *Why doesn't she turn me on anymore? She's got a fabulous body, a marvelous voice, and she knows just how to...*"

"So for the next little while how about I sleep in the guest room?" she says, immensely relieved to finally be making the suggestion. "We'll see how we feel not living so close to each other all the time."

"Some nights I'll sleep at the store," he says, fascinated to feel so swiftly aroused.

"We'll be much more independent," she says, kissing his throat. "Maybe even date other people."

"Sweetheart," he moans, throbbing with pleasure.

"Ooo, Lord," she says, taking command of him. "I knew we'd get this straightened out."

The day dawns warm and still. Lord lies on his back listening to Jenny in the shower, the roar of the downpour lulling him into a dream of making love with...*Mrs. Armitage?*

He wakes with a shout—half-terror, half-delight—shocked and thrilled by his vision of mating with the old crone—his imagination endowing her with the body of a young Venus.

Now Jenny—the real thing—emerges from the steamy bathroom

into a shaft of sunlight—naked rosy goddess—and gives Lord a tender wide-eyed look of love. Yet he feels not a glimmer of desire for her.

"Shall I come back to bed?" she asks sorrowfully. "Or do we..."

"Or do we what?" he asks, hoping she'll say what he's thinking.

"You say."

"Need some time apart."

She nods and turns away.

The pale blue door swings inward to reveal a slender Eurasian woman in black pajamas, her feet bare, her fingers free of rings, her black hair extremely short, her earlobes pierced by tiny gold loops, her eyes huge and brown, a mischievous smile on her remarkably symmetrical face—her age impossible to guess.

"Ruby Heartsong?" Lord asks timidly, expecting someone twice the size of this delicately beautiful woman.

She nods to acknowledge his appellation. "Mr. Bellmaster," she says, her accent Vietnamese. "I recognize you from your bookstore."

"Oh..." he begins, struck dumb by the sight of a sumptuous king-sized bed—gray comforter over pink flannel sheets—standing in a grotto of vivacious ferns. "I was expecting a massage table."

"Yes," she says, ever so gently taking his hand and leading him bedward. "My practice is better suited to this larger format."

Ruby and Lord convene in the middle of her bed and face each other. Lord sits cross-legged, Ruby kneels. Lord has removed his shoes and socks, but is otherwise fully clothed—black slacks, black T-shirt, turquoise belt. Ruby has unbuttoned the top three buttons of her pajama top and is fiddling with the fourth and final button.

"What exactly *is* sensual realignment?" asks Lord, absolutely terrified of what he doesn't know.

Ruby laughs a hearty laugh. "May I be frank with you?"

"You mean..." gulps Lord, electrified from head to toe, "you want to be the man and I'll be the..."

"No, no," she says, resting her hands lightly on Lord's knees. "May I speak openly and explicitly to you about our bodies and our emotions?"

"Oh, *that*," he says, breathing a sigh of relief. "Words. Sure."

"Do I appeal to you?" she asks, gazing into Lord's eyes.

"Well," he says, electrified anew, "you mean..."

"I mean, does it give you pleasure to look at me?"

"Yes," he says, really *seeing* her for the first time. "*Big* pleasure. You're lovely beyond lovely. I adore your voice, and..."

"What if you were blind and deaf?" she asks, scanning his face and body. "What if you could only feel me and smell me, but could never be inside of me? Would you still want to be my lover?"

"Sure," says Lord, wholly unaware that he is shaking his head *No*.

Ruby moves her head in mimicry of him. "But wouldn't that be terribly frustrating for you?"

"Not at all," says Lord, nodding *Yes*. "I don't think so."

"You're afraid to tell me what you're really feeling, aren't you?" says Ruby, nodding along with him.

"No way," says Lord, his nodding emphatic.

Ruby touches Lord's chin to stop his nodding. "Lie down, Lord. It's time to undress you."

"I'm afraid of you," he blurts—a gong of truth.

"Now we're getting somewhere," she says, deftly unbuckling the quaking man's belt.

&

Walking home from his first fabulous session with Ruby Heartsong, Lord gets lost a few blocks from the bookstore. Nothing seems to be as it was before. The most familiar sights are new to him. He bends down to pet a friendly cat and his eyes fill with tears at the exquisite lushness of the kitty's fur. He stands up and beholds a world drenched in golden light, a flock of pigeons wheeling in the azure sky—angels on a divine mission to enliven the air with the beating of their wings.

"Didn't I tell you so?" says a marvelous voice—deep and soft and sublimely British-accented. "Didn't I tell you she would change your life?"

Lord turns away from the throng of angels and beholds Alec Guinness, the late great British actor incarnate in the body of Peter Franklin, retired postal employee and habitué of Under the Table Books, looking dapper in a black tuxedo.

"You most certainly did," says Lord, kissing Peter's hand in humble gratitude.

"Welcome to your new everything," says Peter, bowing gallantly. "I recommend you be especially tender with yourself for the next day or so. Those new synapses need settling. New strings on the old piano."

"I'm lost," says Lord, thrilled by the sound of his own voice. "I have no idea where I am."

"Excellent," says Peter, taking Lord by the hand. "Fabulous. I will guide you to the bookstore on my way to the philatelist ball."

Princess In Tower

(further expansions of the boundaries of erotic consciousness)

Mrs. Armitage, hidden beneath several layers of old-lady clothes, arrives at Monica Copia's house on a sun-filled summer morning just as Pinky Jones, a handsome man with a dreamy smile on his face, comes dancing down the stairs from Monica's door, his condition unmistakable — deeply marvelously sexually satisfied.

Mrs. Armitage, her bonnet obscuring her face, glowers at Pinky, for she reflexively associates a man's joy with a woman's sorrow.

"Good morning to you, my beauty," Pinky croons, his sexually enhanced sensory powers espying the luscious body hidden beneath Mrs. Armitage's baggy shroud. "Stunning."

"Who is? What is?" she snarls, shocked to feel him seeing through her disguise. "Mind your own business!"

"But it *is* my business," he says, caressing her with his eyes. "To love the whole truth of you, and nothing but the truth."

"Balderdash," says Mrs. Armitage, terrified of being unmasked.

"I, too, was in hiding for many years," he says, locking eyes with her. "I, too, lived in fear of being discovered. Until one day I realized that what I feared most was not other people, but myself in relation to them." He winks at her and blows her a kiss. "Until we meet again."

She watches the happy man stride away into the brilliant day, and a rosy hue suffuses her cheeks—her long-clenched heart unfurling.

"I know it *sounds* counterintuitive," says Monica, sending forth clairvoyant tendrils to search for chinks in Mrs. Armitage's psychic armor, "but the successful mending of a broken heart almost always requires the heart be broken again, and yet again."

"Explain," snaps Mrs. Armitage—her false persona wobbling.

Monica and Mrs. Armitage are seated a few feet apart in comfy brown armchairs in Monica's sumptuous solarium—songbirds trilling in a gigantic cage in the coolest corner of the sun-splashed room, vigorous green vines sporting sprays of magenta orchids framing crystalline windows, sparkling water splashing down from a white marble urn atop a black marble pedestal rising from a green marble pool adorned with pink water lilies—bright orange fish patrolling the depths.

"When broken bones have mended crooked," says Monica, itching to undress the old lady, "the only way to get the kinks out, as it were, is to break those bones again and set them straight."

"That's me," says Mrs. Armitage, her eyes shut tight. "The crooked mend, if mended at all. I still dream of murdering my ex-husband twenty years after he took everything, daughters and all." She opens her eyes and sneers. "I take pleasure in killing him, though he begs for mercy."

"How old are you, dear?" asks Monica, sensing the old gal is far younger than everyone assumes her to be.

"Oh, I don't know," says Mrs. Armitage, her voice softening. "Too old for anybody's good."

"Younger than I," says Monica, munching a glossy red cherry. "Bet you five billion dollars."

"Don't be absurd. You're young and vibrant. I'm old as the hills and twice as dusty."

"I'm sixty-two," says Monica, spitting the pit in the pool. "I'll bet you could still have a baby."

"Outrageous," says Mrs. Armitage, shrugging weakly. "Oh, what's the use? You and Pinky see right through me. I'm..." She takes a deep breath. "Forty-seven."

"Why the disguise? Who do you think you're hiding from?"

"Men, of course," says Mrs. Armitage, gritting her teeth. "Dirty rotten hurtful deceitful lying ruinous men."

"May I?" asks Monica, untying Mrs. Armitage's bonnet.

Mrs. Armitage squeezes her eyes shut again. "Don't tell anyone."

"Just between you and me and the universe," says Monica, removing the bonnet and loosing a glorious cascade of rich black hair. "Holy moly. You're ravishing."

"*Still?*" says Mrs. Armitage, gazing out from a face every bit as beautiful as Nefertiti. "Damn me. When will it ever end?"

"Shall we take off your clothes, too?" asks Monica, nodding hopefully. "I'll take off mine if you'll take off yours."

"Then what?" asks Mrs. Armitage, dazzling Monica with a smile—fearful excited inviting.

"Oh, we'll think of something," says Monica, bouncing her eyebrows. "Of that we can be certain."

Luxuriating in Monica's rooftop hot tub, the sun's rays deflected by a colossal green umbrella, cold white wine loosening their tongues, Monica asks Mrs. Armitage, "So who are you really?"

"Well," replies Mrs. Armitage, delighted and terrified to be naked with another human being, "I'm an old woman in public, and in the privacy of my apartment I'm that archetype you describe in your book. The Princess in the Tower Waiting to be Rescued."

"By a man?" asks Monica, smiling languidly. "A dirty rotten hurtful deceitful lying ruinous man?"

"No," answers Mrs. Armitage, her voice full of longing. "By a man like no other man."

"Oh, him," says Monica, nodding in recognition of the favorite fantasy of princesses in towers. "So what's got you wanting to change?"

"Well, it began quite by accident," says Mrs. Armitage, her voice deep and alluring—not a trace of the old biddy left. "I'd gone to the bookstore to feed the cats and there was this horrid man taking all the books, stealing them out of pure malice, and I felt...well...I felt this fierce loyalty to the store and the people there..."

"Even the men?"

"Yes, even the men," says Mrs. Armitage, blushing magnificently. "Or maybe even *especially* the men. I found the drama of the situation, the threat to the existence of our family of friends...thrilling. And I felt overjoyed to be part of the resistance. Thrilled to my bones."

"I remember that day," says Monica, recalling the revolutionary fervor that swept the neighborhood and rallied the community to defeat the plunderers. "I donated my entire collection of Mindy Toomay cookbooks and a whole shelf of erotic poetry."

"Yes!" cries Mrs. Armitage, joining hands with Monica. "Then Denny arrived to save the day with his huge bus full of books, and I hugged him. Spontaneously. Deliciously. The first time I'd touched a man in decades. Then I turned and looked at Lord Bellmaster..."

"Lord is *such* a fox," says Monica, nodding her approval. "And?"

"I felt a stirring," says Mrs. Armitage, feeling a similar stirring as she speaks of that previous stirring. "I was in a tizzy for days, and in the midst of my tizzy I came to your workshop, and then I devoured your books, and..."

"Got it," says Monica, gliding through the water and wrapping her arms around Mrs. Armitage. "So tell me, sweetheart, before you were abandoned by your dirty rotten hurtful deceitful lying ruinous husband, who were you at nineteen, seventeen, fourteen, eleven, nine, seven, four?"

"My, it's hot in here," says Mrs. Armitage, swooning. "Must be time to get out."

Monica sits in her comfy armchair and holds Mrs. Armitage like a baby—Mrs. Armitage weeping and weeping about her lonely childhood and her estrangement from her mother and the absence of her father and the cruelty of others to her and her own cruelty to those weaker than she.

Mrs. Armitage weeps and weeps and weeps and weeps for hours and hours—Monica loving her unceasingly—until finally the exhausted girl falls asleep on Monica's breast and sleeps a deep healing sleep.

Loose Bonnet

(string theory manifest in shoelaces and their ilk)

In the aftermath of a cathartic therapy session with Monica Copia, Mrs. Armitage can't keep her bonnet—the apogee of her old-lady persona—from slipping and sliding and coming untied and repeatedly threatening to fall off and reveal Mrs. Armitage's true identity. Her bonnet has heretofore fit ever so tightly, the knot under her chin strong and sure, the pattern of her life static. But now that Monica knows the truth about her, Mrs. Armitage's fingers tremble when she ties her bonnet strings, rendering the knot insecure.

And so engrossed is she in musing about Debra and Carla, her long-lost daughters, that she bumps into the back of a wheelchair.

"Watch out!" cries the occupant of the chair, twisting his torso to see who rear-ended him.

"Sorry," says Mrs. Armitage, hurrying around the chair to apologize to the driver—a legless one-armed Aztec Ethiopian man, his hair shiny black, his hand bejeweled with silver rings.

"Got to watch where you're going," he says gruffly, his drawl distinctly Louisianan, his eyes lighting up as Mrs. Armitage's bonnet falls away and her raven black hair cascades around her dazzling face. "Whoa, baby. An' all this time Wolf thought you was just a angry old lady."

"*Am*," she growls, snatching her bonnet from the sidewalk and jamming it onto her head. "It's a wig, I tell you, and this is a mask." She pokes her cheek. "Rubber. See?"

"Wow and zow," he says, grinning ecstatically. "Wolf knew there was a reason he didn't die over there in that useless war so one day he see the old cat lady turn into you. Honey! Please take off your bonnet and let Wolf see you a little bit longer? Por favor?"

"Of course," she says, humbly removing her bonnet.

"He Wolf," he says, touching the mole in the center of his forehead. "Walk to the park with Wolf, he show you a miracle."

Wolf and Mrs. Armitage stop on the cement shore of a small man-made lake—an island at its center.

"Wood ducks live over there," says Wolf, gesturing at the island. "Lay they eggs in peace over there. Wolf come watch here every day, rain and shine. Chase them dogs away they hassle the birds."

"Guardian of the isle," says Mrs. Armitage, musing aloud.

Wolf smiles sheepishly. "How'd you know his secret? They Wolf's special friends those wood ducks. Sleep at his feet some days."

"I can feel how much you love them," she says, wanting very much to take his hand and kiss his fingers—but she is afraid.

Now a wood duck hen swims toward them—her brood of seven ducklings following her through the murky green water.

"Life springs eternal," says Wolf, scattering breadcrumbs upon the tiny waves. "Ain't they the most precious innocent things you ever seen?"

"Precious and innocent," says Mrs. Armitage, distracted by voices of children playing on the nearby swings.

Time does a backflip and Mrs. Armitage is twenty-four. Debra is three and Carla is five, playing on the swings and calling, "Mommy! Mommy! Push me, Mommy. Push me," and she goes to push them and they look up at her in surprise and terror—not her daughters.

Struggling madly with her bonnet, Mrs. Armitage enters a neighborhood of pink and yellow and green and white buildings, the air redolent with cooking smells—rice and beans and chicken and pork—gardens blooming ecstatically, doors and windows open to the sweet evening breeze, couples and families promenading on the sidewalks, seeing each other and being seen.

The bonnet slips away once more and Mrs. Armitage's hair breaks loose—a black torrent.

Two girls in red belly shirts and shimmering green pants stop to gawk. They, too, have long black hair. Their navels are pierced with gold loops. Their red sandals show off shiny red toenails. Their faces are painted to make them look old enough to buy beer.

"*Ay, madre,*" says the elder of the two, staring in wonder at the younger Mrs. Armitage emerging from the carapace of a crone. "Why you in that old-lady costume for?"

Time flips again and the girls become Mrs. Armitage's daughters.

"Debra! Carla!" cries Mrs. Armitage. "Oh, my darlings."
She moves to embrace them.
They cry, *Loca!* and flee from her.

Midnight, riding in the back of an empty bus, her bonnet on cockeyed, Mrs. Armitage gazes out the window at the passing blur and wonders what will happen now that she has shared so many of her secrets with Monica—secrets composing the very fabric of her existence.

The bus stops. A man climbs on and takes a long time fumbling sufficient coins into the toll box. He is of medium height and wearing black motorcycle boots and black jeans and a black T-shirt overmatched by his big tummy. His thinning hair is going gray, his mustache comically lopsided, his exhaustion palpable as he collapses into the seat across the aisle from the driver.

"Quiet night," he says, smiling affably at the driver—a regal brown woman named Cassandra. "Rode out into the country to watch the eclipse and my motorcycle broke down. Nine-mile walk to here, and these boots aren't made for walkin', that's for damn sure."

Time does a backbend with a twist, and Mrs. Armitage freezes in horror. The man is her ex-husband—he who so cruelly abused her and betrayed her and turned her daughters against her.

"Eclipse?" says Cassandra, her sonorous voice sending shivers up and down Mrs. Armitage's spine. "Of the moon?"

"What else at night?" says the man, laughing pleasantly.

"You neglected to mention what time you rode out," says Cassandra, laughing with him. "Might have been high noon."

"True, true," says the man, closing his weary eyes. "But it was the moon at dusk, a great pearly egg half shadowed by the earth as she rose into the gray-blue sky over Mount Diablo."

Mrs. Armitage unfreezes. Her ex-husband may have been a

charmer, but he was no poet, no lover of earth and sky.

"I once saw an eclipse that changed the moon to golden brown," says Cassandra, easing the bus onto a narrow street. "You could see the craters with your naked eye."

"She's closer than we think," says the man, folding his arms and closing his eyes. "Very much closer."

Mrs. Armitage descends from the bus at twilight and nearly collides with a rangy man—his corncob pipe glowing in the dark as he tokes of rich tobacco—Denny the book scavenger.

He mumbles, "Excuse me," and walks on.

Mrs. Armitage grows drunk on her memory of that delicious moment when Denny arrived in the nick of time to save Under the Table Books from the plundering book thieves.

When I hugged him my fortress began to dissolve, my castle to crumble.

So she calls to him in her undisguised voice—Cupid's *eros*—and her siren's singing of the lonely man's name strikes the lonely man in the heart of his heart.

Gifts From Our Past Lives

(Tomas attempts to elucidate the unspeakable)

Do I believe in reincarnation? Well, that depends on your definition of reincarnation. Have I ever had a clear recollection of something—anything—that was unquestionably from a past life of mine, and mine alone? No. Then how dare I speak of *Gifts From Our Past Lives*?

I dare because I am convinced that creative illumination springs from a vast reservoir of *collective* experience and knowledge. When I say *our* past lives, I mean a *library*, as it were, of all the knowledge and talent there has ever been from which we may draw upon in *this* lifetime.

Where is the library located?

We're living in it.

For instance, my sudden knowing of how to mitigate migraine headaches when I was seven years old without anyone teaching me how to mitigate them—without my ever having *thought* about headaches—came to me because I *very much wanted* to help my sister. I emphasize those three words because they are crucial to understanding my theory of how past life talent manifests in *this* life.

I do not believe that I, Tomas, human being, am necessarily someone who cured migraine headaches in a previous life. But I do believe that when those people who *were* such healers died, their knowledge and skill did not die with their bodies, but entered the immortal collective consciousness (or unconsciousness to use the Jungian term) which became available to me when I *very much wanted* to help my sister. I have no doubt whatsoever that this gift of migraine mitigation has migrated into countless other humans and has been amplified and enhanced by many of us.

I contend that this invisible library of talent is accessible to anyone. We can borrow anything from the library for as long as we live. I further believe that musical prodigies and the extravagantly multi-talented are extraordinary because their *access* to this trove of previous experiences is less inhibited by neurosis and self-doubt than is the access of the erroneously labeled "less talented."

Is there a way to test my theory?

I think so.

Choose something you'd love to do that you have heretofore told yourself you don't have the talent for. For example, tap dancing. Before you try to tap-dance, close your eyes and imagine entering a building full of light, a place that fills you with joy and hope and excitement.

Do you see that shaft of golden light slanting down through the center of the room? That is an emanation of all the accumulated tap-dancing talent and necessary related talents since the beginning of human history. Go stand in that column of light and allow your body and being to be flooded with tap-dancing experience and spirit.

Doesn't that feel great?

Denny's Confusion

(over pints of winter wheat ale at the Rubicon Circus Pub,
the music almost but not quite deafening)

Moustafa, a princely black man wearing a burgundy Under the Table Books T-shirt, his many beaded braids grazing his shoulders, takes a first long drink of the potent brew—known locally as liquid cannabis—and sits back with a contented smile on his handsome face.

"Oh, my," he declares in his mellifluous voice. "From the oncoming buzz I'd say I've had quite enough, so please allow me to bequeath what's left in my glass to you."

Denny, a rangy white man with longish red hair, quaffs his pint in a trice and says, "Moustafa, do you think I'm weird? I mean, of course I'm weird compared to...I don't know...most people, but am I *strange*? Is there something inherently unattractive about me? Something organically off-putting? To women in particular, maybe?"

"Why do you ask?" says Moustafa, studying Denny's troubled face. "Are you still thinking about the woman who left her falcon in exchange for a pile of provocative poetry?"

"She's definitely part of the equation," says Denny, growing swiftly drunk. "No doubt about it, but here's the thing. When I got home a couple months ago, I'm barely home a week when I meet this wonderful woman at Arno's. Exquisite. Smart. Funny. Really seemed to like me. And we were just about to get it on when she says, 'You know what? This doesn't feel quite right.' When I ask her why not, she says, 'Feels like we're moving too fast too soon.' So I split."

"Yet she implied if things were to develop a little more slowly between the two of you perhaps..."

"Nah," says Denny, finishing Moustafa's pint. "She was there to get laid. Just not by me. Then there was the falcon woman who seemed *real* interested in me, but she completely disappears, and now..." He takes a deep breath. "Just between you and me."

Moustafa raises his hand to attract Ginger, the star waitress of the cacophonous pub. "Just between you and me."

"Well, last night," says Denny, glad for the loud blaring blues, "I'm walking along J Street and the bus pulls up and Mrs. Armitage gets off and calls to me, and her voice..."

Ginger—gorgeous brunette with big brown eyes and comely curves in blue jeans and a green-and-gold Oakland A's belly shirt—slow dances to their table. "Hey, you book guys," she drawls, anointing them with her honeyed voice. "What now?"

"I'd love some hot black tea," says Moustafa, smiling at the golden Buddha perched in Ginger's belly button. "Denny?"

"Another pint of the same," he says, so eager to get on with his tale he is oblivious to the striking presence of the young goddess.

"So...her voice," prompts Moustafa, watching Ginger saunter away—never in a hurry but always on time. *Remarkable.* "Mrs. Armitage."

"Her voice was so...I don't know how to describe it, but...it struck deep in the heart of my heart and I was...even though I *know* it's coming from an old lady, I...I'm turned on, Moustafa. Seriously turned on."

Moustafa arches an eyebrow. "There is nothing so alluring as a well-tuned voice well aimed."

"But this is an *old* lady," says Denny, writhing passionately in his chair, his anguish rising above the din. "Remember when I came home after months of scavenging and the vitriolic crazy guy was taking all the books? She...Mrs. Armitage was the first person to hug me hello, and the thing was, she didn't *feel* like an old lady to me. She felt young and strong and I thought, 'Man, I've been on the road *way* too long if this old gal feels this good.' So last night when her voice was so..."

"Sexy," says Moustafa, smiling as Ginger approaches with his tea.

"Exactly," says Denny, nodding affirmatively. "Sexy."

"You book guys are *so* complimentary," says Ginger, kissing the air in Moustafa's direction. "I love it."

"You are grace incarnate," says Moustafa, nodding thankfully. "Please come lunch with us at the bookstore. You will be most welcome."

"Tomorrow too soon?" asks Ginger, giving Moustafa a look that makes his heart skip a beat—in a good way.

"So *anyway,*" says Denny, exasperated by the interruption, "Mrs. Armitage calls out to me and I...I..."

"Fall in love with her," says Moustafa, sighing as Ginger departs.

"Moustafa," says Denny, feeling a deathly sobriety in the pit of his drunkenness. "I walked her home. She held my hand. And I swear to God it was the most exciting seven blocks of my life. I felt like... well...like we were making love the whole way to her apartment. Not foreplay. I'm talking about full body electrifying..."

"Two bodies as one," intones Moustafa. "Doubt extinct."

"Right," says Denny, breathing hard. "So... is that weird or what? She's ancient. I'm thinking maybe the luscious woman at Arno's and the bountiful falcon woman, who were both *very* attracted to me at first but then suddenly retracted their attraction, I'm thinking maybe on some female intuitive level they sensed I have an unconscious desire to have sex with an old woman, and *that's* what turned them off about me. They could *sense* I'm into old ladies." He grimaces. "Could that be?"

The soundtrack changes from blasting blues to Eva Cassidy singing *Autumn Leaves*, the jam-packed joint going relatively quiet.

"My dear friend," says Moustafa, gazing into Denny's eyes. "Here is what I think. Life is forever presenting us with opportunities to love and be loved. These opportunities have absolutely nothing to do with our age or the age of the other. For the most part we are totally unaware of most of these perpetual opportunities because our eyes and our hearts and our minds are closed to them. We are deafened by ignorance, blinded by illusion, deluded by misconception, and immobilized by fear. My own experience has been that the more genuinely I practice friendship, the more obvious the opportunities for love become. As to Mrs. Armitage specifically, I have observed her with the bookstore cats on many occasions. Her zesty love for them, her delight in them, seems ageless and sensual and irresistibly seductive."

"So..." says Denny, at a loss for words.

"What happened when you reached her apartment?"

"She invited me in," says Denny, gulping his brew. "She put her arms around me and invited me in."

"Yes," says Moustafa, smiling sublimely. "She invited you in. Such a generous woman. And..."

"I split," says Denny, waving wildly for another pint. "Scared out of my mind."

"Yes," says Moustafa, finishing his tea. "There is your answer."

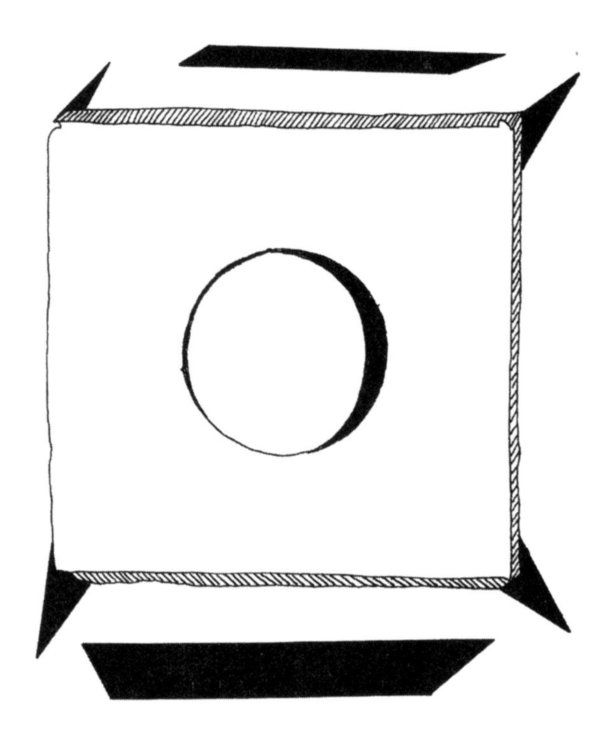

Jenny's Letter

(written on her thirty-third birthday)

Dear Gram,

Thank you for the box of your special oatmeal cookies. I love how some have chocolate chips and some have raisins, so every first bite has the excitement of the unknown. Moustafa would love to have your recipe. And thank you so much for the five dollars. I hope you aren't depriving yourself on my behalf. I can imagine you using the same tea bag three times instead of your usual two so you can justify sending me money. That's why I'm enclosing a box of your favorite Darjeeling tea.

So now I am thirty-three. When you were thirty-three you had four children with a fifth on the way. When Mom was thirty-three she had three children with me on the way. I have no children and none on the way. Until this year I rarely thought about having children, but now I think about having a baby all the time. Or maybe it would be truer to say I *feel* about having a baby all the time. I don't think I will have a baby any time soon, but it is fascinating to find myself so frequently taken over by such primal urges.

Yesterday a teenaged guy came into the bookstore, goonish and repulsive, but when he came to the counter to ask me where the comic books were, his young male scent was so overpowering I had this wild fantasy of seducing him so he could impregnate me. Eek!

Speaking of sperm donors, the big news in my life is that Lord and I have separated. I'm in the process of moving out of our apartment into one of the bedrooms at Under the Table Books. I still love Lord and I'm sure he loves me, but living as a couple was making us both miserable.

The biggest part of my misery had to do with our persistent lack of money. During the three years I lived with Lord, we almost never had enough to pay the rent until right before our rent was due. So nearly every month I went insane with worry, while Lord acted like we had millions in the bank. True, the money always did materialize just in the nick of time, but the stress was killing my love for Lord and killing our sex life, so...

The day we decided to end our "marriage" I got dolled up and went looking for work. By the end of the day, I'd been hired by a huge accounting firm to be their morning receptionist. At the end of two weeks, I told Myra the office manager I was quitting. She immediately offered to double my salary. So I stayed on until I couldn't stand it any longer and told Myra I could only work three mornings a week. She not only agreed to three mornings, but gave me another raise.

"Why are you being so nice to me?" I asked suspiciously.

"The big bosses love you," said Myra, glancing around to make sure no one could overhear her. "The clients love you. You make everybody happy and you add so much *class* to the operation."

"Myra, I answer the phone. I facilitate client flow. I..."

"You melt people with your smile and your voice. All the men are in love with you. Please don't quit. They'll blame it on me."

So yesterday, Kevin, the most charming of the senior partners, asks me to go to dinner with him and I surprise myself by saying *Yes*. He takes me to this swank restaurant and I drink way too much wine and then he drives us in his enormous new car up into the foothills to see his gigantic new house. As we're strolling in the moonlight on the shores of his private lake, he makes this impassioned speech about how all his life he's been looking for the perfect woman to be his wife and the mother of his children and how he's absolutely certain—after three hours with me during which time I have said almost nothing—I am that perfect woman.

So I tell him about Under the Table Books and our operating philosophy of creative anarchy and recycling and sharing, and that *his* way of life is the ruination of the planet.

And *he* says, in all seriousness, that his sister was brainwashed by a religious cult, *too*, but that with proper counseling and effective antipsychotic medication she was saved—his exact words were "returned to the fold." Then he took my hand and said that if I would marry him, he would move heaven and earth to restore my sanity.

So I'm unemployed again, though I don't feel

unemployed. I feel like I narrowly escaped the jaws of death. This morning I got in bed with Lord to snuggle, and one thing led to another and we made love. He has always been a good lover, but this morning he was positively divine, so I couldn't help asking if he had a new lover.

"No," he said, smiling mischievously. "Not *yet*."

Which opened up the subject of whether or not we could still be lovers if we had other lovers. Oh, Gram, I like the *idea* of sexual freedom, but imagining Lord with someone else infuriates me. *I* certainly don't have a desire to sleep with anyone else as long as I'm committed to Lord, which, even though we're supposedly breaking up, I am.

Monica Copia—I sent you her essay *Illusory Delusions*—says what we fear most about our lover having another lover is that we will be compared to the other lover and judged inferior and then abandoned. Jealousy, she believes, is a profound reflection of how little we really love ourselves. Certainly one of the most maddening things to me about Lord is my knowing he wouldn't mind if I had another lover. I don't think he has a jealous bone in his body. He's so incredibly trusting. It's one of the many things I love about him and can't stand about him. He's so self-contained, so content with so little, so...passive. Yet he's always doing things and going places and...oh, who knows? I want him to be exactly who he is and someone else, too.

You asked how my art was going since The Big Fire. Mostly going internally these days. I feel pregnant with whatever comes next, but I have no idea what that might be. In the meantime I'm dancing with Natasha, cooking with Moustafa, gardening with Derek, and practicing the piano every day for at least half an hour—just like you do.

Love,

Jenny

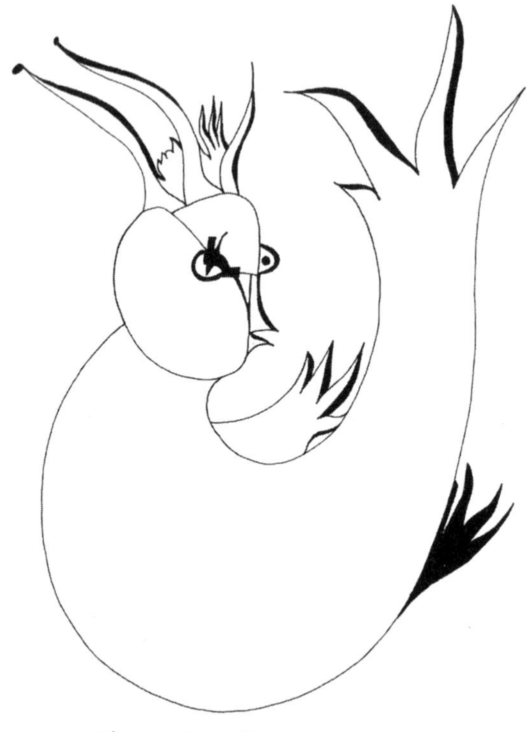

My bird is fine.

Capture

(of birds and boys and cats—autobiography from a distance)

Mrs. Armitage wakes at dawn, her parakeets singing their greatest hit *We Want Breakfast*. She opens the two large cages and allows the seven tiny birds to flit about the sunny kitchen while she brews a cup of coffee and tries to decide whether to alter her public personae in one fell swoop, or slowly but surely. She is tired of hiding her lovely shape under baggy dresses. She no longer wishes to wear a bonnet. Her feet are sick of being entombed in combat boots.

"Soon," she vows to her birds, "I will no longer go forth as an old-world crone. It is time to change. Difficult, but necessary. If I hadn't seemed so old to Denny last night I'm sure he would have..." She blushes. "You know...come in for tea."

In the privacy of her apartment, she wears a red silk bathrobe and allows her luxurious black hair to be free. Hers is a primeval beauty—her body strong and lithe from the religious use of barbells while dancing to groovy music from around the world.

Mrs. Armitage, her very name suggesting old age, known as the Cat Lady to the habitués of Under the Table Books, has no cats at home in deference to her parakeets. She has not had a lover in twenty years, though every day she practices tantric exercises so she might one day prove an admirable partner for some really lucky guy.

To support herself—she lives on almost nothing—Mrs. Armitage writes easy-listening erotica—the softest of porn—which she mails through the old-fashioned post office to an agent in Detroit who syndicates her sexy words on various information highways.

> Virginia stands by the window, watching crows hunt for leavings in the snow. She is waiting for Malcolm to come up behind her, to cup her breasts in his big warm hands, to whisper those deftly wicked words that never fail to arouse her. Her silky blouse unbuttoned, her nipples swollen in anticipation of his touch, she senses him behind her. But something is different tonight. She has never known him to hesitate. A delicious dread consumes her. *Has his lust for me diminished? Must I now seduce him? What a joy to be the aggressor once more!*
>
> She turns from the window, not in the least disappointed to find him standing naked on the bed, the supreme ambassador of his passion poised at the perfect altitude for her hungry kiss.

In Under the Table Books, the beguiling octogenarian identical twins Iris and Leona Spinelli are humming a sweetly atonal rendition of *Take the A Train* while alphabetizing the *Hollywood Heart Throbs* section. Wearing matching sky blue kimonos, their identical white hair is piled on top of their identical heads and held in place with identical black chopsticks, making differentiation impossible for any but their closest associates.

Hint: Iris chews gum, Leona does not.

Behind the counter, the boy Derek nimbly inputs data into a wheezing old computer unearthed by Denny in an abandoned warehouse and repaired by Moustafa and Natasha. The software is Neanderthal, the available fonts few and prosaic, but the ancient machine is ideal for keeping track of the contents of the bookstore refrigerators, and may yet do the same for the incoming and outgoing streams of books and things, if only Natasha can figure out how to add more memory.

Mrs. Armitage enters the bookstore without saying hello to anyone—a shocking departure from her usual behavior—and gathers the bookstore cats around her in the Reading Circle. She kneels on the frayed carpet and dispenses one enormous scallop, lightly simmered in sunflower oil, to each of the cats. The kitties do not quarrel over these delicate morsels, abiding by the Cat Lady's Supreme Rule of Dispensation: *Wait your turn politely or you don't get a turn at all.*

Watching George, the enormous orange tabby, swallow his scallop, Mrs. Armitage absentmindedly removes her bonnet and allows her glorious hair to *publicly* tumble down over her shoulders. "I am approaching innocence," she murmurs. "My penance is ending."

George and Girly Girl and Valentin and Boneyard meow longingly for a bit more seafood and rub themselves against the revered Howdy Doody lunchbox from which so many delicious meals have emerged.

"All gone," she says, petting each of them. "I've been a bit preoccupied of late. Sorry, my dears. But I'll tell you a story if you'd like."

"May I listen?" asks Derek, standing on the edge of the Reading Circle. "I love your stories."

"Of course," she says, holding out her hand to him. "Join us."

"I've heard you telling them stories before," he says, awestruck by her transformation, "but I didn't want to intrude."

"How considerate of you," she says, smiling into his eyes. "You really do have the loveliest of souls. Sagittarius Leo Aries. I've told you that before, but have I told you why you reincarnated this time?"

He slowly shakes his head, mesmerized by her new visage.

"To facilitate the healing of humanity," she says, drawing him near. "Through the fostering of a much kinder economic paradigm."

"I never would have thought you had such long hair," he says, sitting cross-legged beside her, entranced by the splendid fall of her black tresses. "I thought for sure it would be white or gray. I mean...you don't seem very old at all now."

"Slowly but surely the truth is revealed," she says, kissing his cheek. "You're one of the first to know."

"My mother had long hair," Derek whispers. "But she wasn't as beautiful as you are."

"Once upon a time," says Mrs. Armitage, keeping hold of Derek's hand, "there was a young cat named Missy. Her first and only litter was small. Just two little girl kittens. She loved them very much, but she was too young and inexperienced to protect them. When the kittens were only a few weeks old, they were stolen from her by a big tom and his mean wife. Heartbroken, Missy roamed far away from the place of her birth, and after many months of living in constant fear of being captured and enslaved, she entered a dark forest."

"Oh, great," says Derek, squeezing her hand. "I love it when the main character enters a dark forest."

"Yes," says Mrs. Armitage, putting her arm around him. "She made her home in a hollow tree, living alone for many years, mourning the loss of her daughters, until one morning, while hunting mice, she heard the desperate cry of a young cat. She snuck through the ferns and came upon a frightening scene—a young boy cat cornered by a vicious dog. With no thought for her own safety, she leapt at the dog and scratched his nose and face until the dog ran away howling in abject terror, never to be free of pain for the rest of his life."

The bookstore cats, now certain there will be no more scallops today, begin cleaning themselves.

"Then what happened?" asks Derek, spellbound by the new and improved Mrs. Armitage.

"Then Missy and the young cat became best friends and lived in the forest together hunting mice and living in peace ever after."

"What was his name? The young cat?"

"Derek," she says, her eyes filling with tears. "Though Missy just called him Dear."

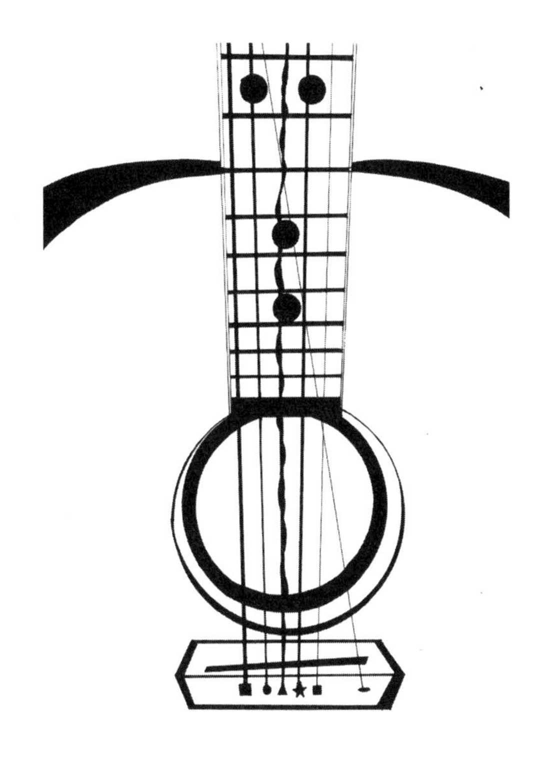

Music and Sex and Love

(Tomas on sonic aphrodisiacs and the varieties of relational experience)

I am not so much ashamed as chagrined to admit that when I woke this morning—the sun striking my eyes through the one missing Venetian blind I have vowed to replace for the last ten years—I knew I was sharing my bed with someone, but I wasn't sure who that someone was. Twenty years ago I would have blamed my memory lapse on the deleterious effects of marijuana and alcohol and a relatively promiscuous lifestyle. But now I blame age and time and synaptic patterning, not necessarily in that order, for it has been at least two years since I spent the night with anyone. Thus, my waking self simply didn't know how to react to the presence of a woman sleeping beside me.

I got up to pee. The woman slumbered on. In the bathroom, looking in the mirror, the events of last night came back to me along with the identity of my bedmate: Tantha Fidelos, singer songwriter accordion player extraordinaire. I'd spent the afternoon playing guitar and piano with her at Temple Groove recording studio, Dr. Frankenpeter at the controls. Tantha is putting together her second album of original songs, having played accordion on hundreds of other people's albums. I feel both honored and baffled that she chose *me* to play with her when she can have her pick of any musician on the planet. But I digress.

The larger issues, at least the ones looming largest as I stood in my bathroom and perused my old-man's face, my jowls seeming more jowly than ever, my wrinkles more wrinkly, is that Tantha is half my age—I am fifty-five—and I made a vow ten years ago to never again get sexually involved with anyone more than a dozen years my junior, for all sorts of good reasons, and just because.

But there I was, having made love with Tantha—no hesitation on either of our parts about climbing into bed with each other after a splendid meal at *Cuatro Hermanas*. Tantha had a beer, while I, in my eleventh year of sobriety, had an excellent glass of lemonade to accompany our scrumptious catfish tacos.

We were higher than kites from a recording session Tantha called *astral, juicy, heartbreaking,* and *impossible*. I know what she means. I was never for an instant aware of thinking or trying as we played together. She would begin a song and some moment thereafter I found myself playing along with her, and eventually the song would end, our final notes ringing as one, the synchronicity of our timing impossibly juicy, the music compelling and mysterious and achingly beautiful.

Thus age and jowls and wrinkles were not on either of our minds as we floated down the hall from the recording room to hear the playback in Dr. Frankenpeter's digital den. We sprawled side by side on a plush sofa and drowned together in music so sexy and spiritual, we *had* to fall in love with each other.

Yet I am fifty-five. Tantha is twenty-seven. I live in a small apartment above an anarchist bookstore in a noisy crowded city, having failed three times to make the transition to a more rural life. I have a few hundred dollars to my name, a fine guitar, and a not so fine piano. That is all. My hair will soon be completely gray. I am no longer the lean and muscular man I used to be. Tantha has long thick red hair. She *is* lean and muscular. I am, relatively speaking, a musical nobody. She gets calls every day to play with people so famous it hurts my head to think about them. She is on the verge of superstardom, whereas I make more money mitigating migraine headaches than I make as a studio musician.

But none of that mattered when we made love. Our bodies, fueled by the energy of the divine tender juicy heartbreaking astral impossible music we created, worked perfectly well together.

I *never* thought she would want to make love with me again in the light of day. But she did. She was eager and happy and appreciative and magnificently uninhibited, and I forgot all about my jowls and wrinkles and her *lack* of jowls and wrinkles. We just had the best time together, laughing and loving and marveling at how good it felt to be so freely lusty with each other.

Then we took a long shower together and made love again in the downpour. Then we donned bathrobes and took possession of the kitchen. She made eggs and toast. I made coffee. As she whipped the eggs in a dark blue bowl, she said in her confident way, her Finnish accent utterly beguiling, "Wow, Tomas, I am so totally digging you, I'm feeling we should get married and have a kid or two. Yeah?"

Before I go any further with this tale, I wish to reveal some of my personal history, and some of Tantha's, too, so you will better understand why I responded in the way I did to her spontaneous marriage and kid-having proposal, and why she then responded to my response as she did.

I have tried on numerous occasions to remain sexually monogamous for more than a year. I have even twice married with all the legal sanctions, the church weddings, the official honeymoons, the houses and health insurance and cars. And in every relationship, legally sanctioned or not, either I or my partner, and sometimes both of us, fell in love with someone else—misery ensuing for everyone concerned.

At the age of forty-seven, following the absolutely shattering dénouement of my relationship with the woman I believed to be the greatest love of my life, I declared myself a permanent soloist. My sexual liaisons since then have been few and unsatisfying. My fears of being hurt again or hurting someone else have kept me from making any serious effort to instigate relationship.

Now here is something fascinating. During my eight-year hiatus from physical and emotional intimacies, and possibly as a *result* of this self-imposed singularity, I have experienced what Lord Bellmaster calls "the quantum flowering of my music." Moustafa says he no longer hears the meshing of the gears of my intellect when I play. And it's true; though I was a highly competent musician for over thirty years, it has only been in these last eight years that my playing has become effortlessly expressive. My music, if you will, has become the undisputed love of my life.

Hence, when Tantha heard Brisco Murray's slow dance jazz folk album *Poo On My Shoe (Again)* on which I played both piano and guitar, she was moved to call me from Hollywood where she was recording her accordion parts for the soundtrack to the blockbuster science-fiction outer space remake of *Mutiny On the Bounty*. Following our awkward hellos, she played her accordion and sang into her phone while I played along on guitar into my phone. Three minutes later, despite the totally funky sounds of our music coming through phones lying on beds four hundred miles apart, Tantha declared, "I am *so* in love, Tomas."

Tantha hails from a small village in Finland a few miles below the Arctic Circle where for millennia women have married men thirty and forty years their seniors. Tantha's mother, for example, was sixteen when she married Tantha's father who was fifty-three. Tantha's older sister Resmia, who just turned thirty, recently married a man in his sixties. Why do they do this? No one knows. But thus it has been for countless generations among her people. And thus Tantha not only prefers older men to younger men, she does not consider males under the age of forty-five to be fully formed human beings.

"So that means there must be lots of widows among your people," I said, trying to wrap my mind around the connubial realities of Tantha's tribe. "Since the wives would almost always outlive their husbands?"

"Of course," said Tantha, nodding complacently. "The widows, you see, take younger men for their lovers to prepare them for marriage."

We return now to the moment following Tantha's proposal of marriage to me.

"What a sweet and flattering thing for you to say," I said, unable to keep my hands out of her bathrobe. "Are you crazy?"

"No. I think you're the perfect age for me. You are just what I like in my bed. And the music we make..."

"But I'm old enough to be your father."

"Not where I come from."

"I'm a pauper."

"I have a house with fifty acres and a herd of seventy reindeer. I earn very good money."

"I'm a Californian. Snow terrifies me. I would perish in Finland."

"We will only spend our summers there. The rest of the time we will live here among your people."

"I've never had a successful long-term relationship. I don't think I'm capable of such a thing."

"Don't be silly. Of course you are."

"But you hardly know me."

"Tomas," she said, putting her arms around me and looking deep into my eyes. “What are you afraid of? Happiness?”

And I said, “It’s a long story.”

And she said, “We have all the time in the world.”

Merlin

(a bird in the hand might be every bit as good as a burning bush)

"...then she ever so slowly removed the blindfold," says Lord Bellmaster—Moustafa and Denny hanging on Lord's every word—"and I swear it was like I was back at the beginning of my life. The very beginning. Only I was as old as I am now. Then she took hold of my earlobes..."

Derek, ten years old, saunters into the kitchen, a sleepy smile on his face. Lord clams up, believing the details of his fabulous session with Ruby Heartsong unfit for the ears of one so young as Derek.

"It's okay," says the boy, opening the refrigerator and taking out a carton of eggs. "I've been listening from my bed the whole time anyway. So then she took hold of your earlobes..."

"You heard the part about the brandy snifters?" asks Lord, blushing ferociously. "The crème de cacao? The owl feathers?"

Derek nods. "Listening to you is like watching a movie. So then she took hold of your earlobes and..."

"To be continued," says Lord, giving the boy an implausible frown of disapproval. "I've got to open the store."

"We await the conclusion of your rebirth with open libidos," says Moustafa, rising to check the morning loaves.

"Hey, and don't forget to find me that book on falcons," says Denny, glancing at the hat rack atop which sits a snowy white falcon, the legacy of a beautiful buxom blue-jeaned belly-button-baubled blue-eyed blond from Belgrade who recently stole Denny's heart and traded the gorgeous raptor for an armful of erotic poetry. "This little guy hasn't eaten in a week."

"Who wants some omelet?" asks Derek, expertly cracking eggs into a large white bowl.

"I," says Moustafa, setting the bread timer for five more minutes. "Shall I pick chives and cilantro and..."

"Three large green onions. Please," says Derek, continuing his cracking of the eggs. "Denny?"

"Food?" says Denny, coming out of his reverie about the aforementioned buxom belly-button-baubled blue-eyed blond. "Always."

"I'll have some!" calls Lord from upstairs. "Many thanks in advance oh wondrous waif."

"Me, too," says Mr. Laskin, a grizzled ancient in jeans and Harvard sweatshirt entering through the sliding glass doors. "What I'm doing here before two in the afternoon is a mystery, but here I am, and you make the best omelets since those long-ago days in my Tuscany villa."

"Hey," says Denny, rolling his eyes because he believes the old man to be a crazy coot with delusions of bygone grandeur, "Tomas is quite the bird guy, isn't he? You think he knows anything about falcons?"

"Family *Falconidae*," says Mr. Laskin, seating himself at the kitchen table and nodding gratefully as Derek serves him a brimming cup of ink-black coffee. "Sixty-three known species worldwide. Seven known to breed in North America. I kept seven falcons at my Scottsdale digs back in the day. And there is nothing, I repeat, nothing like the sight of a mature gyrfalcon streaking through the desert sky at a hundred and seventy-five miles per hour to break the back of a fleeing pigeon with the force of his blow. A truly awesome spectacle."

Denny rolls his eyes again, but can't help asking, "So what kind is the white guy on the hat rack?"

"That," says Mr. Laskin, taking a luxurious gulp of the bitter brew, "is an incredibly rare female albino merlin. Judging by the vestiges of her youth, I would guess her to be four years old. Typically brownish—the males are more of a slate gray—she is commonly known as a pigeon hawk, but the Latin *Falco columbarius* does her more justice. She is by far the most exquisite albino of her kind I have ever seen. She would fetch a king's ransom in Abu Dhabi. Those sheiks go wild over topnotch birds of prey."

Moustafa enters laden with chives and cilantro and green onions and a dozen cherry tomatoes. "We are wondering how to feed the bird," he inquires, smiling quizzically at the old man. "We have tried various raw meats, but she is disinterested."

"Depressed, more likely," says Mr. Laskin, finishing his coffee and smiling hopefully for more. "Needs to fly. Waiting to be taken out to those wide-open spaces. Aren't we all? No doubt misses her master and is cowed by the city. How did you come by her?"

Denny rolls his eyes yet again and says, "I'm pretty sure Tomas knows something about falcons."

Derek's little jaw sets in anger—he hates it when his friends doubt Mr. Laskin—but before he can come to his mentor's defense, Lord Bellmaster skips down the stairs with a big book entitled *All About Falcons* full of glossy color photos of the fierce little raptors.

"Listen to this." says Lord, infested with joyful exuberance from his fabulous session with Ruby Heartsong. "Family *Falconidae*. Sixty-three known species worldwide. Seven known to breed in North America. Here's a picture of ours, a rare albino merlin. Only the females are trained for hunting. Typically brownish—the males are slate gray—merlins are commonly known as a pigeon hawks. The albino shown above, *Falco columbarius*, recently fetched a king's ransom in Abu Dhabi."

Denny retires to the garden to enjoy a smoke—organic tobacco in a corncob pipe—and before settling into the big blue hammock, he places the merlin on a branch in the black walnut tree.

Derek follows shortly with a bucket of compost, which he sets down beside a recently harvested potato patch. "Hey, Denny," he asks, trying to contain his simmering anger, "may I ask you a question?"

"I know what you're going to ask me," says Denny, blowing a succession of smoke rings into a nascent breeze. "How come I don't believe your old fart was ever a rich guy?"

"Well, that's only part of it," says Derek, fetching a spade from the tool shed. "I understand why people have trouble believing a man who spends so much time in dumpsters was once the richest person on earth. But what I *can't* understand is why people, especially *good* people who range far and wide in solar-powered school buses gathering books for the experiment of sharing and love that is Under the Table Books, can be so rude to a kind old man who saved my life." Derek's jaw begins to tremble. "I mean, let's say he *is* crazy and never had anything. Is that a good reason to treat him like he's *bad*? Is that a reason to call him a fart and crazy and roll your eyes every time he says anything? And there was one time you called him a loony old leech, when he finds us gourmet cheese to eat all the time." Derek sniffles back his tears as he digs a hole for the compost. "And the worst part is he really likes you. Especially you, Denny. He says you remind him of his old friend Frank Lloyd Wright, whoever *he* was."

"Hey, man, I'm sorry," says Denny, slowly shaking his head. "I… you know what it is?"

"What?" asks Derek, startled out of his sorrow by the falcon dropping to the ground to snag an earthworm from the freshly turned soil.

"He reminds me of my old man," says Denny, taking a deep breath to quell an upsurge of long-suppressed emotions. "My pompous know-it-all father who never let me get a word in edgewise and told me to get the hell out and go to hell when I was sixteen. They could be twins."

"But they're not," says Derek, unearthing another worm for the hungry bird. "Hey, look. She's eating."

Denny sits up—his heart cracking open at the sight of the falcon eating from the little boy's hand.

Mr. Laskin and Derek and Natasha and Denny and Tomas are standing in a vast field of mustard and thistles bordering Otter Creek, the sky overcast, Merlin poised on Mr. Laskin's gloved right hand.

"Now *fly*," says Mr. Laskin, launching the bird with an expert flick of the wrist.

Merlin rises swiftly, her wings beating the air as she circles higher and higher until she is nearly out of sight in the gray sky.

"*So* beautiful," says Natasha, smiling in wonder at the fantastic ascension. "And to think we got her for just a few hot love poems."

"Do you think he'll come back?" asks Denny, holding his breath and thinking of the buxom belly-button-baubled blond from

Belgrade. *Oh, please come back for your bird. I won't be afraid of you this time, I promise.*

"Merlin is a *she,*" says Derek, gleefully clapping his hands. "Of course she'll come back."

"Look," says Tomas, pointing eastward toward the snowcapped Sierras, barely discernible above the valley haze. "Mourning doves. A big gang coming this way."

"Ah," says Mr. Laskin with a glint in his eye. "Prepare yourselves for a deathly miracle. Keep your eyes on the falcon if you can."

Now Merlin plummets from the sky—a blur of white descending unimaginably fast to strike the trailing dove and break the hapless bird's back with an audible pop—the leading doves scattering with peals of hysterical hooting.

"What do we do now?" asks Denny, looking to Mr. Laskin.

The old man frowns in confusion. "About what?"

"The falcon," says Denny, trying not to see his father in the old man's face. "Do we go get her or wait for her to come to us?"

"I don't remember," say Mr. Laskin, frowning in confusion at Tomas. "Do I know you?"

"Yes, Grandfather," says Tomas, putting a hand on the old man's shoulder. "We meet now and then at the bookstore."

"Where the hell are we?" asks Mr. Laskin, looking from face to face until he comes to Derek's. "Ah, my little friend. Almost two, isn't it? Sandwich time?"

At which moment, Merlin leaves off feasting on her prey and rises into the sky, winging swiftly eastward for a long moment before she banks off a northwest breeze and returns to the humans—alighting with remarkable delicacy onto the shoulder of the worm boy.

Pinky On Stage

(wanting to sing for his friends)

Under the Table Books has been host to many fabulous performances over the years. Hundreds of poets and writers and visionary thinkers have performed for audiences large (over fifty but under a hundred) and small (over two but under five) since Lord Bellmaster took the helm of the cavernous store lo these many (twenty-three to thirty-five depending on whom you talk to and *when* you talk to them) years ago.

Lord: I guess you could say I took the helm, but as soon as humanly possible I instituted a system of helm sharing that quickly evolved into the ambiguous format of governance (laughter) currently helming hereabouts.

Musical performances, however, were infrequent in the bookstore until a year ago because

Leona Spinelli: The acoustics in here sucked.

Iris Spinelli: Leona! I'm shocked to hear you use that expression. It's so unspecific.

Leona: On the contrary, I mean it literally. There was a sucking up of the music into the rafters or the corners…something. Remember that Russian guy? The one with all the hair? When he started pounding away on Grossman's Steinway, Tchaikovsky or something, it sounded like he was at the bottom of a well?

Iris: You're right. The acoustics sucked.

That was before Jenny and Moustafa made it a priority to improve the barn-like acoustics of the high-ceilinged enclosure. After several months of research and experimentation, they installed what we now call The Hanging Blankets of Babylon.

Jenny: They aren't actually blankets, but king-sized down comforters. I think we were influenced most profoundly by Buckminster Fuller's writings on tensegrity and Herb Kritzer's musings on the interplay of The Loud and The Muffled.

Moustafa: The hangers are replicas of standard metal hangers. We made them with half-inch rebar.

Lord: Performances at the bookstore are staged in the Reading Circle. We recommend you bring a pillow. No chaise longues, please, unless you are absolutely certain (how could you be?) the audience will not exceed twelve (which includes large dogs.)

Derek: I've looked and looked, but I've only been able to find seventeen chairs in Under the Table Books, including four plastic ones from the garden. Of those seventeen, I would say ten are sort of comfortable. The other seven are pretty terrible unless you use a pillow. I think we should build a stage in the empty warehouse next door. We could show movies and have concerts and lectures and everything.

Lord: An admirable vision. Alas, we are currently two months in arrears with our rent. Hence such a grandiose expansion is not in the offing.

Derek: What does "the offing" mean?

Mr. Laskin: The near future.

Lord: Oh, maybe expansion is in the offing.

Moustafa: We remain open to myriad possibilities.

A goodly crowd is gathering for Pinky's concert. The piano, an exquisite seven-foot Steinway grand borrowed from Murray Grossman (Lord Bellmaster's maternal uncle) has been placed at the south end of the Reading Circle and tuned to Tomas's satisfaction, the Hanging Blankets of Babylon are in place, Moustafa's chocolate chip cookies and Natasha's mango *agua fresca* are going fast—the eight o'clock curtain drawing nigh.

Three members of the audience are newcomers to the bookstore: a Very Famous Movie Star, a Very Powerful Media Mogul, and The Last Woman Pinky Slept With Before He Went Off Into the Wilderness to Die thirty-some years ago. This woman, Petra Bernadette, is now a Formerly Very Famous Movie Star, her legendary beauty and *joie de vivre* barely discernible in her many-times surgically altered visage.

Petra and the Very Powerful Media Mogul learned of Pinky's impending performance from the Very Famous Movie Star as a result of the unfathomably complex and unerring principles of cosmic interconnectedness, erroneously known to dualistic thinkers (good/bad, right/wrong) as An Amazing Coincidence.

Natasha's footloose mother Florence was attending an exclusive wild party in a castle in Scotland. She had just received a letter from Natasha that morning written on the back of a flyer for *Pinky Jones Live.* Said flyer just happened to fall out of her handbag while Florence was deftly eluding the passionate overtures of the aforementioned Very Famous Movie Star, who then picked up the fallen flyer and nearly had a heart attack when he saw the headline *Pinky Jones Live.*

Thus, the Very Powerful Media Mogul, the Formerly Very Famous Movie Star, and the currently Very Famous Movie Star have come to see if *this* Pinky Jones could possibly be *the* Pinky Jones (long thought by everyone to be long dead) who was the making of each of them in their early days in Show Biz.

How was Pinky their making? (Can that possibly be grammatically correct?) Well, it was Pinky, a wunderkind singer songwriter comedian, who spotted Petra waiting tables at Torquemada's Bar and Grill (famous for their rack of lamb) on Sunset. Pinky saw beyond her beguiling beauty and recognized a fellow comic genius—a preternatural clown. When he was offered a sit-com lead, he insisted that Petra be given the part of his quick-witted smartass sexy-in-an-unconscious-sort-of-way girlfriend. They were an instant hit together ("...a hilariously idiotic dyad." *Los Angeles Times*) but once the dominant overlords of The Biz got a gander at Petra in a bikini, she was removed from television and placed in a series of blockbuster extravaganzas in which she played, well, super-hot prostitutes, of course. What else?

The Very Famous Actor was another of Pinky's discoveries. Pinky was filming an insultingly moronic white-cop black-cop buddy film bank heist kidnap comedy romance, *We'll Look Back and Laugh About All This Someday*, when his co-star buddy walked off the set in a huff. Pinky had long admired the physical grace and snappy repartee of the black guy who worked the morning shift at Jagged

Psyche espresso bar on Pico where Pinky stopped every morning on his way to the studio. Pinky insisted said espresso guy be given a shot at the huffily vacated black cop buddy part. The movie was a monstrous success, and another star was born of Pinky's intuition and clout.

The Very Powerful Media Mogul owes everything to Pinky. They met the day Pinky arrived in Los Angeles. A forlorn teenager, recently orphaned, scared out of his wits, seventy-seven dollars to his name, Pinky was hoping to parlay his guitar playing and singing into a career. The future media mogul was dealing dope—and not *good* dope—out of the motel room adjacent to Pinky's motel room. When he heard Pinky singing through the paper-thin wall, he had a flash of inspiration. "What you need, kid," he said, knowing nothing about show business but a great deal about greed and avarice and human frailty, "is a manager." And he rode Pinky Jones all the way to the top of the heap.

The houselights dim. Lord, looking very much like James Dean in *Rebel Without A Cause* (blue jeans and white T-shirt) only older and with a darker more Italian Magyar countenance—and come to think of it, all in all, much more attractive than James Dean ever was—steps into the ersatz spotlight (Derek and Moustafa and Natasha standing on stools shining powerful flashlights) and the audience ceases to murmur.

"Welcome to Under the Table Books," says Lord, smiling gratefully at the full house (estimated crowd: 97). "It is my enormous pleasure to present Pinky Jones accompanied on piano by Tomas Petruchio, both of whom live upstairs and are forever filling the cosmos with their exquisite tones and tunes. I wince to speak so mercenarily, but as most of you know, our rent is long overdue. Fortunately, our landlord is incredibly wealthy, spends most of his time out of town, and no one else wants to rent this space, knock on wood, because the neighborhood is considered dangerous, which is both ironic and bizarre since it's just *us* around here, and we're loveable as can be. Nevertheless, we encourage you to drop some cash in our stash if you dig the show. Blessings and thanks. Here he is. Pinky Jones."

Tomas, wearing gray slacks and a billowy white shirt, his hair rather billowy, too, slips unobtrusively onto the piano bench as Pinky emerges from the hallway and stands beside the piano. Surprisingly graceful for one so tall, Pinky is wearing black trousers with a red belt, a long-sleeved shirt— fuchsia—with cufflinks made from Chinese coins, and fanciful red slippers with upturned toes. His longish gray hair is brushed back from his handsome craggy face—his eyes shining with tears. He is both comic and tragic, whether he tries to be or not.

"My friends," he begins, holding his arms out to embrace the entire audience, "I am so happy to sing for you."

Now Tomas essays a gorgeous run of churchy bluesy chords that set the tone for Pinky to sing *I Wish I Knew How It Would Feel To Be Free, Summertime, Don't Think Twice, It's All Right, Someone To Watch Over Me, You Are My Sunshine, Some Enchanted Evening, Blackbird, Autumn Leaves, Get Together, Turn, Turn, Turn,* and *Here We Go.*

Finishing over a luscious bed of Tomas's chords, Pinky says, "I ran away from some crazy idea of myself. I wanted to die, but fell in love with the wilderness and lived there for thirty years where poems and melodies came to me every day on breezes large and small. And though I sang with the river and sang with the wind and sang with the roaring waves, I longed to harmonize with other humans. I didn't crave sex or coffee or chocolate or conversation, all of which I *do* love, but I ached to make music with others of my kind. Which is why I came back. So if you're willing, I'd love love love you to sing with me now."

Kneading

(the annual debate—whither goest the pun?)

Lord Bellmaster lies on his back behind the counter, pondering a fundamental koan of Under the Table Bookism: can the worth of anything be quantifiable in burritos?

"The pain is formidable," he groans, wondering who might be in the store to hear him. "I can't move. I was fine a moment ago, now it feels like I've got a knife in my spine. Hello? Anyone out there?"

A woman leans over the counter and frowns down at him. It is Mrs. Armitage, the Cat Lady, though Lord barely recognizes her from his unique perspective. "Mrs. A? You look positively angelic from this angle. Not that you aren't angelic from other angles, too, but from *this* angle you resemble some sort of fabulous sex goddess, and I mean that in the friendliest way, of course. Forgive me if forgiveness seems called for."

"Are you hurt?" she asks, pleasantly aroused by his compliment. "Did I hear you moan?"

"More of a groan, I think," says Lord, grimacing. "It even hurts to talk. My back is on fire. Can't move. Came on suddenly and inexplicably. One minute I was whistling a happy tune, the next I was growling *Stormy Weather* with lightning bolts running up and down my spine, runnin' round my heart, runnin' round my brain."

"I'll get someone," she says, trying not to laugh. "You're delirious."

"No, no, I always talk this way. Besides, I'm learning so much from down here. Who knew?"

"How so?" she asks, removing her bonnet and allowing her raven tresses to tumble down—every lovely feature heightened by the black frame of her hair.

"My pain cannot be wholly physical," he says, shocked by her metamorphosis, "but symptomatic of a need to make big changes."

"Such as?" she asks, loving the caress of his voice and the penetrating pleasure of his non sequiturs.

"My relationship with Jenny, for one. Imagine a traffic jam as far as the eye can see, not a whisper of movement, the cause of the jam beyond our perceptions. She's moving out, and so am I, but the tendrils of dependency entangle us still. Who knows what's hers or how is mine or where why what when which was whose originally?"

"Tell me more," she says, her voice growing deep and husky and lusty. "I love the way you mangle meaning."

"This bookstore," he says, his voice creaking like a rusty hinge. "This assemblage of spirits. This frigate of hope in a sea of despond. We need coats of paint, more windows, a sofa in the Reading

Circle. Hey, you were Cat Lady. Now you…oh, I don't know… more live music. Impeccably tuned instruments. Perhaps a theater in the adjoining abandoned warehouse. There's so little time. Or too much of it. Less clothing. More touch. More fearless kissing. A storewide clearance sale."

Mrs. Armitage disappears from above and reappears beside Lord, her skirt brushing his arm as she kneels beside him, her scent elixir to the fallen bookstore guy. She puts her cool hand on Lord's forehead and sends a thrill of pleasure down his spine to mingle with his pain. "You're feverish. You should be in bed."

"I am in a state of revelation," he proclaims, conquered by her touch. "I love the feel of you on me. My pain is mentor, therapist, travel agent, and you the muse sent to…where have you been all the years you were someone else? What have you done with the old lady? Be gentle with her. I'm sure she meant no harm. Logic is insufficient. The worm *is* the butterfly. Lately, I've been catching glimpses of a previous life in which I died before I could fulfill the promise of…my promise."

"You're molten," she says, moving her hand from his forehead to his wrist—his pulse the *bossa nova*. "I'm taking you to bed."

"What a good idea," he says, smiling despite his agony. "If only I weren't in so much pain, I'm sure we would have a splendid…"

"Shh," says Mrs. Armitage, running her fingers through his hair. "I'll see who's downstairs to help me lift you."

Her skirt swirls about him as she goes for help, and Lord shudders with pain as a long-locked door to a cubicle in his heart swings open and out rushes his memory of running on a beach chasing the first woman he ever really loved.

With a heroic burst of speed, Lord catches up to his inamorata and shouts over the roaring waves *Marry me!* as he takes her in his arms.

But she shakes him off and obliterates his love with three angry words: *Get real, doofus.*

Mrs. Armitage stands in the doorway between the rumpus room and the kitchen, arrested by the awesome spectacle of a glistening black man, naked to the waist, tenderly lifting a massive swell of dough from the kneading board and lowering it gently into a huge white bowl.

"Moustafa," she says reverently. "Lord hurt his back. Can you help me get him into bed?"

"Of course," says Moustafa, bowing to her. "Look how lovely your hair, your face, your posture. Old lady gone."

"My bonnet..." she begins, feeling deliciously self-conscious in the presence of the half-naked god. "Won't stay on anymore."

"How could it?" he asks, brushing the living dough with olive oil. "Too much life to contain with such flimsy fabric."

"Why do you say that?" she asks—stabbed in the back by daggers of pain. "What's happening to me?"

"Go into the garden," he commands. "Take off your shoes and lie down on the earth."

"Yes," she says, holding out her hand to him. "Help me."

Moustafa takes the stairs two at a time and finds Lord on his feet—perplexed and amazed by the swift cessation of his suffering.

"It's a miracle," says Lord, grinning at Moustafa. "One moment agony, next moment fine and dandy."

"Memorize the sensation of the cessation of your pain," says Moustafa, reaching down and picking up a passing kitty cat to gently rub her soft round tummy. "For the next time she comes to visit you."

Lord Bellmaster's Sorrow

(teetering on the abyss, parachute store closed, he writes of himself…)

He sits immobile, occasionally blinking one or both eyes. Less occasionally, he sniffles. It is freezing outside, yet tropically warm in Weatherstone—a den of coffee drinkers, the soundtrack Brandenbergian, the women undoubtedly wild and willing beneath their languid exteriors. If only he spoke their language—even a few salient words of it. He wants coffee, but he's on the wagon, so he's having peppermint tea.

He doesn't want to be his age, but he doesn't want to be older or younger. He longs for the past, for the perfectly imperfect woman.

He longs to be a perfectly imperfect man adored by vibrantly attractive women. He longs to be invited by one or more vibrant women to share in her (their) life (ves) she (they) forgiving him in advance for his frequent and often lengthy disappearances into aloneness.

In the meantime, he mourns his disconnection from Jenny, his now probably previous lover, wishing she could ease into blameless friendship with him, which would then free him to openly pursue the newly metamorphosed Mrs. Armitage, a divine tigress inhabiting the body of a human female; her touch, her scent, her voice, her eyes, her lips, her cheeks, the way she ever so slightly squints and chews on her lower lip sufficient to drive a man insane with lust, to fill him with a wildly illogical longing to reside forever in the warmth of her embrace, to be *born* to her, to draw milk from her breasts, to be surgically attached to her—and even in death remain one with her.

Lord Bellmaster sips his peppermint tea and feels cheated by the Almighty. Why create such a thing as coffee, and permit some Italian genius to invent Cafe Latte—steamed milk seducing blissful bitterness from black espresso—only to render the brew a curse upon the nervous system of the likes of Lord Bellmaster?

He considers changing his name to Desire. "Hi. My name is Desire. I'm a previously owned literature personage."

"Double latte," sings Cecily Considine, the diva of Weatherstone, her billowy white blouse all but unbuttoned as she stands at the counter, a fire engine red espresso machine pulsing and hissing behind her—an appealing vision of a perfectly ripened succubus in an only slightly expurgated version of hell.

Lord Bellmaster groans. His peppermint tea has the punch of a sickly two-year-old, as satisfying as...well, nothing.

"House latte. Two shots," croons Cecily, aiming her words at Lord's exquisitely sensitive ear.

He questions his sanity. Why remain in this atmosphere dense with the divine stench of coffee, the walls echoing with the jittery jabber of unglued humans zooming on fresh infusions of zingy brew—anxious voices rising and falling around him underscored by Vivaldi—the sirens of Arabica calling to the half-mad captain lashed to the mast of his badly listing ship?

Caffeine-tossed psyches, he thinks, glaring at Cecily. *I blame* you *for my allergy to the powerful pith of the bean. Makes of me a chattering caricature.*

"House latte. Two stupendous shots of jazzy jolt," she says, smiling lasciviously, sensing how close to collapse Lord's rag tag defenses.

He leaps to his feet and heads for the door, determined to break free of the evil Babylon of Colombian French Kenyan Italian Brazilian Costa Rican Moroccan Turkish Guatemalan alchemical conspiracy.

"House latte? Two shots?" she calls again, and something in her voice—a plaintive generosity?—stays Lord Bellmaster.

"Last call," she says, her words striking his taste buds—well-flung Frisbees of doom. "House latte. My best since...forever. If I do say so myself. And I do. I really do. Two *enormous* shots of concentrated love power. Going once. Twice..."

Time hangs suspended. Slowly Lord turns, his eyes locking on the dark green bowl topped with a meringue of frothy foam—cream steamed into an ethereal inhalant. He knows the latte is his for the taking. He knows Cecily's next line as well as he knows the date of his birth, his telephone number, and the whereabouts of dandelions in July.

She will say, "House latte. Two shots. On the house."

He will move swiftly to claim the potion of his downfall.

For truly, I am but a pawn of desire. Or possibly a knight.

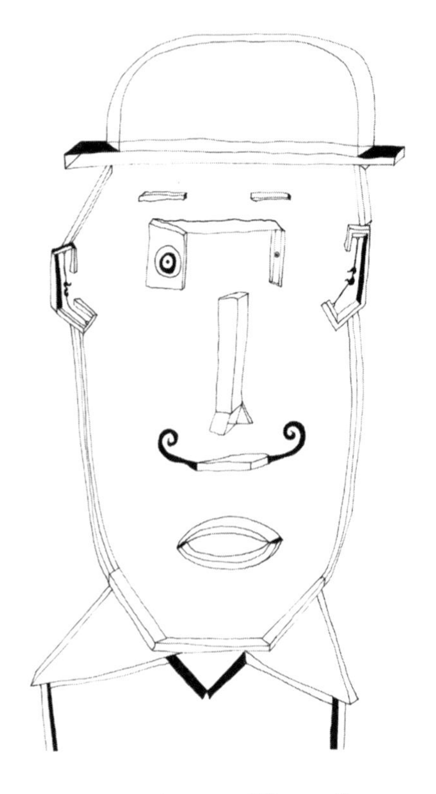

Landlord

(somnolent flamenco guitar)

Someone raps impatiently on Mrs. Armitage's door. She slips out of bed and dons her red silk bathrobe, wondering if the knock was real or merely the end of her lurid dream.

She opens the door to find Peter Franklin, her landlord, a dead ringer for the late great Alec Guinness, staring bug-eyed at the exquisite vision before him—a goddess with raven black hair tumbling in waves over her shoulders, her bountiful breasts all but fully revealed.

"Good god," he blurts. "You... you... you..."

"Yes?" she says, touching her black mane and realizing she's out of costume. "Is something amiss?"

"Your hair," says Peter, formidably aroused. "Your body. Your face. Your...the whole package, as it were. My god, you're magnificent. You take my breath away."

"Come in," she says, her accent becoming his—pleasantly British. "Tea? I have a lovely Ceylon and the freshest of cream."

"Don't try to butter me up," he says, hoping she will. "You're two months late with your rent. I've tried to be patient, but now with complaints of strange men coming and going all hours of the day and night, well, I've bent over backward, as it were, but unless we can think of some mutually satisfying method or technique, if you will, by which you can make good on your debt to me, I..."

"There must be some mistake," says Mrs. Armitage, enjoying the sensation of her favorite actor looking her up and down. "I've paid my rent a year in advance. As for strange men, the only..."

"Oh, no you don't, cutie pie," he says, wagging his finger at her. "I wasn't born yesterday. I only have *one* tenant who pays a year in advance, and that's Mrs. Armitage. Believe me, I keep extremely precise records. Having very little else to do. At my age. Though I would be hard-pressed to tell you what that is. My age. Keep records. However, I have it written down on my calendar. In the kitchen. My age. But as I say, my only tenant who pays in advance is..."

"But I *am* Mrs. Armitage," she says, touching the rosy flesh just above her glorious cleavage. "Though not for long."

"Mrs. Armitage lives at 431," says Peter, leaning back to scrutinize her apartment number, "and this is...oops. 431. God, I'm sorry." He shoves his hands into various pockets, searching for something. "I'm...hold on. Ah. Here." He brings forth a small plastic bottle—a single pill rattling around inside. "Damn my memory. I had your number mixed up with another number. Please forgive me."

"Come in," she says, taking his hand and drawing him inside. "I'll give you some water to take your pill."

&

Peter sits wearily at Mrs. Armitage's kitchen table and swallows the big yellow tablet. "341," he says disconsolately. "Not 431. I should sell one or the other. At my age, whatever my age happens to be, it's ridiculous to have three confusingly numbered properties. 431, 341, 143. We bought them thirty-five years ago when her father died. He left her a big duplex on the river. Or did I buy the duplex with my movie money? In either case, I traded the duplex for three smaller units. For the rental income." He smiles at her parakeets—seven in a row on the windowsill watching the world go by. "Lovely birds." He frowns. "Do I allow pets?"

"Yes, you do," she says, suddenly remembering what happened last night. *Unless that was a dream.* "Allow pets."

"I would," he says with a brilliantly dramatic sigh. "Allow pets."

"Tea?" she asks, gazing into his twinkling eyes.

"Can't," he says, rising gallantly. "If I stay another minute I will be so hopelessly infatuated with you, my only option will be to make a further fool of myself. Besides, if I am to have bread on my table, I must hurry to 341 and tell that girl to pay up or get out. I don't think she's actually a whore, but rather an exceedingly vivacious young woman. Mrs. Lipman tends to blow things out of proportion."

"Mrs. Lipman?"

"The neighbor with big ears and inquisitive eyes. The very worst sort of person to have next door. If you get my meaning."

"If I hadn't read his obituary, I would bet anything you really are Alec Guinness. Himself."

"The resemblance is uncanny," he says, hesitating on the threshold. "The voice only a fair rendition."

"Please come again," she says, ushering him out. "I so very much enjoyed our conversation. Your accent becomes me."

"If this ever happens again," he says, gravely inspecting the number over her door, "just say, 'Look at the number, Alec. Look at the stupid number.' Good day."

Mrs. Armitage crawls back into bed with Lord Bellmaster.

He stares at the ceiling—his previous notions of reality obliterated beyond recognition.

"What are you thinking about?" she whispers, hooking her leg over his chest.

"You, of course. Us. We. Making love. Wondering what might happen next. Never wanting to leave. Loving the sound of your birds. British people talking in your kitchen. Paradise." He takes her foot in hand and kisses her toes. "I woke to a voice saying, 'Honey is the root of all evil.' Must have meant *money*. Yes?"

"Do you think evil actually exists as a free-standing entity? As something separate from circumstance?"

"Is anything separate from circumstance?" asks Lord, throwing back the covers to reveal the splendors of his body.

"It's dangerous having you in my bed," she says, loving how naked he is. "Go away."

"Why? Something I did?"

"We," she says, gently gripping his impressive tumescence. "I need to become someone else before I let you in again."

"But you're so fine as you, darling," he says with an unmistakably sexual sigh. "The real fabulous you."

"Go," she says, letting go. "You're much too easy to love. My work demands no distractions, and you are definitely distracting."

"May I write to you? Please?"

"No!" she shouts, pulling the covers over her head. "I have all the information I need at this time."

Who Let The Bird Out?

(doing things with a warm-hearted mind)

Merlin, the albino falcon given to the bookstore in exchange for an armful of erotic doggerel, is absent from her cage in the darkest corner of the kitchen.

Derek, nearing his eleventh birthday, a slender child possessed of startling intelligence, and one of the more emotionally stable members of the eclectic collective known as Under the Table Books, frowns at the open door of the spacious cage and wonders who let the bird out, and why.

Moustafa, a loquacious brown man, his long black hair configured in seventeen braids strung with cylindrical glass beads—blues and yellows—arrives to shape the morning loaves: sourdough French and cinnamon raisin rye.

"Merlin's gone," says Derek, peering out the glass doors onto the brick terrazzo. "Was she in her cage when you went home last night?"

"She was there," says Moustafa, lifting the heavy bowls of risen dough onto the long oak table where he and his helpers make the daily bread. "She seemed particularly agitated."

"Restless," says Derek, nodding grimly. "Mr. Laskin said she was overdue to go flying again in the wide-open spaces. He says these kinds of falcons are like race horses and need to be flown or they..." His frown gives way to a hopeful smile. "Hey, maybe Mr. Laskin took her flying."

"Let us hope so," says Moustafa, stretching his arms skyward. "Shall we make our bread?"

"We shall," says Derek, joining Moustafa at the floury table.

They work in silence, enjoying the noises of their various friends awakening and arriving. From one of the more remote bedrooms comes the sound of Carl Klein striking a match on the piece of sandpaper he has pinned to his wall for just this purpose—the lighting of his pipe. From on high comes the telltale click and creak of Lord Bellmaster unlocking the street-level door and entering the bookstore, his footsteps resounding in the quiet. Bedsprings whimper in the bedroom nearest the kitchen—Jenny racing to the bathroom before Carl gets in there and camps for an hour as he does most mornings. Delivery trucks rumble by on High Street, their loudness proving Lord left the front door open. And now comes Natasha's fabulous soprano as she enters the bookstore in full song, Lord joining her with his dusky tenor.

I give to you

you give to me

we plant the seeds

to keep the garden growing

"Life is so good here," says Derek, looking up at Moustafa. "I wonder why more people don't live this kind of sharing life."

"We are not taught to share in our society," he says, gazing at the boy. "Rikyu Chin says that generosity is the tenet of Buddhist philosophy that Americans have the most difficulty integrating into their lives because we are programmed from an early age to expect a return for what we give—gratitude at the very least. But giving to get something is the antithesis of generosity."

Derek pauses in his shaping of a loaf to recall the golden moment when Mr. Laskin said to him, "You can live with me," the old man speaking without forethought, his spontaneous generosity obliterating the terrible fear that had dogged Derek every moment of every long day since his mother fell ill and lost her job and could no longer feed her three young children.

"Sharing is the best," says Derek, wondering where his mother and younger brother and baby sister might be now. They were living in his mother's dead car in the glass-strewn parking lot of a boarded-up strip mall south of Fresno when he ran away so dizzy from hunger he could barely see. "Even burying compost is sharing, huh? Food for the earth."

"Yes, my friend," says Moustafa, resting his hand on the boy's shoulder. "You know, the social worker came again yesterday when you were playing in your fort, so she didn't find you. But soon we must take proper action so you can stay with us. This will require an attempt to locate and contact your mother."

"I was afraid of that," says Derek, his vision blurred by sudden tears. "Denny says my being here could be a disaster for the collective, that the authorities could accuse you of..."

"No," says Moustafa, lifting the boy into his arms. "Your being here is a great blessing. I am prepared to do anything necessary to keep you with us. Please don't be afraid."

"Okay," says Derek, turning at the sound of the back door opening.

Enter Leona Spinelli—a sprite in green dungarees and a puffy blue jacket, her curly white hair blown every which way by the petulant October wind.

"Cold out," says Leona, closing the door behind her. "Saw Denny with the falcon. Said he was going to the flea market. Said the falcon was a curse."

Derek and Moustafa are just coming out the bookstore door when they see Denny coming home sans falcon.

A rangy redhead, Denny forestalls their questions by shouting from a distance, "I sold him for five hundred bucks. Good riddance."

"Denny," says Derek, clenching his fists, "how many times do I have to tell you? Merlin is a she."

"Well, she's gone now," says Denny, ashamed yet self-righteous—a nauseating combination of emotions. "She was driving me crazy."

"The falcon was no longer your responsibility," says Moustafa, speaking angrily to Denny for the first time in their decades of friendship. "She was Derek's pet and you stole her. Take us to the person you sold her to."

"I don't know who they are or where they went," says Denny, stunned by Moustafa's fury. "It was some guy in a burnoose. I could hardly see his face. He shoved the money into my hand and took the bird and disappeared."

"How could you?" asks Moustafa, wanting to strike his friend.

"I'm sorry," says Denny, bursting into tears. "I was desperate. I…I didn't know what else to do."

"It's okay," says Derek, bowing his head. "I know how you feel. I stole things, too, when I was desperate for something to eat. It's okay. I forgive you."

"I just…I couldn't take it anymore," says Denny, wringing his hands. "Every time I'd look at that bird I'd think about my wasted life, how I don't have anybody to love, how…"

"It's okay," says the boy, touching Denny's hand. "It's nobody's fault."

The wind abates. Dark clouds disperse. Sunlight floods the earth.

"Oh, Derek," says Denny, falling to his knees. "What have I done? Why did I want to hurt you so?"

"I don't think this is about me," says Derek, putting his hand on Denny's shoulder. "You're just trying to take care of yourself."

Dusk. A hard rain falling. The bookstore deserted. Jenny, a lovely lass of thirty-three, sits on the stool behind the counter reading *The World's Greatest Poems About The End Of A Relationship*. The bell above the door jingles. Derek enters in a shiny yellow raincoat and red rubber boots, having spent the entire day roaming the soggy city in search of the falcon.

"There you are," says Jenny, coming around the counter to give her boy a hug. "I was worried about you. Shall I run you a hot bath? You must be freezing."

"I am kind of cold," he says, his voice hoarse from calling and calling and calling to Merlin. "Moustafa here?"

"He went to the store." She takes him by the hand and leads him down the stairs. "He'll be back soon. Butternut squash and goat gouda cheese and sunflower rye for supper."

"Did Mr. Laskin come for his two o'clock sandwich?" asks Derek, allowing Jenny to help him out of his sodden clothes.

"I'm not sure." She starts hot water running into the old claw-foot tub. "I was gone for most of the day until late afternoon. But judging by our cheese supply, he probably came. Stupendous cheddars."

"He shouldn't be out in this cold," says Derek, waiting for Jenny to look away before he takes off his underpants and climbs into the tub.

"I would leave you alone, sweetheart," she says, lingering in the doorway, "but I'm worried you'll fall asleep in the bath."

"You're right," he says, wearily closing his eyes. "I might."

Derek wakes in his little bed to the sound of laughter from the kitchen. For a brief scary moment he doesn't know where he is, but now he remembers he lives at Under the Table Books, not in a tract home in Fresno, not in a derelict car, not in a cardboard box in an alley full of garbage, not in the bushes by the river.

He starts to get up, but he is so weary from searching for Merlin, he drifts back to sleep, lulled by the sonorous voices of his friends.

Claim

(poets loyalty love timing)

Finely tuned by his acupuncturist (in trade for *Joan of Arc* by Mark Twain) Lord Bellmaster strides exuberantly into the bookstore and finds Jenny on the verge of tears.

"What?" he asks, fearing the worst. "What's wrong?"

Jenny blinks at her lover and wants to say, *I know you have a new love and I'm heartbroken,* but lacks the courage. Instead, she smiles bravely and says, "A man just gave us ten thousand dollars in cash for a beat-up paperback edition of *Kim*."

"Kipling?"

"He didn't tell me his name." She sniffles and wipes her eyes. "Just gave me the money. A hundred hundreds. In this shoe box." She taps the top of a faded Keds box. "He said it was his father's."

"The money?"

"No. The book. His father died when he, the man who gave me the money, was seven. He'd never had anything that belonged to his father. So imagine his surprise when he was browsing the *Greatest Geniuses of All Time* section and came upon his father's signature on the inside front cover of *Kim*. He said he was happier than he'd ever been in his life just to hold the book and know his father had held it, too."

Lord glares at the mass of moolah. "Whoa. What do we do with so much cash? This tops the old record by a mile."

"Call a meeting?" suggests Jenny, pressing close to Lord for solace. "Mmm, you smell nice. Massage oil?"

"No," he murmurs, distracted by the stacks of bills. "Some sort of mugwort goo she use in conjunction with the needles. A meeting? We've only had one of those in all these years and it was a disaster. Remember? Massive incongruity seasoned with threats of secession. Lets just put the cash somewhere safe and think about it for a while."

"Well, we certainly should pay the back rent," she says, perusing Lord for signs of sexual satiation. *But is that glow in his cheeks from sex or acupuncture? Hard to tell.* "That leaves eight thousand."

"Oh, the rent," says Lord, wistfully. "How quickly we forget."

"And Carl needs new glasses," says Jenny, thinking of the much-glued frames of their kindly old friend. "Desperately. Shall we give him five hundred?"

"Fine," says Lord, swelling with bravado imparted by the lucre. "Carl shall have new glasses, which will surely enhance his vacuum cleaning. Furthermore, let it be known that the Spinelli sisters shall not suffer through another summer without shade trees in front of their deforested duplex. Give them two hundred."

"Moustafa needs a new conga drum," says Jenny, starting a list on top of the money box. "Costing how much? Three hundred?"

"Agreed," says Lord, pounding the counter. "A new conga it is. In addition, henceforth let it go out into the land that..."

The bell over the front door announces Bernie—pudgy and forlorn—a locally renowned sandwich maker bearing seven volumes of poetry by Numero Uno, the locally renowned poet and penny-ante investment broker. Each volume is a first edition in mint condition, personally inscribed at length by Numero.

"Wow," says Lord, reading the dedication scrawled on the title page of *Eat My Tendons.*

> To his Bernaciousness magician of sandwiches beyond the call of the wild blue yonder of unconscious genius love. Yummy great gigantic good. Sinew synapse recharge! Keep up the tongue-tantalizing combos. Samba cuisine! Kosher dill and what was that mustard? Brazilian. Yow! Numero Uno

"Each one signed most specifically to you, Bernie," says Jenny, peering over Lord's shoulder. "Amazing. These must be worth a small fortune. Emphasis on *small.*"

Bernie lowers his voice. "My dream is to get five or six thousand dollars for these, quit my job and go to Mexico and walk on the beach and eat in cantinas and learn Spanish and date a few señoritas. I thought I'd give you guys first crack before I go to the big-dollar stores."

Jenny gazes wistfully at the money. "Five or six? Which?"

Bernie thinks for a moment, calculating train fare and cheap rooms and shirts and pants and shoes and food and miscellaneous whatnots. "*Seven* thousand," he decides. "Though just among the three of us, if you twisted my arm, I'd take six."

Jenny looks at Lord. Lord clears his throat and nods. Jenny removes three thousand dollars and hands the box with the rest of the loot to Bernie. "Should be seven in here."

Bernie blanches. "No. Wait. Really?"

"Not prepared for your dream to become reality?" asks Lord, smiling ironically. "I know the feeling. The dream is so vivid the actual thing pales in contrast. On the other hand, your timing is impeccable, which bodes well. Ten minutes later that money was *spent.*"

"Wait. Wait," says Bernie, staring at the blur of green. "This is *verifiably* seven thousand dollars? Truly? You mean I could actually do what I just said I wanted to do?"

"Or not," says Jenny, her eyes brimming with tears. "That's the beauty of it. You can do whatever you want. It's all yours."

"Need to sit?" asks Lord, solicitously. "A cup of tea? Or how about a beer? I seem to recall you're something of a beer drinker."

"No, thanks," says Bernie, fitting the top on the shoebox. "I'll take this to my bank, to my favorite teller, Eva. She's always so friendly in that extra delicate way like maybe you have some terminal illness because they can see right there on the screen exactly how little money you have, and I rarely have *any* money, so this will be a whole new experience for me. *And* for her. I might even...no."

"Oh, yes!" cries Jenny, caught up in his fantasy. "Ask her out."

He shrugs painfully. "Oh, but she's so beautiful. I'm not exactly the man of anybody's dreams. I don't think."

"I'll give you a haircut," she says, clapping her hands. "Have a seat while I get my scissors."

"I will lend you my magic turquoise shirt," says Lord, winking at Bernie. "It will harmonize superbly with your new aura."

"Why are you being so nice to me?" asks Bernie, backing away. "You're after my money, aren't you?"

Lord nods emphatically. "That's right, Bernie. We gave you the money so we could try to get it back from you. Makes perfect sense to *me.*"

"Perfect," says Jenny, her attention diverted by the bell announcing the arrival of Numero Uno himself—the bookstore's poet laureate, one of the last of the original (lesser) Beats, his accent Bronxian, his eyebrows *way* out of control.

"These books," says Numero, his voice quavering as he fingers the pristine volumes of his poetry. "Where did you get them?"

"From the man you once called his Bernaciousness magician of sandwiches," says Lord, gesturing to Bernie. "The renowned sandwich maker from Steve's Stunning Sandwiches."

"Bernie?" says Numero, aghast. "You're *selling* my books?"

"Sold," says Jenny, smiling admiringly at Bernie. "Now he's off to Mexico with Eva."

"Or not," says Lord, grinning at Bernie. "This money seems to have rather curious mojo, if you catch my drift."

"God," says Numero, grimacing. "I wrote my guts out to you in here." He opens the good-as-new copy of *Next Guy Calls Me Fatso, I Deck Him* and reads, 'To his Bernaciousness on high, sandwich guru savior of my dumb beast body squeezing words from sponge of anguished soul such beauty from your tender turkey gooshed with zenith avocado and twang of Ukrainian mustard on rye. I love you old friend. These poems are *for* you and *of* you and made in concert with your culinary handfuls, my ambrosia, gracias grande. Numero Uno.'"

"I'm sorry." Bernie sobs, "but I'm dying here, Numero. Dying."

"I forgive you." says Numero, gathering up the books. "I claim these volumes from this anarchist quagmire utopia in excelsius in exfahrenheit. Goodbye."

"I still love the poems. I do, but..."

"Bernie," says Numero, waving away the apology. "Enough said. A book is to be shared. No expectations. It must be given, and given free, or it means nothing, not a thing. The same is true of love. You may quote me." He bounces his eyebrows. "Please. Quote me. Quote me."

"Your haircut," says Jenny, hurrying away to find her scissors. "You want it short or short short?"

"Handsome," says Bernie, waving farewell to Numero. "Make me as handsome as feasibly possible."

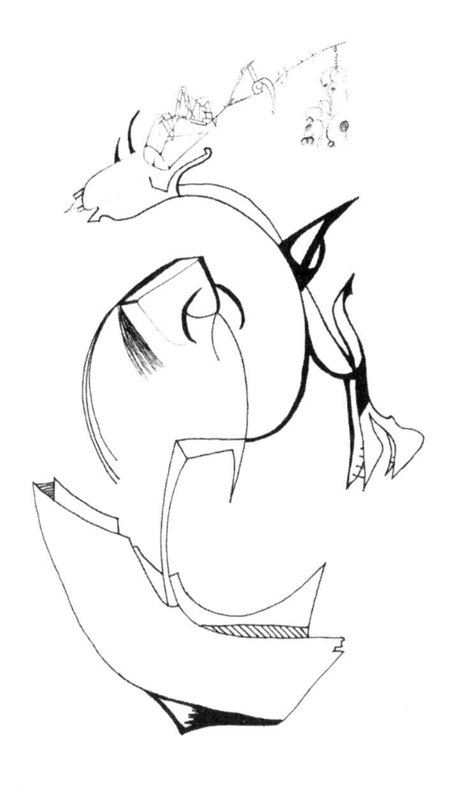

The Return of Mashman Z

(time providing space for evolution)

Mashman Z—young gifted black and *really* good looking— steps off the 84 bus and breathes a big sigh of relief because nobody in this part of town wants to shoot him. He steps behind a hedge of oleanders and changes from hoodlum gear to the soft gray twills of coffeehouse cool, his dark glasses replaced by simple wire frames.

"Took me a while to get myself back here," he croons, finding his stride and narrating his story as he nears Under the Table Books. "Mama so needy and debts to pay, but finally came around to be today. Now to lay mine eyes on sweet Natasha."

Under the Table Books is particularly warm and cozy today, the cavernous anarchist haven basking in a kindly October sun, the old place filled with the scent of freshly baked cinnamon swirls.

"Me likes this joint," says Mashman, leaning down to pet a big orange cat. "Mama never let us have cats for the fleas." He scans the profusion of books, chuckling in wonder at the verbosity of humans. "Just think of all the good stories must be out there."

The Spinelli twins, Iris and Leona, spry octogenarians in paisley pinafores, move in opposite directions through the *French Diatribes* section, alphabetizing and dusting, while Napoleon Diaz, seventy-seven, a handsome Cuban with a rakish mustache and wavy black hair, stands on a ladder peering into a wooden cage hanging from the central rafter.

Mashman Z smiles up at Napoleon and asks pleasantly, "What's hatching, daddy-o?"

"You work here?" asks Napoleon, frowning down at Mashman. "You Moustafa's boy?"

Mashman stiffens. "Excuse me? I don't see any boys around here. You want to rephrase that question?"

"Sorry," says Napoleon, shrugging in slow motion. "No offense. Thought maybe he was your father."

"Never met the man," says Mashman, mimicking Napoleon's shrug. "And no, I don't work here. Not yet anyway."

Napoleon taps the cage. "This crow is not well. Last thing I need is the health department closing my building on account of a sick bird."

"Actually," says Iris, gazing up at Napoleon, "Butch is a raven, and he's only living here until he recuperates from the terrible shock of almost being hit by a bus."

Napoleon rolls his eyes. "Why I keep this place I don't know."

"You own this paradise?" asks Mashman, obviously impressed. "Allow me to compliment you on your choice of employees, especially the divine Natasha."

"I own the *whole* building," he says with an imperious gesture.

"I'm the landlord. Got nothing to do with these people. But I can't have sick animals on the premises. So many cats bad enough."

Leona glares up at Napoleon. "Cats are every bit as good as people. Humans are *not* the end all and be all of evolution. You think you're superior to a two-thousand-year-old redwood? Can you fly like an eagle or swim from Mexico to Alaska every year like the whales do?"

"Excuse me," says Mashman, bowing gallantly to Leona. "Would you by any chance know the whereabouts of one lovely brown woman known as Natasha?"

"She's not here," says Iris, clutching a copy of Dubonnet's *Treatise on Treatises*. "Probably cooking at Chez Ben, her brother's cafe."

"Far from here?" asks Mashman, smiling quizzically. "Chez Ben?"

"Best food in town," says Napoleon, coming down the ladder. "Where's Moustafa? Smells good in here. This place isn't licensed for a commercial bakery, you know?"

"Moustafa is no doubt monitoring the progress of his current batch of cinnamon swirls," says Iris, pointing to the stairway down. "I'm sure he'd be delighted to have a visit from you, Mr. Diaz. Or if you prefer, we can give him a message for you."

Napoleon glares at her. "Tell him to fix the crow or get rid of it. Lease or no lease, we can't have sick birds in here."

"Yes, your royal imperial highness," says Leona, curtsying ridiculously to Napoleon as he struts out of the store.

"So Natasha's a chef?" asks Mashman, pursuing Iris. "Tell me more. Tell me everything."

"Are you in love with her?" asks Iris, shelving *Treatise on Treatises* and pulling out Count Burgundy's *Seventy-six Arguments For the Elimination of Prisons*. "I hate to disappoint you, but you're not the only one."

"This I assumed," says Mashman, grinning at the twins. "What else about her? Talk about her constantly, please."

"She loves to dance," says Iris, thinking fondly of Natasha cavorting around the Reading Circle. "You know that kind of dancing where your arms go all over the place and you don't need a partner? Whatever she wants to do, she does."

"Chez Ben is where?" asks Mashman, eager to go there.

"Come with us," says Leona, nodding enthusiastically. "We're almost done with the diatribes."

On the street, Leona to his right, Iris to his left, Mashman says, "Kind of ironic my walking along so friendly with the two of you."

"Life is ironic," says Iris, nodding. "When it's not being absurd or delightful or poignant or dismal or...variable."

Leona frowns at Mashman. "How did *you* mean kind of ironic?"

Mashman shrugs. "Well, when I was punk, used to jump old ladies and grab their purses."

"That was then," says Iris, speaking factually. "Now you'd never."

"Correct," says Mashman, "but wasn't long ago what I'm saying."

"Every journey begins with a single step," says Iris, taking Mashman's hand and giving it a goodly squeeze. "The *Tao*."

"The who?"

"Not *The Who*," says Iris, shaking her head. "We like *The Who*, too. I'm speaking of the *Tao*. The book of changes."

"Ancient Chinese brain twisters," says Leona, taking hold of Mashman's other hand. "Here's one I especially like. *The greatest force lives in the not doing*."

"Me likes," says Mashman, partial to the unexpected syllable. "That's in a book?"

"The *Tao*," says Iris, sensing something special flowing through the handsome young man.

"Ah, here's Chez Ben," says Leona, gazing fondly at the sign above the bright blue door. "May we treat you to a smoothie?"

"If you tell me what's in it," says Mashman, arching an eyebrow. "If it sounds remotely edible, just maybe so."

"A Chez Ben smoothie," says Iris, closing her eyes, "is an ambrosial mixture of fresh fruit and yogurt and spring water and spine-tingling secret ingredients."

"A Chez Ben smoothie," says Leona, taking her sister's free hand, "is the quintessential milkshake without milk or ice cream."

"A Chez Ben smoothie," says Iris, opening her eyes, "is the gateway to contentment."

"And," says Leona, starting the three of them turning in a circle, "you'll find the interplay of raisins and cinnamon pure poetry."

"There's something primordial about a Chez Ben smoothie," says Iris, licking her lips. "Something of mother's milk."

"I thought you said no milk," says Mashman, confused and delighted by the old gals. "Didn't you just say no milk and no ice cream?"

"No *cow's* milk," says Iris, loving the influx of warmth coming from Mashman's big beautiful hand. "Turns out humans can't easily digest cow's milk or anything *made* from cow's milk. We evolved eating fruits and nuts and vegetables and the occasional hunk of meat, but not cow milk."

"We've been sold a bill of goods by the poop heads," says Leona, her eyes narrowing in anger. "Beware the dairy industrial complex."

"How do you two know so much?" asks Mashman, wishing he could take them home to meet his mother. "How'd you get so smart?"

"We're eighty-eight," they sing in harmony. "Eighty-eight times two is what?"

Iris & Leona

(a twin saga)

Iris

I was married for eleven years to a relatively nice man named George Albers. We lived in Santa Rosa. He was a carpenter, specializing in kitchen cabinets and front doors. He was seventeen years my senior. We met at church. Methodist. I was twenty when we married. Extremely shy. We tried for seven years to have children, but I never got pregnant. I suggested we adopt children. He said no. Definitely not.

After those first seven years, he stopped touching me and started sleeping on the sofa in the living room. Otherwise, very little in our lives changed. I continued teaching kindergarten and keeping house. I had a fine rose garden with thirty-seven heirloom varieties. I had the best yellows in town. He kept on being a carpenter. We talked about the usual things over supper. Work. The weather. Food prices. He had only ever touched me for sex, every week or so, which hadn't been enjoyable for me because he did it without any apparent feeling for me, quickly, often before I was ready, so I was more relieved than sad when he stopped.

Then four years after he stopped touching me, in November, the week before my thirty-first birthday, a woman came to the kitchen door. This was during the Depression, so at first I thought she might be looking for something to eat, but it turned out she was George's mistress. He had taken up with her after he stopped touching me. She had five children by her first two husbands, and she said George was supporting her so she would have a child with him. But she couldn't get pregnant by him either. She said he was behind in his payments to her. She said he was impotent. And all this time he had insisted something was wrong with *me*.

I packed a suitcase and took a train to Los Angeles to stay with Leona. She was working for Columbia Pictures as a set decorator. She borrowed a truck from the studio and we drove to Santa Rosa, packed up my things, and drove back to Los Angeles. George kept the house and married twice more before he died without having any children.

Leona encouraged me to sleep with lots of men, but I never felt comfortable about that. She had a new boyfriend every week. They would have sex everywhere in the house. I would stay in my room, which made me feel like a prisoner. After about three months with her, I moved north again, to San Francisco. I got a job teaching kindergarten in the Fillmore, which was an Italian community at that time. I had several suitors almost immediately. I didn't have sex with any of them, but I did do lots of kissing before I made my decision.

I finally chose Manny. He was not as handsome as Carlo or Enrico, but he was a wonderful conversationalist and an excellent cook. He loved to go to the beach. He was also a fine gardener. He seemed to think I was pretty wonderful. He grew most of the flowers he sold in his grocery store. I'll never forget the moment I decided he was the one.

I was standing on the little patio behind his house, soaking up the October sun. He came to me from the garden with his arms full of purple and yellow mums. It was so beautiful, like a vivid dream. He kissed my cheek, being careful not to crush the flowers between us. Then he said, "Choose the blooms you want. I will sell the rest and take you to dinner. Anywhere you like to go."

I got pregnant two weeks after our wedding. Who knows how many children we would have had if he hadn't gone to war to drive the Germans out of Italy. But four was enough, each a blessed miracle.

Leona

I'm so glad Iris had children. When I moved up to San Francisco in 1943, after she got the news of Manny's death, it felt so natural to be there, to help with the kids and to keep the grocery store going, to help her get through the darkest days of her grief. She loved Manny so much, and he was wild about her. Every time I came to visit before he died, the house would shake during the night when they made love. It seemed so unlikely after her sexless life with George.

By the time I moved to San Francisco, I was through with men. I officially entered my Gertrude Stein phase in 1945. I tried to get Iris to switch, but she wasn't interested. When she married Gunnar in 1950 and moved to Norway with the kids, I thought I'd never see her again. But four years later when the cannon on his whaling ship exploded and killed him, she moved back to the States and we've lived together ever since.

The amazing thing about Iris, and this has been true since we were little children, is that she never criticizes people, never speaks a harsh word, and always looks for the good in everything. It's not in her nature to be negative. I'm the exact opposite—a critical cynical cranky old bitch—though lately Moustafa has been helping me practice neutrality and I'm starting to experience some pretty nifty results from holding my tongue; no easy feat for the likes of me.

If we were fruit, Iris would be a sweet papaya, whereas I'm more of a crab apple.

Chez Ben

(the nature of quality)

Leona and her sister Iris, identical twins with curly white hair and pinkish white skin, commandeer the one and only window table in Chez Ben, their guest a gorgeous brown man called Mashman Z.

Mashman is questing for the princess Natasha with whom he had one scintillating encounter some months ago—and he's been pining for her ever since. Leona and Iris have brought him to Chez Ben where Natasha plays close-harmony second fiddle to her older brother Ben, the creator of some of the tastiest culinary concoctions in human history.

"We're in luck," says Leona, pointing at the *Specials* scrawled on a triangular chalkboard nailed to the wall behind the makeshift counter—two wooden doors balanced on cinder blocks. "Fresh blackberries today. Ben is a savant with berries."

"You did say you were buying, didn't you?" asks Mashman, batting his eyelashes. "I'm currently a bit under-funded."

"Fear not," says Iris, intuiting something extra special about their dashing young guest. "We have oodles of credit here. We clean Chez Ben in exchange for unlimited yum."

Ben pops out of the kitchen, a smile breaking through his persistent despair. "Be right with you. I'm just pulling scones. Hold tight."

"Ben is Natasha's brother," says Leona, whispering to Mashman. "He's a child prodigy world-class chef. And the hits just keep on coming."

"Wait wait wait," says Mashman, frowning severely. "We mustn't be talking about the same Natasha. Mine is a tall chocolate brown. This dude is short and white and..."

"Same Natasha," says Iris, winking playfully. "She and Ben have the same mother, different...oh, what's the expression, Leona?"

"Bio dads," says Leona, sharing Iris's perception of Mashman—his essential magnificence echoing through the caverns of her intuition.

"Aha," says Mashman, raising a declarative finger. "Natasha has a white mama. That explains everything."

"How?" asks Leona—the young man's genius a palpable current. "How does having a white mama explain everything?"

"Explains why Natasha isn't sure what color to be," he says, sounding oh so sure. "Because, see, if her mama was black she wouldn't have a question."

"In my experience," says Iris, gazing fondly at Leona, "there's no end to the questions, no matter what color your mama."

"Though it is true," says Leona, returning her sister's gaze, "that mothers usually do most of the early shaping, and Natasha hardly had a mother at all, other than Felix. And he's a man, and white to boot."

Ben emerges from the kitchen to take their order, his frizzy hair tied back in a stubby ponytail, his big nose dominating his boyish face, his pink T-shirt proclaiming CHEZ BEN YUM.

"Hello, Benjamin," says Iris, wrinkling her nose in greeting. "This is our special new friend Mr. Mashman."

"Welcome," says Ben, preoccupied with innumerable weighty matters. "What can I get for you?"

"We'd like three of those scones you just pulled," says Iris, her eyelids fluttering in anticipation of the coming feast. "And three smoothies. Shoot the works."

Ben nods wearily. "Give me five minutes."

"Excuse me, monsieur," says Mashman, taking a deep breath, "is Natasha here today?"

"She went to the store," says Ben, taking his familiar place behind the counter. "We were low on currants and buckwheat and rice syrup. I expect her within the hour."

"Gracias," says Mashman, scanning the funky room—a derailed boxcar. "Nice place you have here."

"It's for sale," says Ben, nonchalantly tossing myriad comestibles into the massive blender. "I'm going into a monastery."

Leona places a hand on her heart and gazes in anguish at Ben. "How much are you asking?"

"Equipment and recipes and the name—five thousand dollars." He opens a jar of esoteric yeast. "But for you, Leona? Five thousand."

"A monastery?" says Mashman, wincing at the thought of celibacy. "To be like a monk?"

"A Buddhist monk, yes," says Ben, dumping a swarm of glistening blackberries into the mix and topping the swarm with a dollop of glimmering seaweed. "Assuming I can hack it."

A gargantuan tear rolls down Iris's cheek. "No more Chez Ben. What a tragedy."

"We've had a good run," says Ben, not one to mince words. "Nineteen months of unparalleled cuisine. History made. Life goes on."

Iris smiles bravely at Mashman. "I'm so glad you'll get to taste some Chez Ben yum before they close."

"Me, too," says Mashman, watching Ben approach with a plate of humongous blackberry scones and three towering bluish green smoothies. "It's that good, huh?"

"Beyond good," says Leona, transfixed by what she is about to put in her mouth. "Life-changing."

Mashman bites into a scone and his taste buds sing hosanna. "Baby," he groans, squinting hard to keep his beliefs intact. "It *is* beyond good. This...this is...revelatory."

"Taste the smoothie," Iris moans, swallowing her first glorious gulp. "I swear it takes me back forty years."

Mashman sips the fruity brew and a delicious breeze rushes through his veins, cooling his persistent anger and giving him a crystal-clear vision of a highly creative and sexually satisfying future. "Yo. This stuff shatters every previous notion of what food can be. Don't stop."

"Sorry," says Ben with a regretful sigh. "Old hat to me now. A reflexive response to fabulous ingredients. But to what end, you know? I need something else besides the alchemy of edibles."

"You think you're gonna find something better than this in a monastery?" asks Mashman, drinking deeply of the regenerative brew—a thousand good ideas clambering to be talked about. "What could be better than Chez Ben Yum?"

"Not better," says Ben, resolutely folding his arms. "Not better or worse or bigger or smaller. Simply..." He turns and walks away. "Else."

"Wow," says Mashman, beaming at Iris and Leona as they beam at him. "I just had a most amazing..."

"Epiphany," says Iris, nodding.

"Realization," translates Leona, nodding synchronously with Iris.

"About my name," says Mashman, drinking the last of Ben's elixir.

"Tell us," say the twins, each taking one of Mashman's hands.

"No more Mashman," he says—tears spilling from his beautiful eyes. "Only Z from now on."

"Zee," sing the sisters in pleasing harmony. "Zeeee."

Mr. Laskin

(The News)

I don't have much, but there's one thing I treat myself to every Wednesday, and that's a newspaper, fresh from the rack. No one else has touched it. The news is absolutely fresh. You can smell its freshness. The folds of the pages are sharp and clean. This is my greatest luxury, my last strong link to civilization. It may not seem like much to you, but for me buying the Wednesday news is absolutely, without question, the zenith of my week.

Furthermore, it is absolutely essential that I pay for it. If someone gave the newspaper to me, it would have no importance whatsoever. I must get my news through ritual.

Every Wednesday I wake up early, wherever I happen to be, and I take a bath. Sometimes I bathe in the river. Sometimes I use a garden hose, if there's no one around to tell me not to. Sometimes I am somewhere with a shower, and now and then I find myself in a house with a bathtub. That, of course, is the ultimate luxury, to soak for a while in a tub full of truly hot water.

Then, once my body is washed, I put on my cleanest clothes and set forth to find a newspaper rack. I do not buy my papers from vendors or in stores. I want my news direct, no middlemen. When I have located a rack I like the look of, I approach it slowly, with solemnity. I do not allow myself to read the headlines. To know anything at this point would destroy the purity of the experience.

I take two quarters from my pocket. Fifty cents still buys the news in this town, thank God. I will have had these quarters since the day before, at least. I will not beg on Wednesdays. No, the day I buy my paper is a day of dignity for me. On this day I am as good as any other man, even the president, even the pope.

I hold the quarters, heads side up, between the thumb and index finger of my right hand. I read aloud the dates on each coin. Lately, I've been getting lots of those bicentennial ones. 1776 –1976. George Washington on one side, a Revolutionary War drummer on the other. On the George side it says LIBERTY up above his head, and then in smaller print under George's chin it says IN GOD WE TRUST. If we didn't know better, we might think George was a mannish-looking woman, hawk-nosed and severe, with silly curls and sillier ponytail, with a ribbon in it yet. There is no mention anywhere on the coin that this person is George Washington. Somehow we know. Or maybe it would be more appropriate to say, somehow we have not yet forgotten.

I put the quarters in the slot, give the handle a pull, and listen carefully as the quarters roll, then fall into the change box.

Sometimes the chamber is empty and the quarters clonk against the bottom in a sad hollow way. Other times the coins settle gently onto a good pile of fellow coins, making a beautiful clinking sound. I sometimes think the sound my quarters make going in is more important than getting the paper itself. If I am sad, that beautiful soft musical sound can cheer me up. And if I'm happy, that hollow clonking can leave me doubting everything.

There are times when the paper on top of the stack is damaged, dog-eared or torn. I take the next one down, or the next. I want perfection of form if I can't get it from the contents. And sometimes only one paper remains, the paper held against the glass by the metal frame. I do not like these papers as well. They have been looked at by countless passersby and handled roughly by the person stocking the rack. I take them, but those Wednesdays are never quite as good as the Wednesdays when the quarters fall just right, and the papers are many and fresh, smelling strongly of ink, hot off the presses, still warm from the ovens of thought.

I tuck the paper under my arm and go in search of a place to read. I need a table, sunlight, and good coffee. I will not drink cheap coffee on Wednesday. Fortunately, there are many good places to go in this town, many good cups of coffee to be had. I am known in these places. On Wednesday I am not a bum, a freak, a shopping-cart person. My shopping cart is hidden somewhere safe. I am free of my few things on Wednesday. I have a dollar to spend, a morning to dedicate to my god, the news. If all my days could be like Wednesday there is nothing I couldn't accomplish.

I read the paper in order, front page to back. I read every word, save for the Classifieds section, and on a rainy day I will read that, too. I study the advertisements. I ponder the editorials. I read every comic strip, every statistic in the sports section, every letter to the editor, every shred of gossip. I meditate on my horoscope. I scrutinize the photographs and wonder at the movie reviews. I fall in love with the fashion models, devour the food section, second-guess the business experts, and check my stocks, the ones I would have bought a year ago when the market was way down and the time was right.

All in all it takes about four hours. Then I carefully reassemble the paper and carry it to my friend Leopold who meets me in front of the library, downtown, every Wednesday at one o'clock. Sometimes I get there before him. Sometimes he is waiting for me, leaning against the old stone building, holding it up with his strong little back.

I give him the paper. He always asks, "Anything good?" I usually say, "A few things." Though once I remember the paper was as empty of anything good as I have ever seen it, and I said, "No, Leo, not a goddamn thing." To which he responded by putting it directly in the recycling bin, without so much as a glance at the sordid headlines. And once, yes, once I said, "Oh, Leo, it's incredible. You won't believe all the good news." To which he responded by hugging the paper to him like long-lost best friend.

And then, with or without Leo, depending on his mood, I walk to the post office where I purchase a postcard on which I write a brief note to the president, which I then send. Now and then I'll include a poem, if a good rhyme comes to me. Sometimes I'll quote an editorial or a news item. Whatever I write, it is inspired by the news I have just read.

One time I wrote him a postcard that said, "Dear Mr. President, it is clear from the news that you have lost touch with the will of the people. As they grow more and more desirous of a peaceful world, you grow more and more vituperative, angry and irrational. I urge you to take some time off to search your soul, to listen to the inner voice, lest you drift too far from your purpose."

And the very next week the headline read PRESIDENT IN SECLUSION. Had he heard me? Did he read my note? I don't know. I only know that he canceled all appointments for three days and went into seclusion. To think. To ponder. Perhaps to study the news.

I like to think he reads all my notes, and looks forward to my postcards as I look forward to the Wednesday news. He listens to me. He didn't at first, but now he does. Now his aides sort through the avalanche of mail to find my cards. They know my handwriting now. And I mark my notes in another way, too. I take a quarter, with the bust of George face up, and I press the postcard down onto the coin and then I take a pencil and I color in over the quarter, so that George and LIBERTY and IN GOD WE TRUST and the date come through, like a temple rubbing.

I'm not insane. I don't believe the president listens to me. I am a man who lives for Wednesdays. I once owned fleets of cars, now I push a shopping cart, which I did not steal. I found it by the river where the shopping carts grow. I will return it someday. Perhaps the day before I die. I have never stolen anything. I fathered three children. I had tens of hundreds of thousands of millions of dollars. I lived with a woman, my wife, and could not love her.

What am I saying? Why have I told you this story? Because though the news itself may be a mass of lies and half-truths, rising above it, every Wednesday, is a tone, a feeling, a universal hum. And it helps me. It allows me to go on, to hope.

Some find salvation in prayer, some in music. I am not saved yet, but if I am ever to be saved, if I am ever to find the peace I seek, I know where I'll read all about it.

J30

(Cassandra, Olivia's mother, carries the people)

Downtown. High noon. Swirling autumn leaves. Honey-brown Cassandra sits down behind the shiny black steering wheel of the massive bus, knowing by the height of the chair that it was Maxine who just ended her shift and left the bus all warm and toasty. Cassandra is so pleasingly voluptuous, even her starched brown uniform cannot obscure the loveliness of her figure—long golden teardrop earrings making upside-down exclamation points to her fierce beauty.

She adjusts her seat and mirrors, closes her eyes, and starts to sing, the bus ringing with the power of her astonishing voice.

Now she opens the door and her song strikes a young black man—hungry lonely out of work—as he climbs aboard and drops his quarter in the pay box. He bows to Cassandra, hoping to make eye contact, but that won't happen. She's singing, true, but she's a fortress. The young man takes a seat ten rows back—Cassandra's song ending on a high trembling note that leaves the young man completely undone.

Now she ignites the mighty engine and eases her coach into the lunch-hour madness, inching through the jam to the corner of Ivy and Vine where a half dozen severely retarded men and their supervisor clamber onboard and race to find seats, save for Dapper Dan—a wizened old man forever young in his mind—who lingers in the doorway, gazing in goofy wide-eyed wonder at Cassandra.

"Will you you you marry me?" asks Dapper Dan, innocently grabbing his crotch and grinning at Cassandra. "I I I promise to be be be a good good good husband. You you you won't be be be sorry."

"Not today, Sugar," says Cassandra, her voice sharp with impatience. "Come on, Danny. Move along. More people getting on."

A gigantic woman hails the bus. She is so huge it takes her a full five minutes to hoist the fantastic bulk of her body up the three steps and into the sideways-facing seat across from Cassandra. Taking up space for three and blocking the aisle with her massive legs, the giantess pants and groans with the terrible effort of breathing.

And before *every* stop, the tortured woman grunts and gasps in agony, "Mine? This mine? My stop? Safeway?"

"No," says Cassandra for the thirteenth time. "Not yet. I'll tell you when. *Please* believe me."

To no avail.

"Mine? This mine? My stop? Is this my stop? Huh? Is it? Mine? Safeway. Is it?"

Finally, after an eternity of such desperate questions, Cassandra roars, "Safeway! Your stop. Safeway. Get. Off. Here. Now!"

"I heard you," says the woman, barely able to rise, barely able to squeeze her way down the stairs, barely able to make it out the door. "I hope I never see you again."

Cassandra waits for her heart to stop pounding before she pulls back into traffic—her daughter coming to mind—sweet Olivia, three years old, already a passionate singer like Mommy. *My baby girl will sing for the world, not just on a bus in the middle of nowhere.*

Only when she comes full circle and stops where she began does she speak to the young black man who rode the whole way with her.

"Sightseeing?" she asks, killing the engine. "I'm not supposed to take you around more than once unless you pay again."

"I was hoping you'd sing again," he says, nodding courteously. "It's just, see, I know a guy in the record business. He'd kill for your voice. You could make it. I know you could. And I'd be like your manager for say twenty-five percent."

"Twenty," she says, though she'll give him any per cent he wants if he can make even a little something come true. "*If* I believed you."

"I could set up a meeting," he says, thinking out loud. "I play a little piano. Comp a few chords. Maybe *Stormy Weather* or *You Send Me*. Something like that. Blow his mind."

"I've got my own songs," she says warily. "I play my own piano."

"Even better," he says, holding out his hand. "My name's Ray. Ray Lancaster. I'll set it up and call you."

"In a professional recording studio," she says, declining his touch. "For a *real* record producer. You can reach me through RT. I'm Cassandra. Afternoon J30. And if you try to con me, my brothers, my *big* brothers, will find you. Understand?"

Ray gets off at the next stop, dizzy with desire. *I do know a guy. Friend of a friend. Be worth a call. Sure. What have I got to lose?*

Cassandra smiles as she pulls up to her last stop of the day and sees Harlan Perkins, skinny white man, dearest human on the planet because every evening at six he takes her place and sends her home with a wink and a smile and flurry of kindly words.

She walks down quiet streets lined with old apartment buildings, the air sweet from recent rain, the sky dotted with puffy white clouds, the sycamores gleaming in the twilight, swallows combing the air for bugs, the beauty of everything calling forth a song from her—the song of going home to her baby girl—the people opening their windows as they always do when Cassandra comes by singing.

The Glider

(rising on the wind of a timely metaphor)

Lord—shaving every other day for the first time in years and staying away from coffee yet again—and Jenny—in another of her black-clothes-only phases, her hair cut boyishly short—are adventuring together, just the two of them, for the first time since they gave up their apartment and Jenny moved into a bedroom at Under the Table Books and Lord moved into a yurt behind Iris and Leona's duplex.

They are on their way to Santa Cruz to pick up a one-of-a-kind balsa wood glider—the commune's gift to Derek for his eleventh birthday.

The glider is the creation of a man named Bobby Screech Owl. Derek heard Bobby being interviewed about his gliders on the radio show *What Goes Up*, and ever since then Derek has been eager to see Bobby's gliders. Well, it so happens that Moustafa, the commune's baker and Frisbee guru, was in a Very Loud Band eons ago with Bobby, so he called his old buddy to arrange for Derek to see one of Bobby's gliders.

After Moustafa made his request, there was a long silence on Bobby's end of the line before Bobby replied in his monotone way, "Oh, yeah, him. He came to me in a dream last night. Cute kid. Smart. I said I was making a glider for him. Come and get it."

"So..." says Jenny, as Highway One unfurls before them, Lord at the wheel of Jenny's electric Rabbit, Jenny gazing at the shining Pacific, "rumor has it you're dating someone named Ruby."

Lord guffaws. "I have twice visited the noted Sensual Realignment and Ignition diva Ruby Heartsong, but I'd hardly call that dating."

"She's a *sex* worker?" asks Jenny, horrified. "You're *paying* for sex when we could be..."

"Not *sexual*," says Lord, bemused by Jenny's misconception. "*Sensual*. She...we...well...she tunes me, my body and my reflexes and my...expectations. It's all about opening more and more to our ecstatic potential without necessarily resorting to intercourse."

Jenny folds her arms and pouts. "I think *I* was pretty good at getting you off without resorting to intercourse."

"But I don't *get* off with Ruby," says Lord, giggling. "Not in the traditional sense. In fact, by *not* getting off in the traditional sense..."

"Are we talking about *coming?*" asks Jenny, begrudgingly admiring the sun-tipped breakers crashing onto San Gregorio Beach.

"By *not* coming," says Lord, warming to his subject, "we find ourselves growing more and more and *more* sensually activated..."

"You're hard the whole time, I take it," says Jenny, rolling her eyes. "Sounds like good old foreplay to me."

"Transcendent of good old foreplay by light years," says Lord, pulling over to allow several speedier autos to zip by. "But don't take my word for it. Go see for yourself."

He hands her a silky white business card.

ONE FABULOUS SESSION

Ruby Heartsong, LOTFLC

Sensual Realignment and Ignition

A dozen miles north of Santa Cruz, the Rabbit leaves the coast highway and ascends a potholed track through slender redwoods—a brisk breeze ruffling the feathery foliage of the tall young trees—the road ending in a cul-de-sac at the top of a hairpin turn where two old pickups share the shade of a sprawling oak.

"Moustafa said we take the southernmost trail," says Lord, gleeful to be so far from the madding crowd. "What a spectacular place to live. Listen how quiet. God, it's fabulous."

"Hold on a minute," says Jenny, hesitating to leave the cocoon of her car. "*Do* you have a new lover?"

"Have I made love to someone other than you since we stopped living together? Yes. Once. Will I tell you who this person is? No. Why not? I don't want to."

"So you slept with her," says Jenny, her eyes brimming with tears, "and you may or may not sleep with her again."

"Yes."

"Now you're supposed to ask me if *I've* slept with anyone since we separated. But you're not *going* to ask me because you don't really care, do you? You're happy to be done with me, aren't you? To finally be free of your neurotic, fear-driven..."

"Jenny," says Lord, exasperated. "We were both miserable, stuck, wanting a change. Both of us. We. Not just me. You, too. Remember?"

She gapes at him. "You think I'm being *rational?* I'm freaking out! I'm grieving and pissed off and crazy. I'm feeling ripped open and abandoned and discarded and forgotten. I still love you. I still want to be your one and only. Okay? I miss hiding from the big mean world together and telling each other lies about what geniuses we are and how we'll grow old together, me a latter-day Georgia O'Keefe, you a modern-day Rudyard Kipling. Blissful delusional ignorance. Okay? *And...*" She takes a deep breath. "...I'm *so* relieved we're not living together anymore. It was killing us, killing our friendship, killing our creativity, killing everything we cherish about each other."

"Well..." says Lord, brimming with boyish hope. "You *are* a genius. Of this I have no doubt."

The southernmost track runs downhill through blackberries and nettles and poison oak to a barely trickling creek. From here the trail climbs through spindly redwoods to a flat-topped ridge occupied by three rough-hewn buildings—the home, guesthouse, and workshop of Bobby Screech Owl, his wife Maria Lopez, and their sons Tigre and Leon.

Gordo, a shorthaired mutt, dun brown with pointy ears, barks sharply to announce the arrival of Jenny and Lord, and sensing their goodness, he approaches them with his tail wagging, hopeful they'll pet him, which, of course, they do.

Bobby Screech Owl, fifty-seven, a thickset *indio*—Ohlone—in blue coveralls, his graying black hair caught in a ponytail, comes out the door of his workshop and raises his hand in greeting. His face is deeply lined—grief having amplified the work of time.

"Welcome to the woods," he says with no apparent enthusiasm. "I was thinking about lunch."

"We brought you one of Moustafa's gigantic sandwiches," says Jenny, scratching Gordo's back. "He said it's your favorite."

"I love that guy," says Bobby, a sheepish grin blooming on his careworn face.

They feast on Moustafa's vittles—broiled salmon with capers and thinly sliced goat cheese and dill pickles and horseradish mustard and lettuce and tomatoes on sourdough rye—at a picnic table in a clearing ringed by twelve of the tallest redwoods Lord and Jenny have ever seen.

"They make a perfect circle," says Jenny, her distress evaporating in the marvelous silence. "And they're all about the same size."

Bobby nods, relishing the last bite of Moustafa's ambrosia. "They sprouted from the fringe of their mother when she was cut down a hundred and fifty years ago."

"You mean," says Lord, gazing at the massive trees, "from the same batch of seeds?"

Bobby shakes his head. "From the stump we're sitting in the middle of. From a tree forty feet in diameter and four hundred feet tall. Used to be thousands and thousands of these big people from here to Oregon. Now there's only a few left. These ones here are babies of the giant." He gazes up at the swaying tops of the mighty trees. "Wind is steadying down. Let's go fly."

"You'll stay the night," says Bobby, leading Jenny and Lord into the workshop—a spacious light-filled room, half given to Maria's pottery, half to Bobby's drums and gliders. "Maria's teaching at university today. Boys went with her to use the library. Book reports. Home school."

"Are there other kids around here?" asks Jenny, imagining living with Derek in these wooded hills.

"Swarming with kids," says Bobby, holding an exquisite open-backed elk-skin drum. "This right here is the best drum I ever made." He hands the drum—two feet in diameter—to Lord. "Just blow on the skin."

"Blow?" asks Lord, daintily handling the instrument.

Bobby nods. "On the skin."

Lord holds the drum not far from his lips, takes a deep breath, and blows on the center of the taut skin.

And the drum begins to hum.

"My God," says Lord, trembling with pleasure at the deep vibration. "Is this for sale?"

Bobby makes no reply, but takes from the wall a brown-skinned balsa wood glider not much larger than a pigeon—more wings than fuselage. "Now this here is for your boy. Best I ever made. I'll show you how she flies."

Tenderly, Lord hangs the elk-skin drum on the wall and follows Jenny and Bobby out the back door into the growing cool of the October afternoon, his heart still vibrating from the hum of the drum.

They follow a well-worn path through the forest to the edge of a westward-sloping meadow—a steady breeze caressing the golden grasses.

Bobby stands absolutely still, assessing the data flooding his senses. Now he raises the glider in his left hand and releases her with the slightest forward motion—and down the hill she glides—Bobby controlling her rudder with a teensy weensy joystick mounted on an itsy bitsy transmitter.

"I thought she'd be bigger," says Lord, delighted by the hawk-like grace of the glider as she banks into the breeze and speeds uphill.

"You're the boy's mother," says Bobby, moving close to Jenny. "You try this so you can show him how."

"Oh, gosh," says Jenny, gingerly taking the controls. "I'm not really his mother, but I'm happy to learn."

Bobby watches the plane heading straight for Lord's head. "Pull back slowly toward you," he whispers to Jenny, "and move that stick a little to your right. Everything subtle. She's sensitive."

"I *love* this," says Jenny—the plane responding to her command by swiftly spiraling up into the blue.

Lord wakes at dawn, deliciously warm, Jenny slumbering beside him. He dresses quietly and steps out of the guesthouse into the encompassing quiet—smoke rising from the workshop chimney.

Bobby Screech Owl is sitting on a stool beside the woodstove, lightly drumming on the best drum he ever made, singing softly in Ohlone, a song about the darkness giving way to the light.

"Spirit says don't give you this drum yet," says Bobby, gazing sadly at Lord. "Says you come another time and see what happens."

The Ben & Natasha Letters

Dear Ben,

Missing you. How goes it? Do you ever think of your little sister? When your mind isn't a blank? Is your mind ever a blank? Can you feel yourself changing?

you in my life every
day for twenty-four
years suddenly
you're gone.

I went to the movies with Z. Great double bill. The Color of Paradise and 32 Short Films about Glenn Gould. Z's turning out to be really nice. I'm not in love with him or anything, but it is kind of exciting to spend time with someone so different from anyone I've ever known. Once without thinking I called him Ben. We're working up a few songs together. He has a beautiful voice. I know it's vain to say so, but we sound fantastic together.

Everyone asks about you. We all miss your yum, Iris and Leona more than anyone. I can see how hard it must have been for you to have so many people depending on you for a certain kind of happiness. I hadn't realized what a burden that must have been. It makes me think you were carrying all kinds of emotional weight I didn't know about when we were growing up. So I want to thank you for that.

Sis

Dear Natasha,

We were encouraged not to write letters for at least two weeks. Otherwise, I would have written sooner. Not easy making my mind blank. So many attractive women here. I know I'm doing well in meditation when I don't have an erection, which is not often. I remember Lord Bellmaster suggesting I might be a bit young for celibacy.

Roshi Segundo gives most of the dharma talks. His is the only human voice I've heard for seventeen days, though my dreams are full of people talking. You, especially. Roshi Supremo, the main reason I came here, is fasting and not available to us. Roshi Segundo is extremely intellectual. I almost always have a headache by the time he finishes speaking. I think he's a bit of a fake. However, this may just be my ego getting in the way, and that's why I'm here, to see if I can replace the buzz of judgment with silent acceptance.

How are you? Say hi to everyone for me.

Ben

Dear Ben,

I think you're so brave to be doing what you're doing. I'm having a hard enough time adjusting to your being gone, and I have all my friends around. I hope you're not too lonely. What do you do when you're not meditating? I think I'd go crazy not being able to talk. I tried to go a whole day without talking last week just to see if I could, and the first few hours were easy, but then I started singing. Are you allowed to hum? How about whistling? I guess I'm kind of mad at you. I feel kind of robbed not having you around. I hope you don't stay there just because you said you would. If it's not working for you, come on home.

Moustafa made twenty extra loaves yesterday, and Z and I went down to the river and distributed them to the homeless guys under the oaks where you and I used to go fishing with Felix. Speaking of whom, he called from Barcelona a few nights ago. Says everything is fine. He has a slight Spanish accent now. It's hilarious. He asked how you were doing. I told him it was pretty weird having both of you gone and it would be nice to have one or both of you home. Soon. Hint, hint.

Sis

Dear Natasha,

Thanks so much for writing. Your letters are shafts of light in this deeply serious place. During morning meditation yesterday, the woman next to me began to laugh hysterically. I thought I might laugh, too, but instead I began to feel nauseated. Strange. She laughed for what seemed like an incredibly long time before she lapsed into silence.

For his dharma talk, Roshi Segundo spoke of laughter as oral farting. That made me laugh. I'd write more, but I'm grossly sleep-deprived. I wash dishes and scrub pots when I'm not meditating.

Say hi to everybody.

Benner

Dear Brother,

Come home. It sounds awful. It sounds like torture. If Roshi Supremo isn't there, and you don't like Roshi Segundo, why stay? I'm worried about you. Things are so interesting here. Jenny and Lord are going through all kinds of heaviosity, Z is learning to work the counter, and we're having lots of luscious November rain.

You've been gone long enough. Felix came home last week with a new woman friend. Hallelujah. She's part Algerian, part French. Very sweet. And can she cook? Oh, Ben, you'd love the way our kitchen smells these days. I'm not trying to tempt you or anything. I'm begging you! Come on home.

Sis

Dear Natasha,

I think maybe I've painted too negative a picture of this place. It is quite beautiful here. Sitting for hours and hours at a time, attempting to transcend the physical associations that define the individual's existence, I drift in and out of memories and fantasies. The present is evasive, even with "nothing else to do."

There are times when I fear I may simply be too young yet to sit in such close proximity to so many vibrant women. They are all beautiful. Everyone is. We are encouraged not to watch each other, but I'm a hopeless case. In the absence of conversation, looking at people is enormously entertaining.

There was a notice posted outside the dining hall about an all-male order up the coast with openings for monk trainees. That may be the solution to my rampant libido, but I'm still holding out hope Roshi Supremo will end his fast and become a presence in the life of this place.

Roshi Segundo, who always seems to be reading my mind, focused his last three talks on the pitfalls of lust, and I don't think it was my imagination he directed most of his comments at me. Despite this, along with the usual aching muscles, I have finally experienced several moments of no-thought, from which I emerge delightfully refreshed. Today, a three-hour sit seemed to pass in moments. Unfortunately (or naturally), I was then assailed with the worry that no-time might actually be the loss of time.

What if love has no intrinsic meaning? What if love is nothing more than a genetic trick to insure the continuation of the species?

Rhetorically,
Brudder Ben

Benj,
on a sandstone bluff above the storm-tossed sea,
angel gulls swooping in the raucous wind,
tears in my eyes from salt spray and missing you,
I hold out my hand and your spirit fills me.
Natasha

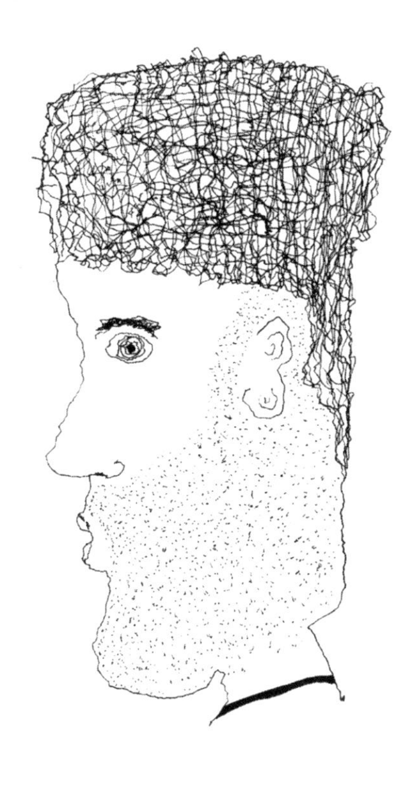

Today

(told to Lord Bellmaster by a guy named Jack who comes into the bookstore every Thursday looking for books on photography and horticulture)

I see a man breaking into a car parked in front of a house where they sell drugs. He's a small muscular man, brown-skinned, but I can't tell if he's Mexican or Arab. He's wearing a red T-shirt and black jeans and black tennis shoes. I'm across the street, waiting for a bus, broad daylight.

He sticks a screwdriver in at the top of the window and forces the glass down a few inches, reaches in, unlocks the door, climbs in, rummages around for a few seconds, climbs back out, closes the door and takes off like he's in the Olympics, which is lucky for him because the second he takes off, the door of the drug house flies open and two huge black guys come out, one with a baseball bat, the other with a gun. They run down the steps, jump in the car and screech away after the guy.

Everything is tied together for me these days. I'm waiting for the bus to take me to the bike shop so I can buy a bike because somebody stole mine, and everybody says it's people stealing to get money for drugs. Everybody says gangs are spreading, taking over more and more neighborhoods, and it's all because of drugs.

I read an article about Holland the other day. You can buy marijuana in the coffee houses there. They have almost no crime, and if you get old or sick, no matter who you are, they take care of you. Nobody carries a gun. They don't have the death penalty. And their economy is fine because they have lots of family farms and businesses and even prostitution is legal, so there's nothing for criminals to get control of.

I have a friend, a masseuse, and for fifty dollars she gives me a whole new lease on life, so I save up and try to go to her once a month. She says you have to realize our government is a criminal organization. Look what they spend money on. Everything is done to create fear and addiction so they can sell more and more guns and bombs and drugs and burglar alarms. That's her theory anyway.

The black guys come back and the one with the baseball bat sees me standing at the bus stop, watching everything. He hands the bat to the other guy and crosses the street, smiling to let me know he isn't gonna hurt me. I'm not afraid of him. Some guys I'm afraid of, others I'm not. I'm not quite six foot, but I'm in good shape. I'll be forty-two next year, but I ride my bicycle sixteen miles round-trip to work every day and I'm in the wrestling club at the Y. It's a good way to stay strong and limber.

So he comes up to me and stops maybe five feet away, which I appreciate. Some street guys come right up close and try to intimidate you. One time, ten years ago, in Seattle, a guy came up to me at a bus stop and got real close to me and acted all chummy, and if I hadn't been mugged before I would have been mugged that time because his friend was coming up behind me with a pipe. He was talking about basketball and what did I think the Supersonics should do about a center, and I caught just a flicker in his eyes and without even thinking I ran right over him like a fullback going over a kid and the sound of that pipe whooshing through the air barely missing my head will be with me for a million years if there's such a thing as reincarnation.

So this big guy, and he's big, I'd say six-five, shoulders wide enough you could get two Chinese acrobats on either side of his head, biceps bulging his fishnet tee-shirt tucked into his silky black slacks smiles at me and says in a buttery voice, "Hey, my man, you been here a while, you see that dude hit my car over there?"

"Yes, I did," I say, matter-of-factly, showing him I'm not afraid. I wonder if he can tell I'm in shape. Only thing showing are my legs down from my shorts, pretty good bicycle muscles, but my Giants sweatshirt covers my arms, so he could think I'm nothing.

"You identify him?" he asks, squinting at me, his smile going to a frown. "If you saw him again?"

"Maybe," I say, shrugging. "I saw his clothes and his hair, but I didn't get a good look at his face."

"But you saw his clothes, huh?" he asks, the smile coming back.

"Yeah," I say, figuring it doesn't matter who I tell what. They're all crazy. They'll all kill you if you get in their way.

"Mexican dude?" he asks, reaching into his pocket, bringing out a pack of cigarettes.

I wait for him to get one in his mouth, but he doesn't. He hands me the pack.

"No, thanks," I say. "I don't smoke."

"This ain't tobacco, my man. This is twenty fat joints, fine shit. Take it, man. Go on. Nothing to fear."

I go paranoid for a split second thinking maybe he's a narc, but narcs don't give you dope, they try to sell it to you, and I realize he's paying me for something he's gonna ask me to do, and he's paying me quite a bit street price, and I wonder how he knew about my special vice. I love a toke when somebody offers but I never buy the stuff because I'd be doomed if I ever made a good connection.

So I take the pack and put it in my pocket. He closes his eyes and nods, and I like him, I know I shouldn't, but I do, and now he says, "I need you for thirty seconds." He opens his eyes and drills me with them, drills me all the way to the center of my brain. "Not a second more."

I'm still not afraid. I'm a little dazed, a little out of my body, and I'm breathing hard, but it's excitement not fear, and I hear myself saying, "I won't go into the house, man. I'll give you back your stuff."

"No, no," he says, reaching out and putting a hand on my shoulder, and the span of his arm and the size and weight of his fingers is amazing. "I just need you to peek at something right out front. Right at the car, something I found, that's all."

I go paranoid again, wondering if they want to make me the fall guy, thinking they got ripped off and now he's planted dope on me and they'll get me over there and bash me and take me to their boss or whoever and say I'm the one took their stash.

"I better just give you your stuff back," I say, putting my hand in my pocket.

He grips my shoulder and steps closer. I prepare to move away. I'm a very good wrestler. I know just how I'll break his hold and take him down, though I'd rather not. I'd dearly love to keep these joints for the secret pleasure. I'd freeze them, yes, I would, smoke one a week and give one to my brother, one to my masseuse, one to my friend who always gives me one for Christmas. I don't want cocaine, it's evil shit, and I don't drink, it makes me sad and sick, but marijuana once in a while is like a pilgrimage for me. I go to a different world without going anywhere. I walk down the street and I understand so many things that stopped making sense so long ago. I see everybody trying to be happy, trying even though they don't know how because they believe life is about doing and going and getting, when it's really about being an honest person and being generous with your love.

I've been married three times. My first wife ran off with a man who promised her a new car and a house. I saw her five years later in the grocery store with two kids. She was swollen and sad and strung out on something and I finally forgave myself for not being able to keep her.

My second wife was a blind woman. I met her because she lived next door to me. I used to help her with her groceries and sometimes she'd come over to talk. I liked her, though I wasn't particularly attracted to her, but we both got so lonely one winter we became lovers and I felt so guilty about sleeping with her I married her. The minute I did, she turned jealous. She was sure I was cheating on her, when I never would. But there was nothing I could say to convince her I was loyal. She went absolutely crazy, and I had to leave. It was leave or go insane with her.

Then a few years after that, I really wanted to have kids. I was thirty-five and all I could think about was having babies and pouring my love into them, and I fell for this woman who worked at the Y. She was *so* beautiful and she and I used to flirt, and I asked her out and we talked about everything and we got so excited about wanting kids we forgot to be in love first and she got pregnant and moved in and we got married and after six months she realized who she was married to and said I was too simple and too content with too little and I was never going to make enough to live somewhere decent and goodbye.

Which is not the *reason* I crossed the street with the guy, but I *do* live alone now, except for my cats, and I don't even think about getting married again. I own the house I live in, paid for. I work my forty hours a week at the nursery. I'm in charge of greenhouse maintenance. I meet women sometimes for sex and because I like going out with them, but I have a big wall around my heart or whatever you want to call it, and maybe someday I'll open up again, but this last time with my baby in her, watching her go, hearing her tell me I was never going to be good enough when I've spent my whole life trying to prove that I *am* good enough, that my father and mother and teachers were wrong, that I could be happy and have a good life, and hearing her say all that negative shit to me and watching her take my child away, it was like being killed, and I was dead for a long time, and I've only recently wanted deeper pleasure again, and this is a pocketful of pleasure and I don't want to give it up, and he *swears* I won't have to go anywhere but over to his car, and it's broad daylight on a busy street, cars going by, and I can see my bus coming about a mile away.

So we stop at the back of the car, a burgundy Cadillac, very nice, shiny clean. He sticks a key in the lock, lifts the lid of the trunk, and here's the guy, the guy who broke into the car. He's curled up on the floor, his ankles and wrists taped together, tape over his mouth, his eyes flashing terror and the lid closes.

"That the guy?" asks the man, frowning at me, watching my face for anything that could be an answer.

But I don't give my face or my body a chance to speak for me because I know this guy's senses are so sharp I can blink and he'll sense the truth. So I say loud and angry like my father lying to my mother about everything, lying to me and my sister and his boss on the phone, lying without hesitation so it seems like the truth, because we stupidly think truth never falters but lies do, "No way, man. The guy was much older and shorter. This isn't him."

My bus is a block away. I meet the man's eyes the way my wrestling coach in high school told me to meet the eyes of my opponents. Over and over again, he'd say, "Remember, Jack, fear conquers from the inside out. It climbs in through your eyes. That's why you have to be invulnerable there. You have to meet their look with all your courage because the match is over if you let them penetrate your eyes. You hold them there or you don't stand a chance."

"You sure?" says the man, his frown deepening. "You sure this ain't the guy?"

"If it is," I say, "he lost fifteen years between here and wherever you found him."

"But he was runnin', man, runnin' scared," says the man, and I hear the doubt in his voice.

"I gotta go," I say. "I been waitin' for that bus for an hour."

Now I wave to the bus driver and dart across the street. I feel strong and quick and I remember the last football game of my senior year, three years on the bench, never once got to play until the last game when all the other backs got hurt, and the coach, sadist idiot, scowled at me and said, "Okay, Jones, get in there, try not to fumble." I carried seven times. And the first five times they gave it to me I got a yard or nothing. And the sixth time, I started to understand the puzzle, and I broke through for eight yards. And then I heard this roaring, and in the huddle they said I would get it and it was our only hope and I *knew,* I knew I would see the way, and they pitched it back to me, and the pieces moved, the colors shifted into patterns and I saw the path twisting through the maze and there was no more fear or doubt in me and I burst through the first wall of them and the second wall of them and ran seventy-three yards for a touchdown and they said it was luck but it was not luck, it was knowledge.

So I get on the bus and sit by the window where I can see the man standing by the trunk of his car. He's hunched over in doubt. I'm fearless now, high up in my shiny bus. I slide open the window and shout, "He's not the one. It was somebody else. I'm sure, man. Different clothes."

We pull away. The cool air rushes in. I breathe deeply and feel the cigarette pack in my pocket and I wonder if there's anything good in there, or if he was just conning me.

Torture

(transformation)

Mrs. Armitage invites Jenny, a fetching Celtic thirty-three, and Natasha, a shapely chocolate twenty-four, to sup with her on Halloween. After a scrumptious repast of stuffed potatoes a la Florentine, chased with an ambrosial pinot noir—a ten-dollar steal at the Wine Club Depot Warehouse—Mrs. Armitage removes her enormous gray bandana and releases a stunning tumble of raven black hair.

"Jesus," says Jenny, gaping at the transformation. "You're gorgeous. And you're young. What's going on here?"

"Whoa," says Natasha, flaring her nostrils at the former old lady. "Who are you?"

"I want you to cut off my hair and shave my head," says Mrs. Armitage, her vowels showing signs of an emerging East Indian British accent. "I am going through a catacleesmic change. I have been thees old woman for twenty years, and now my seervitude is over. I'm almost someone else. Indira. I have veesions of Kali making love with Buddha. I see women running naked across the fields, men watching from the forest, deeply respectful. The change is coming, my daughters. Scrape my scalp and open me to whatever comes next."

"I'd kill for your hair," says Jenny, trembling at the thought of what they're about to do. "Virtually."

"Ditto," says Natasha, loving the silky sheen of Indira's tumble. "Mine's got just enough kink to make me crazy. You have what every woman desperately wants. Great face, great body, *and* great hair. Why did you hide it for so long? As if I didn't know."

"I feared myself," says Indira, bowing to them. "That's why I need your help. I want you to tie me down. Make the knots tight. She'll fight like a demon, old Mrs. Armitage, but don't let her up until the shaving is complete. Swear to me. No matter what she says, no matter how terribly she threatens or reviles you, do *not* release me until the shaving is done. Will you swear to that?"

Jenny and Natasha look at each other to gain courage, and say in unison, "No matter what she says, no matter how terribly she threatens or reviles us, we will not release you until the shaving is done."

"Cross your hearts and hope to die?"

They cross their hearts.

True to her word, once the young women have Mrs. Indarmitage tied down to the bed, the old gal returns in the form of a snarling beast.

"Don't you dare touch me," she growls. "I take back everything I said. Untie me."

"Should we?" asks Jenny, frightened by the beastly verbosity. "She says she's changed her mind."

"Forget it," says Natasha, scowling at Mrs. Armdiratage. "You made us swear on our lives for a reason. We have to honor our vows."

"Touch me, I call the police," says Mrs. Armdira—a terrifying combination of her old and new selves. "Hurt me and you'll rot in jail."

"Not gonna hurt you," says Natasha, taking hold of the long black mane. "Unless you struggle so much we have a little accident. These scissors are very very sharp. We wouldn't want you to jerk suddenly. Who knows what might happen."

"Torture!" she screams. "You're torturing me!"

Natasha cuts off a big sheaf of the strong black hair and waves it in Indarma's face—the poor woman shrieking at the sight of the black coil and collapsing into unconsciousness.

"Quick," says Natasha, prompting Jenny. "Help me cut the rest before she comes to."

"Is this legal?" asks Jenny, her hands trembling.

"Of course it is," says Natasha, cutting and cutting and cutting. "We have a legally binding verbal contract."

"If you say so," murmurs Jenny, dazed and confused and grossly over-identified with the woman losing her hair. "I'll look for a razor."

Indira awakens in a room illuminated by myriad candles. She is lying on her back on her bed, a silky red sheet covering her body. She sits up slowly, her head feeling barely attached to her neck.

Jenny and Natasha are sitting at the foot of the bed, each wearing a crown of braided black hair.

Indira touches her hairless dome and feels a pulsing rhythm. "You did it. *She's* gone. The old crone is gone. Thank God."

"You're not mad at us?" asks Jenny, ineffably sad. "It's what you really wanted?"

"Yes, oh, yes," cries Indira, her East Indian British accent coming and going. "Eet ees wonderful. Thank you my darlings."

"I'll miss the Cat Lady," says Natasha, smiling bravely through her tears. "And I guess so will the cats."

"Indira will not forsake the kitties," she says, rising gracefully. "Now I must see."

They carry candles into the bathroom and behold themselves in the mirror, Indira flanked by two young goddesses. And though Indira is old enough to be Natasha's mother and older than Jenny by fourteen years, she appears younger than either of them—a wild-eyed newborn.

"I like myself with black hair," says Jenny, touching her thick black wreath. "I look so much more, I don't know...earthy."

"We're stunning," says Natasha, enthralled by their reflections. "The sum total is stupendous. We should start a band."

Indira gazes at her reflection for several minutes until her disbelief gives way to clarity. "There I am," she says, her face ablaze with joy. "There I am, at last."

Ben In the Garden

(organic abdication)

Abandoned by his mother when he was six years old and raised by the man most likely his biological father, Benjamin is today a spry twenty-seven. He squats to sniff an early narcissus, a yellow puff on the edge of the monastery garden—a delicious acreage of flowers and leafy greens.

"He met his mother only once after childhood," he says, narrating the story of his life, his vow of silence broken, though he has yet to speak to anyone other than himself. "He was twenty-six at the time. His mother had been around the world several times, living in Paris and London and Lagos and Los Angeles. She had hundreds of lovers. He hated her in an abstract way. She represented eternal rejection. He was furious with her for leaving him, and this fury fueled his life and kept him running a few steps ahead of depression. And even though his diner, Chez Ben, had attained global status as a culinary hotbed—his morning spices legendary—and his run of highly original recipes were forever being compared by food critics to the musical output of Mozart, at his core he felt like a useless pathetic worm—his mother's discarding him proof of his essential worthlessness."

He plucks a leaf of kale and chews it slowly—his taste buds singing the opening lines of a sexy little recipe.

"So is that why Ben is in a monastery? Is that why he traded a life of love and fame and extraordinary food for twelve months of silence and run-of-the-mill vegetarian cuisine? No. He's here because after reading Roshi Supremo's *Nine Ideas That May Not Lead Anywhere (So?)*, he was drawn to Roshi Supremo as if by a powerful magnet. And so began eighty-eight days of silent sitting, interrupted every twelve hours by an ill-conceived vegan meal, the rice routinely overcooked, the chard sadly mangled. The sounds of chopsticks clacking and people wolfing their food haunt Benjamin for hours after each meal, his meditations clogged with the bitter remembrance of foodstuffs too bland for words."

He scans the verdant garden. The heads of cauliflower are as big as basketballs, as white as swans. The beet greens are as high as a heffalump's eye and seem to be growing clear up to the sky.

"With goods like these Ben could make people dance for joy. Eating his food, their prayers would be as pure as the rain in Tibet. He said immodestly yet factually."

Two hundred and seventy-seven more days of silence lie ahead.

Benjamin espies the chief gardener—a pleasingly Rubenesque woman of fifty-nine healthy years, her body redolent and flexible from decades of yoga, her strong arms bare. She is squatting midst the cabbage, pulling weeds. Ben saunters into the field of vegetables, loving the feel of the soil squishing between his toes. He kneels to pull weeds near the chief, stealing glances at her, his cock thickening, the hood of his monk's habit weighing heavily on his forehead. *Two hundred and seventy-seven more days? Of total celibate silence?*

"Excuse me," he whispers to her. "I've been here eighty-eight days without saying a word. I don't even talk in my dreams anymore. But see, here's what I need you to understand. I was a chef before I came here. A rather good one, he says immodestly. I'm going insane. Personally, I find Roshi Segundo a tiresome bore, my resolve is failing, and the only thing keeping me here is the overpowering belief or feeling or something that I'm destined to interact in a more tangible way with Roshi Supremo himself. Wherever the hell he's gotten to. So could you somehow use your influence to make it okay for me to work in the garden? Please? If I have to sit through another group meditation, I swear I'll jump up and perform a really horrible monologue I call *Monks On A Hot Tin Wok*."

The buxom chief laughs pleasantly and beckons Ben to follow her. They traverse the garden west to east, leap over a babbling brook, and climb a red rock hill dotted with baby pines and bonsai oaks. At the apex, a view of the distant sea fills Ben with irrational hope. Now they descend the backside of the hill to a log cabin ringed by dainty ferns and cradled in a semicircle of fruit trees.

"Nice place," says Ben, admiring the fit of the house to the land. "Looks like it grew here."

"Make me something," she says, opening her door. "Anything."

He gawks at her impressive array of copper pots and gleaming knives. "Nice tools," he says, eyes wide. "Garlic? Onions? Zucchini? Basil? Cauliflower? Kale? Mushrooms? Cumin? Ginger?"

"Produce in the sink," she says, pointing to the blue-tiled basin bursting with the finest from the fields. "Herbs and spices alphabetical to the left of the stove. Fungi in the black box under the counter."

"Serious kitchen," he says, squinting reverently at her. "Have we met? Did you take a workshop from me? Or did I take one from *you?*"

"Cook for me, Sugar. Makes no never mind who learned what from whom. I just want to watch you sauté."

"But not in this robe," says Ben, removing his heavy cloak and standing naked before her, his young cock proud and erect. "Kitchens like this totally turn me on. Six-burner stove. Excellent knives. The finest ingredients. And let's not forget the appreciative audience. There could be no better scenario. Particularly for one as gifted and deprived as I. He said immodestly yet factually."

"I'll say," she says, quickly disrobing. "I haven't seen a priapus of your effervescence since…who knows when."

"He is available and free of illness," says Ben, gazing delightedly at his happy dong. "I just love him."

"My name is Luna," she says, pressing close. "My bedroom is also a place you might appreciate."

"Boy," he says, taking her in his arms. "I had this monastery all wrong. Everyone pretends to be celibate."

"Not pretending," she says, kissing him eagerly. "Being."

Transcendent sex eventually finds them back in the kitchen. Ravenous. Luna stokes her woodstove to warm the house against the cold sea air. Ben dices and chops and mixes and matches with the purest intentions, his body aglow with the fire of love, his deftly blended ingredients sweating their juices and changing the flavor of life.

Luna and Ben sit by the roaring fire gorging on food so good each morsel imparts an extra year of life. Luna sets her bowl down, her empty bowl, and gratefully kisses the hands of the young genius. "I'm gonna ask Roshi Supremo to appoint you my official assistant."

"Wait," says Ben, wincing at the idea of anything official. "Can't this just be between you and me for the next, oh, two hundred and seventy-seven days?"

"Doesn't work like that here," she says, tightening her belt. "The hierarchy must be respected, however illusory. Order exists for a reason. Until it doesn't."

"And what reason is that?"

"To inspire moments of calm in the karmic chaos."

"Potatoes," says Ben—visions of organic hash browns dancing in his beleaguered head. "I *must* do something with potatoes."

"Put on a pair of my jeans and one of my sweatshirts," she suggests, opening her door to a chilly draft. "Don't want you catching cold. I'm gonna go speak to Roshi Supremo. He's gotta taste your food."

"But mostly I'll work in the garden," shouts Ben, calling after her. "Yes? Slow toil upon the good earth. Por favor?"

Luna runs swiftly up the steep trail past the prayer wheels and the gray stone statue of Buddha, over the high-arching bridge and under the waterfall to the bottom of the twenty-seven-rung ladder leading to the lofty platform overlooking the Pacific where Roshi Supremo has languished for three months now, meditating and watching the gulls and buzzards keep company with ravens.

"Roshi Supremo," she calls, her voice strong and sure in the silence. "I have found a reason for you to come down. I have found a vital motive for your return."

Roshi Supremo crawls to the edge of the platform and peers down at his beloved Luna. He is weak from fasting to protest what he calls the conspiracy of mediocrity among his fellow humans.

"A motive?" he murmurs, his life force low. "Tell me."

"There is a young god in my house cooking potatoes," she says reverently. "He makes zucchini taste like wild salmon. Come see what he does with spuds."

Money

(initiation to the dance)

Derek, boy wonder, climbs atop the stool behind the counter at Under the Table Books, hoping to remember most of what he's learned from Lord Bellmaster and the other veterans of anarchist exchange—this being his first time tending the counter *alone.*

"But I'm not scared," he says to the curious raven peering down from the bamboo cage suspended over the acreage of books. "Not very."

The bell above the door jingles and a fat man stumbles in. "Money," he rumbles. "Books on money. Where would I look?"

Derek thinks for a moment. "You want fiction or nonfiction?"

"Reality!" shouts the man, red in the face and breathing hard. "Facts about how to get it."

"That would be in the *Facts About How To Get Money* section," says Derek, waving at the entire store. "Over there."

"Terrific," says the man, winking and blinking. "Peachy."

Next to arrive is Mrs. Armitage, her head shaven, a big red dot painted in the center of her forehead, her lovely body visible through the soft cotton of her yellow sari. "I bring cooried cheeken for my keetees," she says, sounding positively Hindi. "You like a leetle bite, Dereek?"

"Mrs. Armitage?" he gasps, mightily confused by her transformation. "Is that you? Where's your bonnet? Your baggy dress? How come you're talking so funny? What happened to your hair?"

"I'm someone else now," she says simply. "Is Lord here today?"

"But you have her *memory*," says Derek, squinting at her. "How else would you know Lord? He's never met you like this. Has he?"

She frowns. "Please don't confuse me, Dereek. I am very much enjoying thees new incarnation. Parteecularly the teekle on my tongue when I talk like thees."

"What I mean is," says Derek, excited by the exotic new Cat Lady, "you're still her but you're also somebody else."

"Mrs. Armitage is *gone*," she says firmly. "Dead and gone. I am Indira and I very much weesh to see Lord."

The cats crowd around their favorite human, her essential scent unchanged, her feelings for felines intact, or perhaps stronger than ever, given the Hindu predilection for worshipping animals.

"Lord should be back any day now," says Derek, transfixed by Indira's baldness. "He's gone scavenging with Jenny. To Santa Cruz and Arcata and then up to Gant's Good Used Everything in Medford. I almost got to go, but I had to stick around for a meeting with my social worker to discuss various educational options and foster-parent parameters."

Indira serves out seven little bowls of curried chicken, the younger cats yowling at the turmeric, the older ones demanding water, pronto.

The fat man huffs and puffs back to the counter with a big fat manuscript entitled

You Get Too Big They Squelch You

Facts About the How Why What and Who of
Getting Money Faster and Faster and Faster

"How much for this?" he asks, bringing forth a bulging wad of hundred-dollar bills. "It's handwritten by a man claiming to have been so rich the powers that be took everything and stranded him on the streets."

"That's Mr. Laskin," says Derek, smiling fondly at the mention of his mentor. "He comes in every day at two for his sandwich. He's very handsome and he has long white hair. If you wait a little while you could probably talk to him. That is, *if* he's in a receptive mood."

"Is it true?" asks the fat man. "He had billions?"

"*Trillions*," says Derek, setting the record straight. "You'll find his book rife with sure-fire moneymaking tips. Took him years and years to write and it's the only *complete* copy in the world, so who knows how much it's worth? Hundreds and hundreds, at least, I would think. Probably."

"I can *meet* him?" asks the fat man, frowning gigantically. "Would two thousand dollars be enough?"

"We were hoping for substantially more than that," says Derek, his heart pounding. "Since it is the only *complete* copy in the entire universe. How about twenty-five hundred?"

"Fine," says the man, peeling off the appropriate currency. "Small price to pay for the work of a lifetime."

"Terrific," says Derek, grabbing the money. "Here he is now."

Mr. Laskin strides purposefully into the store, his shirt oddly buttoned, his zipper down. "Sandwich time," he sings. "Bologna, I hope."

"Mr. Laskin," says Derek, carefully counting the bills, "I'd like you to meet..."

"Mr. Techthin," says Mr. Techthin, shaking Mr. Laskin's hand. "You certainly *look* like a billionaire. I just bought your book and I'd be honored if you'd sign it."

Mr. Laskin grabs the one and only *complete* copy of *You Get Too Big They Squelch You* and scrawls across the title page.

> To whoever you are fly under the radar. I was the richest man on earth and now look at me.
> *Laskin*

"Thank you *so* much," says Mr. Techthin, bowing to Mr. Laskin. "I'll do my best to stay invisible."

"Go over a trillion you're doomed," says Mr. Laskin, glancing at Derek. "Bologna?"

"Coory today," says Indira, squatting beside her snarfling kitty cats. "Cheeken."

"Lucky cats," says Mr. Laskin, rubbing his hands. "But I was referring to my much anticipated sandwich. Bologna?"

"Tuna and green olives," says Derek, raising a hand in farewell to Mr. Techthin. "And there's pie if you want it."

"You don't *ever* want to have too much money," says Mr. Laskin, nodding sagely. "Once you've suckled on lobster Henri Duvernois and munched Betty Rothschild's grapes fresh from her vines in Provence and slept in silk sheets in your own palace on the highest hill of your very own Caribbean paradise, it's no easy thing begging sandwiches."

"You are in no way begging," says Derek, handing Mr. Laskin a nice fat sandwich. "Not only do you keep our larder brimming with fine well-aged cheeses, but you just made a small fortune for the bookstore through the sale of your magnificent tome. And, to quote from your book, which I happen to have a photocopy of minus *The End*, 'Every large fortune, whether fiscal or mystical, begins with a virtually imperceptible wrinkle in the fabric of the economic continuum.'"

"You will be repaid," says Mr. Laskin, wagging a finger at Derek. "Mark my words. There's no such thing as a free lunch."

Indira adjusts her sari, touches the red dot in the center of her forehead, and makes a protective gesture in Derek's direction. "May your day be a blessed one."

"So far so good," says Derek, tapping the money from Mr. Techthin. "Need any dough?"

"You are most kind to ask," says Indira, feeling her persona wobbling, her accent slipping. "But no. I'm fine."

"You're good as either person," says Derek, arranging the bills in order of crispness. "I like you either way however you like to be."

"Is that real money?" asks Mr. Laskin, his mouth full of tuna. "Haven't seen so many hundreds since that awful night in Rio when they knocked me out and switched my identity with that rotten old cipher."

"You want it?" Derek whispers. "It was *your* book he bought."

"Nah, they'll just take it away from me." A smile creases his rugged face. "You mentioned, did you not, something about pie?"

"Rutabaga and pumpkin. I prefer the pumpkin for it's piquancy, but the Spinelli sisters were euphoric about the rutabaga. And they're more your age. If that's at all relevant. Is it?"

"I like the rapid expansion of your vocabulary," says Mr. Laskin, arching an eyebrow. "A good vocabulary is the path to big fun. What would be my chances of getting a piece of *each* kind of pie? So that I might compare them and better elucidate the relevance or irrelevance of age and taste in their regard?"

"Excellent," says Derek, hopping off his stool. "Stay right there. I'll be right back."

"And do tell Moustafa," says Mr. Laskin, calling after him, "I've got the strongest hankering for bologna. Maybe tomorrow?"

Dinner Music

(poem begets poem begets poem)

Z, dashingly professorial in his three-piece twill, watches the wily child Derek leaf through a slender volume of poems—*Dinner Music* by Quinton Duval—while on the customer side of the counter the sad woman wishing to sell the poems bites her tongue and explains, "He was my favorite poet for eons. He signed it to me. See? On the first page."

"Cash or trade?" asks Derek, smiling deferentially. "Trade or cash? Money, tasty comestibles, advice, a song, a dance. You name it."

"What's the difference?" asks the sad woman, brushing the harsh red curls from her eyes. "What could I get in trade?"

"Anything we have," says Derek, gesturing at the contents of the store. "Or a few dollars."

The woman gawks at the sea of books. "Someone told me you have food here, too."

"Three refrigerators full," says Derek, proudly. "Help yourself. Pumpkin pie, potatoes, carrots. And if I'm not mistaken we still have a piece or three of Moustafa's fabulous lasagna."

"Alcohol?" she asks hopefully. "Wine?"

"Not a drop," says Derek, ringing open the cash register. "But here's five bucks."

She grabs the money and hurries out the door.

Derek turns officiously to Z. "Questions?"

"Why five bucks? Why not two or one or three?"

"She was thirsty," says Derek, dialing a gigantic old-fashioned black telephone. "You can't really get anything good for two dollars these days. As Lord says, 'The best way to ride the counter is with a loose rein and an open heart.' I'm pretty sure I can get at least seven for these poems. Maybe more. Watch."

Z opens the volume to a poem called *The Story of Spring.*

> This is the time when everyone looks for love...
>
> at work, in the park on the way home, at the grocery.
>
> There is a deeper breathing and incredible breasts
>
> rise and fall over typewriters and shopping lists.
>
> The men march around with newspapers
>
> over their waists. It's just the season.

"Hello?" says Derek, clearing his throat. "Mr. Duval? Hi. This is Derek at Under the Table Books. I've got a copy of *Dinner Music* here. You signed it six years ago. *To Brigitte with lust. Thanks for the stupendous afternoon. Giggles. Quinton.* Incriminating? That's a hard call, Mr. Duval. Six years is a long time ago. I'm sure your wife would..." He listens. "I could certainly let you have it for..."

"I want it," says Z, dropping a five-dollar bill on the counter and staring raptly at *The Story of Spring.* "This is *fantastic.*"

"Um," says Derek, chortling, "there's somebody here who wants it for five dollars." He listens. "You'll pay ten?"

"Fifteen," says Z, turning to the title poem.

Dinner Music

The things in this dish have each been touched
by your fingers. The dough has marks in it
where you shaped it out round and white
and rising slowly. I remember all this
as I begin to eat. It is exciting
in the light given off by the oil lamp
on the table. I smell the kerosene,
your perfume, and the scent of the food you made.
I am touched by the wonder of it all. I mean
your hands are in my mouth even as I eat
what you have made, like other things you make.
After dinner your lips open quietly to the dark
passage down inside you. What is all this,
this odd food we give away? We eat each other's
love and feel amazed and full.

"Twenty?" says Derek, repeating Quinton's last bid. "You'll pay twenty, Mr. Duval? Well..."

"Twenty-five," says Z, desperate to possess the bountiful words. "Thirty!"

"Fifty?" says Derek, smiling enormously into the phone. "Terrific, Mr. Duval. We'll hold it for you."

"Damn," says Z, reluctantly relinquishing the book. "I dig this."

"We've got two more copies in the *Greatest Not Yet Famous Enough Poets* section," says Derek, winking at Z. "Take your pick."

"You are one shrewd little mouse," says Z, mussing his mentor's hair. "No wonder this place survives."

"Here," says Derek, hopping off the command stool. "You take it for a while. See what happens."

"But you'll hang out?" asks Z, nodding anxiously. "In case I run into something beyond me?"

"I'll be right here," says Derek, patting Z on the back. "Live one at twelve o'clock."

The bell clangs raucously as Miss Kelso, the big band chanteuse and poodle groomer charges into the store, races to the *British Romantics (female authors)* section, grabs ten books with the word *lust* in their titles, dashes to the counter, thrusts a hundred-dollar bill at Z, and hurries out, panting.

Z snaps the bill to test its authenticity. "Nice work. But she could have taken those books for nothing. Right? That's the part I don't get. How do they know what to leave?"

"Do you need that money?" asks Derek, leafing through a stack of old *Alphabet Threat* magazines. "If you do, you can keep it."

"Could use fifty," says Z, thinking of his mother and how good she'd feel if he planted some legal green on her. "Can I make change?"

"Doubt there's fifty in the till."

"So what do I do?"

"Lord says try not to think about what we need until we're done with our stint. That leaves us free to ride the shifting fortunes."

"In other words?"

"There's no telling what might happen next."

At which moment, Indira—her shaved head painted pale blue, her gorgeous body cloaked in a red silk chemise—dances through the door carrying a cardboard box—plaintive mewing emanating from within.

"I found these babies," she says, her voice choked with tears. "May I trade them for a potted plant? My spider needs a mate."

"As a matter-of-fact," says Derek, smiling adoringly at the Cat Lady, "Leona scored seven perky aloe vera plants this morning in exchange for a falling apart but complete and eminently reparable copy of Maurice Maeterlinck's *The Life of the Bee*. Do you know if these kittens have had their shots yet?"

"I seriously doubt it," she says, whirling around in a burst of grace, filling the air with the scent of cloves and curry. "But they are most devastatingly cute."

"Take this hundred," says Z, deeply entranced. "Get their shots and keep the change."

"How generous of you," she coos, curtsying alluringly. "And then I will bring them back."

"Sure," says Z, dizzy with desire. "Why not?"

"Fascinating," says Derek, watching Indira sashay out the door. "I'm beginning to understand what Lord means when he says you have to watch out for the hypnotic effect of certain individuals. Even *I* find Indira hypnotic, and I'm not quite eleven."

"Help me," says Z—the room spinning. "Every time that woman comes in here, my brain goes on the blink. She defies all previously documented schemata, yet she appeals to everybody. Wonder why she stays in this old backwater when she could be the queen of Hollywood, the toast of Broadway, the cat's..."

"Meow?" guesses Derek, frowning quizzically at Z. "Pajamas? I'm pretty sure she and Lord have something going on with each other, though they mostly pretend they don't, but they do."

"How do you know?" asks Z, arching an inquisitive eyebrow. "Little birdy tell you?"

"No, but sometimes early in the morning when we're shaping the loaves, Lord comes in to talk to Moustafa, and before he's had his coffee Lord tends to be fairly oblivious to preternaturally quiet boys."

"How long have you lived here?"

"Seven months," says Derek, lowering his voice to a whisper. "I was homeless before that."

Z gently touches Derek's shoulder. "Little king of survival."

The bell jingles. Lord and Moustafa enter with a *Gonzo Records* bag bulging with ancient photographs of men and women and children at the beach in boxy black bathing suits.

"Any idea of the worth of these?" asks Moustafa—a lordly brown man—bowing deferentially to Z. "From *way* before television."

"People sure haven't changed much," says Z, inspecting the pictures. "Hate to say it, my brother, but I find no black folk in here."

"We could ask Jenny to touch them up," says Lord—a charming white guy in need of shave—perusing a picture of a man holding his nose and jumping off a pier. "She's a master at transforming images. She could *fill* these shores with black people."

"Where did you get them?" asks Derek, gawking at a photo of a woman riding into the surf on a man's shoulders.

"We were walking by the abandoned house on J Street," says Lord, his voice so calm it would soothe lions, "and we heard someone cry out."

"A woman," says Moustafa, reverently. "So we rushed inside, but the place was empty."

"Just this bag of old photos," says Lord, shaking his head. "The floor was thick with dust. No footprints other than ours."

"Oh, yes," says Moustafa, bowing his head, "and there was a mother cat so recently dead she was still warm, no sign of her kittens."

"*We* know where they are," says Derek, holding up a picture of four naked boys, their faces smeared with ice cream. "We just sent them off with Indira to get their shots."

Moustafa turns to Lord. "You called it, my friend. You said five-to-one the kits would end up here."

"I watched an old cat die once," says Z, gazing at Moustafa. "I'll never forget the cry she made at the very end. Sounded just like a person. Exactly like a person."

Derek

(speaking for himself)

Sometimes when Carl goes to Mexico to watch winter league baseball and Jenny is staying over somewhere else, and we don't have any guests staying at Under the Table Books, which isn't very often, I get kind of scared being here alone, so Moustafa lets me sleep in his bus with him. And some nights when it's not too cold or wet, I sleep in the cave we dug next to the bookstore garden. Sometimes Pinky sleeps in the cave, too. We've got it fixed up pretty nicely with a mattress and a table and two chairs and a kerosene lamp for reading or playing cards.

The scariest part about being homeless was not having a safe place to sleep. Now that I live in the bookstore building, I feel safe most of the time. I love hanging out with Mr. Laskin when he's not in a bad mood. At one time he was the richest man on earth and now he has hardly anything, but even so he seems pretty happy as long as he has plenty to eat.

Some nights I have a fire at the mouth of our cave and Mr. Laskin comes and we talk until I fall asleep. He says he doesn't sleep much anymore, and usually he isn't there in the morning but sometimes he is and we have breakfast together, but he says it's strange being at the bookstore in the morning because he likes to keep things in a certain order and he prefers the bookstore to be where he gets his afternoon sandwich. But lately he's spending more time here, which is fine with me. He's my idol along with Lord and Moustafa and Indira, who used to be Mrs. Armitage, and Jenny and Natasha, who are the best friends I could ever have, but Mr. Laskin is *way* the most important person to me.

I'll never forget the first time I saw him. I ran away from my mother because there was never enough food and I was really hungry. For the first few months I hung out with some tough kids but they beat me up sometimes and I couldn't trust them not to rip me off. Then I lived alone for five months hiding under houses mostly and scrounging for food in garbage cans at night until one day I saw Mr. Laskin talking to a policeman in Plaza Park. Something about the way he was standing so proudly made me want to hear what he was saying, so I got close and the first thing I heard him say was, "Until you see yourself as a servant of humanity, you'll never be a good cop." And I just knew if I could get to know him I wouldn't be afraid anymore.

So I followed him after that, and every day at two he came to the bookstore and they gave him a sandwich, and almost every night he went down to the river and slept under a big oak tree with his friend Leopold, and I'd sleep in the grass nearby.

One day Mr. Laskin met a lady in front of a coffeehouse and

he took off his hat and bowed to her and they started talking and laughing and he went home with her instead of to the river, which is when I got desperate and came to the bookstore and Lord let me stay here. The lady Mr. Laskin went home with turned out to be Iris Spinelli, who is now practically my grandmother, but at the time I didn't know who she was.

The thing is, now that I'm settled and Jenny teaches me art and Natasha teaches me cooking and dancing and Moustafa teaches me numbers and history and baking and Frisbee, and I've learned how to work the bookstore counter, and I hang out with Mr. Laskin every day, I'm starting to see maybe what I'll do when I grow up.

I think we should move to an island and have a boat and a garden and a big house and a school for kids who don't have families. We'll teach them how to grow vegetables and fish and play baseball and make their own clothes and bake bread and carpentry and music, along with how to manage their money. Lots of practical stuff mixed with fun stuff.

After the school gets going, I might start a band because Denny taught me some fundamental minor seventh chords on the piano and the other day I started writing a song Indira heard and said was beautiful. I'm not sure how it's going to end, but I'm pretty excited because the song just came to me while I was improvising and Jenny says creations come to you when they recognize you're an artist they can express themselves through. So maybe that's what I'll be, some sort of artist with a school for kids.

Last night by the fire at my cave, I sang Mr. Laskin the start of my song. At first when I finished singing he didn't say anything. He just stared at the flames for a long time, and then he added a few twigs and said, "Derek, the thing is, you've begun to bear fruit, and that, above all, is our purpose here. Bless you and bless your song. Don't ever listen to anyone who says you aren't a perfectly wonderful soul."

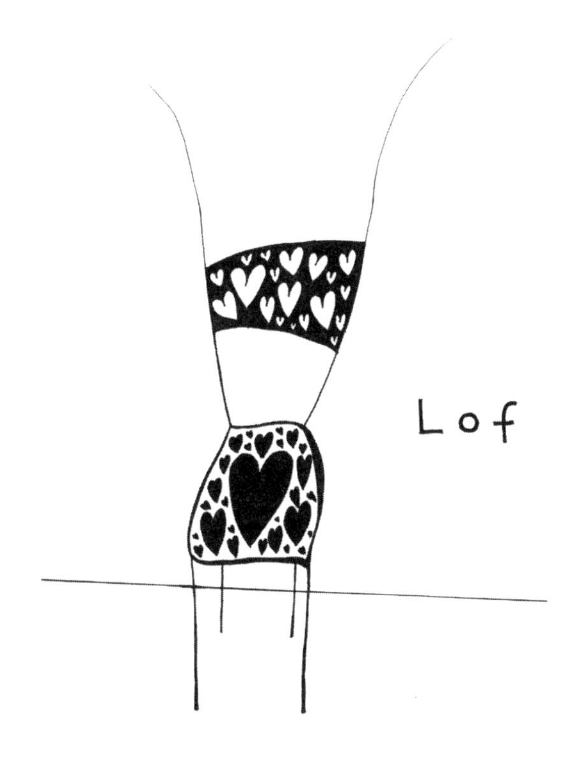

Time and Again

(in the course of infinite transformations)

Indira

Dusk is settling over the city. I step from the doorway of the bookstore into a cool mist from the distant sea. My mind is full of fantastic orchids and iridescent hummingbirds and golden toads and other wonders I have just seen in a book about the cloud forests of the upper Amazon.

I hear footsteps—a certain unmistakable cadence that brings my consciousness fully into *Now*. I raise my eyes and see Him walking toward me—the man I love—and I feel I may burst into flames.

Lord

She walks right by me, her shoulder brushing mine, and I think *My oh my what a bewitching Hindu babe.* For in the absence of her long black tresses and her formless old dresses, and due to the elapsing of a long week out of town since I last felt her amorous caresses, I'm on the threshold of Under the Table Books before I realize *My God, those eyes, those deep dark eyes are the eyes of Mrs. Ar...the* former *Mrs. Armitage with whom I made love, and with whom every corpuscle and synapse and peptide in my body wishes to make love again.*

Indira

He passes me, giving me only the barest of glances, and I stiffen with anguish, my hopes dashed. *How could He not know me? I who opened my body to Him as I have never opened to anyone.*

I touch my shaved head, touch the red dot in the center of my forehead, feel my body cloaked in a sari, and I realize how unlike my former self I must appear. So I come to a standstill in the October mist and send my desire swimming through the air to catch Him, trusting his higher mind, his deeper memory, his cellular wisdom, to remember our love that blurred all boundaries between us.

Lord

Derek is behind the counter having a spirited discussion with Moustafa about whether yeast has consciousness. I love the juxtaposition of Derek small and slender and blond and rosy with Moustafa tall and muscular and brown with braids so black, Derek's voice high and eager, Moustafa's deep and resonant. And though I missed them tremendously while I was off scavenging with Jenny, and I *really* want to stay and chat, I barely have time to say *Hello* before I am pulled backwards out the door by an invincible force and find Her standing in the October mist waiting for me, her freshly shaved dome and illimitably lovely face glistening with beads of mist, her bountiful lips slightly parted—the reason for everything swimming around in her sparkling eyes.

Indira

I am certain He will take me to my apartment, for that is where we made love that one incomparable night (and again in the morning) in those first bewildering hours of my renaissance. But the gods love nothing better than demolishing our certainties, and before I can find my voice to proclaim my devotion, He parts the flap of his yurt and beckons me to enter the delectably round room with Persian carpets on the floor and red and gold blankets covering the walls, a sumptuously pillowed king-sized mattress and a falling-apart leather reclining chair and a teak coffee table the only furnishings beneath a ceiling draped with blue paisley sheets.

As He busies himself boiling water for tea on a propane camping stove, I curl up in the recliner and open a volume of Ann Menebroker.

> Everything about you
> is soft and electric.
> I will pluck
> to see if I can strike
> a chord.

He serves us black tea in *raku* cups and we study each other. He traces the curve of my dome with his eyes, his eyebrows lifting hopefully when my tongue sneaks out to moisten my lips. He likes how my breasts are calling to him to get their nipples in his mouth. We allow our eyes to meet and stay in the meeting until we both look away to catch our breaths.

Calmer now, I return my gaze to his luscious mouth, imagining his lips kissing mine, imagining him suckling on my breasts, his tongue flicking my nipples. I smile at his grandiloquent nose and can't help but think of his glorious *tumba*. I love studying him studying me, imagining what he might be imagining. Such communion is most enjoyable and inspiring.

He speaks of his travels with Jenny, of the marvelous people they met on their way, of the books they found, of the joys and sorrows of not knowing what they will be to each other now.

I tell him it was Jenny and Natasha who cut my hair, and I rejoice to learn that Jenny made no mention of my shearing, for she promised to tell no one. I describe how Mrs. Armitage fought like a tiger to escape the clutches of the goddesses—my love for Jenny and Natasha boundless now.

Lord tells me of making love to Jenny on their journey, a kind of loving he has never known, a tender friendly lovemaking with only a hint of the torrential passion he feels for me. Those are his words *torrential passion*, and I swoon as he kneels before me kissing my fingers and wrists and forearms and shoulders and throat and chin and lips and eyes, as he whispers his special brand of fabulous nonsense and I go blind with pleasure and lust.

Lord

Finding ourselves esurient following our divine toil, Indira dons my jeans and T-shirt and leather jacket—outrageously sexy—while I wrap myself in her pink sari and we walk in the rain to David's Beau Thai, the next best thing to Moustafa's cooking.

Awaiting our zesty comestibles, we share a goblet of Indian wine, deliciously dry with a tea-like finish, and get so turned on watching each other sip we change our order *To Go*.

Indira

We walk home as fast as our legs will carry us, the gods sending rain and wind and thunder and a hilarious (in retrospect) warping of the time-space continuum to make it seem an eternity before we get back to Lord's place—our lust transmogrified into ravenous hunger.

Lord

Oh, what a feast! Succulent prawns in blazing red curry, roasted eggplant and string beans sautéed in spicy butter, scallops flash-seared in sesame oil with garlic and basil and puffy brown rice.

We eat so much, sex is impossible, so we bide our time with a game of Scrabble, Indira winning with *NEXUS*, her *X* on a triple letter square.

The bells of St. Ambrose toll the midnight hour. We stand naked outside my yurt—planets and stars revealed in transient clearings midst the scudding storm clouds.

Shivering, we scurry to bed.

Indira

Heaven as he plows me deep.

Lord

We fall asleep entangled.

Indira

I wake in darkness free of fear.

Lord

I wake to the quiet of aloneness. Tendrils of dreams play about me—none strong enough to carry me back to Morpheus.

Now the flap of my yurt bursts open to sunlight—Indira entering with a basket of eggs and peaches and berries and plums—her sari pink, her darling dome anointed with cocoa butter.

"Stay in bed," she commands, trumping my impulse to rise. "Rest while I make our breakfast."

"With pleasure," I say, rolling onto my side to watch her.

She squats at my table and lights the stove, a lusty smile on her tired face. "I want to feed you, Lord, to give you strength to ravish me."

She prepares turkey sausage and scrambled eggs. She cuts up fruit and stirs the juicy chunks into a bowl of yogurt. She sings a song in praise of the sun and soil and rain and seeds and plants and flowers and fruit and cows and turkeys and chickens and eggs.

Spontaneous Therapy

(woof and twill and weave and warp and waft—
and who knows who gets healed)

Not much there thinks Jenny, glancing sadly at her reflection in the steamy mirror. *I am not much of anything.*

Just outside the bathroom, Jenny bumps into Carl Klein, a jovial (when he's not in a foul mood) potbellied former minor-league baseball player turned soldier turned cactus rancher turned iguana breeder now retired and living in one of the more remote bedrooms of the collective known as Under the Table Books.

Carl peers at Jenny through the very thick lenses of his incredibly dirty new glasses and says, "Oh. Jenny. I barely recognized you. These new glasses are terrible. I can't see a goddamn thing. The old ones may have been taped together, but at least..."

"Carl?" says Jenny, having accompanied him to the optometrist's three times to help him get the new glasses he so desperately needed. "Your glasses are filthy. I can barely see your eyes. No wonder you can't see. May I?"

"May you what?" he asks, unaware that she is slowly reaching for his glasses.

"May I clean them for you?" She smiles fondly at Carl and thinks of her father—a man she never really knew—who would have been just about Carl's age had he survived the senseless war that ended his life when Jenny was ten. "Your glasses?"

"How come my other ones didn't get so dirty all the time?" he asks, following her into the bathroom where she rinses the lenses under the tap and dries them thoroughly with *her* towel—the only towel in the communal bathroom she knows for certain is clean.

"Because you never *went* anywhere when you had your old glasses." She places the new ones on his face. "Now that you can see again, you're all over the place, including Derek's very dusty cave."

"We're digging for quartz crystals," says Carl, grinning in wonder as he looks around at the suddenly clarified world. "And I've got a feeling we're about to strike a major vein. Hey, these new glasses are great."

Jenny climbs the stairs to the bookstore and finds Natasha engaged in a spirited debate with Peter Franklin, a dashing older man who resembles precisely the late great British actor and memoirist Alec Guinness. Peter is arguing that culture—books movies music art drama—has devolved into a cesspool of soul-sapping mind-shrinking mediocrity. Natasha strenuously disagrees, arguing that the artists of her very much younger generation employ technologies so radically different from those used by the artists of Peter's generation that his point of view is hopelessly antiquated.

"And thirty years hence, will you and your age peers sit around campfires singing *rap* songs together?" asks Peter, *sounding* exactly like Alec Guinness, too. "I daresay not. You will, at best, be singing Beatles' songs learned from your parents and grandparents. But not rap."

"What does sitting around campfires have to do with culture?" says Natasha, waving her arms in exasperation. "And besides, rap is only one of a thousand parts of our culture. What was the last movie you went to, anyway? *The Horse's Mouth*?"

"I beg you not to bring Alec Guinness movies into this discussion," says Peter, wincing at the myriad levels of meaning evinced by the evocation of that seminal film. "I find him...Alec...me...his...my...our sameness highly confusing." He clears his throat. "Though you must admit he was fabulous in that film, which, by the way, he also wrote. And no, that was not the last film I went to."

"Truce," says Natasha, kissing Peter to make things sweet between them. "I'm due at the recording studio to sing with Tantha and Tomas. Ultra-melodic. Possibly campfire material thirty years hence. No kidding."

"Believe me," says Peter, calling after her, "my critique of the current epoch has nothing to do with you. I adore you. Your ideas, your feelings, your grace, your face, your splendid body, the way your magnificent hips sway as you walk along the boulevard, the timbre of your voice, the..." He turns to Jenny. "I hope I didn't offend her."

"Fear not," says Jenny, taking Natasha's place on the stool behind the counter. "She adores you every bit as much as you adore her."

"I knew her mother well," says Peter with a wistful sigh. "Very well, indeed. Dear Florence. To quote the late great rap maestro Nine Ice J Slick Daddy Oh Girl, with only slight alterations to the original text, 'she make me hard day and night and day, sexy thing with sexy way..."

"You're kidding," says Jenny, shocked by his recitation. "You made that up, didn't you?"

"For me to know and you to wonder about," says Peter, gallantly doffing his hat—a classic English bowler—and exiting stage left.

Jenny straightens the till and counts the cash, musing about Natasha's mother Flo, renowned for her lifelong sexual escapades with a dizzyingly large cast of lovers—apparently quite healthy and happy in her middle-aged nymphomania, living in Great Britain these days throwing parties for the rich and famous and sleeping with most of them, certainly not the shattered wreck the textbooks say she's supposed to be.

Whereas I *cringe at the idea of ever sleeping with anyone other than Lord ever again for the rest of my life.*

The bell above the door announces one of Jenny's dearest friends, Monica Copia, a buoyant curvaceous love machine and world-famous psychosexual therapist. Author of the classic neo-post-feminist feminist texts *I Like Kissing You Out Of Bed* and *A Little Lie Down With Chocolate*, her latest opus *Come On In, Big Boy* is due out any day now from Double Random Knopf Bantam Viking Harpers Schuster Penguin Day House.

"Hi, Jen," says Monica, resplendent in a jade green sarong, her long gray hair shiny from a recent henna rinse and haloed with a *lei* of heavenly scented gardenias. "Seen Pinky today?"

"I think he's at the studio with Tomas and Tantha and Natasha. Vocal tracks for Tantha's new album."

"God, does Pinky love to sing," says Monica, a rosy tinge creeping into her cheeks as she speaks of her lover. "Sings all the time we're making love with a deep steady hum."

"How nice for you," says Jenny, her envy palpable.

"Oh, sweetie," says Monica, frowning in sympathy. "You're all closed in on yourself. Lord with Indira got you blue?"

This unexpected (and precisely accurate) diagnosis shatters Jenny's pretended cool and bursts her into tears.

"Guess so," says Monica, the maitre d' of emotions. "Come around here and get a hug."

Ensconced on the biggest of beanbag chairs in the Reading Circle, Monica holds Jenny in her arms—mother sister cradling daughter sister—and listens to Jenny give the plaintive speech Monica has heard ten thousand times and often made herself until a decade ago when the truth of her fabulousness finally triumphed over her delusions of inadequacy.

"How could we be *so* happy together," keens Jenny, "and then he chooses her over me? She *must* be better than me, or I'm just not good enough for him, or something. It isn't fair. I thought we'd patched things up. I thought we were back together again. I thought he loved me. But if he *really* loved me, how could he just drop me like that?"

"Sweetheart," says Monica, her voice a soothing rumble, "you were happy together because you were happy together. And you're *more* than good enough. You're marvelous. And you *did* patch things up, and you *were* back together. And now it's now, and..."

"But how could he *do* that to me?" cries Jenny, leaping away from Monica and pacing the Reading Circle like a caged lion. "It makes me feel so...expendable, so...interchangeable, so...*un*special."

"None of which you are," says Monica, struggling to extricate herself from the clutches of the beanbag.

"But I *can't* be any good if he would do that to me." She clenches her fists. "I must be shit. I must be. Shit."

"My friend," says Monica, taking a deep breath and resisting her impulse to comfort Jenny with yet another hug, "I know you feel terribly hurt, but here is what I believe to be the heart of the matter. Our thoughts are a form of action, and the universe, this miraculous unfathomable thing we call life, is flawlessly and comprehensively and instantaneously *reactive* to our actions. Some call it karma. I call it dancing. We may choose to dance with conscious grace, and to love ourselves and others, or we can bewail our imagined fate and in so doing *tell* the universe just how badly we want things to go for us."

Jenny unclenches her fists and nods in understanding. "I know you're right, Monica, but what I know and what I feel are still so far apart. I mean, you've got Pinky, Tantha's got Tomas, Indira has Lord...and you're all *beaming* with happiness, so it's hard for me to..."

Monica laughs. "I haven't got Pinky any more than he's got me. We're lovers without borders." She takes Jenny's hands and does a slow *cha-cha* with her. "All in good time, sweetheart. Little by little awareness dawns. You'll find your way out of this."

Weeping as she sits on the stool behind the counter, Jenny waits for someone to spell her so she can go downstairs and crawl into bed. Hence, she barely looks up as Jack steals into the store as he does every Thursday afternoon, seeking books on photography and horticulture.

A robust good-looking man with brilliant blue eyes and a heroic chin, his head shaved to complete the work of balding, his voice a smoky tenor, Jack has been infatuated with Jenny for years now. Having heard through the grapevine that Jenny is single again, he has every intention—if he can work up the nerve—to ask her to go out with him.

Jenny mechanically removes a piece of purple paper from the side of the cash register and holds it out to Jack. The purple paper is supposed to contain a list of books on photography and horticulture that have come in since Jack last checked the shelves—a service provided by the bookstore staff for their most regular of regulars.

"Thanks," says Jack, scanning the piece of purple paper, "but I think you've got me mixed up with somebody else."

Jenny looks at him through a blur of tears—his beautiful blue eyes the only distinct features of a phantom.

"Someone else's list," he says with laughter in his voice. "*Sex and the Single Surfer. The Babes of Daytona Beach. Love In the Dunes. Out Out Damn Sand.* I'm photographs and trees and flowers and..."

"Oh, sorry," she says, reaching for the errant list. "I don't know where yours is."

"No problem," he says, proffering the piece of purple paper in such a way their fingers have to touch. "I actually didn't come in for books today. I came to see you, to see if you'd go out with me some time. To a movie or something. Or for coffee. Or..."

She blinks to clear her eyes of tears, but he remains a blur—her vision veiled by grief.

Loony Bird

(the wounded psyche returns)

Saturday morning. A cold rain falling. The bookstore toasty. Lord behind the counter—black pajamas and a jester's cap—playing gin rummy with Natasha—gray sweats from her Frisbee workout with Moustafa. Baking and socializing and tea drinking underway downstairs. Books flying out three times faster than they're coming in. Mysteries and nostalgia extra-popular as Thanksgiving approaches.

The jingling bell above the door proclaims the entrance of one of the angriest men on earth, an avowed enemy of the bookstore, a snarling fellow with flaming red hair and heavy black-framed glasses.

"I'm back," he growls, unzipping his shiny black leather jacket to reveal his *The Word Spiritual Nauseates Me* T-shirt. "I'm back and I'm gonna shut this bullshit bookstore down. That's right. You heard me. Ten days from today I will put you people where you belong. On the streets."

"Say it isn't so," says Lord, grimacing. "Napoleon is selling the building to *you?*"

"For a cool million," snickers the man with flaming red hair and heavy black-framed glasses. "Unless *you* can come up with the money first. Diaz is giving you ten days, but you idealistic idiots probably don't have fifty bucks, let alone a cool million."

"Not true," says Lord, smiling bravely at Natasha. "How much have we got? Roughly."

"Seventy-seven dollars," she says, checking the till *and* the tip jar. "Plus change."

"Have fun," says the man, sneering at Lord. "I'm *emptying* this place first of the month. Disinfecting it."

"You know," says Natasha, trying to remain calm as she addresses the vituperative stranger, "I don't know you, but you seem terribly upset, and I have a friend, a most excellent therapist who might really be able to help you. I'd be happy to introduce you to her. In fact, I could give her a call right now and see if..."

"Save it, sister," snaps the malicious man, gritting his oft-gritted teeth. "The party's over. There's nothing wrong with *me*. I've got the cool million. You don't. So it's *you* who are in trouble now."

"What are you talking about?" asks Jenny, emerging from downstairs with a carafe of freshly made lemonade, Derek following with a basket of peanut butter cookies. "What did we ever do to you?"

"You're sickening," spits the spiteful redhead. "You sit around pretending to be Buddhists and anarchists, but it's all bullshit. You only survive because capitalism works so well it supports lazy slobs like you feeding off the hard work and sacrifice of decent responsible people. And then you try to say *your* way works because you're on some sort of cosmically correct path. Like you're somehow better than the rest of us."

"*Us?*" asks Lord, aghast at the man's contempt. "Who is us if not we, and you included in there with me?"

"The people who *work* for their money!" cries the crazed conformist. "My father busted his butt for fifty years to earn what I inherited from him, and you guys just screw around all day. It's not fair! So I'm throwing you out."

"Doubt it," says Natasha, wrinkling her nose. "Ten days is a long time. Virtually infinite. You could have a revelation tomorrow and become the next Saint Francis. Or at least turn into a fairly nice guy."

"You sicken me," says the man, heading for the door. "Ten days from now you'll all be exactly where you should be, standing at freeway entrances begging for change."

"Not me," says Lord, shaking his head. "Grocery store parking lots, maybe, but I draw the line at freeway entrances. Deadly fumes."

"I hate you," says the man, his eyes jittery with rage. "I hate how smug and superior you act. I hate you."

"You are my teacher," says Lord, bowing to the man. "I trust your astounding animosity has a purpose yet to be revealed."

"Eat shit!" shouts the man, storming out of the store. "Scumbags!"

Derek sets the basket of cookies on the counter and asks with undisguised anguish, "Sell? They're gonna *sell* the building? Where will I go? Maybe he just said that to scare us."

"I'm afraid not," says Napoleon Diaz, their dashing Cuban landlord. He stands in the doorway—appearing several decades younger than his seventy-seven years—a surly smile on his rakishly handsome face. "My wife is in desperate need of new joints. Hips, elbows, knees, ankles, shoulders, neck. She's a wreck and I'm feeling younger than ever. These operations could give her twenty more good years. But see, new suspension don't run cheap. We want the best. A cool million barely covers it. I'm not trying to gouge you. I don't mind so much having your bookstore and your commune or whatever you call it here, but life is life. Nothing personal. You have ten days to raise the money. I'll take yours before anybody else's. That much I can promise."

"I know who can help us," says Derek, hopping up and down. "Mr. Laskin. He wrote the *book* on making money faster and faster."

"Mr. Laskin is a loony bird," says Napoleon, squinting at Derek. "He's diving for rotten cheese in the dumpster behind Andronico's. He's a total cuckoo."

"In *your* opinion," says Lord, winking at Derek. "For our money, to use an expression I think we can all agree is particularly appropriate to the subject at hand, he's far saner than that terribly sad fellow to whom you intend to sell the building."

"Nuts," says Napoleon, turning to go. "Laskin is a delusional schizophrenic nutcase. You don't actually *believe* he was a billionaire?"

"Trillionaire," says Derek, nodding emphatically. "So then they squelched him. You go over a trillion with even slightly left-leaning politics and it sets off a red alert in the bowels of the hidden domain of the secret global warlords."

"I loved that book," says Jenny, her eyes filling with tears as they so often do these days. "How he fell in love with Conchita Herrera, the sugar magnate's daughter, those long kissing scenes in the canoe in the mangrove swamp. His refusal to fight a duel with the wicked drug lord. Conchita's suicide. It would make *such* a great movie."

"But he knew too much," says Natasha, moving to the top of the stairs. "I'm late for a recording session. See you all later."

"You see, Mr. Diaz," says Lord, gesturing skyward to the mysterious powers of the universe, the beneficent spirits, and any other agents of cosmic largesse who might be listening, "we have no reason *not* to believe in Mr. Laskin, whereas..."

"Ten days," says Napoleon, rolling his eyes. "You might want to have a clearance sale."

"But nothing here is for sale," says Lord, bemused. "You knew that, didn't you? People leave whatever they think a book is worth, though I suppose we could ask them to leave half of that."

"No," says Jenny, daubing her eyes with a burnt sienna handkerchief. "You can't have a sale if nothing is for sale."

"So is it okay if *I* raise the money?" asks Derek, gazing up at Lord. "With Mr. Laskin?"

"We would be delighted," says Jenny, giving her boy a hug and smiling at Napoleon. "Denny caught a huge flounder yesterday. We're having a major feast tonight. Would you like to stay for supper?"

"Please do," says Lord, waving out the window to a passing unicyclist with a large raven on her shoulder. "I'm making my famous carrot salad with raisins and sesame oil."

"You're all crazy," says Napoleon, turning to go. "Ten days is all I can give you. And then this party is over."

Derek catches up to Napoleon on the sidewalk. "Pardon me, Mr. Diaz. May I speak to you for a moment? Ask your advice?"

"Sure," says Napoleon, shoving his hands in his pockets. "But don't try to talk my price down. We need a cool million. All new balls and sockets. Top of the line. Best surgeons money can buy. A cool million and she'll be able to do virtually everything again. So they say. In the bedroom. If you catch my drift."

"I'm not quite eleven," says Derek, nodding. "But the social worker said I have an immeasurably high IQ. Whatever that is. So I kind of know what you're talking about. Let's call it an inkling."

"Well, let's just say my wife has been incapable of certain physical endeavors," says Napoleon, lighting a big cigar, "which has necessitated my going elsewhere to fulfill the needs of this body that won't seem to get old. And, see, I dearly love my wife. So if she could have again the fun we used to have, it will be worth selling this old building. Nothing personal. I don't mind you folks so much. I just need the money. Simple."

"And you're pretty sure Mr. Laskin is crazy? You don't think he ever had lots of money?"

"He's a loony bird," says Napoleon, spitting into the street. "Loco. Nobody owns whole cities like he says he did. I one time let him talk to me for two hours. Just to see what he'd say. Claimed he invented a secret formula that made everyone happy. He says he had so much money..."

"I know, I know," says Derek, a lump in his throat. "I read *You Get Too Big They Squelch You*. Twice." His eyes fill with tears. "The part where they changed the formula for joy into one that made everyone depressed? That part was *so* sad. And look...it all came true."

"He's a lunatic," says Napoleon, glowering at Derek. "I'd throw money down the toilet before I'd let him play with it."

"What a waste," says Derek frowning at Napoleon. "There's gotta be at least one chance in a trillion he's telling the truth."

"*No* chance," says Napoleon, biting his cigar in half. "Don't you get it? Crazy street people are not ex-billionaires. It doesn't happen."

"We were rich once," says Derek, nodding sadly. "My dad was an engineer. We had a house and everything, and then they phased him out and moved the company to Haiti and he...he died, and then my mom got sick and the insurance wouldn't cover her medicine and she had to sell the house and not too long after that we were living in an old car and then I ran away because there was never enough food."

"But you weren't *billionaires*," says Napoleon, patting Derek's head. "That's the difference. His book is a crock of shit."

"I had my own bedroom," says Derek, seeing his room—the *Star Wars* posters, the clothing marked with logos of major supranational corporations, the empty hamster cage. "And a super-fast computer with tons of memory. I must have been pretty happy."

"Look," says Napoleon, tiring of the parable. "The price is a million dollars. Go tell somebody else your sob story."

"It's not a sob story," says Derek, glaring fiercely at Napoleon. "I'm explaining to you why I believe in Mr. Laskin. I thought I was the richest kid in the world. I know *just* how he feels."

"He's a demented psychotic," says Napoleon, climbing into his massive new utility jeep truck—two miles per gallon. "Might as well flush your money down the toilet. That's if you had any money to flush."

"Actually, I do," says Derek, smiling slyly. "It's money from selling the one and only *complete* copy of Mr. Laskin's book. I put it in the bank."

"The toilet!" says Napoleon, gunning his engine.

"I'll try Mr. Laskin first," says Derek, shouting over the engine's roar. "Wish me luck?"

"Vaya con dios," says Napoleon, handing him a five-dollar bill. "Treat yourself to some good enchiladas. You'll need the energy."

Cipher

(the powers of zero)

Derek finds Mr. Laskin, tall and straight-backed with long white hair, picking through a dumpster in the alley behind Andronico's Extremely Expensive Food Shoppe.

"Mr. Laskin?" says Derek, hoping the old man is in a good mood. "I know you said you didn't want to see me until the afternoon, but it's kind of important. It's about your two o'clock sandwich."

"You're out of place, Derek," says Mr. Laskin, squinting at his favorite human. "You don't belong in this phase of my life. You're a second-half-of-the-day person. I've been slipping lately, combining the phases. Dangerous behavior for my personality type. So… see ya later."

"The thing is, Mr. Diaz is going to sell our building," says Derek, unable to conceal his distress. "Where the bookstore is? Unless we buy it. He wants a cool million. None of us has any money except me. I have twenty-five hundred plus interest in the bank from selling the one and only *complete* copy of your book about making money faster and faster. And I was thinking since you told me you could turn a dollar into a thousand easy as pie, that with twenty-five hundred you could probably…"

"Get away from me," says Mr. Laskin, glowering. "I made my trillions and they stole my life. I busted the bank. And I'm talking about the mother of *all* banks. I owned whole nations. I was about to buy this one: America. I had *that* much, and they bopped me over the head and switched my identity to that mindless cipher in New York."

"What's a cipher?" asks Derek, taking out his trusty notebook to make note of the new word.

"Nothing," says Mr. Laskin, warming to his tale. "I solved the essential problem. I was moments away from making corporations functionally obsolete. So they demolished me."

"Well, then, how about if you tell *me* what to do?" asks Derek, nodding hopefully. "They don't have to know it's *you* making the money."

"Don't be absurd," snorts Mr. Laskin, tugging angrily on his ponytail. "My touch is unmistakable. Why just last year I bought thirty-nine cents of Peruvian copper futures. I had forty thousand dollars in two days, so they mugged me. They're brutal. They don't want me anywhere *near* money. Why they don't just kill me is an ongoing mystery."

"But all I want to do is turn twenty-five hundred into a cool million, buy the building where the bookstore is, and live happily ever after. Is that so much to ask?"

"You don't wish to accumulate capital?" Mr. Laskin squints at the boy. "Are you saying this would be a one-time only purchase for the greater good of humanity?"

"For the greater good," says Derek, nodding solemnly. "So we can keep the bookstore and you can have your sandwich every day. That's what's really on the line here. Your every-day-at-two-o'clock sandwich."

"Now that's a horse of a different color," says Mr. Laskin, climbing out of the dumpster, a look of fierce determination on his craggy face. "I draw the line when they start messing with my lunch. Take me to a working television."

"Huh?"

"A television," says Mr. Laskin, handing Derek a bag of odoriferous cheeses. "Mass media. The pulse of the lowest common denominator of the group mind. The glittering glamorous torrent of greed."

"We don't have a television at Under the Table Books," says Derek, trying to remember the last time he watched one. "But we do have a transistor radio for ball games and an FM radio to pick up KPFA in Berkeley. The leftist pinko radical hip-hop jazz salsa soul station?"

"Won't work," says Mr. Laskin, licking his lips. "I need mainstream American television. The great murky middle muddle."

"Why?" asks Derek, feeling the first twinges of doubt about Mr. Laskin's sanity.

"To predict from," he says, flagging down an old Fiat driven by Mr. Techthin, the corpulent owner of the only existing *complete* copy of Mr. Laskin's treatise *You Get Too Big They Squelch You.*

"Mr. Laskin," says Mr. Techthin, rolling down his window and smiling admiringly. "What a pleasure to encounter you again. How are we on this fine frosty morning? Well, I hope."

"We need a television," says Derek, bowing graciously to Mr.

Techthin. "Could we possibly come to your house and watch one?"

"An honor," says Mr. Techthin, arching his chubby eyebrow. "Onto something, Laskin?"

"Need a cool million quick," says Mr. Laskin, jumping in the backseat with Derek. "Step on it. My lunch is on the line."

In Mr. Techthin's tidy living room, Derek and Mr. Laskin stare with mouths agape at beautiful naked women acting out mildly shocking sex on a liquid crystal screen. Fifteen minutes into the soft-focus porn, Mr. Techthin ventures to ask, "What exactly are you hoping to see?"

"Seen enough," says Mr. Laskin, rising quickly. "To a penny-ante broker. Pronto."

"I'll drive you," says Mr. Techthin, taking a deep breath. "On one condition. That you allow me to invest identically to you."

"I don't care if you wipe your butt with seaweed," says Mr. Laskin, barging out the door. "Just get me to a penny-ante broker."

Moustafa Kahlil, Frisbee guru and master baker, and Numero Uno, a feisty unrestricted free agent of a poet best known for his erotic culinary haiku, sit in their mobile solar brokerage school bus house, playing with poor people's pennies on the great electronic stock exchange accessed through jerry-rigged black market computer clones.

Numero Uno buys nine dollars worth of African gold shares and sells them two minutes later for a sixty-cent gain. "Yes!" he cries. "Showed *those* greedy guys."

Moustafa scores with an Icelandic volcano company. "Forty-five cents in twenty-eight seconds," he chuckles. "Let's take a break."

"Stay right where you are," says Mr. Laskin, striding into the brokerage bus with twenty-five hundred plus interest, chased nimbly by Derek and the breathless Mr. Techthin.

"Never fails," says Numero Uno, shaking his head. "Declare a truce, all hell breaks loose."

"I want this money," proclaims Mr. Laskin, "on your absolute rock bottom cheapest deodorant stock. Something in the sixteenth of a cent category. Or lower."

"No problem," says Moustafa, tapping his keyboard. "Demur Odorology, makers of odor-suppressant pills. Forty-two shares per penny. But I must warn you. The company is not long for this world."

"Give me two thousand five hundred and sixty-two dollars worth," says Mr. Laskin, glowering at the computer screen. "Quick."

"107,604 shares," says Moustafa, making the buy.

"I want the same," says Mr. Techthin, dropping his cash on Numero's keyboard. "Exactly."

"Yours," says Numero, thinking of a recent poem. "Yours and therefore mine, for I am surely you."

"Good news," says Moustafa, smiling up at the elderly gentlemen. "You two just bought the entire company. Demur is *all* yours."

"Ah," says Mr. Laskin, turning to Techthin. "I run the show. Agreed?"

"Yes," says Mr. Techthin, bowing submissively despite his girth. "With pleasure."

"Give me one of your shares," says Mr. Laskin, tapping his foot. "Hurry, man. Time is of the essence, ephemeral though it may be."

"Of course," says Mr. Techthin, directing Numero to make the transfer. "Give him *five* of my shares. We'll consider it his commission."

"Done," says Numero, grinning at Moustafa. "Isn't this great.

They own an entire company. However chimerical it may be."

"Chimericals?" says Derek, frowning at the word. "I hope they're not poisonous."

"Now to send a fax," says Mr. Laskin, grabbing Derek's hand. "Techthin, you stay here. If our total approaches a million before we get back, sell ours. I don't care *what* you do with yours."

"Got it," says Mr. Techthin, gazing into Numero's screen. "I have a lock on the graph of our investment."

In the fax shop, Derek sits at the composing console, entering whatever Mr. Laskin dictates.

"Alexander Laskin, eighty-seven-year-old controlling shareholder of Demur Odorology...no. Start again. Ruben *Laskowitz*, the one-hundred-year-old CEO of the oral deodorant giant Demur, announced, mere moments ago, a startling breakthrough in body odor research. A Demur exclusive. A deodorant composed of two *distinct* odors, one female and one male that ignite each other during foreplay to create an aphrodisiacal scent guaranteed to inspire big long orgasms for all concerned."

"Five dollars," says the fax girl, taking the completed memo from Derek. "For broad release."

"Damn," says Mr. Laskin, slapping his forehead. "We forgot to keep some cash on hand for publicity costs."

"I have exactly five dollars," says Derek, searching his pockets. "Mr. Diaz, our landlord, told me to buy enchiladas to give me energy."

"Consider our two o'clock sandwiches enchiladas," says Mr. Laskin, snatching the bill and handing it to the fax girl. "Mission accomplished."

They arrive back at the brokerage bus just in time to see their holdings roar up over the hundred-thousand-dollar mark. At four hundred and eighty-seven thousand dollars, Mr. Laskin yells, "Sell! Sell!" and Moustafa types in the command as fast as he can, but his order is delayed thirty seconds due to info highway overclog and they don't get out of the game until they have three point seven million dollars.

Mr. Techthin stares at Numero's screen, his face contorted in disbelief as his fortune soars up and up beyond seventy million and disappears into a single blinking zero.

"What happened?" croaks Mr. Techthin, numb from head to toe. "Nothing? I have nothing and *you* have three point seven *million?*"

"No," says Mr. Laskin, putting a hand on Mr. Techthin's shoulder. "*You* have three point seven million. May we borrow a cool million, please? Forever?"

"But I *lost* all my money," says Mr. Techthin, white as a sheet and terribly thirsty. "I should have pulled out when you did."

"We're giving you ours," says Derek, nodding enthusiastically. "Minus a cool million so we can buy our building."

"Say yes," says Mr. Laskin, rubbing his stomach. "It's nearly two. Coming on sandwich time."

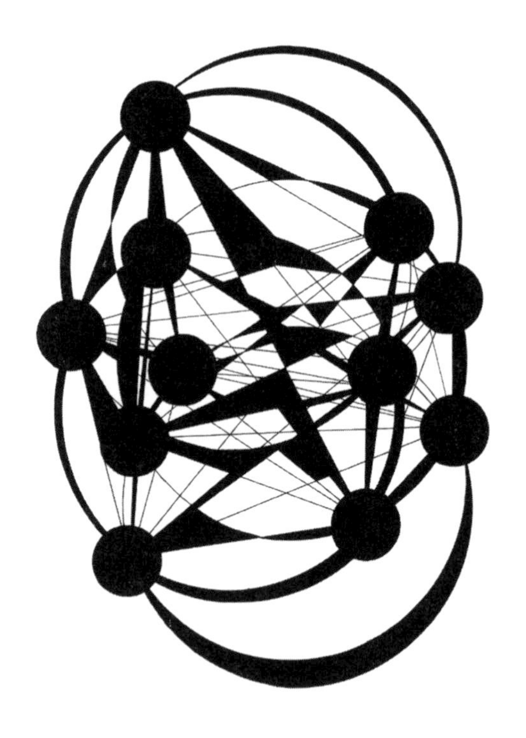

Freedom

(celebrating the purchase of an old brick warehouse—
petri dish of infectious creativity)

"Welcome," says Lord Bellmaster, standing at the podium on the edge of the Reading Circle, his audience the hardest-core stalwarts of the anarchist collective. "We are gathered here tonight for our second official meeting in seventeen, no, eighteen, no...many years. Our last meeting was a disaster, but as someone once said, probably Shakespeare, 'The past is prologue.' Anyway. So. Here we are. Thanks for coming. We are now among the landed. We who have for large portions of our lives owned nothing now own this thousand-ton building and the land under it and around it and the air space above into the stratosphere. How bizarre! So."

"What's the meeting about?" asks Moustafa, smiling curiously at his old friend. "The building is ours. No one can take it away from us so long as we pay the taxes. Need we say more?"

"Well, the thing is," says Lord, doing a rather impressive jitterbug, "I keep thinking about us doing something momentous to celebrate our newfound relationship to this blessed building. Something like..."

"How about a party?" suggests Denny, recently returned from a scavenging binge through greater Los Angeles. "I'll make my famous garlic potatoes and be happy to play drums in a house band, too."

"I can play a little bass," says Z, thumping his notebook with his thumb. "Run a little rap?"

"And I," says Pinky Jones, nodding assuredly, "will hand out programs and escort people to their seats. I have just the outfit and just the persona I've been wanting to try. I'll give you a hint. Polka dots."

Peter Franklin rises slowly to add his thoughts to the public imaginings. "I propose we preface the party with a reading."

"Poetry?" asks Lord, recalling the last lines of his latest poem. *I am occupied territory/her arms about me/I don't dare (don't really want to) move.*

"If you will," says Peter, bowing graciously, "though most audiences prefer stories. It's in our genes, I believe, to love a good story."

"I will be happy to read," says Lord (this being his secret intention all along). "From my latest collection of unfinished gems *Not Quite Yet Almost.* The shorter funnier ones."

"I could *tell* one," says Mr. Laskin, chewing on the end of his long white braid. "I've got a story I've never told anyone. As far as I know. Have no fear. It's not the one about being the richest man on earth. No, this is a whole other story from so long ago you won't believe it actually happened to me, but it did." He chuckles. "I'll give you a few hints. A parrot, an orchid, a silver locket, and two hard-boiled eggs."

"Oh, boy!" says Derek, clapping his hands. "Let's have the party tomorrow night. I *love* stories! Maybe Mrs. Armitage, I mean Indira, would tell one of her kitty cat stories."

"Hey, I'll go ask her," says Lord—visions of Indira dancing in his head. "Right now."

"Hold your horses," says Jenny, glaring at Lord. "We haven't decided anything yet. Have we?"

Natasha taps Moustafa's wrist. "You gonna read, Moustafa?"

"I'll do something," he says, entertaining myriad possibilities. "Bake bread at the very least."

"I will be happy to accompany anybody who wants such on piano and/or guitar," says Tomas, ever ready to tickle the strings of either.

"While I and my able assistant Monsieur Derek will be delighted to create a persuasive poster," says Mr. Laskin, giving Derek the thumbs up. "We'll fax it everywhere."

"I can run lights," says Jenny, recalling a long-ago high school triumph. "I ran the light board for *The Diary of Anne Frank*. When the Nazis came at the end, and the cast was frozen in fear, I slowly dimmed the lights until everyone and everything disappeared."

"I'll definitely play congas and dance," says Natasha, leaping to her feet and swinging her arms as she leaps around the Reading Circle. "Maybe sing a song. Maybe write a story. And read it, too. We'll see. I might be too shy, but probably not once I get going."

Numero Uno, the garrulous poet, rises authoritatively and stands on his chair. "Listen to me people. I've done a thousand readings, from hoity-toity literary soirees to busking for dimes in the gutter, and if I've learned anything, it's that you gotta be honest with your audience or they'll despise you. They can smell a hypocrite fifty yards away."

"And yet," says Peter, blinking curiously at Numero Uno, "one of the beauties of fiction lies in its freedom from the so-called truth."

"I'm talking about *poetry*," says Numero, his voice ringing with passion. "I'm talking about words naked and undefended by the subterfuge of verbosity, right there on the gigantic page."

"Oh, let's not quibble," says Indira, appearing in the doorway, her head unfettered by a single hair, her pleasing curvosity cursorily cloaked in a flimsy white shift. "Sorry I'm late. Did I hear someone say something about stories? I have a good one to share. Poignant, evocative, with a cunning twist at the end."

"Yippee!" shouts Derek. "Stories! Heaven on earth."

"And may I further suggest," says Mr. Laskin, enthusiastically licking his lips, "that the company make the magnanimous gesture of serving *sandwiches* to our adoring public at this *soiree* as Señor Poet Numero suggested we name our grand affair? Shall we say bologna on Russian rye with thick slices of Muenster cheese, big smears of Bulgarian mustard atop crunchy romaine lettuce? As part of the culinary array?"

"We could have a gigantic potluck," says Derek, racing around the Reading Circle, leaping and spinning. "Come as your favorite dish."

"We'll do our medley of Bob Dylan tunes," says Leona, nudging Iris. "We still have our cowgirl outfits from our last trip to the Fillmore."

"Or maybe we'll come as beatniks," says Iris, her green eyes sparkling. "Leotards and berets. What could be better than that?"

"Or beatnik cowgirls," says Leona, bouncing her eyebrows. "The best of both archetypes."

"I feel the stirrings of inspiration tickling my mind," says Moustafa, bowing to one and all. "I must go to my bus now and make copious notes. Excuse me. Please."

The room empties fast—everyone fleeing to his or her den or sofa or cave or bedroom or duplex to prepare for whatever the Big Show turns out to be.

And presto, Indira and Lord are alone with each other, the sun setting over the copper dome of the cathedral of Saint Francis, a female muezzin calling out her evening prayers from the top of the Oddfellows building, her voice rich with yearning, her lyrics a mix of Joni Mitchell, Rickie Lee Jones, Harold Arlen, and D.R. Wagner.

"Hi, hi, hi, hi, hi, hi, hi, hi," Lord stutters, *so* glad to see his most inspiring friend. "It's been epochs since I last laid you, er, eyes on you. Two hours at least almost. I missed you."

"You," says Indira, slipping her hand under his shirt. "Is there a mattress or a chair or a wall nearby we can use?"

He grabs her hand. "Follow me. Be careful on the stairs."

"Stairs can be fun," she says, slowing him down. "I think you'll find the conveniently juxtaposed elevations highly conducive to certain propitious explorations."

"I love it when you use the words *juxtapose*, *propitious*, and *conducive*," he says, pulling her close for a good long kiss. "Indeed, the juxtaposition of your propitious vocabulary and the allure of your inestimable nonverbal parts is undeniably conducive to various and sundry erotic tendencies."

"Juxtapose," she whispers in his ear. "Juxtapose. Conducive. Propitious."

"Temptress," he murmurs, standing one stair below her and burying his face in her breasts. "You conducive propitious vixen, you."

"Juxtapose, juxtapose, juxtapose, juxtapose."

"I'm warning you," he growls, finding nothing but flesh beneath her flimsy shift—his hands gripping her magnificent butt. "Precariously balanced on a steep stairway or not."

"Juxtapose, juxtapose, juxta...mmm. Oh, Lord. Ooo, yeah."

Writer's Bloc

(coming soon to an anarchist bookstore near you)

Roseate fingers of dawn tap tap tapping on her window, Natasha—long brown luscious beauty—leaps out of bed, grabs pen and paper, and swiftly writes the first four pages of a story about two men lost in a jungle, stopping herself with the thought *I can't do this. I've never written anything longer than a page or two. And that was poetry. Who do I think I am?*

Yet the story continues to unfold seamlessly, vivid scene by vivid scene. So she banishes doubt and fills three more pages, her narrative voice growing stronger with every word she writes.

But now her doubts reemerge, their ferocity trebled, the words of her story drowned in the roar of the question *Who do you think you're kidding?*

Seeking solace from Moustafa—charming brown Frisbee savant and master baker—Natasha finds him in the hammock on the terrazzo doodling in his sketchbook.

"How goes the opus?" he asks, sensing Natasha's agony.

"I've never written a story," she says, feeling shy with him for the first time in her life. "Yet I seem to know how. Or am I deluding myself?"

"I have little experience with the art of story writing," he says, beguiled by her shyness. "My understanding is that every story has its own particular way of wanting to be told. They choose us, say the great writers, these stories do. We don't so much make them up as let them through."

"Will you read my first seven pages?" she asks, nodding hopefully. "Give me some feedback?"

"Not today, my darling," he says, tapping his sketchbook. "I'm working on my own story and I fear your words would get mixed up with mine. Talk to Lord. He's a past master at making things up."

Natasha finds Lord sitting on his high stool behind the counter in Under the Table Books banging away on an ancient Smith-Corona manual typewriter, hunting and pecking with his index fingers, his fabulously changeable face changing fabulously as he composes.

"Let me finish this thought," he says, concluding his paragraph with a vivacious flourish—typos be damned. "Yes?"

"My inner critics," she reveals, "have the advantage of me. How do I shut them up?"

Lord ponders Natasha's dilemma, knowing it to be his own, and says with a wistful smile, "You know, I once wrote a twenty-page story so fast I didn't know what I'd written until I read it. Knew it was great and sent it off without changing a word. And by golly the editor who rejected it at *The New Yorker* called to say it was the best story he'd read in years. Then the editor who turned me down at *Esquire* flew out from New York to shake my hand and tell me face to face my story was a masterpiece. And finally the *publisher* of *The Atlantic* wrote me a long and passionate handwritten rejection letter proclaiming my story the best he'd *ever* read, and included a personal check for a thousand dollars. So you see, sometimes the great ones just pop out fully realized, which is what your story is trying to do. Pop out. Fully realized. So I suggest you identify your inner critics, hunt them down, and kill them."

"But I've never written a story," says Natasha, biting her fingernails for the first time since junior high. "I keep stopping myself because I can't believe how well it's going."

"Happens to me all the time," says Lord, thinking of women and art. "We aren't taught to trust our instincts. On the contrary, we're taught to mistrust them. So here you are feeling great about what you're writing, and these voices are shouting, *No, no. It can't be any good. You like this too much. You must be insane.* Which is why most artists quit trying and fall off the path before they ever come close to fully flowering."

"Or we keep our creations secret," she says, lowering her voice.

"But what about this?" he says, raising his cup of tea to make a toast. "How about believing the things we create are not ours to hide?"

On the veranda of the yurt Indira shares with Lord, the sun dancing in water glasses, Natasha holds her breath and watches Indira, a bald nearly naked woman, read the seven pages composing the start of Natasha's story.

"Tremendous," concludes Indira, tapping the last word of the last line. "However did you think of it?"

"Don't know," says Natasha, shaking her head. "Just came out that way. Though I've never been in an actual jungle."

"Or maybe you have," says Indira, thoughtfully sipping her *chai*. "Our fears cripple us, and fear is composed of thoughts, and these thoughts are made of memories, which is why so many of the most famous writers drank or took drugs to block out the past that so painfully impinged upon their ability to hear the stories wanting to be told."

"It's true," says Natasha, bowing her head in shame. "I'm mostly afraid other people won't like it."

"Forget about other people," says Indira, gesturing to a passing dragonfly. "Write your stories for the spirits."

Z, dark and handsome, takes over for Lord at the counter in Under the Table Books, opens his brand-new big fat notebook and starts scribbling madly, inventing a zany fantasy adventure frolic.

The bell over the door sounds and Z looks up, his bedroom eyes flashing at the sight of Natasha, the premiere love of his life.

"Yo best of everything," he croons. "You who with every gesture makes sense of chaos. Yoo hoo, baby."

"Writing a story?" she asks, frowning curiously at his furious scrawl. "So am I. Or I was."

"I don't know for sure if it's a story," he says, looking down at the sea of symbols, "but it sure is gushing out and I'm gonna *let* it gush until it stops. Then I'll see what I've got. See what I might make of it."

"Oh, thank you," she says, catching his hand and pressing it to her breast. "That's *exactly* what I needed to hear."

Now she dashes out the door, leaving Z stunned, his heart thudding, his train of thought derailed.

"What'd I say?" he murmurs, dazed. "Can I get a witness? Somebody, please. What did I say to make her give me so much love?"

Derek—moments away from being eleven years old—emerges from the *Myth As History* aisle. "You rang?"

"Did you hear me talking to Natasha just now?" asks Z, his mind so full of his beloved he can't remember a single word he said to her. "She pressed my hand to her...um...because of something I said. You gotta help me out here, Derek."

"I would if I could," he says with an apologetic shrug, "but I was so deeply engrossed in *O'Henry's Greatest Hits* the only word I *think* I heard you say was *gushing*."

A Selection of Four Stories

(CAREFULLY CULLED)

from

The MOTHER of ALL UNDER THE TABLE BOOKS *Fiction Soirees*

UNLIMITED FICTIVE OUTBURSTS

Conga Creations Ink

proudly present

a full moon fiction

EXTRAVAGANZA

singing, drumming, dancing, feasting

& Admission As Per Usual &

In Mexico

(Denny recounts a formative adventure
from long ago in his scavenger's life)

The boy is waiting for me on the street outside the bakery, the loaves being brought out fresh from the ovens for those of us knowing to be here before the flies descend on the bread and taint it with their diseases. He has been following me since I pulled into town—San Miguel. I would say he was seven years old, but many of the poor children of Mexico remain small for lack of food. He might be as old as ten or eleven.

"Gracias," I say, smiling at the round little woman as she hands me my big bag of rolls. I give her an American dollar and she tries to give me change. "No, no," I say, "yo quiero pagar un poquito mas. I want to pay a little more." She thanks me profusely.

On the street, a dozen boys swarm around me. I pass out the rolls, saving one for myself and one for the boy who has been following me. He stands apart from the others, refusing to beg. I try to catch his eye, but he will not look at me. I explain to the children, "Yo no tengo mas. I don't have any more." My accent is good, my vocabulary small.

I have been in Mexico for three months. I am running away from California, searching for another California. I am running away from the disastrous end of a misguided love affair, searching for a way out of my shame. I am losing myself in the process of escape. Sometimes the adventure is exhilarating, but more of the time I feel frightened and falling apart inside and out.

I wander down the sunny side of the street, following a divine scent. Someone is cooking something I would very much like to eat. I have little money, but in Mexico, especially in the small towns, I am wealthy. If not for a spinal condition that disqualified me for military service, I could easily have died or been maimed in one of the latest American wars. Or I'd be living in Canada. Or rotting in prison. Or living here, in Mexico.

I have friends who died in Hue and Da Nang, friends who went crazy, friends who killed themselves rather than live besieged day and night by nightmares of carnage. I have friends who died in Afghanistan, a friend who lost his legs in Baghdad. I marched against all those wars, ran from riot police, and went to jail time and again for adding my body and my buses to blockades of induction centers and federal buildings. I helped young men become conscientious objectors. I smuggled dozens of lads into Canada. But the warmongers stay in power and the wars keep going.

The divine scent leads me to the terrace of a large brick house not far from the town plaza. A servant is cooking breakfast on a barbecue. I stop to get a good look. A beautiful middle-aged woman, her face a mask of sorrow, sits in an iron chair at an iron table, waiting to be served. Huge phallic cacti loom above her. She is wearing a pink robe. A cup of coffee steams in the morning sun. The servant brings her a plate of chicken and corn. She heaps on the blazing salsa of her people. Yellow birds flutter around the bulbous red flowers on the cacti shafts. The salsa drips from her mouth as she gorges on tender flesh.

She looks up and sees me. A smile transforms her sorrow into hungry love. "Buenos dias," she cries, licking her lips, her voice trembling. "Are you from United States?"

"Yes," I say, bowing. "Followed my nose. Food smells fantastic."

She thinks I have smelled *her*. She thinks my animal has come for her animal. I can see it in her eager eyes. She invites me to join her. I do. The boy waits for me in the street. I eat a huge breakfast. The woman watches me eat, devouring me with her eyes. She talks and talks about her last visit to Los Angeles, her trip to Disneyland, the beauty of California, her wish to live there.

When I have finished eating, she quietly asks me if I would like to come to bed with her. She is a widow. She is starving for a decent man. There are no good men in town, only lechers and perverts. She loosens her robe as she speaks, allowing me to see her breasts.

"Lo siento," I say, smiling at her. "I'm sorry, but I cannot make love with you. You are very beautiful and I'm honored you would ask me, but I'm still trying to get over a woman I..."

She glares at me, her dark eyes fierce. "I want you, *now*," she whispers, gripping my wrist with her warm fingers. "Why should you deny pleasure for both of us?"

"Lo siento," I say, trying to think how best to explain my reluctance, for the truth is I have longed for just such an invitation, but...

The boy is standing in the street, watching us. He is tiny and brown, a bonsai of a boy, his brown shorts tattered, his yellow shirt free of buttons, his bare feet gray with dust. His legs and arms are little more than bones encased in skin. His head seems too large for his body. He has the face of a little man, his eyes huge and dark.

"Get away from here!" shouts the woman, shaking her fist at the boy. "Get away from here you little bastard."

"I'm sorry," I say, standing up. "He followed me here."

"They laugh at me," she says, pressing her body against mine. "They say horrible things." Her arms encircle me. "Please, señor? Please come to my bed. They torture me."

I pull away from her before I become too aroused. I jump over the low wall that separates her terrace from the street. I wait for her to curse me, but I hear nothing as I stride down the road. The boy falls in behind me. And now an ear of corn, warm and wet with butter, strikes the back of my neck. I don't look back. I hear the sound of the boy eating the corn.

I am sleeping beside a creek south of town. The water is dense with tiny fish. In the morning I will scoop up hundreds of these fellows with my colander and fry them in butter and garlic. I will eat like a king.

The boy is curled up on the ground a few feet from me, close to my fallen fire. I am warm in my sleeping bag. He has no shoes or socks, nothing but his rags.

I do not know he is there. I will wake up and find him so very cold, and I will bring him into my sleeping bag, and we will become friends.

He walks beside me now. We share our meals. I buy him a pair of sandals. We make our camp more permanent. My bag is not big enough for two, so I buy him a sleeping serape. He takes me to the site of an Aztec grave. We hunt for stone carvings, but find only shards. The days go by. He teaches me secret songs at night by the fire. His name is Miguel.

Today, after our morning banquet of fish and beer, Miguel tells me I must go back to the widow's house because she will kill herself if I don't ease her aching sex.

"How do you know about something like that?" I ask him. He seems to be repeating words without comprehending their meaning.

"El Corazon told me," says Miguel, digging at the dirt with his sharp stick—the wooden sword he carries to defend himself. Someday, he often tells me, he will have a gun.

"The heart?" I ask, translating El Corazon, touching my chest.

"No, no," he giggles. "The blind man."

"How would be know?"

"His mind floats in the sky over the city," says Miguel, matter-of-factly. "He knows everything."

"Take me to him. I am eager to meet such a mind. I have many questions to ask him?"

"What questions?"

"Who am I? Where should I go?"

Miguel laughs sweetly. "You are you. You should go where you want to go. I'll come with you."

"Is that what El Corazon will say?"

"How should I know?" says Miguel, wrinkling his nose. "*He* is the mind reader. Not I."

"How much does it cost for a reading?" I ask, my question a reflex in Mexico.

"Not money," says Miguel, disappointed in me.

"What then?"

"Flowers. He loves flowers."

The blind man is not much bigger than Miguel. He lives on three squares of pavement near the train station. His squares are situated between the squares of the woman without legs or arms, fluttering her shoulder fingers, and the squares of the blind couple from Oaxaca, singing so beautifully. Arrayed around the blind ones are diminutive Indian women in colorful blouses and long skirts sitting cross-legged beside piles of chili peppers and potatoes and mangos, crying out their prices.

People come from far and wide to hear the latest gossip from the blind man, to listen to the blind couple sing, to stare in fascination at the pesticide mutant.

"Listen," says the blind man, pointing at me before I can hand him my red roses, "she is near death. Only your man can save her woman."

Everyone is fascinated by his proclamation. I am now the main attraction of the morning market. A hundred women stare at me, many of them nodding. There are few men about because they are in the fields. They are scratching the tired earth, coaxing the corn, and trying to ignore the thunderous rumbling of their empty bellies.

"Go to her," says the blind man. "Go now!"

His command is so direct, so clear, I find myself *running* through town, leaving Miguel far behind.

Her servant leads me down the hall to a massive door. I hear her moaning within. The servant goes away. I open the door. Her bed is dark mahogany, canopied with a cloud of silk. Sunlight streams through her windows. She is naked in her white sheets. Her moaning ceases when she sees me. I take off my clothes and lie down with her and give myself to her.

In the morning, Miguel is waiting for me in the street. The widow has extracted my promise to return in the evening. I don't put much stock in the future, but I will probably honor my promise.

We go to the bakery to buy bread. I feed the army of little boys. Miguel and I find breakfast en *el mercado*. Chicken tacos, *frijoles negros*.

Miguel looks up at me and asks, "You like her. Yes?"

"Perhaps," I say, wishing to keep our sex a holy secret.

Miguel's shoulders shake with laughter. "El Corazon shouted each time you came into her. So many times, hombre."

Women flirt outrageously with me. I walk around on a wave of murmuring. Old men applaud as I pass by. Celebrity alarms me. At sunset, a crowd of people watches me enter the widow's house. They cheer when the front door closes.

The widow is wearing an elegant red gown and red high heels, her hair piled high on her head. She is aflame. We feign an interest in supper and drag each other to her bed.

We make love sleep wake love sleep love wake sleep

At breakfast I ask her, "May Miguel come in the house with us?"

"Miguel?" she says, laughing heartily. "He hates to sleep inside. He prefers the ground."

"How can you say that?" I say, a fierce anger welling up in me.

"Because," she says, showing me her sharp teeth, "he is my son."

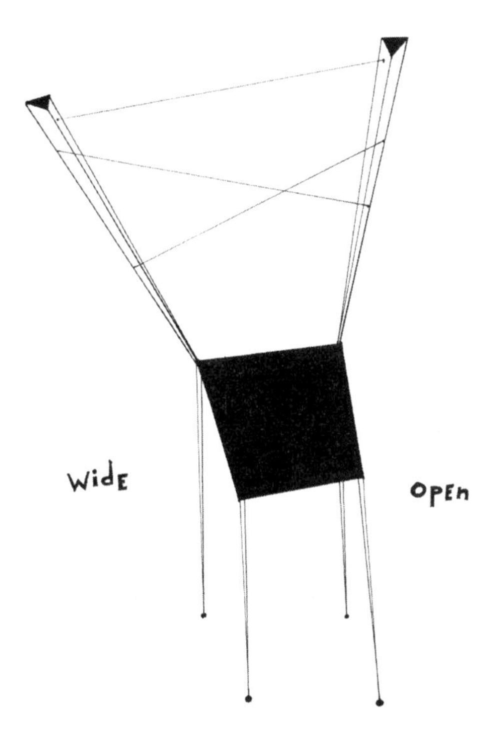

I Was Not Much Interested In Poetry

(Numero Uno writes true fiction)

I was not much interested in poetry. Oh, once, when I was a child, I wrote a poem for my mother on her birthday. The last line was *I love you.* I don't remember the rest. I remember, though, that her eyebrows jumped ever so slightly when she looked at it, that she gave me a fake smile, kissed the air in a way I despised, and put the poem on the arm of the sofa, from where it fluttered to the floor.

She unwrapped the rest of her presents, kissed my stepfather after each unwrapping, exclaimed over a box of chocolates from my stepsister, gathered up her gifts and went to do her face before going out to a champagne brunch. The poem remained on the floor until late that afternoon when my mother and stepfather returned from their waffles and bubbly. My mother, a tidy person, snatched the poem from the floor, saw it was nothing of importance, crumpled it up and threw it away. She had no idea I was watching her. She assumed I was watching television.

And, of course, in high school and again in college, poems were inflicted upon me, my task being to interpret them and relate them to whatever it was the teacher thought they related to. The worst case of this was a philosophy professor who wanted us to find Descartes in Robert Frost. I anguished over the assignment for a week, dropped the class and eventually dropped out of college.

I didn't blame poetry. I merely associated it with unpleasant parts of my life.

And yet I went to poetry readings. Not to hear poems, God, no. In those days I would rather have listened to AM radio. I had never understood a poem read out loud. I could barely understand the poems I had systematically analyzed in school. Besides, most of the poets I heard mumbled when they read, or they made their voices sound unnatural, or they pronounced words so they didn't sound like words, or they would stop sentences where no natural sentence would ever willingly stop, and they read too fast or too slow, and in between poems they would tell inane stories about where they got the idea or who they wrote it for or why it was funny. That, I think, was the most repulsive thing they did, tell us in advance that the thing was supposed to be funny, when it never was, and we were supposed to *try* to laugh, which was like trying to be turned on, or trying to be happy.

But the worst thing of all, yes, this was the worst for me, was when they would proclaim their extreme and unique sensitivity, implying that their pain was somehow greater than yours or mine, their fears more profound. Their love, their desire, their joy, their visions were stronger and better than any we could ever hope to experience. And in that way they reminded me of my mother and her fake smile and her fake kissing of the air and her fake love and her fake husbands and fake life.

Yet I went to poetry readings. Why? Because I enjoyed everything about them, other than the poetry and the reading of the poems. I enjoyed the arrival of the audience, the enthusiastic milling around, the finding of seats, the avid anticipation. And most of all, I enjoyed watching the people listening, or, as in my case, the pretending to listen.

And my hope, the force that launched me into the night in those days, was that a woman would appear at the reading, and in the milling around, and in the finding of her seat, she would reveal herself to be desirable to me. Should this hope be fulfilled, I would attempt to position myself so that during the period of anticipation and during the actual reading of the dreaded verses, I might watch her listen, and hope of hopes, entice her to look at me, to introduce myself with a smile, to convince her I was worth at least a hello during the deliciously long poetry reading intermission.

This happened more often than you might imagine. True, these relationships rarely lasted much beyond the hellos, but once, yes, once, the hello took root, and before I realized what had happened, the garden of my soul, if you will, was rife with the Bermuda grass of love.

Thereby hangs this tale. A poet would make short work of it.

A man, desperate for love, goes to a poetry reading, though he despises poetry. The place is crowded, despite the rain. The man has never been to a poetry reading where more than twenty people showed up. He wonders what could be so special about this particular reading. Moments before the poems are to be read, he spies a woman entering late, a woman of such clear beauty, such honest proportions, such an intensity about her that the lights of the room seem to be focused on her, or do they emanate *from* her?

It is impossible for him to know anything except that he has been struck deep in his heart by the desire to love her.

She, much to his surprise, meets his gaze with a smile of sweet surrender. Or so it seems. They exchange several exceedingly long glances during the first set, in which one poet reads with no sense of rhythm, and another reads with no sense of anything. Or so it seems.

At the break, the man and woman approach each other, she all smiles and welcome, he grinning like a fool. They exchange names. Harriet Jones. Alan Webster. They share a cup of coffee. They banter happily about everything and everyone they see. Suddenly she becomes horribly preoccupied and excuses herself, leaving him desolate and alone. Years later, the intermission ends.

He returns to his seat, baffled and hurt. The woman does not return to her seat. *How*, he wonders, *can such highs and lows coexist in so small a space, on such a flat plane as this?*

Moments later, the master of ceremonies announces, "Now for the star of our show, the poet we are so very fortunate to have in our midst tonight, the incomparable Harriet Jones."

Never, let me repeat that in case you missed it, *never* have I listened so intently to poetry. I hung to and clung to and licked and chewed and swallowed and digested and integrated into my mind and heart and stomach and lungs and blood all her beautiful phrasing and tempo and clarity and honesty and humor and pathos and hope. And when she delivered her last line, culminating forty of the most intense minutes of my life, and that line was *I love you*, and the audience rose as one in a tumult of joy, I was a confirmed lover of poetry and have been so to this day.

But to then say that she came to me, threw her arms around me and said, "I have never read so well in all my life, and it was because of you," well, death might have come for me then and I would have greeted it like an old friend, content my life had not been ill spent.

We went to a bistro, Harriet and I and eleven of her fans. I sat between my darling Jones and a fat smelly man with a mustache. He started each and every one of his innumerable diatribes with the phrase, "Okay, so here's the deal." And though the repetition of these words drove me to the brink of madness, I barely minded because Harriet's hand was on my arm, squeezing it every time he said, "Okay, so here's the deal." And then I began to associate the words with the squeezing, and I learned that if I peppered him with questions he would *have* to begin again and again with, "Okay, so here's the deal," and she would *have* to squeeze me, and it was, all in all, a delicious way to survive.

Out on the street, three in the morning, Harriet took my hand and said, "It was great meeting you, Alan. I'd love to see you again."

"Why not now?" Everything I had ever thought or been told screamed at me to take her in my arms and kiss her. I moved to do so, guided by my overriding desire to consume her.

But she transformed my aggression into a mutual embrace, whispering, "I'm happily married, Alan. I do love you. You make me feel more alive than I've felt in years, but I only sleep with my husband and he only sleeps with me."

Then she kissed me on the mouth, and I felt her passion for me, and her acceptance of me, and her love for me, but not sexual love. It was a revelation. It was the beginning of a new life. It was, in truth, an inoculation, an inculcation, a brand burned on my lips forever that reads

**THIS MAN
IS THE PROPERTY
OF POETRY**

When He Was

(Tomas gives his life a story)

He celebrates his thirtieth birthday by moving his few possessions into the apartment above the bookstore. He invites Sally over after she gets off work at the coffeehouse. A fiercely hot night, they fill his claw-foot tub with cold water, smoke dope, listen to Miles and Cannonball, drink champagne, and immerse themselves in the cool until midnight.

They make love in front of an open window on his new mattress, a whisper of a breeze kissing their sweaty bodies, Sally humming her delight as he loves her with urgent slowness.

He leaves her snoring atop the sopping sheets and tiptoes into the bathroom to take a cold shower. He peers at the face in the mirror, smiling and frowning in dim recognition of what he has become. "What are you now?" he asks quietly. "What will you be a year from now?"

His sideburns are uneven. His left foot is one size larger than his right. He loves spicy food, though it causes him heartburn, still he loves it.

When he was six years old, he kissed a girl named Diana and experienced a profound sexual longing, a heavy heat in his chest and loins and throat, though he had no idea at the time this was sexual longing. There was a depth to Diana's kiss, a hot truth, a prescient familiarity that subsequent kisses did not bring him until he made love to the wife of his sociology professor, one bright night in a redwood forest overlooking Monterey Bay. She was thirty-three, he was nineteen.

Her legs around him, her back cushioned by a sloping mound of redwood duff, their tongues engaged in a dolphin dance of mutual admiration, he felt as if he had finally made his way back to the unknowing wisdom of his childhood. She spoke softly, instructing and complimenting him, and giving forth a hearty groan as he released himself inside her.

He adorns the walls of his apartment with posters of paintings that make him feel mildly uneasy. "I am trying to overcome my aversions," he explains to the women he brings home for sex and conversation.

One of the paintings is Picasso's *The Three Musicians*. "The thing feels full of death," he says to Sally one night, the rain rapping on the bedroom window.

"Where?" she asks, reluctant to release him, loving his weight in her arms.

He gets out of bed and moves slowly toward the painting. "There," he says, pointing fearfully at the face of the white-capped flute player. "And there. And there."

"All the faces," says Sally, sending him a silent plea to rub her aching feet.

He sits on the bed and reaches under the covers. "And their clothes, and the shadows. The whole thing."

"You were a musician, weren't you?" she says, sighing with pleasure at his strong tender touch.

Her question bores into him like the twisting seed of a wild oat.

When he was six years old, he sat down at the first piano he was allowed to touch, and he played the most beautiful music he had ever heard, glimpsing in that moment of unconscious creation a glorious parallel universe inhabited by naked dancers.

When he was twenty-four, perpetually enraged, a user of desperate young girls, his hair a black snarl splashed with yellow paint, slave to a money-hungry manager, addicted to hashish and speed, he shaved his head and took a sledge hammer to his electric keyboards and synthesizers and amplifiers and microphones, smashing them into tiny bits.

His birthdays are often days of action and change for him. On his thirty-seventh, he and two friends wrestle an old piano up the narrow stairs to his well-worn apartment above the used bookstore. He strains his back in the uphill tussle and has to lie on ice for two days before he can even dream of sitting at the piano to see what he might do.

He touches middle C and realizes he is now four years older than his sociology professor's wife was when he made love to her on that glorious night eighteen years ago. He limps to his ancient refrigerator and drinks three dark beers, imagining himself finding his sociology professor's wife's telephone number and calling her, arranging a rendezvous, flying to Iowa—*why Iowa?*—hitching a ride in the back of a pickup through endless fields of ripening corn to her lovely Victorian farmhouse, her husband sitting in his wheelchair among the pansies, a docile invalid now. She is luscious and adoring, and immediately leads him to her bed.

"I gotta tune my piano," he murmurs, closing the refrigerator.

Forty-four.

"Four and four is eight," he says, gulping his third pint of beer.

It's *Grateful Dead* night at the Rubicon brewery, the sound system blasting out a bootlegged recording of Jerry and the boys doing an old *Moby Grape* tune. *Would you let me walk down the street, naked if I want to?*

"Eight," he says, snapping his fingers. "I was eight and now I'm forty-four." He snaps his fingers again. "Just like that."

Ariana, so young she might be his daughter, her eyes lit with strong dope, takes his hand and peers at his palm. "I see sex in your life." She grins gigantically. "As soon as we get home."

"Home," he says, seeing the rooms of his apartment above the bookstore, the walls white, a single word in small black letters printed in the center of each massive rectangle. LOVE SING COOK WATER BREATHE KISS. "Ariana, you called my apartment *home*."

"Who said we were going to your place?" she replies, unwilling to fight him. "I have an apartment, too."

"You have roommates," he says, leering at her. "We can't moan and groan and shout when we fuck at your place."

"They don't mind," she says sullenly. "You're the one who minds."

"Let's go to my place," he says, lurching to his feet, praying that in coitus everything will be set right, the confusion ended, his guilt dispelled, the tender truth revealed.

But he is too sick to make love. He drinks a quart of bubbly water and sits on the toilet, feeling old and trembly. Ariana comes to the bathroom door naked, a red ribbon around her waist, a floppy bow covering her pubic hair, her long honey-brown mane escaped from braids. “Happy birthday,” she says softly. “I’ll be in bed. Your bed.”

He climbs the stairs to his roof garden and pees on his marijuana plant that shares a redwood tub with a voluptuous cherry tomato vine. He holds his penis and closes his eyes, imagining his old lover Sally waiting for him in bed, but he cannot quite recall the contours of her face.

The kettle whistles, rousing him from an involuntary nap. “How the fuck did I get down here?” he asks, surprised to be sitting in his kitchen. He peeks into the bedroom. Ariana is sleeping soundly, humming softly with each exhalation. He brews a cup of ginseng tea and tells himself he’s feeling better now, tells himself he will drink the tea, pee once more, rouse Ariana and make love to celebrate his forty-fourth. *To prove what?*

“That I can?” he says, rising slowly to his feet, feverish and frightened.

He gulps the scalding tea and returns to his cannabis bush.

“I wish I had a garden,” he says, opening to memory.

He is seven years old, roaming the wooded lot across the street from the apartment building where he lives with his mother. His feet are tough as leather. He has a long wooden spear. He imagines he is an Indian brave. He eats ants and insects and wild seeds, knowing instinctively to chew them well before swallowing. In a fern-clogged gully canopied by an old oak, he makes little fires and holds long conversations with the spirits who grow more and more trusting of him with each passing day.

He lights a bundle of sage, and as the sweet smoke fills the gully, spirits come to him. Here is Ee Jima the horned toad lizard and Lucky the crow and Jumasa the hummingbird and Tuk the gopher snake. And here, too, are the unseen ones riding on gusts of wind and rising from the earth through the roots and stems and brilliant purple flowers of the never thirsty thistles. The spirits come to hold council with him—the great mystery power manifesting in clouds above him—floating topographies of love.

But now Father, deathly drunk, finds him in the gully and beats him mercilessly. "Teach you to play with matches," says Father, dropping him in the dust and peeing on the sacred fire.

For his forty-ninth birthday, he treats himself to a massage from Sally. He hasn't seen her in five years. A renowned masseuse now, Sally greets him at the front door of the midtown Victorian she shares with her two husbands, Arthur and Felipe. She is three months pregnant, her hair as white as snow, her voice an octave deeper than he remembers. He stares at her in disbelief until she calls him by his secret name.

Her massage table stands beneath a tulip tree in full bloom. She watches him disrobe, carefully studying his posture and movements. The process feels oddly familiar to him, though it is wholly new. He lies face down on the cushioned table. They do not speak.

Her hands are strong. He forgets she was once his lover. He forgets a woman is touching him. She finds a tangle of muscles in his back and undoes it with her strong fingers, and when the last knot gives way around the central nerve, he weeps and weeps and weeps.

"Rest now," she whispers. "Drift away."

He is six years old, playing on the pull-up bar in the doorway at home. He swings his legs up in front of him and the bar disengages and he falls to the concrete floor, crushing four of his vertebrae, his father cursing, "Shit, I was gonna fix that."

Sally returns with two cups of tea. They sit on a porch swing and she says, "This is the tip of the iceberg, you know. There is so much more to get out, to be free of. If you want to keep working with me, I'll give you a great price break. For old-time's sake."

Fifty-five, staying in a cottage on the coast, he lies on his back on the floor beside the fire, his eyes closed. A woman sits cross-legged beside him, playing her accordion.

He is journeying across a vast prairie, riding on the back of a huge tiger, his naked thighs gripping the beast. They move through high grass to the edge of a dark jungle. The tiger says silently, "This is a place of great suffering."

They find a three-year-old boy in a crib, the baby's forehead pressed against the bars, his eyes squeezed shut in terror, his mother looming above him, her hair a mass of hissing vipers, her eyes dripping blood, her demon voice growling, "Die, you little monster. Die, you thief of my life!"

He chases away the demon and lifts the baby boy from the crib, holding him firmly in his strong arms, mounting the tiger and flying with the child into the great void.

"But how will I live without her?" asks the baby boy. "I am so small. I can barely walk. What will I eat?"

"I will feed you," he replies. "You will grow strong and brave. I will never abandon you."

He stands on a hillside above the sea, the sky rich with stars. He yearns to touch his mother, to make a final peace with her. He brings a slender stick to his lips, kisses it, snaps it in two.

I Remember You

(Felix reenacts the high point of his thirtieth high school reunion)

Here we are together again. Do you remember me? Think back. Remember in the first grade, the day I arrived? I tickled someone during nap. He tickled me first, I tickled him back. He giggled, I got caught. Teacher had me up in front of the class. I looked out and saw you, just as I'm seeing you now. Your eyes haven't changed. Decades it's been since that first day, and I could still dive into those eyes and swim forever. Which is what I did way back when. I dove in and swam and swam and whatever the teacher said to me felt like fine mist. Didn't hurt at all.

You don't remember.

How about second grade? I sang aloud when everybody else was quiet. We were singing *Rock My Soul In the Bosom of Abraham*, and when we got to the word *bosom* no one would say it because they thought it was naughty but I didn't know it was naughty so I sang *bosom* real loud and everyone laughed and I looked at you and I could see in your eyes you thought it was fine I sang it loud and I've never forgotten that.

You have.

Okay. Third grade. Folk dancing. Square dancing. Four boys, four girls, best in the class, you and I among them, you were partnered with Mike Watkins, I was with Christine Chan. May Day festival. The whole school was there, hundreds of parents, teachers, brothers and sisters. I wore a cowboy hat too big for me and cowboy boots too small, and you were so lovely in your red madras skirt, your lips glossy with red lipstick. And you'd painted your fingernails red and your hair was in a long ponytail tied with a red ribbon.

And just as the boys met in the middle, touching our raised right hands together and walking in a circle, the girls circling the other way around us, each of us waiting for the caller to shout, "Break that circle, find your gal" just before his voice might have covered my shame, I farted. And this was no ordinary fart, but a trumpet blast from deep within that stunned the crowd and caused my fellow cowboys to pull their hands away from mine and point, yes, they did, they pointed at me and the multitudes laughed.

And you wouldn't look at me.

You don't remember? Amazing. That event is burned so deeply into my mind it may be the last thing I ever remember. I can see myself on my deathbed, reliving that awesome square-dancing fart.

Maybe this will do it. Sixth grade. I kissed you. I was waiting in line to play tetherball, to challenge the reigning champ, Darcy Wainwright. Surely you remember Darcy, the golden boy with billionaire parents. He took private tetherball lessons. He had his own court. He trained with professionals so he could dominate us prols at recess. I was standing there, watching him obliterate some girl, itching to get my fists on the ball, when Joey Turner came up to me and whispered that you and Sheila Dempsey were in the bathroom selling long kisses for fifty cents, and I said, "How long?" and Joey said, "Minutes."

So I ran up there to the highest wing of the school and followed the cigarette smoke to the boys' room and got in line and watched Sheila Dempsey with her enormous lips kiss one boy after another, thrusting her tongue into their mouths.

But I couldn't look at you. I didn't want to see you kissing other boys. I wanted to pretend you were mine all mine. And when it was my turn, I stood before you and said, "If I had fifty dollars I'd never let anyone else ever kiss you."

And you said, "Fifty cents, please."

And I noticed you were sad. I had always been too smitten and never close enough to see your sadness. I looked into your eyes and gasped at the depth of them. I wanted to fall into you. I was ten years old and I wanted to merge with you, knowing nothing of sex.

You picked the coins from my sweaty palm, dropped them into a sequin change purse, put a practiced hand at the back of my head, and drew my mouth to yours. And then you pried open my lips with your strong little tongue and gave me the thrill of my life.

You remember the kissing, but you don't remember me. No, no, I'm not offended. Absolutely not. You processed us like cartons of milk. Why would you remember me? Well, I'll tell you. Enough early childhood. Come back with me to high school, to those hormone-clogged corridors of that stifling prison of our puberty, that concentration camp of conformity that killed all but the strongest impulses of creativity. Surely you'll remember those tortuous years, the murderous tedium, the nauseating burden of senseless homework and the crushing stupidity of television.

My friends called me Saint because I was allergic to alcohol and because I took it upon myself to drive my drunken buddies home after dances and parties. I enjoyed it. It fulfilled my cab driver fantasies and made me feel useful.

There was one guy, Phillip Johansson, ring a bell? He claimed to have been your first lover. I see by your eyes that this is probably not so. I thought not. A liar he was, but Phillip was my friend. We shared a love for early Ray Charles albums and Nat King Cole. Phillip smoked marijuana, a taste I had not yet acquired, and when he was high, we would talk deeply about things important to sixteen-year-old boys.

What things? Oh, we mostly talked about why the most wonderful girls always had such brutes or idiots for boyfriends, and why we sensitive, witty guys could only manage neurotic liaisons or none at all. Our favorite theory was that wonderful girls secretly wanted to be with us, truly, but feared retribution from their peers, or their mothers, or possibly from the brutes themselves.

We talked about what we'd do after high school, what we would become, what our lives would mean. I was going to be a playwright actor, famous at twenty, a national treasure at thirty, a global force at forty. Phillip was going to be a great guitarist, composer, Zen Buddhist polygamist. He would marry a black woman, a Chinese woman, and a Peruvian princess, become a master of mescaline and write an opera of such intense beauty and power that music as we knew it would be changed for all time. He would live in a castle in Spain overlooking the ocean. He would travel by hot-air balloon from concert to concert. I would live in San Francisco when I wasn't in Katmandu.

Phillip would get so drunk some nights I had to carry him from the car and put him to bed. His parents had given him their garage as his world apart. The walls were papered with Avalon Ballroom posters, my favorite being Jimi Hendrix in a purple haze, leaning back in ecstasy as he played. Phillip burned incense and kept his clothes in two neat stacks, one dirty, one clean. His stereo system was monumental, each speaker the size of a man. He had piles of esoteric magazines, a big old Turkish water pipe, and huge paisley pillows for furniture. His bed was a mattress on the floor. His sheets were tie-dyed blue and red and green.

I would carry him to bed, take off his shoes and cover him. And then I'd stay for a while, perched on a pillow, watching him sleep, wondering how he would survive without me, wondering how any of my friends would survive.

And then I'd think about you and tell myself that on Monday I would speak to you and ask you to go out with me. You would be pleasantly stunned and say something like, "Well, it's about time, Felix. God, I've been waiting for years and years." Then I'd imagine our first date, the awkward hello, the funny drive into the city, the pool hall spaghetti, the poetry reading, our first amazing embrace on the hill overlooking the fairy tale lights of the city I would one day conquer with my play about...something I couldn't quite yet elucidate. But I would get it, yes, I would, as soon as I was free of school and rules and parents.

And then, of course, we would kiss, and you would say that it had never been like this, so dizzying and addictive that we should never be parted, not even by death.

I realize now, as I refused to realize then, that my vision of us joined like that was hardly unique. You were desired by hundreds of boys at our school, and not merely because you were so lovely, but because of the way you looked into our eyes and remembered our names. Over the years I've run into dozens of guys from the old days, and you are always the first person they ask about. And they always mention that you remembered their names and would say hello to them in the halls when no other beautiful girl would give them the time of day. But you always did give them that little bit of your time, which must have lifted their spirits as you did mine.

You know all this. I know you do, and I appreciate your allowing me to go on like this. You'll be relieved to know I am fast approaching the denouement, that moment I don't *think* you could have forgotten, but then maybe you have. I can only imagine, and not in any profound way, what it must have been like to be you, a young woman so desired and so misunderstood. Perhaps this largest of my teenage memories is only a flicker in the vast universe of your experience. I suppose, things being what they are or seem to be, it doesn't matter whether you remember me or not, but I hope you do.

I was driving home, having discharged the last of my discombobulated friends, Phillip, as it happened. I was rehearsing what I would say to my mother when she asked me why I had stayed out so late.

I said, "Mother, the time has come for this nonsense to end. I am no longer a child, I'm a man. If I choose to drive about on a summer's night, what difference does it make if I come in at one or two or three?"

I knew this was weak. It was her car, after all, and she worried and didn't sleep when I stayed out late. It was her house and I was her child, grown or not.

So I said, "I'm sorry, Mom. Something has me wild and jittery these days. I'm too restless to sleep, too restless to stay home. I hope you understand it's not about you. It's about *me*. Me. I'm changing into something else. I feel...too big for this body, like I want to shed my skin and start all over again."

And as I said that, I came to the stop sign where a right turn would take me to the river. It was a turn I never made at night. There were killers and crazy people down by the river. I heard my mother's voice saying, "Only a fool would go there alone at night."

"I'm a fool," I said, making the turn, wondering if I would have the courage to park the car and venture down to the water's edge.

And oh, what a heart-thumping shock it was to see your car parked there on the levee, that Mustang I knew so well, having watched you get in and out of it a thousand gorgeous times, and you barely knowing I existed.

It never occurred to me you might be with someone. It never entered my mind. I parked my mother's car beside yours, forgot to be afraid, and went in search of you. I moved swiftly through the high grass, instinctively heading south.

I found you sitting by the river, barely visible in the faint moonlight, talking to the air. You were drunk and slurring your words. You said, "Oh, God, it's such a mess and I'm sick of it. I'm sick of it. You hear me? Sick of it. I pray and pray and pray and you send me guys who just want to do it to me. Nothing else. They don't even see me, they don't even hear me, they don't care what I think, they just want to get on and get off. I pray and pray to you and now my favorite teacher touches me when nobody's looking and says he's gotta have me. I beg you and beg you and beg you and there's always somebody else wants to get on and get off, and I'm sick of it. Sick of it."

You stopped talking. The river rushed by. I heard a metallic clicking and I knew you had a gun, so I called your name.

"Who is it?" you asked, whispering harshly. "Leave me alone."

"It's me. Felix."

"What are you doing here?"

"I saw your car. I thought you might be in trouble."

"You sure...you sure you don't just wanta do it to me?"

"I'm sure."

"Come here then, mister hero, lemme see which one you are."

You illuminated me with your cigarette lighter. I took your wrist and moved the flame so I could see your eyes, your huge brown eyes, wet with tears.

"I know you," you said. "Felix, right? Funny guy in English. I'm drunk. Sorry about that. I'm a mess. I really am."

"May I have the gun?"

"No, Felix, you may not. This is my ticket to ride. My way out. This is the end and good riddance."

"But why?"

"Because I feel horrible. All day and all night, Felix. Every day. It gnaws and gnaws at me. I'm nothin' but a thing, Felix. I'm nothin' but a thing and I'm sick of it and I'm gonna stop it right now."

"Well, I've never thought about you in that way. I think of your voice, how even just speaking it's like a beautiful song. I think of your eyes, how you're never afraid to look right into the heart of things. I think of your face, your mouth, how incredibly honest you are when you talk in class and say exactly what you think without ever worrying about looking stupid, which you never do. And I love the way you move. You're a dancer through and through, and sometimes I walk beside you in the halls without you knowing it and I feel like Fred Astaire with Ginger Rogers, about to take your hand and swirl away with you."

"You're just being nice to me to get what you want."

"No. It's truly how I feel."

"So now I'm supposed to say, 'Oh, Felix, my hero, you're so different from the other animals, let's get married.' Right?"

"Right. Except first we kiss and the heavens open and..."

"Don't say heaven. Don't say God or love or any of that. Okay? Just don't say it. I'm sick of it."

"Why?"

"Because there is no God, Felix. I pray to God all my life and nothing good ever happens to me. Only bad and worse and worse all the time and now the pain is so horrible I can't wait to be dead. That's not how it would be if there was a God, Felix. It wouldn't be this way. I know it wouldn't. So could you please leave? Please?"

We sat there for maybe an hour, maybe ten minutes. Impossible to know. We were suspended in space, a dark cloud obscuring the moon, the universe rushing by.

Finally I said, "If I can prove to you there's a God, will you give me the gun and promise to live for at least one more day?"

And you said, "If you can prove there's a God, I'll make you feel so good your life will never be the same."

"And you will live another day?"

"I'll live forever if you prove it."

So I told you everything. I told you about the first time I saw you, about the bosom of Abraham, the fart, the fifty-cent kiss, the years of silent adoration culminating in a moment when I took a road I had never had the courage to take before.

What brought me there at that precise moment? What gave me the strength to turn? I don't know, and I don't know if I believed in God until then, sharing the darkness with you, seeing clearly for the first time that my destiny was to talk people out of death, to convince you, however I could, that life is an incredible intersection of miracles, and that we are all empowered by God or Nature or whatever you want to call it, to heal ourselves, and to heal each other.

Then, as they say in all my favorite stories, we talked until dawn. And as the light came upon the earth, I hurled the gun far out into the river. We walked to our cars. You held my hand. We did not kiss. You lived another day.

Yeah, that was me. And that was you. So here we are, together again. How have you been? I mean, how are you?

Alfredo de San Francisco

(formerly known as Myron Weinstock)

"I am seeking warriors to join me in the fight to save the rainforest," says Alfredo de San Francisco, addressing Mr. Laskin. "And not just any rainforest. The last pristine tropical rainforest on the planet."

Ensconced on his favored bench in Plaza Park, Mr. Laskin, a handsome white-haired man wearing tennis shoes, blue jeans, white dress shirt, and a brown suede jacket, looks up from his newspaper and squints at the person standing before him. The morning sun is directly behind Alfredo de San Francisco, so to Mr. Laskin the man is little more than a black blob against a blindingly bright background, a palm tree sprouting from the top of his head.

"I once owned the greater part of the Amazon basin," says Mr. Laskin, clearing his throat. "But they took it all away from me when I passed the trillion-dollar mark. But that was then and now is now. And speaking of now, you're blocking my light."

Alfredo de San Francisco, a chubby man of fifty-seven wearing brand-new camouflage combat fatigues, squints at Mr. Laskin and says with appealing urgency, "If we don't save the rainforest, there's no hope. None. It's over."

"So what else is new?" says Mr. Laskin, glaring at a picture of a house on fire. "And what is it you're hoping *for?* Salvation? Love?"

"Oxygen," says Alfredo de San Francisco, clenching his fists. "They're cutting out the lungs of the planet."

"You know what your problem is?" says Mr. Laskin, nodding slowly to confirm his assessment. "You're thirty years too late."

As if drawn by a powerful magnet, Alfredo de San Francisco finds his way to Under the Table Books, arriving at the moment Natasha bequeaths control of the cash register to Lord Bellmaster. The front of the bookstore is bathed in sunlight, the seven bookstore felines sitting shoulder to shoulder in the doorway awaiting the street-sweeping monster that goes by every fourth Wednesday.

"What *is* this place?" asks Alfredo de San Francisco, awestruck by the cavernous store and the lovely brown woman placing a green visor on the head of a handsome white man in need of a shave.

"Welcome to Under the Table Books," says Natasha, bowing to Alfredo de San Francisco. "Epicenter of anarchist exchange."

"Certainly more than meets the eye," says Lord, wrinkling his nose at Alfredo de San Francisco's getup, combat fatigues particularly tiresome to Lord. "Let me know if we may be of assistance."

"I am seeking warriors to join me in the fight to save the rainforest," says Alfredo de San Francisco, standing as tall as his minimalist height will allow. "And not just *any* rainforest, but the last pristine tropical rainforest on the planet."

"We have a bulletin board where you can post a flyer," says Natasha, disappearing down the stairs. "See you later, Lord."

"Break a leg," says Lord, tapping the *Open* button on the gigantic old cash register, curious to see the contents of the till. "She's auditioning for a major motion music video. That woman can dance."

"I love the vibe of this place," says Alfredo de San Francisco, gazing rapturously around the store. "There's something so sixties early seventies about all this."

"Would that be the *nineteen* sixties or the *eighteen* sixties?" asks Lord, pleasantly surprised to find so many bills and coins so neatly organized.

"Nineteen, of course," snorts Alfredo de San Francisco, frowning at Lord. "How would I know about the eighteen?"

"Books, past lives, imagination," says Lord, dealing a hand of solitaire. "Hungry? We have three well-stocked refrigerators down the hall, and just past the refrigerators you'll find the bulletin board and the inspiringly clean unisex bathroom."

"May I confess something to you?" asks Alfredo de San Francisco, feeling an irresistible urge to tell Lord Bellmaster the story of his life.

"That's what I'm here for," says Lord, nodding in appreciation of the hand he's dealt. "It is my destiny to hear your confession."

"Until I had my vision seventeen days ago," says Alfredo de San Francisco, looking around for something to sit on, "I always walked the straight and narrow. Fearfully obedient, college, graduate school, career, marriage, children, houses, cars, money." He sighs. "I fulfilled my parents' every expectation of what their son should think and be and do."

"Do be do be do," says Lord, liking the way the cards are falling.

"But then two years ago on March fourth, my fifty-fifth birthday, everything started to come apart. At the seams. Nothing made any sense. Then the nightmares began and I kept waking up not knowing who I was. My wife became a stranger to me and when my daughter came home from college I couldn't remember her name."

"That might be just as well," says Lord, slapping down the jack of hearts. "Kids these days are forever changing their names."

"In desperation I went into therapy," says Alfredo de San Francisco, biting his already masticated fingernails. "I began with a Freudian, then transferred to a Jungian, and finally to a Pharmaceuticalist. He put me on massive mood neutralizers to bring down the highs and lift up the lows, but I continued to feel..."

"Lost," says Lord, gathering up the cards mid-game as the bookstore cats begin their ecstatic mewing at the impending arrival of Indira, Lord's beloved: AKA She Who Feeds The Cats.

"More than lost," says Alfredo de San Francisco, frowning in annoyance at the urgent cries of the kitties. "I felt certain I had wasted my life. Utterly. Every minute of it."

"I was there, too," says Lord, gazing doorward as Indira's shadow falls across the threshold. "But no more."

"Because you found a purpose for your life," says Alfredo de San Francisco, smacking his fist into his palm. "As have I."

"Yes, yes, yes," says Lord, his mouth falling open in voracious adoration as Indira follows her shadow through the doorway—her *sari* gold, her perfectly round head freshly shaved, the center of her forehead dotted neon blue, her right hand raised in an elegant *mudra* of sexual generosity, her left hand gripping the red and white ice chest containing a feline feast of *flan aux fruits de mer*—a veritable seafood potpourri.

"*Bon jour mon amour*," says Indira, her accent and syntax thickly French this morning. "I am so very much needing kisses from you on every part of me."

"*Mon plaisir*," says Lord, flying to her side. "I'm famished."

"But we only ate an hour ago," she growls into his ear—his lips touching her throat.

"Eternity," murmurs Lord, diving into her heavenly cleavage.

"We are closely observed," murmurs Indira, swooning at her lover's touch. "By *un petit gendarme*."

"Oh," says Lord, reluctantly disengaging from his lover. "May I present Alfresco de Santa Barbara."

"Al*fredo* de San Fran*cisco*," says Alfredo de San Francisco, bowing as gallantly as his camouflage fatigues will allow. "I am seeking warriors to join me in the fight to save the rainforest. And not just *any* rainforest, but the last pristine tropical rainforest on the planet."

In a twinkling, Indira's dreamy smile changes to a fierce frown. "Are you serious," she asks, taking a step closer to Alfredo de San Francisco. "You're not just another nutcase are you?"

"I…I don't think so," says Alfredo de San Francisco, stunned by the intensity of Indira's gaze. "I had a vision. A waking dream. Followed by a crystal-clear-cut epiphany. I was floating above the earth and…"

"You saw the forest burning," says Indira, taking another step away from Lord toward Alfredo de San Francisco. "And you knew the entire planet was on fire."

"Yes," he says, frowning suspiciously. "How did you know?"

"I dreamt the same dream," she whispers passionately. "And I joined a band of renegades to fight the despoilers. We became denizens of the forest. We had nothing but our loyalty to each other and our fierce desire to save the last splendors of Eden."

"From your lips to God's ears," says Alfredo de San Francisco, beaming. "My first recruit."

"And maybe your second," says Lord, aching to spend the rest of his life with Indira—at any cost.

The Courtship of Z and Natasha

(collision bafflement awareness compassion adjustment
confusion frustration anger avoidance remorse
reunion acceptance forgiveness love)

Z, a devilishly handsome young black man—sexy fizz of hair, brilliant smile, easy grace, gorgeous hands—wearing the latest in jumpsuits, a Flash Gordon burgundy affair, pulls up in front of Under the Table Books in the newest of Jaguars, the blazing black paint so fresh it still looks wet, the engine purring like ten thousand contented cats, the stereo pouring love jazz into the sultry summer evening.

Young brown Natasha, dressed way beyond the nines in a shimmering white dress clinging to her glorious curves in such a way she seems more naked than if she *were* naked, her wavy black hair glistening from a henna wash, her feet shod in red Romanesque sandals, her kiss-me lips danger-zone red, comes dancing out of the store with big brown eyes growing huge at the sight of Z's exquisite ride.

Derek, a slender white kid in gray dungarees and a green *Save the Biosphere* T-shirt, his dirty blond hair in need of a trim, follows Natasha out to the curb to gawk at the snazzy car and gaze adoringly upon Natasha—the first serious crush of his little-boy life.

"Wow, Z," says Derek, gushing with admiration. "What a beautiful car. Is it yours?"

"Until midnight," he says, gallantly opening the door for Natasha. "Then it turns back into a pumpkin."

Natasha kisses Z's cheek. "I *love* you referencing Cinderella. This whole dress-up thing is *so* much fun."

"Wait," sings Lord Bellmaster, more unshaven than ever as he emerges from the store with a huge old box camera acquired in exchange for a pristine first-edition volume two of *The Collected Short Stories of Somerset Maugham*. "Posterity. Incongruous juxtapositions. You and that new car and this old store and the night and the music fill me with photographic desire. You and the night and the music so bright means I love you."

"I never thought we'd leave," says Z, his patience sorely tested by the photo session. "I think that man's got designs on you."

Natasha gives Z a withering look. "Ex*cuse* me? Designs?"

"Lust," says Z, frowning at the road ahead. "Easy to see Lord wants to get you in his bed. Moustafa, too."

"*You* don't lust after sexy women?" says Natasha, folding her arms. "I think you do."

Z grips the steering wheel and snarls, "Well, I don't happen to appreciate other men looking at my woman like that."

"Stop the car," says Natasha, holding her breath. "Stop this car *now* or I will never speak to you again."

Z pulls over in front of a derelict warehouse, the flat-topped roof a roost for myriad pigeons, the boarded-up windows plastered with posters for a reggae concert ten years ago.

"Oh, let's not get into a fight, baby doll," he pleads. "We're way late for the party as it is."

"*Baby* doll?" she says, gaping incredulously. "*Your* woman? Z, I got news for you, I'm not your baby doll *or* your woman. And if you think you *own* me now because I slept with you one time and we had barely adequate sex, then you apparently haven't heard a word I've said since first we met." She opens the door and jumps out. "See you later. *Much* later."

Z turns off the engine and bows his head. "No no no. Let's rewind and take that again. Please."

B*arely adequate sex* reverberates in his brain—deafening lyrics to the rap song of his life.

He grows tense with fury and vows never to return to Under the Table Books, never to speak to Natasha again.

Now his fury becomes a deeper loneliness than he has ever felt. He loves that old bookstore—the fabulously funky amalgam of spirits dancing in the bodies of humans and cats and plants and books.

Now his rage returns and he wants to kill Lord Bellmaster and Moustafa—sees himself walking into the bookstore, guns blazing.

Now his fury ebbs into sorrow once more and he desperately wants to talk to Moustafa, to say, "Oh, my teacher, my friend, help me overcome this terrible rage inside me."

Without being conscious of what he's doing, Z snorts a tiny spoonful of the cocaine he bought especially for partying with Natasha—though she *did* say she never used the stuff—and feeling a reassuring rush of confidence, he snorts a bit more, whips out his mobile phone, and calls his ever ready flame Charisse.

"Mashman?" she coos, her voice dreamy sexy. "Where you been, big boy? My girl parts been missin' your boy parts *so* much."

"I pick you up, baby doll," he says, reveling in her uninhibited availability. "Lush party at Sammy D's. Dress hot. Twenty minutes. Come out, yo. I'm a black Jag."

"Oh, yeah, Mash. Ooo, yes. Pronto. *So* ready for you."

Late morning. To rain or not to rain, that is the question. Z trudges along the sidewalk to Under the Table Books, hoping to speak to Natasha and beg her forgiveness. Seriously hung-over and deeply chagrined, he keeps remembering the impossible promises he made to Charisse in the throes of drug-propelled sex.

He finds Lord at the cash register, the bookstore crawling with customers, Natasha nowhere in sight. Z fervently loves this place, though after months of working sleeping eating laughing crying here, he still feels unhinged most of the time; the rules here (or lack of them) so contrary to the rules of survival at Ground Zero, the hood where Z was born.

"Lord," he says, raising his hand in greeting. "The joint is jumpin'. Coffee to be had?"

"Indubitably," says Lord, pointing to the stairway down. "Quite a gang assembled in the kitchen. I suspect another harmonic convergence. You may have to brew some fresh. If you do, I'd love a cup. Light cream."

"Natasha around?" asks Z, hoping to sound convincingly blasé.

"Out of town," says Lord, smiling at the approach of a woman laden with books on trout fishing. "With Moustafa."

Z stiffens with rage. "Moustafa? Are they...?"

"Hold that thought," says Lord, turning his attention to the trout-fishing books. "Aren't these lovely? The price? First time here? Whatever you think they're worth."

Z staggers down the stairs, his jangled mind flooded with images of Natasha naked with Moustafa, the man's muscular limbs perfectly matched to the woman's voluptuous curves. He finds Jenny and Denny and Derek and Carl at the kitchen table playing a riveting game of Hearts.

"You have arrived at the crucial moment," says Carl, squinting at his cards, hoping to see something that isn't there. "Two outs, bottom of the ninth. A full count. The tying run at third."

"Translation," says Denny, biting his lower lip. "Jenny is on the verge of shooting the moon."

"And only I can stop her," says Derek, smiling hopefully. "Maybe. If nobody else, you know, blows it with an ill-timed move."

"Dream on," says Jenny, watching Z search in vain for coffee. "I'll brew some new after I trump these chumps."

"Take that, confident wench," says Denny, slapping down a puny six of hearts.

Derek slowly shakes his head and releases a great sigh of defeat. "I *really* wish you hadn't done that, Denny. You've flushed the last moderately high heart held by Carl, the ten, I believe, so now there's nothing to stop her from having her way with us."

"Such is life," says Denny, stretching his arms skyward. "We are all of us ever unknowingly flushing the last high heart."

Which pronouncement drives Z out into the garden to weep.

Jenny, easily sunburned, lies in dappled shade in the garden hammock while Z paces around and around the carrot patch trying to talk his way out of his confusion about Natasha.

"...and after we...after we...you know...made love, I felt so... *empowered*, except it wasn't the new me, the new Z that was empowered but the old *Mashman* Z from Ground Zero where the proof of power is in things we possess, control, dominate—which most definitely includes possessing and controlling and dominating *people*. So here I am with exquisite Natasha building this friendship knowing full well unless we are absolute *equals* there's no chance for us to be any kind of We, and I start thinking she's *mine*, and I'm scoring coke and renting hot wheels I can't afford to show her off at the palace of some gangster kingpin, and I'm lucky she *didn't* go to that party because it was the gateway to hell, and I'm only barely speaking metaphorically, Satan himself would have wanted Natasha, and he was *there*, so..."

Z stops his pacing, arrested by a magnificent black butterfly fluttering down out of the sky to feed on a blazing orange torch tithonia.

"The good news is she loves you," says Jenny, smiling at Z. "And she's the most forgiving person I've ever known."

"Are they lovers," he blurts, his body hot. "She and Moustafa?"

"Have been," says Jenny, nodding. "Might be."

"None of my business," he says, recalling his long night with Charisse. "Me, the king of double standards."

"Don't be too hard on yourself," says Jenny, closing her eyes. "It's a complicated dance we're learning here, and you're a marvelous dancer."

❦

Z brews his skinny mother a cup of strong black tea and sets it on the rickety table beside the grandiose armchair in which she spends most of the hours of her days, her hips sorely afflicted with arthritis. Afternoon sunlight slants through her heavily barred windows—the room ringing from a recent outburst of neighborhood gunfire.

She nods gratefully to her only child and says, “I always know what you’re thinking, Xavier. So I know you’re thinking you should move me to a safer place. But I say all in good time. You’re doing just fine for a man growing up in a war zone. I am so gratified by how you care for me.”

“Speaking of which,” he says, taking his familiar place in the lesser armchair beside her, “there’s a most commodious apartment coming open over the bookstore. Pinky Jones is moving back to the coast. I’ve put in a bid for the place. I think you’d like it there. Good people. Quiet. Safe.”

“How we gonna afford that Shangri-la?” she asks, scowling. “Can’t hardly pay for this little prison in the worst part of town.”

“I can afford it, Mama,” he says, grinning in wonder to be an integral part of Under the Table Books. “I work there, see. It’s a collective. We only give money when we have some to spare.”

“I’d be a fish out of water,” she says, sipping her tea. “You say it’s upstairs? How am I gonna get up and down with my arthritis?”

“Mama,” he says, his tears on the rise, “these gracious people will wait on you hand and foot.”

“Now why would they want to do that?” she asks, squinting suspiciously. “No such thing as a free lunch.”

“It’s just their way, Mama,” he says, a distinct *Click!* resounding in his mind—no need to remain another day in the line of fire. “You’ll see.”

Natasha, wearing a gray three-piece suit and a purple paisley tie, her hair in a severe bun, her reading glasses perched on the tip of her pretty nose, stands behind the bookstore counter, her notebook open before her, her umpteenth attempt at a letter to Z stalled again.

> Dearest Z,
>
> It has been a month now—seems an eternity—since I left you in that Jaguar and ran back to the bookstore to try to forget all about you. Except I love you. I think I know what was happening to you, and I'm sure you know why I had to...

The bell above the door jingles. Z comes in from the rain. He, too, is wearing a gray three-piece suit, his paisley tie blue, returning from a brilliant job interview at the super-mega bookstore Bornders und Norble.

Eyes meet. Hearts melt.

"Hey, Nash," he gurgles. "How you?"

"Up and down," she murmurs, closing her notebook and demurely removing her glasses. "Better now."

"You've heard, no doubt, I'm hoping to move upstairs here with my mother when Pinky goes. Got the okay from everybody but you. Don't want to wreck the mood for you around here. So, please..."

"Okay by me," she says, coming around the counter, aiming to kiss him. "Save you the commute."

He opens his arms and sings, "God in heaven, you're the loveliest."

Lord and Indira Fully Inhabit Their Bodies

(not really a sexual primer,
but feel free to use it as such)

Neither of them anticipates what happens. Quite the contrary, both are feeling the first Large Doubts about their dyadic potential since that transcendent moment of Recognizing Each Other. And though they remain absolutely perfectly suited to each other for optimal lovemaking—sex drunk for weeks now—they have barely scratched the psycho-spiritual surface of the other.

It is Indira's intention, therefore, *not* to make love to Lord on this spectacular summer's eve, but to *talk* about how she is feeling. It is Lord's intention that they go somewhere together other than bed—a bistro or the cinema. And they are both feeling cranky—one might even say pissed off—about these parallel nonsexual intentions.

Thus we come upon Lord about to knock on Indira's door.

Handsomely proportioned, his antecedents British Greek Egyptian Polish, Lord is, by nature, unkempt—a more romantic word might be *tousled*—but clean. He has only vague notions of what he looks like, and he is so unconscious of his clothing (save that it should be comfortable) it is commonplace for people to say to him, "Nice shirt," and for Lord to have no idea what they're talking about until he peers down at his chest and sees what he's wearing. He is odd, certainly, but in an attractively harmless way. He often speaks in sentence fragments and seeming non sequiturs. From a distance, homosexuals often take him to be one of them. Up close, he is dispositionally and pheromonally heterosexual. He likes everyone. Only the most persistently rotten person can hope to gain his enmity. He saddens easily, but rarely cries except at movies with soundtracks of haunting piano music. He has always felt Separate, and comfortably so.

Lord's mother, in one of the more riotously attended lectures at Under the Table Books—*Before Lord Was Lord*—said of him, "In kindergarten he would climb to the top of the jungle gym and perch there like a hawk watching the other kids playing, yet he rarely played *with* them. He especially liked watching girls. One day he announced to me over his after-school snack that, 'Girls are more complex than boys. Much harder to predict what they'll do next.'"

His relationship with Indira is an anomaly in the relatively tame history of his love life. He has never before felt so equal to his mate; not that he previously felt superior or inferior, just not particularly equal, and he finds this feeling of equality with Indira astonishingly sexy. What's more, their lovemaking amplifies this sense—no, it is more than a sense, it is *actual*—of equipollence, which further fuels his desire to...what?

What do I desire from with of her? he wonders as he listens rapturously to her footfalls approaching the door upon which he has just knocked. *Sex? Yes. Love? Yes. Marriage?* He frowns so deeply his eyes ache. He is struck hard by the realization that he still knows very little about her. *Is that the source of the attraction? The intoxicating mysterious persistent not knowing anything about her? Or is it the ferociously exciting possibility of a revelation about who she is and what we are destined to be together? Or is this merely the zenith of sexual connections? Merely, indeed!*

For her part, Indira...well, virtually everything she seemed to be not long ago, she is no longer. The angry crone is now thoroughly transmogrified into a dark-eyed voluptuous erotic baldheaded henna-tattooed sari-wearing diva of sensual delight. Furthermore, let it be told that even *before* the woman previously known as Mrs. Armitage ceased all sexual activity some twenty years ago at the age of twenty-seven, she had *never* experienced satisfying sex, her mates stunningly inept in the arts of *Eros*, so that at best sex was a shared ordeal that might, and this was the most exciting part for her, lead to pregnancy. Thus, to characterize Indira as sexually born *again* would be highly misleading, for her recent commencement of a fulfilling sex life is the *first* in her current incarnation.

Indira—Olive on her birth certificate—was an only child, a gawky girl who knew nothing of being beautiful until she was sixteen and her previously disparate features came into sudden pleasing harmony. Theretofore an isolated bookworm with an immeasurably high intelligence, Olive was mightily perplexed by the sudden disappearance of invisibility and the onset of unanimous popularity, for she was more than pretty, she was bewitching. By the end of her junior year in high school she was the dream of all the boys and most of the men in town.

Her mother—sad angry divorced embittered overworked—was eager for Olive to marry, and to that end encouraged her daughter to date college boys, which Olive was happy to do, finding them more to her intellectual liking than the mentally stunted native oafs. Nearing the end of her senior year in high school she lost her virginity to a college junior. The sex was awful, and though on paper the young man was a promising catch—old Chicago money with a guaranteed position in the family banking business—she broke with him in hopes of finding someone who could at least approximate the better lovers she read about in the popular novels of the day.

She tried her luck with a few more disheartening college boys and was on the verge of her own university career, when she met a smooth operator named John who was no great shakes in bed but at least he wasn't terrible. They were married when she was nineteen—four months pregnant—and he was thirty-two. John, a Realtor, was never faithful to Olive, and when their lovely daughters were eight and six, he officially left Olive for the woman he'd been involved with before and during his marriage, and took his daughters with him.

Olive, already seriously deranged by eight years of marriage to a pathological liar, suffered a massive nervous breakdown when her daughters were taken from her. She did not regain functional consciousness until four years later when she woke to find herself in Colorado, locked away in a toxic institution for emotionally disturbed adults. Skillfully eschewing the massive daily doses of tranquilizers designed to subdue every independent tendency, and assessed by her keepers to be a moron incapable of escape, she walked away a few days after her awakening, assumed the persona of a cantankerous old lady, and eventually found her way to California where she took up residence a few blocks from the anarchist collective known as Under the Table Books wherein there dwelled the young Lord Bellmaster.

Lord takes a deep breath and sighs impatiently, wondering why his beloved hesitates to open the door to him. They have been apart for—he looks around to gauge the time of day by the quality of light—twelve hours, and he physically aches from a lack of the sight and the sound and the scent and the *feel* of a real live Indira. And now it dawns on him *I'm addicted to her. Not to sex, but to her. Specifically her. Indira. Yikes.*

Indira feels an oceanic momentum to open the door. Yet she does not turn the knob. Instead, she stands very still, inundated by the power of her desire.

Lord says to Indira's door, "I have an idea."

"Do tell," she replies, barely able to suppress her laughter.

"Let's talk for a while with the door closed between us. See what our voices think of each other."

Indira is moved to sing a wordless song expressing her love and admiration for him—Lord humming a resonant harmony.

Lord sits cross-legged facing Indira's door, Indira sitting likewise within. They share their earliest memories of themselves and their earliest memories of each other. They tell about the times in their lives when they felt most betrayed, most admired, most afraid, most confused, most happy.

They begin to laugh, laughing until their bellies ache, until they are exhausted, yet they keep laughing.

They sit in the afterglow of their laughter feeling light and carefree, as if they have expelled a million admonitions *not* to laugh. Lord thinks back over his life, recalling those other marvelous women and men with whom he laughed uproariously, while Indira realizes she has never, until this moment, laughed with anyone in this wildly joyful way.

Darkness falls. The door opens a crack. Indira hands out a white votive candle and a *Strike Anywhere* match. Lord lights the candle and sets it on the *Welcome* mat. Indira does not close the door.

Lord says, "I'm growing a bit esurient. You know, peckish. Shall I fetch a couple burritos from Rodrigo's Incomparable Mexican?"

"Chicken for me," says Indira, her voice rich with gratitude. "Pinto beans, no cheese, extra guacamole."

"Hot sauce?"

"Please."

Midnight, burritos digested, many more momentous moments from each of their lives revealed, Lord says, "I'm ready to see you now. We needn't touch. May I come in?"

"In a moment," she says breathlessly. "I'll call when I'm ready."

Lord enters her apartment, the few small rooms lit by flickering candles, the walls adorned with the shadows of leaves of her myriad potted plants, a translucent reddish paisley sheet dividing the living room in half. Indira's shadow looms large on the fabric scrim, for she is backlit by candles, naked, her arms at her sides.

Lord disrobes and stands so he, too, is backlit by candles, his silhouette large and vivid to Indira through the diaphanous fabric. He wants to ask *What now?* but resists the urge to speak, trusting the *What* of *Now* to manifest without the prompting of a question.

Indira moves so her shadow and Lord's shadow become one shadow. "We cease to be you and I," she intones, "when we become us."

"Is that a bad thing?" asks Lord, frowning at the nondescript blob of their conjoined silhouette.

"Not bad or good," she says as their shadows individuate. "Just what happens."

"You're so lovely," he says, moving so his shadow engulfs hers.

"All gone," she says softly. "No more me."

He moves so they are two again.

"These are but shadows," he protests. "Not the real things."

"Come closer," she whispers, standing with her breasts and knees touching the pellucid partition.

Lord moves swiftly, stopping inches away from her.

They feel the other's heat. They smell the other. They hear the other's breathing.

"Imagine this is all we can ever be to each other," she says, taking a deep breath. "Not quite tangible phantoms."

"Why imagine such?" he asks, straining not to touch her through the gossamer shield. "Why..."

"For now," she whispers. "For a time. Just be here like this with me and imagine this is all we shall ever be to each other."

He tries to do as she says, but the effort angers him. He wants her. He wants to pull down the curtain and cover her with kisses and be inside her. *Why must I play these games in order to...*

"In order to what?" she asks, speaking his thoughts. "Is this just foreplay to you? Is this all, in the end, about getting laid? If so, why me? Why not Jenny? Why not Natasha? Why not any woman you desire who desires you? Why Indira, Lord?"

"Because it happens this way," he says, gazing down at his swollen sex. "Because we got lucky. Because now is all there is and here we are and we're ready to go."

"Speak for yourself," she laughs, tearing down the sheet and roaring like a lion.

She is astride him deep inside her when she—her entire enormous self—enters fully into her body and she experiences a wholeness so complete that her previous conceptions of reality are revealed to have been fragmentary glimpses of the transcendent experience of fully inhabiting her body as Lord—his entire enormous self—enters fully into his body and he experiences a wholeness so complete that his previous conceptions of reality are revealed to have been fragmentary glimpses of the transcendent experience of fully inhabiting his body.

Getting Above Things

(text of audio documentary created by Derek
with the bookstore tape recorder)

Derek: Hello everyone. This is Derek reporting from the top of Indian Rock, high above glimmering San Francisco Bay. Wow! What a view. There's Mount Tamalpais and the Golden Gate and the skyscrapers in downtown San Francisco and Angel Island and Alcatraz and Oakland and the Bay Bridge and the Richmond Bridge and sailboats and...

Natasha: Dazzling.

Z: Amazing.

Leona Spinelli: I love being so high above everything.

Iris Spinelli: Ditto.

Derek: We are here to celebrate my being legally adopted by Moustafa so the social welfare people will stop bugging us about an eleven-year-old boy (me) living with a bunch of "scruffy anarchists." That was the description used by the person arguing *against* Moustafa being allowed to adopt me. Lord was *going* to adopt me, but he's probably going to South America with Indira to join Alfredo de San Francisco in defending the last pristine tropical rainforest on earth, and since the adoption people do these regular checkups to make sure the adoption is going well, the new parent needs to be present, which Moustafa will be. Also, Moustafa looks a little better on paper than Lord since he has his own penny-ante brokerage business and an excellent credit rating.

Moustafa: I am now your legal guardian, but you belong to all of us as all of us belong to you.

Jenny: The little brother I always wanted.

Indira: My beloved son.

Mr. Laskin: My two o'clock sandwich man.

Moustafa: It is good to get above things, to view the world from the vantage point of a high-flying bird, to have only sky above us, to breathe the lighter air.

Derek: We are also celebrating Natasha's engagement to Z, and the publication of Numero Uno's latest volume of poetry *Mexican Women Make the Best Novelists.*

Numero Uno: Based on a true story.

Mr. Laskin: Look south, look west, look north. Most of what you see I once owned. What a greedy bastard I was.

Indira: The past is prologue. No wonder everyone wants to live here. It's paradise.

Lord: Before the Europeans arrived, food was so abundant around the bay—fish and game and wild fruit and fungi—war was unknown among the indigenous peoples.

Derek: Do you think food is the cause of war?

Tomas: The fear of starving to death underlies all other fears.

Derek: (whispering) The accordion music you hear in the background is being played by Tantha Fidelos from Finland.

Pinky Jones: Getting food seems to be what most of life is about. When I lived in the wilderness I was constantly aware that until I quelled my hunger and had enough food gathered for the next meal or two, anything else I did, even sleeping, was charged with the urgency of finding something to eat.

Monica Copia: Was that always true? For the whole thirty years?

Pinky: Always. However, I quickly came to appreciate, I might even say *enjoyed*, being hungry because of how keenly it motivated me. My senses were sharpened fantastically by hunger, and that made getting food much easier. And, of course, the more adept I became at harvesting the natural bounty, the less fearful I became.

Derek: Did you kill animals?

Pinky: Oh, yes. I killed rabbits, mice, fish, quail, lizards, snakes, grubs, slugs, worms, insects, frogs. I also ate birds' eggs, and every so often I managed to kill a deer.

Derek: How did you kill the deer?

Pinky: The very first deer I killed was a doe that had broken her leg and could not run away. I wrestled her to the ground and cut her throat. I killed my second deer with a spear. The third deer I killed with a large rock I threw at her while she was swimming across a stream. I knocked her out and she drowned.

Tomas: Do you remember all your deer kills?

Pinky: Vividly. Each deer I killed was a major event in my life because the coming of so much meat meant that I would have many days of *not* having to hunt and kill, which was a great relief to me. A real holiday. I killed twenty-seven deer in thirty years. I commemorated each deer by making a necklace with their teeth and hanging the necklace somewhere near the place of their death.

Jenny: We take so much for granted, the slaughtering done for us, out of sight, out of mind. What a different world this would be if we had to raise our own food and do our own slaughtering.

Tantha: I am of the first generation in my village *not* to raise all our own food and do our own slaughtering. And now half of my age peers are professional musicians.

Pinky: My parents were farmer musicians. We raised chickens and rabbits and pigs, but we hired out the slaughtering and froze the meat.

Mr. Laskin: Avocados, cheese, lettuce, chard, kale, eggs, tomatoes, broccoli, almonds, bananas, apples, oranges, tofu, rice—the occasional watermelon and a cup of coffee. A person can thrive on such foods, rendering the slaughter of mammals unnecessary.

Monica: Not everyone has the wherewithal to buy such things in sufficient quantity to survive and raise children.

Numero Uno: I once lived on rice and beans and carrots for five years. Oh, and beer, too.

Iris: Don't forget the beer.

Leona: Must have had terrible farts.

Numero Uno: We can get used to almost anything so long as we're free to make our art.

Tantha: Tomas. Tell them your dream from last night.

Tomas: It was one of those dreams so real that when I woke, this reality seemed dim by contrast.

Indira: I am sure it *was* real.

Leona: Of course it was real, but we're so afraid of the miraculous nature of reality we have to *say* maybe dreams aren't real, when they are.

Pinky: I think *this* is a dream, being here with you, floating on this massive stone above the earth.

Derek: What was your dream, Tomas?

Tomas: I'm walking naked on a path in a redwood forest.

Monica: I love this dream already.

Tomas: I come upon a grand piano half-buried in a riot of vines and flowers—nasturtiums and morning glories and wild grapes—and I want *so* much to play the piano, but I see no way to reach the keys without trampling the vines. The next thing I know I *am* playing the piano and the vines are all around me and the flowers are swaying in time to the music, a gorgeous lilting samba something, fourths and sixths and sevenths and octaves with my right hand, boogie-woogie with my left, when out of the piano comes this deep luscious voice singing, "Everything is music."

Natasha: Then what happened?

Tomas: I woke up feeling happier than I've ever felt.

Z: I had a dream like that. Or close to it.

Moustafa: Tell it, please.

Z: Well, I'm walking to the bus stop and I hear this voice, this incredible voice singing, not a woman's voice or a man's voice but both. And I think, '*Damn, I'd like to have that voice*.' In the dream I think that. So this cat…and I'm talking about a kitty cat, a big black one with a red beret on his head, I swear to God, looks up at me from where he's sitting on the bus bench and says, "I can get you that voice you scratch my back." So I scratch him and he starts to purr and his purr gets louder and louder until the street and the buildings are shaking like an earthquake, only the shaking is from that purring, and I feel like I'm about to shatter, and then I *do* shatter, and I'm scattered in hundreds of pieces, but slowly I come back together, and when I'm together again I have that voice.

Natasha: So *that's* why you sing so pretty. Endowed by a dream.

Lord: In the beginning was the word. Or as Groucho Marx liked to call it, the magic woid.

Z: However you say it, I'll bet it was singing.

Moustafa: Isn't it good to get above things? To look at the world through the eyes of a hawk, to see everything so flawlessly connected.

Derek: Does anyone else have a dream to share?

Mr. Laskin: I once dreamt I was married to Marilyn Monroe. A beautiful sunny morning and we're in our bathrobes having our morning coffee at the kitchen table. I'm reading the newspaper and Marilyn is watching me. God, she's lovely, her breasts spilling out into the golden light. She's just there, sipping her coffee and watching me, and I feel...I felt thoroughly embraced by her.

Indira: For years and years I dreamt I *was* Marilyn Monroe, and in many of those dreams I was wearing a bathrobe, a white silky thing, and sipping coffee and watching the person I was with.

Derek: (whispering to Lord) Who was Marilyn Monroe?

Lord: Ask Monica.

Derek: Monica? Who *was* Marilyn Monroe?

Monica: Empress of archetypes.

Derek: I'm not sure what you mean.

Monica: Marilyn Monroe was a strikingly beautiful woman with rosy skin and a voluptuous figure. She could shape shift and be whatever her beholder imagined her to be. She could appear to be an innocent girl and the most knowing of courtesans. She could seem to be the most motherly of mothers and the most elusive of nasty vixens. Even her voice would change from deep to high, soft to gruff, sexy to naïve. She was photographed a million times in every kind of light and in every sort of costume. Images of her in all her guises were sent everywhere around the world until she became the most recognizable woman in history.

Indira: Her beauty was heartbreaking.

Jenny: Heartbreaking, yes. But was it her beauty or that deep sorrow beneath the veneer of beauty that broke our hearts?

Mr. Laskin: I met her only once at a costume ball in New York City. She wore a low-cut black sequin dress that made her ruddy white skin seem to glow from within, and a black sequin mask that I begged her to remove as we danced. But she would not oblige me. She was a fabulous dancer with formidable strength in her arms. I would have given anything to be naked with her.

Tomas: What tune were you dancing to?

Mr. Laskin: *Moonglow*.

Lord Bellmaster: I used to talk to her at night when I was a young man. Before I'd go to sleep. In lieu of praying. I wanted to protect her and ravish her simultaneously.

Z: In the hood they say, "Oh, she is *so* Marilyn Monroe." Means like cool virgin sexy tempting yet untouchable.

Monica: Wholly vulnerable, yet unattainable.

Derek: Any other dreams to share?

Jenny: One I've told before?

Derek: Tell again, please.

Jenny: I am drawing a picture of a door and the picture *becomes* a door. I open it and walk through onto a white sand beach, a wild place, far from civilization, the most beautiful place I've ever been. I feel like I've finally reached the place I've been longing for my whole life. I sit down and watch the waves forming and crashing. I watch the shorebirds probing the wet sand for food. I feel such a deep contentment I begin to weep. Now I hear a voice calling my name. There is an irresistible yearning in this voice. I leap to my feet and run in the direction of the voice and the sand turns to concrete and I'm in a city of tall buildings, the streets dense with cars and people. I look back and see the wild beach far in the distance, the sound of the waves obliterated by the sounds of the city. I want to return to that wild place, but the voice has too much power over me, so I plunge on in search of whoever is calling my name.

Tomas: I've *lived* that dream.

Indira: We do live our dreams. That is what we do.

Tantha: Every story my grandmother ever told began in dreamtime and resolved in waking life.

Pinky: We live our dreams and dream our lives.

Z: My voice sings me.

Derek: Moustafa?

Moustafa: (laughing) How glad I am we climbed up here to feel the embrace of the stainless sky, to breathe the briny air from the bosom of the deep blue sea.

Indira & Jenny

(comparing notes from Before and Now)

On a pristine beach in far northern California, a place barely altered by the comings and goings of a few thousand humans over millennia, two barefoot women walk northward on windswept sand. The month is October, the air warm and sweet and clean, the sun appearing to hover over a dense mass of gray clouds a mile offshore.

Indira is bald and muscular, her ancestors Magyar Bohemians. Carrying a large blue backpack heavy with supplies, she wears brown shorts and a white long-sleeved shirt, her freshly shaved dome covered with a turquoise baseball cap. She is forty-seven, though only the most discerning human would guess her to be much past thirty.

Jenny is thirty-three, and she, too, has an ageless quality about her. Slender of waist and small of bosom, with long sturdy legs, Jenny's beauty is leavened with sorrow, her reddish-brown hair caught in a ponytail, her antecedents Irish French. Her backpack is relatively small, for unlike Indira, she is not training to become a guerilla.

They make camp on white sand untouched by the ocean since the last great storm of the previous winter. Unbeknownst to either Jenny or Indira, they have chosen the favorite campground of the Yuki people who inhabited the region for thousands of years before their swift extermination at the hands of invading Europeans.

A crystalline creek transects the beach and enters the sea as a trickle, giving no hint of the torrent it will become when rain inundates the land. Brown cliffs loom above the sand, their upper reaches dotted with the mud nests of swallows. No scent of rain imbues the air. The wind is but a whisper. The women spread their sleeping bags on a silver tarp and gather driftwood for a fire.

They have come here to be alone together, to talk about their lives, to defuse the tension between them regarding Lord Bellmaster, the man who was Jenny's mate and is now Indira's lover.

Not many months ago, Indira was known as Mrs. Armitage, an eccentric old lady who came to Under the Table Books every day to feed the cats. Jenny, the First Lady, as it were, of the bookstore, was always kind and cordial to Mrs. Armitage, and thus she became something of a daughter to the lonely woman. Then Jenny abetted Mrs. Armitage in a cataclysmic shift in persona by cutting off Mrs. Armitage's long black hair, and thereafter they were on a course to become best friends until Lord and Indira fell madly in love with each other.

And now Indira is preparing to go to Brazil to join the fight to save the last of the old-growth rainforest from the chainsaws and bulldozers of an esurient consortium of amoral, emotionally disturbed dimwits: AKA the powers that be.

Sitting in the fire's glow, the night growing cool, they conclude their simple meal of brown rice and steamed vegetables with hunks of dark chocolate and a few snorts of peach brandy.

"Are you afraid of what awaits you?" asks Jenny, referring to Indira's impending departure for Brazil as sub-commandante of the army of Alfredo de San Francisco.

"No," says Indira, her voice deep and confident. "I long to be in the jungle."

"Lord is terrified," says Jenny, aching with jealousy. "One minute he says he's going with you, the next he says he won't."

"All who have gone before us have died," says Indira, adding a log to the fire. "Lord wants so much to live."

"Don't *you*? Want to live?"

"Yes," she says, gazing up at the thousands of visible stars. "That's why I'm going."

"I don't understand."

"To quote our beloved Monica Copia, 'Fear dissolves when we walk with open hearts into the embrace of that which frightens us—the source of our fear revealed to be illusory.'"

"Do you *trust* Alfredo?" asks Jenny, with undisguised contempt.

"Alfredo is a visionary, not a saint," says Indira, taking off her shirt. "He's a catalyst, not a savior. He's a man, not a god. His actions have created a way for me to go where I want to go."

"But they'll be shooting *real* bullets at you," says Jenny, cringing at the thought of Lord and Indira being torn to pieces. "They'll *really* try to kill you. How is that illusory?"

"You're talking about death, not fear," says Indira, stepping out of her shorts. "Join me for a swim?"

"In the creek?"
"In the sea."
"In the dark?"
"Yes. Now."
"The surf is deadly here."
"I'll stop at the edge of death."
"Are you trying to scare me?" asks Jenny, laughing nervously.
"No," says Indira, kissing the top of Jenny's head.

Jenny wades into the surf up to her knees and shivers in agony until Indira emerges from the roaring waves.

They lie on their backs watching falling stars.

"Was Lord your first lover?" Indira whispers.

"No," says Jenny, grateful to be out of the sea, warm and snug in a sleeping bag on soft dry sand. "But he *was* the first and only man I've been married to. Not that we were *legally* married, but..."

"I know what you mean," says Indira, recalling Jenny and Lord as sweethearts, and how she envied them their easy affection for each other.

"Not that I expected it to last forever," says Jenny, remembering Lord in the early days of their togetherness—how young he seemed, how hopeful he was of great accomplishments for both of them. "I think what hurts most is how easily he replaced me with you."

"You have not been replaced."

"I feel that way. I feel abandoned and betrayed."

"I know those feelings. I spent decades feeling abandoned and betrayed. But such feelings are based on the illusion of unworthiness.

Lord has not abandoned you. Nor have I. Nor have we betrayed you. We have hidden nothing from you."

"You're taking him away from us," says Jenny, her voice gruff with anger. "He's only going because he can't live without you."

"He can live without me," says Indira, rolling onto her side to face Jenny. "I am going to Brazil, whether he goes or not."

"Do you *want* him to go? Because if he knew you didn't want him to go, maybe..."

"I will love him whether he goes or not. And what I most want to tell you is that I have discovered my full strength and power *as* his lover. For the first time in my life I fully occupy my body. I am here, Jenny. Here. Completely."

"Why did you most want to tell me that?"

"To explain why your jealousy serves no good purpose. To give you an inspired vision of your potential."

"Which is?"

"To fearlessly occupy your body, to come into your full power through the dissolution of boundaries into a fluidity through which spirit moves with no resistance."

"But which comes first? Dissolution or fearlessness?"

"Oh, Jenny," says Indira, embracing her friend, "they manifest simultaneously, one and the same."

Helping Pinky Pack

(the constant only is change)

When someone makes ready to move away from a close-knit community, everyone in that community, at least for a moment, imagines moving, too. And though Pinky Jones—tall handsome sixty-five former famous actor singer now obscure—has only been a part of Under the Table Books for three scant years, his impending departure has stirred up gales of emotion, the most obviously affected being Derek, a slender lad taking his first steps onto the minefield known as adolescence, quite recently homeless and still besieged by nightmares of having nowhere to live and no one to befriend him.

"Amazing the amount of crap I've accumulated," says Pinky, holding up a pale pink dress to the muted light coming through his north-facing window. "Now who left this? Svelte thing." He buries his nose in the dress, hoping the scent will jog his memory, but no one comes to mind. "When I came out of the wilderness three years ago I had nothing but the clothes I was wearing, four abalone shells, seven really cool rocks, and a headdress of owl feathers. Now look. Tons of mostly useless stuff."

"I *like* your things," says Derek, sitting cross-legged in a rocking chair, watching Pinky sort through his dresser of drawers. "None of it seems like crap to me. It makes the place feel homey."

"You know," says Pinky, perusing an old *You Bet Your Life* sweatshirt and doubting it still fits him, "creating that cave with you was a revelation. Made me realize how much I miss the deeper silence."

"What about Monica?" asks Derek, referring to Pinky's lover. "She told Jenny she's not going with you. Won't you miss her?"

"I know this may sound strange to you," says Pinky, flopping down on his king-sized bed, exhausted from sorting through so much of his recent past, "but the only thing I *know* I miss is silence. You see, my idea of reality changed completely during those thirty years in the wilderness, and despite the most potent of personal predilections to the contrary, I finally came into harmony with the present moment and I've pretty much been here ever since." He smiles warmly. "For instance, right now I'm having a fabulous time visiting with you. I'm not thinking of anyone else. I love the light in the room, the sound of your voice, the tug of your emotions on mine, the first pangs of hunger in my belly. When you said Monica's name, an image of her came to mind, and I felt my body grow a little warmer, a little more predisposed to go in search of her, and I *love* that feeling. But I don't miss her. I love her. I desire her, but I don't miss her. There's a difference."

"Will you come back to visit?" asks Derek, gripping the arms of the rocking chair—wanting to stay exactly where he is. "Please?"

"Probably," says Pinky, jumping up. "Let's get lunch."

Derek and Pinky and Mr. Laskin carry their gargantuan sandwiches and blackberry smoothies to the round glass table on the brick terrazzo at the edge of the vegetable and herb garden—rays of November sun muted by the intervening olive tree. Mr. Laskin, white-haired and weather-brazed, takes his customary seat with his back to the fishpond, gazes fondly at the turkey avocado feta roasted pine nuts sautéed zucchini on dark rye sandwich prepared for him by Moustafa, and proclaims, “Can there be any greater joy than this?”

“Nnnoo,” says Pinky, his mouth full of sandwich.

Derek sips his smoothie and tries not to think about Pinky moving to the Coast or Mr. Laskin dying or Lord and Indira going to Brazil to fight the plunderers or Jenny returning to New York for one more try at selling her art or Natasha and Z leaving for Los Angeles to become singing dancing acting stars. But no matter how hard he tries, *all* he can think about is the disappearance of his beloved friends. So to forestall his inevitable tears, he mumbles something about napkins and hurries inside to make sure Moustafa isn’t planning to go anywhere.

“I don’t know what I’d do without that child,” says Mr. Laskin, watching the lad scurry into the kitchen. “Oh, I’d keep living until I stopped, I suppose, but life would be awfully dry without his intrepid spirit and faithful companionship, plus all the other inexpressible ineffables.”

“Ever have kids of your own?” asks Pinky, humming with pleasure as he devours his sandwich. “Man, oh man, this is good.”

“Three daughters,” says Mr. Laskin, his eyes narrowing. “Each uniquely bright and beautiful. They switched their allegiance to my usurper without the slightest hesitation. I read about them in the news. They each married high among the power elite.”

“I have a daughter,” says Pinky, feeling a twinge in his chest. “I’ve never seen her. She was four months in utero when her mother left me, and six months along when her mother remarried. About to be born when I walked away into the wilderness."

"Useless to blame them," says Mr. Laskin, nodding solemnly. "Hard to fathom, but we're all doing the best we can."

Derek returns with napkins and a plate of scrumptious oatmeal cookies. "Moustafa," he announces happily, "has just started a new *three*-year Frisbee and meditation training program with seven new students. So at least *he's* not going anywhere."

"I love you, kid," says Pinky, laughing for joy at Derek's happiness. "I remember just how you feel."

Pinky hovers on the edge of sleep in Monica's big bouncy bed, her myriad crystals casting morning rainbows on the royal purple comforter. Monica, a buxom babe of sixty-two, cradles Pinky's softening sex in her hot hand and says, "I'll miss this guy most of all."

"Come visit," he murmurs, forgetting her name.

"Too far away," she says, failing to mask her exasperation. "A seven-hour drive on a crazy curvy road."

"Come for a good long week," he says, kissing her unyielding lips. "Sleepy small town. Long walks on the beach. Quiet, quiet, quiet."

"My work is here," she says, pulling away from him. "My friends, my community, my students, my birds, my…everything."

A silence falls. Pinky knows she wants him to reply, but he can't think of anything meaningful to say.

"I'm…" She hesitates. "I'm seeing someone, Pinky. Someone other than you." She gets out of bed. "I hate this part."

"Don't hate it," he says, sitting up.

"Oh, what do *you* care?" she says, glaring at him. "Just so long as it's fun, right?"

"I care," says Pinky, holding out his hand. "You're wonderful."

"Well, I'm mad at you," she says, leaving the room. "For breaking us up when everything was going so well for me."

Early evening. Rain falling. Pinky strolls into Under the Table Books and finds Tomas playing guitar to Iris and Leona and Natasha tendering a superlative three-part harmony *But Beautiful.*

Drawn to the song like a moth to a flame, Pinky blends his burnished baritone with Natasha's rich soprano and Iris and Leona's quavering altos, their marvelous synergy spreading faster than the speed of light throughout the universe.

"So tell me about being famous," says Natasha, enticing Pinky downstairs with the promise of pumpkin pie and eggnog. "Before you wander off to the frozen north."

"Crack cocaine," says Pinky, sitting down at the kitchen table and watching lovely Natasha—sleeveless T-shirt showing off big beautiful unencumbered breasts, eyes and lips and face to die for—cut him a big piece of pie. "Is there rum in this excruciatingly delicious eggnog?"

"If you want there to be," she says, arching her eyebrow and seeing right through him. "This your dinner or dessert?"

"Both," he says, shaking his head in wonder at how mightily she arouses him. "I could eat your whole pie, honey. No problem."

"Oh, Pinky," she laughs, knowing exactly what he's thinking. "I will miss you lusting after me. I do so appreciate your catholic taste in women, as well as your equally admirable decorum."

"I may be forty-two years your senior," he says, laughing with her, "but never forget: there's no such thing as a dirty old man, just horny young men trapped in the bodies of old guys."

"True, true, I know that's true," she says, serving him a towering stein of nog generously doused with rum. "Now tell me why fame is like crack cocaine? Not that I've ever smoked crack."

"Instantly addictive," says Pinky, his mirth subsiding. "And good for nothing but wanting more."

"Think of the good you could do for the world with that kind of clout," she says, brandishing the rum. "You need more spike in your nog?"

"I do," he says, surprised by the strength of his sadness about his show business past. "As for fame, it's quicksand, darling."

"I just might make it big, you know," she says, deaf to his warning. "I've got the voice, the looks, the style, the songs, the heart, the soul. And if I *do* make it big, I swear to you, I won't let them change me."

"Them?" says Pinky, laughing. "Who do you think *them* are?"

"The ones with the power. The...you know...those people *you* used to know."

"Oh, Natasha," he says wistfully. "If only you could realize you already *have* the power. That singing we did upstairs just now? *But Beautiful. That* is the heart of the heart of the heart. The rest is delusion."

"I'm too young to believe that," she says, serving his pie. "You and Tomas and Moustafa and Monica had your flings with fame and you all turned out fine, so why not see what might happen for me?"

Pinky breathes deeply of the pumpkin pie and prays, "May angels watch over you, Natasha."

On a foggy morning in mid-November, Denny and Lord and Moustafa help Pinky load his furniture and a few dozen boxes of various and sundry into the cavernous hold of Denny's huge turquoise bus, the words BOOK SCAVENGER written on the sides in block letters identical to letters that previously spelled LODI UNIFIED SCHOOL DISTRICT.

When every little thing is securely packed away, they retire to the kitchen where Natasha and Jenny and Tomas and Tantha and Mr. Laskin and Carl and Peter Franklin and Iris and Leona and Indira and Derek have gathered for Pinky's going-away brunch of waffles, spuds, scrambled eggs, and freshly squeezed orange juice.

At meal's end, before everyone disperses to their various walks of life, Lord says, "I remember the moment I first laid eyes on Pinky. I was putting the APARTMENT FOR RENT sign in the bookstore window when this wild-eyed man carrying a battered backpack stopped on the other side of the glass, arched his eyebrow, and gave me a look that spoke volumes. Thus we communed for several hilarious moments before I took down the sign and Pinky moved in."

"I was worried at first," says Tomas, taking up the narrative, "because I like my privacy and I like it quiet up there, and Pinky, as you know, loves to sing. So I feared he might drive me crazy. But he didn't." He smiles at Pinky. "You never sang too loud or for too long and your choice of songs and your interpretations invariably matched my moods."

"Come visit me," says Pinky to no one in particular—oddly detached. "When you need a break from city life."

Denny drives in silence—*the clarity of Cal to break your heart*—fields giving way to rolling hills giving way to coastal mountains, blue skies turning cloudy, rain kissing the windshield—the click and snap of the wipers adding rhythm to the somber mood.

Denny grins at Pinky and says, "I totally identify with you."

"Yes," says Pinky, returning the grin.

"We're loners," says Denny, nodding as the road straightens out—empty as far as he can see. "No matter how hard we try, no matter what starts to happen, we ultimately end up alone."

"We are never alone," says Pinky, gazing out at the gorgeous interconnectedness of everything—thrilled to know he lives here.

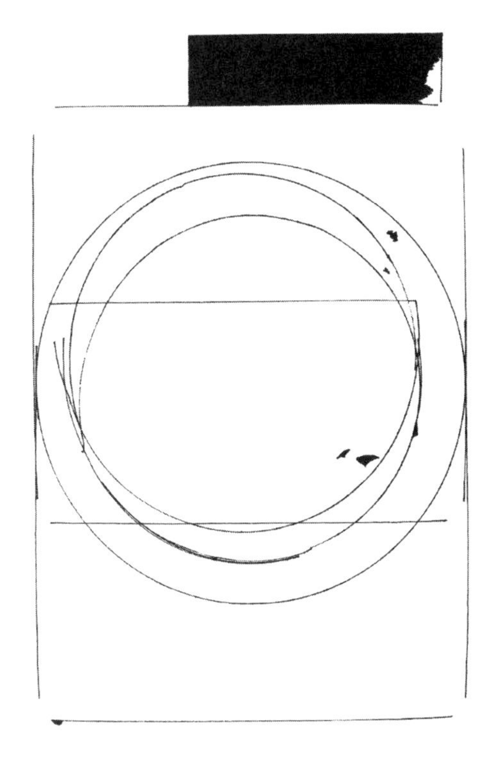

Ben's Escape

(as told by Roshi Supremo)

Benjamin left us yesterday. I couldn't bring myself to eat today. In his nine months as head chef of the monastery, I have grown plump again, brought back from death's door by his tasty comestibles. Now what?

Contemplate.

Why did he go?

"I am trapped in a repetition of my past."

Those were his last words to me.

He came here to break the pattern of his compulsions. He came here to transcend the ideas that defined him. Through silent meditation and silent living, he hoped to overcome his feelings of superiority. Yet in the womb of this sanctuary, he found a kitchen, a lover, and exquisite fresh produce. He demolished our austerity with his cuisine. Laughter overtook the bleak seriousness of our practice. We loosened our belts. Women and men became women and men. Our dreams were full of sex. I, myself, was so relieved to be free from the yoke of pseudo-intellectualism and mock knowledge, I gave my monks and nuns tacit permission to couple. Enlightened conversation supplanted silence and pomposity. Hundreds labored happily in the fields, *his* fields, and their sweat was rewarded with banquets beyond our imaginings.

I am eighty years old. I had not experienced an erection since my forty-ninth year. Yet night after night, morning after morning, the scent of his food made me hard. Should I have banished him? No. He was a rushing tide—the high tide of physical ecstasy and communal fecundity.

Now I will institute a year of silence and austerity. Our food will go unspiced. We will taste the potato unembellished, the carrot simply washed. I will bless those couples wishing to remain coupled and ask them to find their way to new homes. I will oversee the ebb.

I miss him. I am human. Last night, I dreamt Benjamin and I were eating a simple meal prepared by his masterful hands. Bread and chocolate and blueberries.

I said to him, "There seems to be no end to the joy you bring us."

Here is the note he left me.

> Beloved Roshi,
>
> I love making people happy with delicious, healthful food. But it's a trap. I keep thinking I'm special because I can do this food magic. I have no sense of not being special—in the kitchen, in bed, in the garden. There is nothing to refute this.

I'm hoping to find a place where fresh produce is hard come by, where the soil is mean and rocky, where the women are uninspiring, the weather awful. I honestly believe Buddhism is as good as organized philosophy gets, so please don't take this personally, but I need to find out who I am without people adoring my vittles.

Namaste,

Benj

Luna did not go with him. She was in the garden today, as always. She was harvesting garlic. When I approached her, I saw she was weeping. "Can you imagine," she asked me, "what Benj would have done with these cloves?"

They were huge, larger than any I have ever seen. Their scent filled the air, reminding me of my childhood in Shanghai. In my mind's eye, I saw Benj quickly dice them and fry them in olive oil with broccoli and cauliflower and a touch of cayenne.

I, too, began to weep.

termevong

Government

(such as it is)

Moustafa Kahlil and Numero Uno sit in black armchairs facing a panel of United States senators. They are answering questions pertaining to the Demur Deodorant scandal, a twenty-three-minute fiasco that erased seventy million dollars from the gross national product.

“Where did the money *go*?” asks Senator Barbara, glaring at Moustafa’s rasta tumble. “You facilitated the transactions, did you not?”

"Demur was a company in name only," says Moustafa, enjoying the senator's sultry snarl. "The corporation was nearly defunct when we found it on the electronic bulletin board. Barely a scent left. Pun unavoidable. Two men bought the entire company for five thousand one hundred and twenty-eight dollars. Their stock portfolio rose to seventy million before evaporating into zeros."

"*People* lost seventy million," says Senator Jane, glaring at Numero Uno drowsing in his seat. "Where did it *go,* Mr. Numero?"

He yawns. "Please. Call me Uno. See, the first thing you have to understand is that *money* is a group hallucination. The system is full of black holes. You've heard of Orville's Suction Theory of Economics? Somebody somewhere got every cent of it. A hacker in Gnome? A Buddhist racecar driver in Dresden? Impossible to know. *They* may not even know they've got it. It might be sitting in somebody's home computer, beeping away. Even as we speak."

"We can't allow this kind of thing to go on," says Senator Grainditch. "People were hurt by this."

"Life hurts," says Moustafa, nodding slowly. "As Buddha said, 'There is no torrent like greed."

"Did *you* take it?" asks Senator Hatcher, known for his idiotic directness. "Huh?"

"If I had seventy million," says Numero Uno, smiling at the senator, "I'd get twenty-seven flipped-out poets elected to congress and blow your shit away."

"And I would contribute heavily to their campaigns," says Moustafa, bouncing his eyebrows.

"We have no further questions," says Senator Hatcher, twirling his finger around his ear to denote insanity. "Case dismissed. I mean, court adjourned. I mean, this hearing is over."

"Wait," says Numero Uno, leaping to his feet. "I want to recite a poem. I beseech Senator Barbara to intercede. We flew all the way from California, after all, and boy are our arms tired."

"Let him read," says Senator Barbara, popping another coffee drop. "But please Mr. Uno, make it short."

Numero Uno closes his eyes and waits for the voice to rise from his loins through his stomach to his throat out his lips. "This comparison thing eats time—the snail slowly mowing baby lettuce knows nothing but her urges—blessed be her reincarnations as I crush her shell and send her back to the soil. The young man desperate to love the willing girl does not stop to consider what might come after. He is mindless, therefore sure. Blessed be their children, born of biology. We so often sit in our black robes, trapped in the cuffs of logic, knowing less than nothing. Far less. Blessed be those timely accidents with their great influx of pain from which we learn the truth, however fleeting. The world harmonious twill. Woof."

"Anything else?" asks Senator Hatcher, continuing to twirl his finger around his ear to denote insanity.

"Yes," says Moustafa, rising gracefully. "I hope one day you will realize that money is simply your *idea* of it. I pray that each of you will be able to embrace another person and love them deeply, for such depth of feeling is the greatest form of wealth."

Baking Bread

(ingredients of the world unite)

Mid-December. Cool morning. Rain falling on the warehouse district, most of the old brick buildings fallen into disuse.

Derek, eleven, pushes an empty wheelbarrow, freshly painted blue, down High Street with Moustafa, fifty, walking beside him. Derek is slender and white-skinned, his curly hair blond, his coveralls blue, his rain boots yellow. Moustafa is broad-shouldered and brown-skinned, his long black hair arrayed in seven beautifully beaded braids, his trousers black, his raincoat burgundy.

"Not many years ago this couldn't have happened," says Moustafa, gazing fondly at Derek. "A black person adopting a white child. A single man, no less. Unheard of when I was your age."

"I think it helped to have Jenny and Leona and Iris come to the meetings," says Derek, smiling up at his new father. "I think they thought you and Jenny were probably a couple and Iris and Leona were like grandmothers, which actually they are."

"This is true, but even so..."

"I guess there's still lots of prejudice," says Derek, with a sad shrug. "At school the Chinese kids mostly play with each other, and the white kids mostly play with each other, and the black kids mostly play with each other, and the Latino kids mostly play with each other, and it's so *tense*."

"Does anyone tease you about...about having a black father?" asks Moustafa, his life and Derek's only recently conjoined by law.

"A few of the less enlightened children have occasionally misspoken themselves," says Derek, winking at Moustafa. "But we'll soon rectify that situation."

"How so?" asks Moustafa, delighted by Derek's perspicacity.

"I'm going to invite them over to bake bread with us," says Derek, stopping at the loading dock of Murray's Bulk Organics. "I was thinking maybe two at a time. Of differing ethnicities."

"Excellent," says Moustafa, ringing the bell. "Parents, too?"

"No," says Derek, smiling mischievously. "Without their parents it will be much more of an adventure."

Moustafa pushes the heavily laden wheelbarrow back up the hill, the sun making a brief appearance to illuminate the cargo of flours and seeds and raisins and nut butters and date sugar. Derek trudges along beside Moustafa, his knapsack bulging with twenty avocadoes destined to become the latest batch of Moustafa's legendary guacamole.

"You know," says Derek, breathing hard as they crest the hill, "I just realized it was *right* after we bought the building when Lord and Indira and Jenny and Natasha and Z and Pinky all decided to leave."

"I have been pondering this very phenomenon," says Moustafa, wheeling their wheelbarrow down the alley adjacent to the enormous three-story warehouse they call home. "And I think it must be that in *knowing* their base won't disappear at the whim of someone outside our community, they feel more free to fly."

"Of course," says Derek, leading the way to the kitchen door, "because they'll *always* have a place to come back to."

"Aha," says Mr. Laskin, a venerable gentleman in faded cowboy denims, opening the door for them. "Your timing is impeccable. Even as we speak, Jenny is flipping her incomparable flapjacks and Denny has brewed an ambrosial pot of Costa Rican coffee the likes of which I haven't tasted since the rumba first became the rage way back when."

"How am I feeling?" asks Jenny, her lovely Irish eyes meeting Derek's Danish blues. "Changeable. One minute calm. Next minute freaking out. Why move to New York? Why not stay here with you? Why am I so drawn to that crowded island of concrete and heartbreak? I don't know. But I am, and I have to go."

Mr. Laskin sips his second cup of coffee and says, "It is the crowning misconception of youth that the marketplace is where the goods are made. But the calf is not raised in the market, she is fattened on distant fields and brought to town to be sold. Thus it is with art."

"There's something else," says Jenny, wishing she could describe how she felt when she first walked the streets of Manhattan. "I need to feel that energy, whatever it is, again."

"Yes," says Mr. Laskin, pointing skyward. "That is what I meant to say. The communal craving, the longing of the group mind for a new and improved culture definitely creates an impetus, a critical mass, if you will, though such collective desire should never be confused with originality."

"Certain humans long to bring the boon of their creations to a larger audience," says Moustafa, measuring cup after cup of pastry flour into a colossal stainless steel bowl. "For thousands of years artists have migrated to cultural meccas to see what might be made of their talent."

"I wonder why," muses Derek, adding four cups of raisins to the mix. "Why to a larger audience? Why not just to each other? To whomever is right here?"

"I'm drawn there to create," says Jenny, gazing out the window at rain dappling the surface of the fishpond. "I...I can't explain. It's..."

"A ferment," says Mr. Laskin, his voice trembling with emotion. "A mass of dough dependent for its rising on the yeast of artists."

"Yes," says Jenny, turning to him in wonder. "I want to be some of that yeast. At least."

"Speaking of yeast," says Moustafa, exchanging knowing smiles with Derek, "may I have the catalyst, please?"

"I have it right here," says Derek, proffering the warm black bowl.

Tantha Fidelos, having just completed a most satisfying telephone conversation with her mother in Finland, having reveled in her native tongue and the heartwarming colloquialisms of her village, sits on a wooden chair on the terrazzo outside the bookstore kitchen, playing an enchanting melody on her accordion and singing in Finnish. She is tall and broad-shouldered, her braided red hair sporting many a silver strand, though she is not yet thirty—a genetic trait of the women of her lineage. When she smiles, which is often, her brilliant green eyes narrow to sparkling slits and her lips seem huge beneath her somewhat flattened nose. Among her people she is considered a rare beauty. In America, the two words most often used to describe her are *handsome* and *exotic*.

The rain has ceased. In the last light of day the temperature drops precipitously, bringing further joy to Tantha, for the growing cold reminds her of the revivifying winters of Finland.

Derek, bundled up in Moustafa's down jacket, sits a few feet from Tantha, mesmerized by the haunting tone of her accordion and the aching tenderness of her voice. And though as far as he knows she might be singing in Martian, he knows exactly what she's singing about—her longing for home.

Inside, a huge pot of turkey and potato and shiitake mushroom soup simmering its way to perfection, Tomas, Tantha's betrothed, studies seven letters on the little rack before him—*E A T V E N I*—the Scrabble board blank, Moustafa, Jenny, and Lord awaiting the first word.

"Do you know what she's singing about?" asks Jenny, finding Tomas terribly attractive now that Tantha has claimed him. "Are you learning Finnish?"

Tomas forces his mind away from the array of letters to listen to Tantha's song—the glass door slightly ajar. "Seeds slumbering beneath the snow dreaming of the flowers they will become."

He resumes his perusal of his seven letters, and laughs triumphantly as he spells

N A I V E T E

Supper dishes done,
dough rising slowly
atop the warm stove

Moustafa stands in the hallway outside Derek's bedroom, listening to Jenny read aloud from *The Prince and the Pauper*. She is a masterful reader, imbuing the words of the fabulous tale with a clarity and passion that would have warmed the cockles of Mark Twain's heart.

Moustafa tiptoes closer to watch Derek sitting up in bed, his little boy eyes wide with wonder as the timeless tale unfolds before and around and *in* him—genius igniting genius igniting genius.

Heading For Hollywood

(Natasha and Z speed southward in pursuit of fame, fortune, and…)

Midnight, the asphalt darkened by recent rain, the scattering storm clouds revealing an enormous half moon hanging over the hills, traffic heavy and insanely fast, cool piano jazz—sultry sexy samba blues—the soundtrack for this show-biz saga.

"Wow," says Z, setting the cruise control of their Haul-It-Yourself van at seventy miles per hour, a veritable snail's pace on the California interstate. "That was some week, huh? Years and years crammed into seven little days. How *did* we do it?"

"Finally on our way," says Natasha, hugging her knees to her chest and gazing at her handsome boyfriend, a little taller and a few shades darker than she. "Those long goodbyes. So many tears. I'm exhausted."

"Got Mama settled in her new pad over the bookstore," says Z, meeting the gaze of his beloved. "Got myself transferred to the Pico Boulevard Bornders und Norble, got us a sublet in Studio City, got three auditions set up for tomorrow, two more auditions the day after..."

"Can we not talk about auditions right now?" says Natasha, feeling a fierce pain in her swiftly beating heart. "Need to chill. Okay?"

"Fine by me," he murmurs, trying not to sound hurt. "Just excited. So many dreams coming true so fast."

Natasha looks away from the blazing taillights and peers into the darkness through which they are falling falling falling down a long incline to the bottom of the state, to the sprawl of intermingled cities where her mother fled so long ago.

"Oh, my God," says Natasha, sudden tears burning her cheeks. "Is that what I'm doing? Chasing my mother?"

"What, sweetheart?" whispers Z. "You thinking out loud, or did you want to talk some more?"

Hot rage masses in Natasha's chest. "Why are we doing this, Z? What the hell are we doing?"

"We're going to Hollywood," he says, feeling kicked in the stomach. "We're gonna sing our songs for people who can open doors, give us a chance to bring our stuff to the big show, share our magic with millions. That's our dream. Remember? I've been working night and day to set up these meetings. I've put it all on the line. For you."

She closes her eyes and tries to take a deep breath, but fury chokes her. "Stop. Please? Need to touch the ground."

They take the Lost Hills exit and park beside a solitary tree—an oak at the base of a round hill—silver gray in the moonlight. Z kills the van lights and sits back feeling betrayed. He folds his arms, clears his throat, and is about to deliver a passionate defense of his strategy when Natasha opens her door, leaps out, and walks away.

Z, stunned and wounded, swallows his impulse to curse her.

Natasha sits on the ground with her back against the oak watching a vivid preview of the life to come, the men in ascending positions of power drunk on her voice and face and body, each demanding possession of her in exchange for passage to the next higher place on the slippery slope of fame, her formidable voice diminished with each horrific gain.

Now she watches a trailer for Z's life, her gracious talented lover told by one record exec after another to muffle his genius with the fluff and drone of sameness. She winces as he pares away the brave new style that makes his songs unique. She watches him betray his muse for bigger and bigger money in a futile attempt to keep her from leaving him—as she inevitably must—for the men with ultimate clout.

She watches their relationship, so full of promise and collaboration, collapse under the weight of emotional isolation. She watches their sweet togetherness break apart in the absence of a nurturing community, in the absence of loving sisters, in the absence of open-hearted men, in the absence of meaningful work.

And at the climax of her chilling vision, she sees herself and Z atop a desolate island in a sea of smog, bowing to a glittering god, a monstrous vampire insatiable for the blood of hopeful artists.

Now she hears Pinky, he who stood atop the Hollywood heap, saying with quiet clarity, "If only you could realize you already *have* the power. That singing we did upstairs just now? *But Beautiful.* *That* is the heart of the heart of the heart. The rest is delusion."

Z grows restless in the van, so he steps out into the night, the oak's shadow black against the moonlit ground, the air rich with the scent of soil touched by recent rain, the incessant growl of the freeway a defamation of what might otherwise be the deepest silence Z has ever known.

He gazes at the brilliant moon and thinks of his mother safe at last in the embrace of his new friends, the first people in his life, other than his mother, to really know him and appreciate him and *believe* in him. And in thinking of Under the Table Books, he has a powerful epiphany—that the love of his new friends was about to render his old ambitions obsolete, ambitions that had sustained him, *defined* him, for all the dangerous years of his previous life at Ground Zero where he could never let his guard down, never relax, never just be.

So is that what I'm doing? Resuming the old hustle that only looks new because Natasha's with me now? Am I afraid to give up my bullshit flash and bravado once and for all and become...what? A baker of bread? A gardener? A seller of books? A devoted friend to those crazy good people at Under the Table Books? Why must I play out this myth of the slave becoming the star? Am I afraid to be...me?

He laughs as he recalls bumping into Leona in the hardware store day before yesterday, how they stood in the light-bulb aisle working out a harmony for *Someone To Watch Over Me*, how fantastic it felt to fit his strong young voice to her quavering falsetto, and how they *got* it, they really *got* a divine melding of tones maybe better than he'd ever gotten a harmony before—his body tingling with the thrill of a wholly unexpected alchemy of sound—how all over the store unseen listeners broke into applause.

"Natasha," says Z, speaking into the darkness. "You hear me?"

"Yes," she answers—so near and yet so far away.

"What are you thinking about?"

"Oh, everything. You. Me. The bookstore. How much Derek will miss Jenny and Lord and Indira, how much he loved working the counter with you, what a brave person he is, how happy it makes me knowing we were able to help him."

"Like you helped me and my mother," says Z, his mind growing marvelously clear, his soft focus fantasies of being a Hollywood hotshot shrinking to little dots and disappearing. "Love given so freely."

"You chose us, we chose you," she says, laughing her deep warm laugh. "Remember the day we met? Me trying to push you away and you bursting into song about me watching the Cat Lady, life just pouring through you and turning into music?"

"As long as I live," he says, on the verge of song again, "I will never forget that moment."

Myrtle, Z's mother, a skinny brown woman hobbled by arthritis, her wiry gray hair going every which way, sits at the kitchen table in a blue kimono embroidered with yellow dragons. She is cursorily skimming the morning paper, her flimsy reading glasses perched on the tip of her nose as she sips the best cup of coffee she has ever had in her sixty-five years on earth, though she feels shy about saying so.

Derek, glorying in a day off from school, stands on a footstool at the stove tending a zucchini and goat cheese omelet, while Moustafa, in his baker's whites, fries a mountain of hash browns made from spuds harvested mere moments ago, while Jenny in black pajamas—even her toenails painted black—uses chopsticks to turn sizzling sausages in a big black skillet, the torrents of luscious smells causing Myrtle to declare, "You people eat like this *all* the time, or you doing this special for me?"

"Truth be told," says Derek, exchanging smiles with Jenny, "we *do* eat rather well here most of the time, *and* we're going a little overboard since this is your first time coming downstairs to eat with us."

"You have a way with words, young man," says Myrtle, gulping her coffee. "Reminds me of my Xavier when he was a child. Mm hmm. Which of you culinary wizards made this java? Might be better than the best I ever had."

"That would be me," says Denny, calling from the rumpus room where's he's doing a headstand. "It's all about the beans."

At which moment the back door slides opens and Z and Natasha come in out of the rain, tears in their eyes, smiles a mile wide, everybody knowing in an instant they've come home to stay.

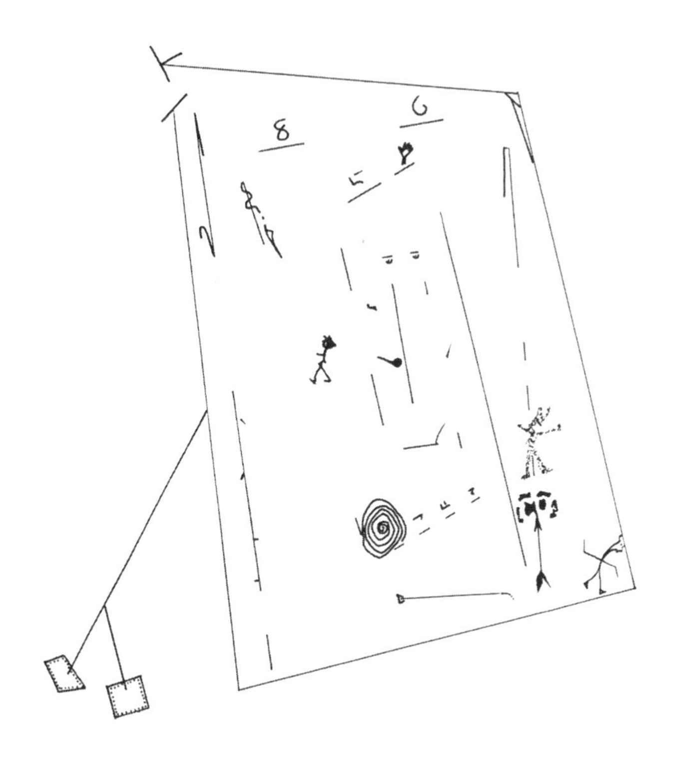

Going To New York (Again)

(this time she takes the zephyr)

Jenny thought—in the surprise and joy of Natasha and Z changing their minds about moving to Los Angeles—that she might change her mind, too. But here she sits in the observation car of a transcontinental express train, gazing out at a painted desert somewhere deep in the heart of Utah, being carried eastward on hundreds of steel wheels rolling on steel bars sending forth countless expressions of sound merging into one grandiloquent rhythm.

No she imagines Moustafa saying as he listens to this marvelous cumulative clickety-clack *I cannot clap that beat, but we could certainly find a sympathetic rhythm to go with it. Almost anything will.*

She gazes out the window at the desert spreading unbroken to a horizon of clouds, and she is keenly aware that had she stayed in the embrace of the commune, she might never complete the daunting task of becoming wholly her own person.

Two magnificent pronghorn antelope appear on the alkali stage and race the iron serpent for a mile or so before they swerve away and disappear in a cloud of dust.

Dear Lord,

I will drop this in the mail during our layover in Chicago. Barring some postal faux pas you should get this before you leave for Brazil. Or maybe you won't go. Maybe you'll change your mind and show up unannounced at my door—whatever door that turns out to be—in New York. But probably you will go to Brazil with Indira, and maybe you'll die and we'll never see each other again.

Whew! Had to take a break to cry. I already feel like a widow and you haven't even left yet. Of course I was also crying about losing you as my lover partner best friend and all those yet-to-be-resolved emotions I still occasionally encounter in the widening wake of We becoming You and I.

But deeper than that is my fear sorrow anger at the possibility of your disappearing from all our lives, from the life of Under the Table Books. Life without Lord Bellmaster? Oh, sure, we're all going to die someday, but you're so young, so funny, so generous and silly and wise.

I see you on your stool behind the counter listening to yet another lost soul confessing his hidden feelings, his long-held secrets, his dreams and hopes and burning questions. And I see you, as always, reassuring him with your smiling eyes and open arms, your voice so friendly calm telling him he's not alone, not insane, and best of all that he is welcome to hang out, to have a bite to eat, a book to read, a place to sit and rest for a time without fear of censure or being asked to leave. You created that safe space for us, Lord. Or, as you would say in your humble way, you got the ball rolling.

Anyway, I just wanted to say I love you, and I will be forever grateful for everything you invited me to be part of.

Jen

Penelope, a short buxom woman with braided black hair takes the seat next to Jenny in Chicago. She is delighted to find that Jenny speaks Spanish. By using a mixture of English and Spanish, they are able to communicate quite well. Penelope tells of her harrowing journey from El Salvador to the United States, how she crossed into Texas with five other women whose husbands were established in

New York and arranged for their wives to be smuggled in the back of a truck carrying tons of garlic from Mexico to Manhattan.

"I no eat garlic for long time after," says Penelope, laughing gaily. "I no can go train before *yo tengo* el green card. *Y ahora pronto* we bring *los hijos* to America."

"*Cuantos hijos tiene usted?*" asks Jenny, relieved to have someone to talk to, someone so warm and friendly.

"*Tres*," says Penelope, her smile becoming sad. "No see my children for seven years."

"Will they have to ride in the back of a truck full of garlic?"

"No," says Penelope, opening the basket at her feet and bringing forth a supper of tortillas *con frijoles y pollo y* blazing salsa to share with Jenny. "*Par avion*. We are citizens now. *Libre*."

Penelope's husband Pedro, a burly man with glossy gray hair, is not surprised to find his wife returning with a new friend, a tall woman—*muy bonita*—dressed in black with a backpack and two big suitcases.

In the beautiful language of their remote highland village, Penelope tells Pedro about Jenny.

Pedro turns to Jenny and says with deep respect, "You are an artist. *Que bueno*. Our house is full, but we can make room for you."

"*Gracias*, no," says Jenny, blushing with pleasure. "I'm staying at the Y for a few nights until I get my bearings."

Penelope takes Jenny's hands. "You have my phone number. You call us if we can help you. Is hard to start new life here."

In her little room on the seventh floor of the YMCA building, the grime of her long journey washed away in a warm shower, she puts on her pajamas—the blue ones with green frogs—and slowly unpacks her suitcases into the small dresser of drawers.

She is too excited to sleep, so she opens her window and the fantastic roaring of the great city rushes in on the freezing air—a roaring that shakes her bones.

But rather than close the window, she listens to the bellowing city and decides she must find a place where the roar is muted, so her sleep will be deep and restful. *How else can I survive here?*

She tallies up her money for the umpteenth time—two thousand six hundred dollars—a total that emboldened her to make this daring move from a lesser city, but in Manhattan seems a paltry sum.

A job. I've got to get a job. I don't want to live someplace dangerous. But what can I possibly afford? A room. I'll rent a room in a quiet neighborhood. Doesn't have to be a big room. I'll be fine. I'll meet people. A job. A room. Then...oh I have to stop thinking about this and get some sleep.

She crawls into bed and shuts off the light, but sleep won't come. So she turns on the light and tries to read. Impossible. Her mind is buzzing like an angry bee. She gets out of bed and rummages in her backpack for her sketchpad. *Drawing relaxes me.*

A bright orange envelope falls out from between the pages—an envelope she doesn't remember packing

From Lord Moustafa Natasha Numero
Derek Z Leona Carl Iris Bernie Indira Denny
Monica Tomas Peter Tantha and Mr. Laskin

Dearest Jenny Friend of All the World,

Knowing Manhattan to be no low-rent paradise, we rounded up a hundred dollars and turned Mr. Laskin loose for twenty minutes on The New York Stock Exchange (appropriate given your proximity to Wall Street) facilitated by Moustafa via cyberspace. Enclosed you will find his winnings transformed into a cashier's check made out to you for seven thousand four hundred and seventy-seven dollars and seventy-seven cents.

"Losing my touch," said Mr. Laskin, though he was obviously pleased to be of help to you.

Our love for you unlimited forever

The Road To Brazil

(Lord and Indira gathering momentum and still very much enjoying wearing each other's clothes)

Indira ceased shaving her head in January. Now that March has given way to April, her lustrous black hair is three inches long and growing fast. When she wets her lovely mop and combs it straight back, she becomes a most exotic Elvis, wildly appealing to homosexuals of either gender, especially when she wears combat fatigues and big brown jungle boots—one very sexy soldier.

As sub-commandante to Alfredo de San Francisco, Indira has seen their band of eco-warriors swell to seventy-four—deployment to Brazil looming as the last pristine rainforest on earth is about to be decimated for the enrichment of a handful of men who already have more money than anyone else in the world. Not only are these greedy guys planning to cut down thousands of ancient trees, but in doing so they will immolate *billions* of the rarest and most enchanting plants and animals and reptiles and amphibians and birds in all creation—*unless* the tiny army of Alfredo de San Francisco can keep the plunderers at bay until...

Until what? Lord wonders, frowning at the pile of clothing he hopes to fit into a small canvas duffel bag, each soldier allowed thirty pounds of gear to be packed by mules into the jungle. Lord is committed to going because he can't imagine living without Indira, but he wishes the whole adventure didn't feel so blatantly suicidal.

Indira enters their yurt wearing a black raincoat over blue jeans and a San Francisco Giants sweatshirt. Speaking into a mobile phone, her side of the conversation is the stuff of existential comedy.

"Balloon," she says officiously. "Incendiary confetti." She laughs musically. "Martinis with Swedish meatballs? Never again."

"What news?" asks Lord, not really wanting to know.

Indira falls onto the bed. "We leave for Costa Rica tomorrow."

"Flying?" he says, his stomach gurgling.

"Ground," she says, closing her eyes. "They're onto us, Lord. They've already arrested three. We're down to seventy-one."

"On what charge? We're just a bunch of environmentalists at this point. And who is *they*?"

"We've been labeled potential you-know-whats by the corporate political powers that be. They want to lock us all up until they're done with their dirty work."

"Costa Rica," he murmurs, lying down beside her. "I think I may be taking too many socks. How many pair are you taking?"

"We'll convene in a location yet to be announced," she says, reflexively fitting her body to his. "From there we'll caravan to Venezuela, whence we'll make our way to positions in Brazil."

"When you say *positions*...I mean *ground*," murmurs Lord, forgetting about his socks and wanting only to be naked with Indira, "do you mean car or bus or train or missionary or..."

"You're *so* sexy," she says, forgetting about saving anything. "Let's disrobe, yeah?"

In the first blush of dawn, Lord driving, Indira riding shotgun, they depart by rented car for the Santa Cruz mountains where Lord hopes to pick up a drum made by Moustafa's old band mate Bobby Screech Owl—a magic drum Lord craves for succor and inspiration.

Indira is more than a little miffed by their detour from the straight shot down the center of California to Mexico, but when they leave the hustle and bustle and muscle and tussle of the urban freeway and climb over the hill to Pacifica, her first sight of the majestic ocean takes her breath away and she kisses Lord in thanks.

"We'll get there when we get there," she says, rolling down her window and filling the car with sweet briny air.

"And," says Lord with a hopeful shrug, "maybe taking the less-traveled road is our best bet for going undetected by the powers that be."

"Border crossings," she says softly. "Those will be challenging."

Bobby Screech Owl, a barrel-chested Ohlone man, takes an elk-skin drum down from a peg on the wall in his workshop. He gazes at the silver-gray skin stretched taut over a wheel of alder and says with a sigh, "This drum doesn't want to go with you."

"Why not?" whispers Lord, longing to hold the instrument.

"Spirit says South World not home to this skin," says Bobby, tapping the drum and making it ring like a gong. "But this drum likes you and wants to live with you someday."

"I don't understand," says Lord, immobilized by sadness.

Bobby closes his eyes and speaks for the drum. "We all live in watersheds, and now every watershed is in danger. There is big work for us wherever we live. I want to be the drum of your people. I am not a traveling drum. I am a drum of the hearth, of the family. Where you go to fight is not my place. You will find something there for making music. I will wait for you to come again."

On a freeway in Los Angeles, millions of barely moving cars suddenly stop—completely. Indira takes her hands off the steering wheel and closes her eyes. The air outside their car is brown, the sky above a murky gray, no clouds in sight. Lord rolls down his window to get a sense of the outside temperature. The stench of burning rubber and diesel fumes enter the car on a hot dusty wind.

"Here's a watershed in trouble," he says, quickly rolling up the window. "Maybe Bobby's right. Maybe we don't need to go to Brazil to make our stand."

Indira opens one eye. "Would you please stop using the royal *We* when expressing *your* doubts. I am not in doubt."

"I was talking about the larger *Us*," says Lord, stung by her retort. "Not just you and me. Everybody."

"Speak for yourself," she says, taking her foot off the brake to let their car roll forward a sixteenth of an inch.

Midnight. A cheap motel on the outskirts of San Diego.

Lord sits on the bed staring dumbly at a television, images of fire and flood and war and starvation and rising seas interspersed with advertisements for cars and beer and computers and razor blades and insurance. And in every ad the men are young and strong and surly, the women young and slender and busty, the message clear: if you want to be that young man and have that young woman, or vice-versa, you *must* own that car that computer that beer that insurance that razor blade. Then, and only then, will you be fulfilled.

Indira pockets her phone and says, "Turn that shit off."

Lord falls to his knees and gropes blindly for the OFF button, the screen going blank just as the busty babe and the surly stud arrive in a cloud of dust at the edge of the Grand Canyon in a shiny black jeep truck the size of a house, the name of the vehicle appearing in huge gold letters on the darkening sky—*VICTORY*.

"We'll have to sneak across the border," says Indira, giving Lord a hand up. "They've caught thirty more of us. We're down to forty."

"Wow," he says numbly. "Maybe we shouldn't go. Maybe..."

"I'm going," she says, looking into his eyes. "Leaving now."

"Now?" he says, utterly drained. "We need to sleep. We need..."

"Lord," she says, forcefully enunciating her words. "They are closing in on us *now*."

"It's a nightmare," he says, bowing his head. "I don't know if I have the strength."

"It is not a nightmare," she says calmly. "This is actually happening. They will kill the earth if we don't fight them."

"They may have already killed her," he says, his eyes brimming with tears. "It may be too late no matter what we do."

"Maybe so," she says, smiling mysteriously. "But maybe not. So I'm going. Come with me if you will."

Dawn. Tiny waves, barely more than ripples, lap gently on the beach of a secluded lagoon some five hundred miles south of Texas.

A man and a woman dressed in peasant garb sleep together on the golden sand. They have few possessions, and these they carry in small canvas packs. They wake to find themselves in each other's arms, though they were not touching when sleep claimed them.

"Lord," says Indira, kissing her lover's chin. "You awake?"

"I am," he says, breathing deeply of her scent. "You dream?"

"Yes," she says, pressing her lips to his throat. "We were in the bookstore, Tantha playing her accordion, everyone dancing because..."

"Yes?" he says, imagining the joyful scene. "Because..."

"It was our wedding," she says, disentangling her body from his and sitting up. "Hungry?"

"I had a dream, too," he says, sitting up with her. "Want to hear?"

"Of course," she says, bringing forth a bag of peanuts. "I'm just suddenly starving."

"We met some people with a beautiful schooner," he says, gazing out to sea as the very boat of his dream comes sailing into the lagoon. "And we sailed with them all the way to Colombia."

They munch peanuts for a time, musing on their dreams and watching a jaunty fellow wearing a blue skipper's cap lower the sails and drop anchor not fifty yards from shore.

"Shall I make coffee?" asks Lord, rummaging in his pack for their little stove.

"Please," says Indira, thinking of her wedding dress in her dream—what it might mean that she chose white.

Now the jaunty fellow on the schooner spots them on the beach and calls out in Spanish adulterated by a thick French accent, "Hello. Do you know of any fresh water hereabouts?"

"There is a clear flowing stream at the southern end of the beach," replies Indira in excellent French. "We can guide you there."

"We are saved," says the skipper, clapping his hands. "My wife is making breakfast. Would you care to join us? I will fetch you in our skiff."

❦

Dear Moustafa,

I am writing this by the light of a kerosene lantern hanging from the boom of the fifty-foot schooner Désir Fatal. We are moored in an inlet off the western coast of Panama, the jungle a hundred yards away in the pitch-black darkness, the warm air thrumming fantastically with the voices of billions of insects. I am sipping a glass of fine red wine made of grapes from a vineyard owned by our incomparable hosts, Jean Pierre and Claudette. I am listening to Indira and Jean Pierre and Claudette speaking French in the galley below. There is nothing about any of this to distinguish it from a lucid dream.

The sky is different here so far south from you—full of stars and constellations I have never seen before. The trees are different, too, as are the birds and many of the fish. I am struck again and again by the ferocity of the beauty here—the source of the ferocity unfathomable.

We should reach Colombia in a few weeks. From there we will find our way to Brazil. I have no doubt now that we will have our chance to place ourselves between the destroyers and the forest they wish to destroy. Somewhere along our way my fear left me. I have been at peace now for many days.

I want to tell you and everyone at Under the Table Books how much I love you, how grateful I am for your tolerance of my massive idiosyncrasies. I hope someday to return to you, though I have no expectation I will.

I enclose a new poem.

Indira sends her love.

I close my eyes and listen to the thunder of the insects and I can see you so clearly I know I am not imagining you or remembering you, but actually seeing you. So beautiful to know you are always so near to me.

Lord

The Stone in the Rock

the blessed body
encased in the cast
of soil and mud,
the dirt in the clod
drenched in dragons' blood
congealed by the sweet ministrations
of gravity over time,
of ever present love,
of the stone in the rock,
the force in the roots
thrusting to fruition,
the rose of the thorn,
the child of the saint,
the mother of us all.

The hummingbird's tongue
deep in the flower,
the truest word,
and if it cannot be found
we shall surrender
to the blessed silence,
of now and forever,
the song in the song,
the light of the sun,
the stone
in the rock.

Double Date

(Iris and Leona and Mr. Laskin and Peter Franklin
discover the fountain of youth)

"Now, Leona," says Iris, serving her sister a cup of chamomile tea in the sunny kitchen of their Victorian duplex, Leona wearing a baggy gray sweater and orange sweatpants, Iris still in her gossamer nightgown. "I have a question for you. Ready?"

"What I wouldn't give for coffee and chocolate," says Leona, glowering at the herbal tea. "Now *that's* the way to start your day."

"Your adrenals are shot," says Iris, matter-of-factly. "Slowly but surely we're resuscitating them, so coffee and chocolate on Sundays only."

"When will it ever be *Sunday* again?" moans Leona, taking a sip of her tea and making a sour face. "Weeds. Boiled weed juice."

"May I ask my question, please?" says Iris, sitting opposite her twin and carefully tasting her piping hot Postum.

"The answer is probably *no*," says Leona, forgetting she hates her tea and gulping it down with gusto. "That's my role in this dyad, right? I'm the bitter twin, you're the sweet?"

"It's about sex," says Iris, clearing her throat. "You see, I've been wondering..."

"You mink," says Leona, frowning into her empty cup. "Sex sex sex. That's all you ever talk about."

"On the contrary," says Iris, feeling affronted. "I have studiously avoided bringing up the subject with you for over a year now."

"Seems like only yesterday," says Leona, rolling her eyes. "Did you say day after tomorrow for the coffee and chocolate?"

"Oh, I don't care," says Iris, fed up with her sister's adrenals. "Have whatever you want. You're eighty-eight after all."

"So what's all this talk about sex?" asks Leona, jumping up to brew some coffee. "You're eighty-eight, too, you know?"

"Well," says Iris, blushing, "I'm on the verge of getting laid."

"*Again?*" says Leona, staring in horror at the empty coffee jar. "We're out of beans *again*? This is an outrage."

"You know they'll have fresh brewed at the bookstore," says Iris, feeling miffed her sister doesn't want to know about her love life. "I've only *tasted* Denny's dynamite java, but I'm told..."

"It's that Laskin fellow, isn't it?" says Leona, sitting down to lace up her running shoes. "That old rake. I thought you were through with him. And how come *you're* still so sexual when I haven't had a libidinal yearning since I can't remember when? Eons. No doubt related to my blasted adrenals. But I don't give a damn because for me coffee and chocolate *is* sex. Are. If you know what I mean."

"I don't, actually," says Iris, shrugging politely. "Know what you mean. But as far as Mr. Laskin goes, Alexander, I *am* through with him. Carnally speaking. We haven't...you know...done the deed in months. Well...weeks anyway. Several days. But..."

"I don't want to hear about his butt," says Leona, rising urgently—an addict on the trail of her fix. "You coming with me?"

"Leona," says Iris with uncharacteristic force. "Peter Franklin has asked me to...to trip the light fantastic with him. As it were."

Leona shakes her head. "So what's the question?"

"Should I tell Peter about my recent engagement, relatively speaking, with Alexander, *and* should I tell Alexander that I am now..."

"What *difference* does it make?" says Leona, slapping a sunhat onto her mop of curly white hair. "You're a *great*-grandmother. Peter doesn't think you're still a virgin, does he?"

"No, but Alexander and Peter have become such great pals of late," says Iris, wringing her hands. "They play chess with each other almost every day after Alexander's two o'clock sandwich, and I...I don't want to be a wedge between them."

"Sis," says Leona, giving Iris a peck on the cheek. "Don't tell them anything. Neither of them can remember what happened two hours ago, let alone yesterday." She opens the door and steps out into the day. "The moment is all we've got anymore, sweetheart. *This* moment."

Iris sits in the resounding silence that always follows Leona's departure, sipping her Postum and musing on her sister's advice.

I suppose she's right. In the absence of memory, jealousy becomes moot.

Peter Franklin, a dapper and wonderfully fit fellow in his early eighties, smiles his impish smile and says to his opponent, "Am I to assume the move you just made is actually the move you wish to make? Or are you merely pondering the board in its new configuration before finalizing your intent?"

Mr. Laskin, a noble white-haired man wearing a purple leather cowboy hat, squints across the chessboard and says, "Look. I'm either three moves away from checkmating your British dandy ass, or you're about to do me in. Prelude to either scenario, that's my move."

Peter nods graciously. "May I ask a question unrelated to chess?"

"A ploy to distract me, no doubt," says Mr. Laskin, extremely fond of their repartee. "Fire away."

"Iris?" says Peter, glancing furtively at Mr. Laskin. "You..."

"I have and hope to again." says Mr. Laskin, smiling broadly at a salient memory of being entangled with Iris in her big comfortable bed. *Yesterday? Day before?* "But I will not begrudge you her considerable charms, my friend. I have noted the exchange of twinkles between you two, and I would be the last man to impede the course of love."

"How very generous of you," says Peter, about to make the move with his queen that will insure his victory.

At which pivotal juncture, Iris enters looking oh so Kate Hepburn in jodhpurs and a billowy white blouse—small and slender and spry, her cheeks aglow.

Both men reflexively rise to fulfill their gentlemanly prerequisites, each bowing with considerable grace and eagerness.

"Good morrow, fair Iris," says Peter, his heart aflutter.

"Peter," she says with a fetching nod.

"*Bon jour ma chose d'amour délicieux,*" says Mr. Laskin, his voice rich with lust.

"Oh, please don't let me interrupt your game," says Iris, shivering in delight at the sound of French—not so sure she wants to forego Alexander after all.

"Game?" say the men. "What game?"

Leona is belting out *There's No Business Like Show Business* as she walks home toting a pink pastry box containing an ultra-fresh *Brick O' Heaven*—a one-pound cube of the richest bittersweet organic eighty-three-percent cacao chocolate. And balanced atop her pink box is a silver bag containing a pound of glittering organic Maui Kona coffee beans, ready for the grinder and the filter and the boiling water and...

"I am *so* happy," says Leona, supercharged from three massive cups of Denny's potent java.

She stops in front of the charming chartreuse Victorian duplex she owns with Iris, grins enormously at a pair of hummingbirds probing the first fuchsias of spring, and gestures majestically to the whole world. "What a *great* life I have. Eighty-eight and going strong."

Theoretically, Iris lives in the downstairs unit, Leona upstairs, but the truth is they both spend most of their time downstairs and sleep together in Iris's king-sized bed. On those rare nights when Iris keeps a lover overnight, she makes sure to hang the DO NOT DISTURB sign on her front door to warn Leona of any hanky panky that might be underway. Iris's DO NOT DISTURB sign is from the Beverly Hills Hotel, and it always makes Leona think about her wild partying days in Hollywood so long ago.

Seeing no such warning dangling from the pushpin, Leona opens the door to an outburst of laughter—male male female. She steps back, scans the door again for cautionary signage, and seeing only a blank field of pink, she enters.

Iris is sitting between Mr. Laskin and Peter Franklin on the big blue sofa—all of them fully clothed. They are watching the Marx Brothers in *A Night At The Opera* on Iris and Leona's state-of-the-art home movie screen, the volume outrageously loud.

"Good *God*, Iris," cries Leona, her imagination running wild. "A *ménage à trois*? You animal, you."

But Iris and Alexander and Peter are laughing so hard, and the climactic scene is *so* loud, Leona's words are lost in gales of merriment.

And as these hurricanes of hilarity buffet Leona, she raises her eyes from the trio on the sofa to behold Chico and Harpo and Groucho making riotous war on Seriousness, and something enormous shifts inside her—the perennial tightness in her chest dissolving into a pleasing softness as some long-held grudge against life evaporates.

Now her eyes move from the screen to Alexander, and before her cynical self can take hold again, she shivers in delight and thinks *What a great-looking man!*

Now she hears a woman's voice, clear and confident and sweet—*so* sweet she thinks it must be Iris's voice until she realizes it's her *own* voice—saying, "Hey, you beauties. I'm about to make a big pot of Maui Kona to go with a fabulous *Brick O' Heaven*."

These promising words strike Alexander deep—Harpo plucking the strings of his mystical harp—and the handsome man rises from the sofa as if lifted by angels.

"Chocolate and Maui Kona?" he intones, approaching Leona. "You're a woman after my own heart."

Peter and Iris lie abed, their first sexual excursion together something of a letdown—nothing approaching orgasm for either of them—yet promising, for they were both eager and tender and patient, and they both very much enjoyed the gentle intimacy.

Iris is just about to say something complimentary and hopeful, when Peter kisses her face and throat and shoulders and breasts, singing, "Getting to know you, getting to know all about you. Getting to like you, getting to hope you like me."

Alexander and Leona lie on their backs in Leona's single bed, wide-eyed in wonder at what they have just experienced—a prolonged earthquake of simultaneous orgasms spanning eras and epochs and rewriting history to usher in the long-awaited renaissance of humanity.

"Um..." says Leona, taking two of Alexander's mighty fingers in her strong little hand. "I wonder...since it's been, oh God, fifty years for me since...if maybe it was extra- special because...or maybe..."

Alexander rolls onto his side to show her his sparkling tears.

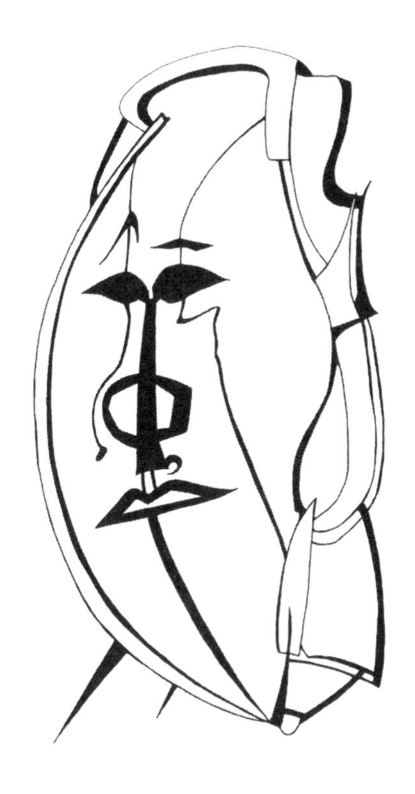

Another Day

(fallen chef, arise)

The morning finds Benjamin sitting in his ratty old armchair, frozen on the edge of a memory. Or is it a memory? He can see the dark oak looming on the edge of his father's property. He was afraid, *is* afraid, of that tree. But why? He is sorely tempted to turn on the television, to drown in the blither of fearful nonsense, but he is still in his pajamas and doesn't want to sink too low. Not yet.

He wanders into his kitchen, the floor begging to be mopped. He aimlessly eats an apple, then another, and their sour taste reminds him of the apple tree growing on the edge of the woods beyond his father's land—the apples full of worms.

He goes into his dank little bedroom and pulls on his dirty jeans, their coldness causing him to wince. He remembers his last lover saying clean clothes never feel cold. She said many things like that. Not exactly proverbs, not necessarily provable—subtle warnings.

In his neglected garden, he stands knee-deep in weeds and recalls life at the Buddhist monastery where he toiled happily for nine glorious months, cooking and weeding and loving with boundless energy, fuelled by the power of friendship. *I could almost go back there. I almost believe there's nothing particularly special about me. But not quite. I still have inklings of some grandiose destiny. I wish to be free of that. How long will I have to go without a decent head of broccoli before I'm humbled? And even then, would my humility last? Wouldn't the first loving woman, the first decent onion, make me feel special?*

He hears a clacking sound—Mrs. Morgan turning her circular clothesline—clackety-clack—hanging up her wash to dry. He wonders if *she* has ever put on dirty clothes in the morning. "Probably not. A day rarely goes by when she doesn't hang something out to dry."

He sits beneath the tulip tree, his bowl of rice steaming in the soft spring sunlight, and he decides to give thanks for the first time since leaving the monastery. For a year now he has rigorously avoided making anything resembling those prayers of gratitude that prefaced every meal in his previous life.

He slows his breathing and begins Roshi Supremo's favorite premeal meditation. He travels in his mind to the field where the farmer uses strength and wisdom to prepare the ground to receive the rice seeds, sun and rain mingling with soil and microbes to bring forth green shoots that grow and grow until their own seeds are gathered by the farmer and carried to the mill where the rice is hulled and the kernels poured into sacks for the merchants from whom Ben purchases the rice.

Now I have cooked these tiny germs of life, thousands and thousands of them, in heavenly water brought to a boil over a flame composed of the essence of ancient plants and animals so I may lift this food to my lips on sticks carved from the wood of a tree that fell to human need. And consider the clay composing this bowl, the potter whose strength and sweat are in this form that holds my meal. Think of my parents who gave me life. And the air, the mountains, the wind, my dreams, the worms—each moment a blessing, every kernel of rice a gift from the beings who live and die so I may live—all there has ever been, all that is, all that will ever be.

Thus prepared, he eats heartily, rejoicing in a vision of returning to his beloved monastery.

Now he takes the last grain of rice into his mouth and remembers standing beneath his father's dark oak—a shivering boy on the cusp of manhood—watching the wind rip the dry leaves from their moorings, stripping the branches bare.

Last

(each and every one of us)

The loveliness of evening, the loveliness of this dream. This is the final test of my faith. *This* is the nick of time. Tomorrow, if we do not stop them at the river, the fight will be lost.

My name is Lord Bellmaster. I am a soldier in the army of Alfredo de San Francisco. There are a hundred of us from around the world strung thinly along the edge of the last fragment of pristine tropical rainforest on earth, home to the last jaguars, the last wild parrots, the last of thousands of plant species. In front of us, across the muddy river, lies the newly made desert where once stood the lungs of the planet.

Soon my beloved Indira will arrive and we will talk and eat and laugh and kiss for what may be the last time in our lives. Tomorrow, our misguided brothers will bring up their armored attack vehicles to destroy us. But not before we fire a few volleys of our own.

An armored gunship moves upstream, laboring against the powerful current. "It is not too late to change your mind," says a man on the boat, his voice booming from a large speaker mounted on the prow. "Do not believe Alfredo de San Francisco. He is a liar and a murderer."

"A murderer, yes," I reply. "A liar, no."

I aim my gun at the boat and pretend to shoot. If I were to actually pull the trigger, as I may tomorrow, the return fire would be instantaneous and overwhelming. Much of the surrounding forest would be pulverized along with me. They aren't taking any chances this time. We are among the last rebels on the planet.

If I were to *change my mind* and surrender, I would be tortured and killed. Why? Because I believe the earth belongs to all living things, not to one species, and certainly not to a few individual humans.

Alfredo came by this morning, stopping only for a moment, wanting to visit all his fighters before tomorrow. He is our spirit and our courage. I need only look into his eyes and my fear of death goes away.

He gave me a postcard, a picture of a watermelon, my favorite fruit. On the back, in his childish scrawl, he wrote,

> Dearest Lord,
>
> I dream we are floating down the river together on the back of a huge turtle. On one side of the river stands the forest we have saved, the mother of our new earth. On the other side, where our ignorant brothers have cleared the land, as far as the eye can see, a new forest grows, planted by the very beings who cut the old one down. The sky is dark blue and the air is rich with

oxygen and we drink the water without fear because humans no longer create poisons. If my dream becomes reality, it will be because you fought with us, you said, "No more! You cannot kill our mother!"

I love you.

Alfredo

Black ants stream through the forest. As the gunboat rounds a bend in the river, the sound of its engine dies away and I can hear the loud whisper of a billion ants moving over the leaves covering the ground.

Clouds spring from the green mass. The sky darkens. Raindrops pelt me. The air cools. Something flares brilliantly on the opposite bank. I dive into my hole. A missile screeches overhead and strikes a huge tree, blowing it into a million fragments, shaking the earth.

The gunboat returns. "It is not too late to change your mind. That missile was a warning. You cannot win this battle. Why not change your mind? You will not be harmed. Alfredo de San Francisco is a liar and murderer. We have every intention of carefully managing the resources of the rainforest."

Many of our people have surrendered in the last few days. Assassins have killed many more of us.

The river is called La Esperanza—Hope. If I were not here in this hole, if I could not see for myself how the river keeps them from crossing, I might think the name a convenient fiction. Indira calls the river The Ribbon. Alfredo says the waters of hope are laced with pesticides. We catch rain and hope it is safe to drink.

But let us turn away from the river. Let me tell you of the towering trees cloaked in great skeins of moss, the royal ferns trembling with life, the slowly graceful sloths and lemurs, the cute little monkeys, the screeching white parrots with their yellow-and-blue manes. Let me tell you of the radiant red flowers as big as a person, of the coal-black butterflies the size of two human hands. Let me tell you of the amazing variety of toads, thousands of them, some so small they can sit on my thumbnail, some as large as basketballs. And let me tell you of our mantis.

There is a praying mantis living in this hole with me. She moved in the day I dug it. She came fearlessly, with the sureness of a queen, swollen with eggs of the next generation. Why the lizards have spared her, why the lightning-tongued toads have let her live, is a lovely mystery. I have seen the monkeys gulping moths and grubs as fast as they can shove them into their greedy little mouths, but they do not bother the mantis. Nor do the parrots. They *see* her, but she is not food to them, not now, not at the zenith of her motherhood.

She sits on my sleeping bag, watching me with her human-like eyes. In my loneliness, in these last naked moments of my life, I believe she is the ear of Nature, that she and her progeny will carry my message to the great spirit of everything.

"Listen, Mantis, you know I would rather not die tomorrow. I would rather live a long time and make love to Indira and eat Moustafa's bread and work the counter with Derek and go roaming with Denny and Jenny, finding books to nourish the souls of our community. But without this forest, the planet is doomed. I've been given so much by you. It's time to walk my talk. To live my truth. To fight for what I believe in."

Mantis cocks her head, blinks a few times, and brings her front feet together in prayer. I close my eyes and hear her say

> There will come a bitter wind
> and many of your kind will perish
> save for those with the new wisdom
> and some of these will survive.

Indira arrives so silently, had she been an assassin, I would be dead. She would make a fabulous assassin, sleek and cunning. She steps into my hole to embrace me. A deeper darkness falls. We cannot eat. We take off our clothes and I suckle on her swollen breasts. She is seven months with child. It may be mine.

Mantis watches Indira straddle me and ride to her joy as I spasm into giving.

My lover whispers, "We will survive," and kisses me.

She sleeps. I eat dried fruit and watch the ribbon of water, lit by moonlight. They are quiet in the camps across the river. I see only a few dim lights, not the usual glare. The cicadas hum. I am overwhelmed with memories of my life in California—the simple joys of walking and talking and breathing and loving, content to deny the horror befalling our planet until I was swept up in Alfredo's fervor to save this last reserve.

Indira wakes and pulls me down beside her. "I had a dream inspired by that most splendiferous loving you gave me."

The mantis walks across my chest and scales Indira's breast, perching there to listen and pray.

"In my dream, you and I were making love on a bed with pink sheets. You were making me pregnant. As you came inside me I was racing up a dark river, my legs straddling a sperm. I came abreast of another woman straddling another sperm. We raced together until she fell behind and I was alone racing toward..."

She stops speaking. We hold our breaths. Someone is moving through the jungle. The mantis jumps from Indira's breast and hides in the deepest corner of our hole. I sense murder in the air—a barely audible whining—but I am not afraid. I am impatient to hear the rest of Indira's dream. I want to say to the murderer, "Come back tomorrow. We are in the midst of sharing our dreams."

Now the person is very near. I want it to be one of our compatriots, but we know it is not.

"Indira," a man whispers. "Indira, are you there?"

Indira does not reply. Nor do I.

Indira rises swiftly and hurls her knife into the darkness.

The man groans and falls to the ground.

Indira lies back down. "Where were we?"

The mantis returns to Indira's breast.

"You were racing up the dark river toward..."

"Yes," she cries. "The incredible egg. And now it looms above me, a fortress so vast, with walls so thick, penetration by me on my wisp of a sperm seems impossible, laughable, and I *do* laugh, Lord. I do. I dig my heels into the flanks of my sperm and laugh as we rush headlong at the wall. And just when I think we will smash against the wall and die, a crack appears, a chink in the armor, and the head of my sperm lodges there and I kick and kick and the tail whips and the wall gives way and we enter."

"Nothing could stop you."

"This child is yours," she says fiercely. "It can only be yours."

"Who was that man you killed?"

"My assassin," she says, placing her hand on my heart. "They know our names, Lord. They know each and every one of us."

Is that the dawn? Yes. The blackness of night gives way to the infinite hues of green, the jungle separating itself from the sky once more to receive the sun, turn water to air, pour trillions of tons of oxygen into the atmosphere to be carried by capillary winds to the distant reaches of the planet.

Indira touches my lips with her finger. "You were dreaming. Can you remember?"

"We were playing basketball," I say, sitting up. "For the first time in my life, the other men were passing me the ball. I couldn't miss." I close my eyes, seeing it all again. "Now the ball is a soft, crumbling sphere of dough, cooked sweet, and I am trying to shoot it through the hoop before it disintegrates. I miss, and miss again. But on my third try, the ball of dough goes through the hoop and leaves the rim coated with cinnamon and there is a woman smiling at me, touching the rim with her fingers."

The sun pours through the canopy of trees, illuminating a leaf shaped like an elephant's ear. Indira carries the mantis to the leaf and we watch her die in an ecstasy of birthing, her eggs foaming out of her.

We ready our guns. The ants feast on the corpse of the assassin.

The wet heat is ferocious today. We drink coffee to stay awake, but finally, when the sun is directly above us, we fall asleep in the hole.

I dream of hordes of starving women and children attacking us. They swarm across the river, eating the forest like mad locusts. There is nothing we can do to stop them.

Indira shakes me. I open my eyes. Alfredo de San Francisco is standing twenty feet away, looking down at the body of the assassin.

"I knew this man," he says, frowning at the corpse. "In college. In California. We played tennis. He had a great backhand."

"I'm sorry," says Indira. "He came in the night to kill us."

"Yes," says Alfredo, nodding. "He would."

But before he can tell us more about the dead man, we hear the amphibious attack vehicles rolling up to the river's edge. We drop into our hole. We point our little guns across the river. Indira takes my hand and kisses it tenderly. I whisper *I love you.*

Alfredo grins at us. "Don't be afraid. It's still not too late for them to change their minds."

Together

(always eternally absolutely)

Derek and Mr. Laskin are walking on an abandoned freeway, the pavement breaking up—weeds and trees beginning the great absorption.

"In five thousand years," says Mr. Laskin, "this will be known as the stony woods. We'll come back here in canoes."

"*We* won't," says Derek, shrugging. "We'll be dead."

"Says who?"

"Scientists."

"Posh," says Mr. Laskin, pointing at two racing clouds. "If you die enlightened, you grab whatever new body you want. Me? I'm gonna be born on Vashon Island. Grow up a rainy water boy. Or girl."

"You can decide?"

"Why not? Nature can't object. It's all a fabulous jumble of possibilities reacting to the ever-changing truth. Nature doesn't allow for long that which destroys her. Everything else is copacetic."

"Copa-what?"

"Copacabana."

"Where's that?"

"Any decent city has a Copacabana. It's where you dance."

"Do we have one?"

"If not, we'll open one as soon as we figure out where we are and how to get back to where we started."

"We're lost?"

"*I'm* lost," says Mr. Laskin, leaning against a young oak rising from the crumbling asphalt. "And very tired. Do you know where we are?"

"I was following you."

"Why?"

"You're my idol."

"Posh," says Mr. Laskin, sighing wearily. "I'm a duddy old fool. Might just curl up right here and die."

"You're a genius," says Derek, rushing to take the old man's hand. "Everything you say comes true."

"I'm no genius," he says, wincing at the moniker. "In ninety-some years you learn a few things."

"Maybe we're *not* lost," says Derek, squinting at their surroundings. "Maybe this *is* the way back."

"Of course it is," says Mr. Laskin, winking. "I was just testing you. No doubt we'll find water and food, too. Any mile now."

"I'm not scared if you're not scared."

"Then I won't be scared," he says, taking Derek's hand. "We'll be brave together."

Heart

(eternal springs of hope)

What is love but the absence of fear? To sit in this room full of books, the cats content on their pillows in the Reading Circle, Derek behind the counter with his girlfriend Kelly, the smell of Mr. Laskin's fried bologna wafting up from the kitchen mingling with the heavenly scent of Moustafa's baking bread, Natasha sitting in her rocker, a big orange cat on her lap, Iris and Leona alphabetizing the *Contemporary Visionaries* section. What could be better than this?

The mailman delivers a big envelope from New York, a painting from Jenny—a burgundy smear over a tangle of gray-black night. Untitled. A short note included.

> Hello everybody. The Big Apple turns out to be a small town with millions of people. I'm giving myself one more year here and then who knows? I have space in my room for visitors. Hint, hint. I have a job in a vegan deli called Burdock For Days. Our kind of people. I'm taking pictures of women with big noses. I ask them to smile, and then to frown. I frame the two images together. A gallery is interested in the concept. Almost all my dreams take place in Under the Table Books. I'm hoping to come home for Christmas. Gotta run. Love you. Jenny

Z saunters in, loosening his tie. He leans down to kiss Natasha. "Hello my reason for living."

"Hello, sweet Z," she says, kissing his hand. "How's tricks in the real world?"

"Suffice to say, selling books for *actual* money is dog-eat-dog. Then again, books have got to start somewhere if they're gonna end up here."

Derek taps the keyboard of the humming computer. "Attention shoppers. We've got a pumpkin pie in refrigerator number two that must be eaten to be believed, and don't forget the fresh carrot juice we got yesterday in exchange for the complete works of Nikos Kazantzakis."

Numero Uno shakes a copy of Lew Welch's *Selected Poems* at Carl Klein. "This is the stuff, Carl. The essence. The man saw God in everything. Don't miss it."

Peter Franklin stumbles in, tipsy from a pint of winter wheat ale. "Let's have another reading. I can feel new poems begging to be born. I need the incentive of public display. Yes? Are we agreed?"

"Not until Lord and Indira come back from the Amazon," says Derek, folding his arms. "It's only been a few months since the battle.

They never found their bodies. They might have survived."

Mr. Laskin comes up the stairs eating a colossal bologna sandwich. Moustafa follows with oatmeal cookies hot from the oven.

"No one survives," says Denny, standing in the doorway to the rumpus room. "I'm off to Santa Cruz. Then maybe up to Canada. The books are calling me. Anybody want to come along?"

Leona looks up from a copy of Buckminster Fuller's *Critical Path*. "A day on the beach in Santa Cruz? What could be better than that? I can be ready in twenty minutes."

"Perfecto," says Denny, relieved to have company. "I'll ready the bus and bring her around."

"But maybe they *did* survive," says Derek, refusing to believe that Lord and Indira are gone forever. "Just because the newspapers owned by the people who attacked them said they were dead doesn't mean they are. The truth almost always comes out years later. Right, Mr. Laskin?"

"The news," says Mr. Laskin, savoring his bologna, "is a tonality."

Iris looks up from a copy of Roshi Supremo's *Don't Just* Do *Something, Stand There* and says, "Derek, my darling, I believe with all my heart that Lord and Indira are alive and will return to us."

"Of course they will," says Leona, reading aloud from *The Wisdom of Insecurity* by Alan Watts. "Nothing is more creative than death, since it is the whole secret of life."

"Still," says Peter, shrugging artistically, "I can't imagine they'd object to our staging another program in their absence. Indeed, I *know* they would heartily approve."

"Maybe you're right," says Derek, warming to the idea. "Maybe if we schedule a performance, it will somehow *inspire* them to show up."

"A very good strategy," says Mr. Laskin, nodding to his protégé. "I refer to it in my book as *chumming for synergy*. There is nothing the universe appreciates more than action. Do you know why that is? Because action is the mother of the whole kit and caboodle."

Scavenger

(Denny hits the road again)

I pull into Tomales, the fog drifting over Highway One and thickening into a dense soup. God, I'm glad to park my bus behind the church and hustle over to Rachel's for a big bowl of soup and maybe a whole lot more.

Her daughter Lisa is there, grown into a woman since the last time I came around—a sweet ample woman—sorry to tell me Rachel is in Portland and won't be back for a week. She serves me soup and bread and stands behind me as naturally as anything in the world rubbing my tired head with her strong fingers, relaxing me to the edge of sleep.

I don't want to go back to my bus. I want to sprawl in Rachel's bed, but it isn't to be. Lisa gives me a loaf of bread and wishes me well. I step outside and the bitter cold strikes me in the heart. I feel my age, fifty-seven, and I wonder how much more of this scavenger's life I can take.

I knock on the back door of Dino's General Store, hoping he'll open up and sell me some wine. He's gone home, smart man, to the warm embrace of Nina. Thinking of love makes me want to drive through the night to Los Angeles, to Maria Esteban's, to see if she still wants to marry me, though she made the offer ten years ago and is probably a mother and wife now to someone far less ambivalent than I.

I crawl into my sleeping bag. I gnaw Lisa's bread until I am calm enough to sleep. I dream I'm driving over enormous boulders until I find myself balanced on the edge of a deep chasm. No way over. No way back. I wake up. The dream didn't frighten me.

I dress and shave and walk back to Lisa's house, though it is not yet dawn. I knock on her door. She opens up to me. I sing a song of thanks for her bread and her soup and her touch. I take her in my arms. We kiss. I ask her to marry me, to settle with me on a farm by a river near the sea. She laughs and laughs and invites me in for breakfast.

We have blueberry pancakes and fresh peaches. She tells me she is moving to Nashville with her lover Lucinda. She says—and she means it—I should come visit them.

On the road again, heading north, my bus running well, I watch the sun rise over the coast range and paint the Pacific with pinks and oranges. I think of Lisa's lips and her beautiful honest laughter.

The Milky Way

We live in a spiral arm of a spinning
Field of stars. We whirl around, a carnival
Ride, full of birds, loves, emotions, endless
Varieties of things unfolding in seasons;
Full of bells and an endless weaving of hearts.

These connections ride upon our consciousness,
Demanding constant performance from us.
Each of us, most royal and majestic as night,
Vile, vindictive and spoiled even before we speak;
Sorrow and joy, the way we sound our name.

We endure all of this, our lips kissing each moment,
Crushed, elated, misunderstood, praised for things
We do as part of ourselves, damned for these same things.

There is no road, there is no plan. Only love
Survives. Everything is forgiven, finally.
Understanding limps behind the parade,
Always late, always burdened with qualifications,
Always abandoning every opinion and argument,
Leaving each of us our place only, describing
This place, the swirling arms, the myriad ways
We twist ourselves to achieve
This weaving, this carnival of love.

D.R. Wagner

Illustration by Brenda Walton

About the Author

Todd Walton was born in San Francisco in 1949. He has published eight works of fiction, including the novel *Inside Moves*, which was made into a motion picture in 1980. His collection of contemporary dharma tales, *Buddha in a Teacup*, was published in 2008. His two nonfiction works are *Open Body* and *The Writer's Path*. A composer of music for piano and guitar, Todd lives in Mendocino, California. His wife is the cellist Marcia Sloane. Todd's website is UnderTheTableBooks.com.

Especial gratitude to:

Quinton Duval

Ann Menebroker

D.R. Wagner

for permission to use their marvelous poetry

Cypress House is committed to preserving ancient forests and natural resources. We elected to print this title on 30% post consumer recycled paper, processed chlorine free. As a result, for this printing, we have saved:

11 Trees (40' tall and 6-8" diameter)
4,152 Gallons of Wastewater
8 million BTU's of Total Energy
533 Pounds of Solid Waste
1,000 Pounds of Greenhouse Gases

Cypress House made this paper choice because our printer, Thomson-Shore, Inc., is a member of Green Press Initiative, a nonprofit program dedicated to supporting authors, publishers, and suppliers in their efforts to reduce their use of fiber obtained from endangered forests.

For more information, visit www.greenpressinitiative.org

Environmental impact estimates were made using the Environmental Defense Paper Calculator. For more information visit: www.papercalculator.org.